CW00549645

REDEMPTION

REDEMPTION

JACK JORDAN

**SIMON &
SCHUSTER**

London · New York · Sydney · Toronto · New Delhi

First published in Great Britain by Simon & Schuster UK Ltd, 2024

Copyright © Jack Jordan, 2024

The right of Jack Jordan to be identified as author
of this work has been asserted in accordance with the
Copyright, Designs and Patents Act, 1988.

1 3 5 7 9 10 8 6 4 2

Simon & Schuster UK Ltd
1st Floor
222 Gray's Inn Road
London WC1X 8HB

Simon & Schuster: Celebrating 100 Years of Publishing in 2024

Simon & Schuster Australia, Sydney
Simon & Schuster India, New Delhi

www.simonandschuster.co.uk
www.simonandschuster.com.au
www.simonandschuster.co.in

A CIP catalogue record for this book
is available from the British Library

Hardback ISBN: 978-1-3985-3155-0
Trade Paperback ISBN: 978-1-3985-3156-7
eBook ISBN: 978-1-3985-3157-4
Audio ISBN: 978-1-3985-3158-1

Typeset in the UK by M Rules
Printed and Bound in the UK using 100% Renewable Electricity
at CPI Group (UK) Ltd

MIX
Paper | Supporting
responsible forestry
FSC
www.fsc.org   FSC® C171272

Dedicated to Martin,
For everything

'*Revenge is barren. Of itself it makes*
The dreadful food it feeds on; its delight
Is murder—its satiety despair.'

— Friedrich Schiller, *Wilhelm Tell*

I

DENIAL

London, spring 2004

'How would you least like to die?'

It's a weird question to ask another person. I'd have been alarmed if it had come from anyone but her. But she asks this inquisitively and innocently, as if she has asked herself the same question many times before and has chosen me as the person to finally think it aloud with. I love nights like these, when it's just the two of us away from the world; when time seems to stop and we can talk about almost anything, no holds barred.

'I'm not sure,' I reply, cheeks flushing. 'I can't say I've ever really thought about it.'

Evelyn lies on her side, her dark hair wild post-coitus, her features soft and unguarded. The sheets drape over her hips, leaving her breasts bare and revealing the soft, tender skin pulled taut over her pregnant belly. She might be the most self-assured person I have ever known. I knew it the second I met her: we were two people in a coffee shop close to campus, smiling as we noticed we were both reading Shelley's Frankenstein. My copy was pristine, without a crease on the spine; hers was battered and dog-eared from years of rereading. She closed hers, knowing the story so well that she hadn't needed to mark the page, and came right over to my table. I think I fell in love with her before she even spoke a word.

'Yes you have,' she says with a smile, dragging me back from the memory. 'Come on, Tobe. Tell me.'

Tobe. Only she calls me that, and my heart jumps every time I hear it. It might seem odd to outsiders that my wife can still make me blush. We met when I was in my first year at university and she was in her second. We were each other's firsts in so many ways, have known each other our whole adult lives, and yet she still gives me butterflies whenever her eyes meet mine. I want to forget the question and kiss her again, but her eyes are so intent on knowing that I stop myself.

'What's yours?' I ask, buying myself time to think of my own answer; one as profound and thoughtful as her.

'To be stranded out at sea,' she replies. Her smile fades. 'The thought of being surrounded by water while dying of thirst; having the same haunting horizon staring back at me each way I look. I couldn't bear going mad like that.'

The room falls quiet. I imagine her lost in the ocean, foaming at the mouth from drinking the water and hallucinating from its salt. By the haunted look in her eyes, I can tell she's dreamt of this more than once. I wonder what it symbolizes. Abandonment, loss of hope, loneliness.

'Plus, there are sharks,' I say.

'Yes,' she replies, laughing with relief. 'That too.'

She raises her hand and strokes my face, smiling as I kiss her palm and the soft skin on her wrist.

'Come on, what's yours?'

She traces my mouth with her finger as I think. I pretend to bite it and she laughs again.

'Betrayal,' I say finally, sucking the joy out of the room. 'It's not the method that frightens me, but the intention. I'd rather be knifed in the front by a stranger a dozen times than be stabbed once in the back by someone I loved.'

'Do you love me?' she asks softly.

I smirk and she hits me.

'I'm serious.'

'It goes without saying,' I reply. 'I adore the bones of you, woman.'

'Then I promise never to betray you.' She leans in and kisses me, soft and slow, before delicately pulling away and taking my hand, placing it above her womb and whispering something, so close to me that her breath warms my lips. 'You are going to be the most wonderful father.'

She kisses me once more and rolls over, and I lie in the dark *thinking of how long we have waited for this. Years of trying for a baby, years of wondering if we were one of those couples who just couldn't conceive despite everything being in working order. We wanted it for so long that I don't think either of us considered how our lives would change the moment we saw the two lines on that pregnancy test.*

I glance around our room, through the open door towards the rest of the flat: a one-bedroom shoebox in Notting Hill that's crammed with books and smells of damp. We've been married three years, lived together for six; we've seen each other through Evelyn's medical degree, redundancies and the death of her mother, her last remaining parent, but this is the first time I can feel our world truly shifting on its axis. I've wanted to be a father for so long that I never stopped to wonder if I'd be any good.

Evelyn rolls back and strokes my chest.

'Stop worrying and go to sleep.'

I smile in the dark. You are going to be the most wonderful father, *she'd said. Picking up on my fears before I'd even dared to utter them aloud. I try to imagine how my life might have been without her, had we not crossed paths that day. What if I'd got up at the right time that morning and made it to class, and not had to head to the coffee shop to wait for the seminar to end? Would we have met another way? Or would my life look completely different?*

Life never fails to surprise me in moments like these. How one's world can flip in an instant by simply crossing paths with another. The joy it can bring, the heartache.

I turn over, hold her and the baby in the crook of me, and close my eyes to sleep.

1

Tobias

San Diego, summer 2024

Sometimes I wonder if I have it in me to kill someone. What my victim would have to do to bring me to the point where impulse overrides morality. What my tipping point might be.

It's not a desire I have. More of a morbid question I ask myself. You hear of regular people snapping under pressure, don't you? Fight or flight. Seeing red. The straw that broke the camel's back. If I were to kill someone, I guess I'd be one of those.

Evelyn woke at five. I felt the bed shift beneath her, despite her attempt to creep out from beside me. I always rouse to her, no matter how quiet she tries to be. I wake when she wakes, and only fall asleep once I hear her first slumbering breath, as if my circadian rhythm is synced with hers. On the off-chance I do wake before her, I like to lie in wait, my gaze flicking between her stoic face and the clock on the bedside table behind her, waiting for 5 a.m. to strike. I eye her smooth and impenetrable skin, illuminated by the glow-in-the-dark digits on the clock. When it hits the hour, her haunted eyes creep open right on cue.

I must have drifted off again, for I wake alone at six. The sheets on her side of the bed are barely ruffled, the slight indent in the pillow where she rested her head the only sign that she was ever there at all.

I should get up, but a sense of dread pins me to the mattress. They smell of us, these sheets. Not perfume or cologne, but the true scent of us: our skin and our hair, the animal pheromones we carry and emit. That's one of the only things that hasn't changed about my wife. The homely scent of her.

I fight the urge to sink deeper beneath the duvet and head into the en suite to empty my bladder. Seat up. Then down again. Flush. Check the floor for any spots of piss that landed on the tiles when I shook off the last few drops. This is the beginning of my morning routine: a mental checklist of tasks I must do in fear of disappointing my wife if I don't. A stranger might think I'm whipped, cuckolded. We stopped caring what people thought of us a long time ago.

I brush my teeth before heading downstairs, a habitual act rather than one of hope. We won't kiss; we may not even speak. It's hard to gauge what kind of mood Evelyn will be in on any given morning. But I do it anyway, ready to seize any sliver of softness in her, a second or two when she drops her guard and lets me in. I try to remember the last time we kissed, and can't.

I stare at the man in the mirror on the wall above the basin. Dark stubble peppered with grey; puffy, bloodshot eyes. I'm forty-seven and I look it. Some men grow into their looks as they age. I might have too, had grief not chipped away at me. The misery can be seen in the lines around my eyes and mouth, the fork between my brows.

The clock on the bathroom wall ticks behind me. I should get showered and dressed, but the growing dread anchors me further. I splash my face with cold water, digging the crust from the corners of my eyes, and rinse the last remnants of toothpaste from the basin. Making my presence known in this house only seems to push us further apart. Sometimes it seems like this is Evelyn's home rather than mine, and I'm merely an unwanted visitor lingering on too long. Often, she will enter a room or cross me in the hall and jump at the sight of me, as if she has stumbled across a stranger. It's better if I make it appear like I was never here at all.

I dress the bed the way Evelyn likes: plumping and arranging the pillows in the right order and smoothing out the creases in the undersheet before fanning the duvet over it, followed by the decorative blankets and cushions. Running my palms over the spot where she sleeps is the closest I get to touching her. I'm sure I can feel the warmth of her body in the cotton, but I know too much time has passed for that to be true. We sleep dressed: I wear a nightshirt and boxers long enough to pass for shorts; Evelyn dresses in pyjamas that cover her from her neck to her ankles, the drawstring double-knotted at the waist. If the bed weren't so big, and there was a chance of us touching, she would have vacated to a room of her own years ago, though we both know what it would mean if we were to start sleeping in separate beds. Still, I see the truth in her each night, her body rigid as she mentally prepares to lie beside me. But that doesn't stop me from lying awake and praying to hear the rustle of the sheets as she turns over to face my side of the room, followed by the feel of her fingers slipping beneath my shirt and the delicate scratch of her nails along my spine. Just like the way she used to, to let me know she wanted me.

Out on the landing, the sun rises on the other side of the window, throwing a warm hue on the hardwood floor and glowing against the array of doors that lead to empty room after empty room, in the house that was never meant for just the two of us.

I head downstairs, watching where I step to avoid the creaking boards. I want a glimpse of her before she notices me. Sometimes, when she is alone, her guard falters. The creases in her brow soften and her teeth unclench. Her eyes are free of that impenetrable glaze. I can see her thoughts, her fears, her grief, and, deep down, I can see her heart. Looking at her in those moments is like looking into the past; it's a chance to remember what I had and lost. I only see it for a few seconds before she senses me near and steels herself, but those few seconds – that wavering hope that the wife I love might one day return – can carry me for days.

Evelyn is in her study, standing before the printer as it chugs out a document in the corner. The blinds are closed, creating the impression that it is still night beyond them, and the desk lamp gives the room a gloomy, secretive air. Even without much light, I know this study like the back of my hand; all of its nooks and crannies, all of its secrets. There is one part of the room that immediately draws attention upon entering: the back wall is covered in photos of Aaron Alexander, the man who killed our son, Joshua, when he was just nine years old. Mugshots through the years up until his final arrest, which changed our lives irrevocably.

He's young. Too young to have destroyed so much and so many. He was twenty when he did it, which makes him thirty-one now. He's on the tall side, standing at six-one or six-two, but despite this he's not intimidating. His bone structure is sharp, but in the photos he still has a boyish youth to his cheeks. I wonder if prison crushed that out of him and what he looks like now as a free man.

There are news articles pinned to the wall among the mug-shots. Headlines shout out at me, exposés detailing the night he killed Joshua.

MAN CHARGED IN HIT-AND-RUN SLAYING

ALEXANDER PLEADS NO CONTEST TO MANSLAUGHTER CHARGES

Then there is a jump to the present day, with articles from the last month detailing his early release; he had been sentenced to over twenty years for an array of felonies but made parole after eleven.

The stories about his release weren't on the front pages; the uproar over our son's death had simmered down by then.

At the centre of all the clippings is a calendar, with violent red slashes through the days leading up to today's date – one month exactly after Aaron Alexander was released from jail. The day my wife has been waiting for. The same day I have lain awake dreading.

The fear returns, twisting my stomach in its fist. I asked her once why she wanted to wait a month before going after him. *I want him to experience freedom*, she'd replied. *I want him to know what he's lost.*

I stare at the wall, at the task my wife has devoted her life to for over a decade. There are private documents pinned there too – health records, prison records. I have no idea how she got them. Sometimes, when it comes to her obsession, it's better I don't know.

Evelyn's hair is tied back from her face, exposing the bare nape of her neck. With her focus on the document in her hands, she reveals a glimpse of her beautiful face: straight-set lips, the profile of her nose, her long eyelashes flicking slowly with each blink. Concentration creases her brow and her jaw is clenched, her teeth grinding quietly behind her lips. My heart sinks. I missed my chance to see the heart within her. It was highly optimistic of me to expect it, today of all days, but even a second's glance would have carried me through.

It always shocks me that grief hasn't aged her like it has me. It seems to have preserved her youth, while mercilessly whittling away at mine. It pads the skin beneath my eyes, droops in the corners of my mouth. Evelyn conceals her pain within; I imagine her insides, black and rotten with it, how I picture a smoker's lungs to look.

She is remarkably fit, far more than when we first met. We were both a bit podgy around the edges when we first lay together. I'd say those so-called imperfections were some of my favourite parts of her. But the last time I saw my wife naked – through the gap in the bedroom door she had left ajar, as I dared to steal a glimpse of her changing – I spotted abs, defined biceps, smaller breasts than she'd had before. She has been training for this day all these years.

I remember staring at her through the crack in the door, how my dick got hard at the sight of her naked flesh and the shame that followed. I felt more like a pervert peering in at a stranger than a husband admiring his wife.

A large black holdall sits at the end of the desk. I watch her check the items inside, crossing each of them off a list as she goes: a handgun, a box of ammo rattling in her grip, a taser strong enough to floor a man twice her size with a single shock. She packed the bag just yesterday. And the day before that. Packing, unpacking and repacking the same bag to make sure she has the drill down, in fear of leaving anything behind. She is just about to consult her list again when a shiver visibly runs down her spine; the feel of my eyes on her, making her recoil. She turns her head ever so slightly, looking at me out of the corner of her eye. When she's working on this, she doesn't like to be disturbed.

Silence swells between us.

'You haven't showered,' she says, her tone thinly veiling her resentment. 'Please don't make us late.'

She turns her attention back to the list. Can she really tell that from her peripheral vision? Or can she smell the sleep on me? No, it won't be that. She'll have been listening for the running of the shower and the gurgling of the pipes.

'I won't,' I croak, my first words spoken aloud.

She nods curtly. The silence that follows lingers like the sting after a slap. I should leave, but I can't stop staring at this woman who seems so new and mysterious, admiring her long, elegant neck and the way her back shrinks towards her newly tight waist.

A body that's foreign and unknown to me, seen only through the crack in a door.

'You're ready for this?' she asks.

It's less of a question, more of an ultimatum. A question that has only one right answer.

Are you ready to murder the man who killed our son?

When I hesitate too long, she turns to face me. Those dark, piercing eyes fix on mine.

'Yes,' I say.

Her glare cuts me open, rummaging around inside me for the truth. Even when she makes me nervous, I can't help but admire her beauty. The tautness of her cheekbones, the fullness of her lips. She nods coolly and returns to her task.

You wouldn't recognize us, had you met us before. We were the couple who were always touching. We'd hold hands in bed as we fell asleep, our fingers interlocked until we woke, and then make love on the sheets that smelled of us. It took me a while to realize that I haven't just been mourning my son all these years; I've also been grieving the loss of my wife. She stayed in bed for a month after his funeral. Thirty days and thirty nights of hiding in the dark. The woman I knew and loved never left that room.

As I stare at her, a question burns away at me. The words linger on my tongue, stinging the wet, pink flesh. They press against my clenched teeth and closed lips, begging silently to be let out into the open.

How did we get here, Evelyn?

I think back to the people we were before all this; the memory of the day we discovered Evelyn was pregnant and the hope we'd carried. The joy that had burst from us was so strong that neither of us could think straight for days. We were embarking on a whole new journey together, a whole new life. And even though the step we're about to take is technically a new beginning, I can't help but feel that it is, in so many ways, the end.

I think of the question I asked myself when I woke; whether I have it in me to kill someone. What my tipping point might be. The truth is, I know I could never take a life. No matter how much anger I carry over the death of our son, and no matter how much Aaron Alexander might deserve a bullet, I couldn't do it.

My wife could, I think, as I watch her zip the holdall shut with a violent flick. *My wife will.*

'I asked you not to make us late,' she says with her back to me.

I silently head back towards the stairs to shower.

*

The journey from San Diego to Beatty spans the desert and crosses state lines. We drive down Route 127 surrounded by nothing but cracked earth and mountains, an odd scattering of long grass that evolved to live without thirst and wildlife that blends seamlessly into the landscape. I eye the occasional dead lizard frying to a crisp on the side of the road, desert hares gutted of their meat by predators after becoming roadkill in the night. Aaron Alexander lives in Beatty. He will die there too, if my wife gets her way.

We drive without speaking. We have been in the car for hours, with several more to go. Evelyn is at the wheel, her determined grip turning her knuckles white, while I sit in the passenger seat beside her with the map. We have the GPS, but they can go wrong, she said. The only judgement my wife trusts is her own.

My phone pings with an alert. The wildfires that began in Spring Valley and San Bernadino National Forest yesterday are growing. I check my news app and read the latest update, the flames burning behind us and ahead of us. They're predicting it to be the worst wildfire season on record for the state of California.

'It's getting worse,' I say.

'It'll be fine,' she replies.

'I can smell the smoke already. We should turn back and wait for it to die out.'

She turns off the A/C and the car speeds up, her foot on the pedal her only response.

As we listen to the purr of the engine and our own thoughts, I stare out at the desert, at the rocky slopes of the mountains, and miss home. Not San Diego. *Home.* When I think of London, with its seasons and green parks and dirty Underground, I feel a pang of longing behind my ribs. Just the thought of its cold winters and tepid springs could bring tears to my eyes. We have lived in America for over a decade, but this land still feels foreign to us. Or perhaps it's us, and we feel foreign to the land. We're not quite British anymore, but not quite American either. Two nomads with no place to call home.

We'd moved for my work. Headhunted for a senior managerial position in advanced manufacturing. Joshua was young enough to acclimatize to new surroundings, and Evelyn and I had lived in the capital for all of our adult lives; it had made sense to snatch the opportunity for an adventure, to grow in new, exciting ways. Little did we know we wouldn't grow at all but become stunted in time.

When my wife notices an American twang to her accent, she visibly seizes up. She doesn't want to grow or change. She wants everything to stay as it was when Joshua was still with us. Changing feels like a betrayal when he isn't here to change with us. It's the same reason we haven't moved back home; we'd be leaving our boy behind. *Come home*, my family has said over and over. Evelyn's parents would have too had they been alive. But what they fail to understand is that without Joshua, there is no home to return to. Our home is here with him, even if he is dead in the ground, hidden by American soil.

America is also the home of Aaron Alexander; that certainly gave Evelyn another reason to stay. To be close by when his prison sentence came to an end. Not that she would have admitted to it to anyone other than me. Hell, she didn't even confide in me about it for the first six years.

*

My wife first mentioned the idea of murdering Aaron Alexander over dinner one August night in 2019. We were sitting in the dining room, at either end of the table large enough to seat eight. Something had been troubling her for days; whenever I looked at her, I found her deep in thought, her eyes moving busily beneath a permanently furrowed brow. I'd felt that same sense of dread I feel now, the undeniable instinct that something bad was coming.

'How can you bear it?' she'd asked at last.

I was so surprised she'd spoken to me beyond a disgruntled instruction that I almost choked on a pea.

'Bear what?' I replied, blinking water.

She put her knife and fork down and picked up her glass of wine. My wife loses her appetite quickly.

'The thought of him being free one day.'

She didn't need to say who or what she was referring to. The topic, it seems, is a conversation we have on a constant loop.

'I try not to think about it.'

She scoffed.

'What?' I asked.

'So you're just going to accept it? That man didn't just kill our son. He left him for dead, for the coyotes to get at him. You can accept that?'

'That's not fair.'

'None of this is fucking fair.'

She pushed her plate aside, the food mostly untouched, and took a cigarette from the packet on the table. I watched her light it hungrily and blow curling, grey smoke into the room. It crept towards me at the other end of the table, and I breathed it in as if it were a part of her, reluctant to exhale.

'We don't have to just accept it, Tobe.' She hadn't called me that for a long time; she no doubt knew what it would have meant for me to hear it again, and I lapped it up like a fool. I remember the tug of longing I had for her in that moment; the urge to hold her and be held by her. To kiss her and have her kiss me back. 'We can do something,' she said.

I stared at her from across the table, at the smoke from her cigarette, as her eyes bored into mine.

'Do what?' I asked nervously.

*

Evelyn sighs behind the wheel, dragging me from the memory.

I sit in silence as she takes a cigarette from the packet hidden in the drink holder and lights it effortlessly with one hand, filling the car with smoke before lowering the window. The hot air sucks out the air-conditioned chill within seconds.

As hard as I try, I can't remember agreeing to kill Aaron. There was never a moment where I definitively said the words. I never plotted with her; I never researched our son's killer like she has. She did all of this alone. But I didn't tell her no, either. My fear then, and my fear now, is that if I did or do, then there will be no use for me anymore. I wouldn't be grieving alongside her; I'd be another person who didn't understand, another person who stood opposed to her and her goal. When she put the idea to me, I knew in a split second that I would lose her by saying no. But it's only now, as we drive hundreds of miles to kill a man, that I know deep in my bones that I will lose her for good if I stand by and let her take a life.

A wave of loneliness envelopes me. It comes at me like that; suddenly and with force. One minute I'll be fine, and the next I'm drowning. How can I be lonely with my wife right here, by my side? How can we be within touching distance, and yet simultaneously worlds apart?

The day we discovered Joshua had died, something in Evelyn seemed to die with him. Her ability to love and be loved was shut off; her capacity for reason and acceptance was replaced by rage and denial. She was a psychiatrist before all this; she of all people should know that she is in denial about our son's death, stuck in this hellish purgatory because she refuses to move through each phase of grief, cementing herself in blind anger and refusing to budge.

Still, I don't think all is lost. Not yet. Would I have stayed if I didn't have hope that one day I might get her back? If not all of her, then perhaps a small part? Probably. But I'm convinced my wife is still in there, buried beneath this new, hardened shell. It's the part of her I creep down the stairs to see in the mornings, that glimpse into her soul that she has become so good at hiding. If she takes a life, I know that any good part of her will be lost forever. I just have to be brave enough and smart enough to stop her.

I watch her drop the end of the cigarette onto the road. She leaves the window open, the breeze playing with her hair and fluttering it against her face.

Evelyn needs to do this. Her plan to murder Aaron Alexander is what has kept her putting one foot in front of the other; the only ray of hope that has kept her rising each morning. Her will to live is intrinsically linked to the death of another, while mine is fuelled by the need to keep her from destroying herself. It seems we couldn't be more at odds.

Through the windscreen, I spot a diner up ahead.

'Let's stop here to eat,' I say, my voice thick and stagnant from the silence.

'We haven't got time.'

'I need the bathroom too.'

She sighs heavily and checks the rear-view mirror.

'Fine, but we're in and out in twenty minutes.'

I nod silently, my heart racing as the car slows and veers towards the diner. I'm terrified of losing her should I betray her, but I fear that if I don't, I'll lose her still. It seems that whatever I do or don't do, whatever I say or don't say, I might lose my wife either way.

The only thing keeping me alive is her. As she pulls to a stop outside the building, dust settling about the car from the spinning tyres, I wonder if she has ever thought the same about me. I don't let myself dwell on it long, unsure if I'd like the answer.

2

Evelyn

I sit in the roadside diner, in a red leather booth that has seen better days, watching my husband eat a fried breakfast with both fascination and revulsion. He cuts the fried eggs until the wet, luminous yolk bleeds onto his plate, and saws the bacon with a quiet tremor in his grip, the blade of the knife screeching on the china. Then he slices off the end of a sausage, skewers the concoction on his fork, and lathers on ketchup before shovelling it all in. I can hear the food in his mouth, the mashing of egg and the mastication of flesh. He chokes slightly on a string of bacon fat before finally swallowing it down. Then he starts the process again, all while I sit fighting the urge to swipe the plate from the table and watch it explode into a thousand pieces against the scuffed lino floor.

My husband eats as if there were a gun to his head. Always has. Joshua did the same. *Little gannets*, I used to say. I don't say anything now; I merely loathe him for bringing up the memory every time he raises the fork to his mouth and chews. I pick up my tea and sip silently. I won't eat: anticipation has filled me up.

The diner is loud. We sit listening to the shriek of metal scraping on crockery, customers talking louder and louder to be heard over one another until they create a deafening, hive-like hum.

There's the trucker in the booth behind us who hacks up phlegm when he laughs. The child missing his two front teeth whining for more syrup on his pancakes. The walking cliché of a waitress long past her prime, sighing resentfully as she tops up people's mugs with cheap coffee that looks like mud, the kind that always leaves stray grains in your teeth. Cars rev by on the other side of the windows, sudden angry growls from their engines making me flinch as they pass. And then there's Tobias's chewing. The loudest sound of them all. I look down and see my hands clenched into fists in my lap, blood squeezed from the knuckles.

'You're grinding your teeth,' he says. 'Dr Roberts said if you keep doing it, you'll end up cracking a tooth—'

'He's my dentist. I know what he said.'

I take a sip of my tea and stare at the bit of yolk caught in the stubble by the corner of Tobias's mouth, glistening when it catches the light. Another wave of revulsion passes through me, which is followed quickly by guilt, stinging like a whisky chaser. The love I have for my husband always appears like a surprise, jolting my heart without warning, before it falls back into the same familiar beat.

Life was so different when we met. We were almost thirty years younger, for a start. That feels like another lifetime to me now. A different couple in a different world. I certainly don't recognize the woman I was then, compared to the woman I am now. My husband, however, is relatively unchanged when one peers beneath the grief. The same values, the same morals, the same trust in others and in life. I often wonder how he managed to keep hold of himself, to keep the grief from swallowing him whole like it did me. Another thing to resent him for. For being able to stay above water while I drowned.

'You can almost see the smoke now,' he says, nodding towards the window.

He's right. The blue sky looks dirtier, thick with the approaching fumes.

'Smoke travels hundreds of miles. It doesn't mean we have to turn back.'

'Not smoke like that. Not smoke you can see.'

'Everyone else looks gravely concerned,' I reply with a sarcastic bite, nodding at the room.

'I just want to keep you safe.'

I look out of the window and tune him out, needing a moment's break from his constant smothering. I come round to the waitress's sigh as she stops beside the table.

'Coffee?'

'Please.' Tobias puts on his best attempt at an American accent.

I avert my eyes, nursing my tea as coffee glugs into his mug.

'Thanks a lot,' he says, with that same American twang.

The waitress grunts in response and shuffles towards the next table, so depressed that she can't even raise her dirty clogs from the floor.

I return my cup quietly to its chipped saucer.

'Why did you do that?' I ask.

'Do what?'

'The accent.'

He takes a sip of black coffee. His left eye twitches from the strength.

'We shouldn't be memorable,' he says quietly. 'We need to blend in. Two Brits sat in a roadside diner in the middle of the Nevada desert are going to stick out by a mile.'

'I don't care about that.'

'I know you don't. But I do.'

Thick, beating veins swell on either side of his neck. He's always holding back what he thinks and feels; a British trait we've failed to shake, I think, as if suffering silently is the noble thing to do, to be. But I'd be lying if I said I didn't notice the array of eggshells around me, and my husband's tentative mission to avoid them. I watch him mustering the courage to speak aloud whatever it is that he longs to say.

'I know I can't stop you from doing this, but it doesn't mean you have to . . .'

He bottles it.

'What?' I push.

I stare at the swollen veins in his neck. His cheeks have flushed so red that I'm convinced he'll burst if he doesn't take a breath.

'You don't have to implode in the process,' he says finally, and exhales. 'You're going into this like a suicide bomber.'

I feel my defences creeping in: muscles stiffening, tongue sharpening. I wonder how long he's been keeping that in. How long he's thought of me as some brainwashed whackjob caught up in the cult of grief.

'We could be more careful,' he says, softer now. 'Doing this doesn't mean we have to destroy our lives completely.'

I cradle the cup of tea in my hands.

'You say that like there's something left to destroy.'

I take a sip.

'Isn't there?'

I hear the hurt in his voice and steel myself against it, looking out of the window to watch the sand billowing over the endless horizon, listen to the tiny granules tinkling against the glass, silently wonder how far off the wildfires are beyond the mountains. I feel his eyes on me, trying to reach me, and resent him for it. I wish he would leave me alone, just for a moment or two. His love, and his need for mine in return, is as persistent as a bluebottle buzzing around my head. One I wish I could crush between my palms.

This was never supposed to happen to us. These things, these tragedies – they happen to other people; to strangers on the news, their grainy faces printed in the papers. And yet here we are, fighting the truth, fighting each other, trapped in the same old cycle. Time, it seems, passes for everyone but us.

'Evelyn . . .' he says.

Suddenly, a car bolts down the highway, disappearing as fast as it appeared. An image flashes in my mind, followed by a sickening sound.

Crack.

The bodily reactions happen all at once. Sweat breaks out all over me, speckling on my face, tingling beneath my arms, warm beads blooming between my shoulder blades. My pulse races and my airways shrink. I look at my husband: he's mouthing something, but all I can hear is an endless, shrill ringing. I blink, and the room explodes with sound. The syrup kid is screaming and red in the face, webs of drool strung between the gaps in his teeth. The waitress is shouting to the kitchen, chasing an order of pancakes, slamming dirty dishes down on the counter as she does so. The trucker is wheezing, phlegm crackling at the back of his throat like a spitting fire. Waves of nausea ripple through me. I try to breathe, but the muscles of my chest have locked in place.

'Evelyn, did you hear me?'

'Are you nearly finished?' I manage.

His frown smooths.

'Are you all right? You've turned pale.'

I ignore him. He knows I hate when he does that; when he answers a question with a question. My heart is beating so fast that I imagine my chest bursting open in a wet explosion of blood and flesh. I just need to breathe.

Tobias places his knife and fork together on his plate as I grab my bag and stand from the booth.

'I'm ready,' he says, realizing my panic. 'I'll get the check.'

'Pay in cash.'

I push past the miserable waitress taking up the aisle, clutching my stomach as if my guts are set to spill out of me, and barge through the swing door. I try to take a deep breath but I'm hit by the heat and the dust instead.

Crack.

I reach the car, hunch over beside it, and spew regurgitated tea onto the hot, broken earth.

Joshua was hit by his killer's car so hard that his skull fractured as it met the road.

Crack.

I heave some more, long strings dribbling from my lips to the ground, tears pattering around the mess. My grief created the scene in my head, conjuring every sound, every frame, and it has haunted me ever since. I see Aaron Alexander's car coming round the bend. Then I see my son's face, the way his eyes would have widened with fear, the way his soft cherub lips would have parted with his last, shocked breath. I hear the screech of the tyres and the slam of my baby's body against the road, ending with the sound of his head hitting the asphalt.

Crack.

Behind me, the door to the diner opens and closes again. I know it's Tobias without looking; his presence is as familiar to me as my own shadow. I wipe my mouth with the back of my hand, bile glistening back at me, and try to compose myself before turning. He comes round to the other side of the car, putting a safe distance and a hunk of metal between us, pity etched on his face and in his eyes. I wish I could pluck it out. Crush the bluebottle to stop its buzzing.

'Do you want me to drive?' he asks softly.

'No,' I snap back.

He opens the passenger door and everything starts spinning. I put a bracing hand on top of the scorching roof.

'Yes,' I relent, a tremor in my voice. 'You drive.'

He nods silently and circles the car, holding out his hand as I slowly unfurl my fist and free the keys. The tips of his fingers graze the soft pad of my palm, sending a violent shiver up my arm. He looks down at my sick on the ground and knows to say nothing. You don't try to stroke a cornered dog; it'll only go for your throat.

Once the driver's door clicks shut behind him, I walk a few steps and stand alone, looking out at the sand and the rock, before closing my eyes to focus on my breathing and calm my racing heart.

Crack.

I open my eyes and blink away the tears.

How can I be haunted by a sound I never heard?

*

I sit in the passenger seat of the car as we continue down Route 127, headed for Death Valley Junction to get to Route 95, wondering to myself how I'll kill him. I think about that a lot.

It's not like I haven't made the decision a thousand times; I'm not one to walk into something without planning every step. But every time I settle on how I'll murder Aaron Alexander – I'll slit his throat, or shoot him between the eyes, or strangle the life out of him with my bare hands – it doesn't feel like enough. A ferocious hunger I can never quite satiate. The more I think about it, the more barbaric and monstrous my intentions become. But whatever I cook up, it's never enough.

A bullet is far too merciful. One second, one bang, and then it's all over, with only a hole in his head and his vacant eyes to show for it. No, I want him to feel it. I want to dangle his death before him until he begs for it, and then make him wait some more. I need him to feel a sliver of the pain I've lived with these past eleven years; a morsel of the pain and fear Joshua would have felt as he died alone on that dark, barren road.

I look in the rear-view mirror, at the slice of Tobias's eyes set on the open highway, seeing him more clearly now than I have in years.

I know I can't stop you from doing this . . .

That's what he'd said in the diner. He hadn't framed it as something we're doing together, or as a goal we share. After years of nodding along, of seemingly agreeing with me, he's finally made his stance clear. Tobias isn't strong enough for this. He never has been. But it's only now that we're embarking on the journey that he's finally found the balls to say the words out loud.

I've been watching him these past few weeks, waiting for the cracks to appear. I think I've known all along that this would happen; the truth has always been there, waiting to be unveiled. Tobias has never been the one to bring up the topic with me, he's only ever responded to my plans when I've mentioned them first, placating me like one might an overimaginative child. All these years he's done nothing but bide his time, hope that the ferocity of my intentions would fade. It's all clear to me now. At best, he is only going to slow me down. At worst, he is going to try to stop me. Two outcomes that I won't allow to happen.

It's gone five. The sun is lowering in the sky and yet the heat is still blazing, rippling across the road, the sprawling desert and the mountains. We've driven almost four hundred miles, from one state to another, with fifty more to go until Beatty. But I have something else to do before then.

Tobias sits in the driver's seat with his hands low on the wheel, his eyes briefly leaving the road to glance at me, before returning to the highway.

'What're you thinking?' he asks, that blue-arsed fly starting to buzz again.

I watch his throat bob up and down with a nervous swallow.

I think you're lying to me.

The silence fills the car like static. My husband never looks at ease when he's around me, not like he used to. I used to feel so much pride when I called him that. *My husband.* Now, the words sit on my tongue like a mouthful of turned meat that I'm desperate to spit out.

He glances at me again, waiting for my response.

'I'm thinking about stopping for the night. There'll be a motel up ahead. We can stop and rest.'

He nods quickly.

'I think that's a good idea.'

Of course you do, you coward. It's one more night for you to summon the courage to try and talk me out of this. As if another night will change anything.

When I think about how he's been nodding along this entire time, judging me, pitying me as he often does, I feel sick to my stomach with the betrayal. I knew he was weak. I knew he wasn't the sort of man to be able to handle something like this. But I thought our son meant more to him. I thought our marriage meant more. When it comes down to it, all that matters to this man, this stranger, is his moral compass – no, his moral *superiority* – because somehow he can think of the man who murdered our child without wanting to kill him in return.

I stare out at the wasteland of the Nevada landscape, spotting tumbleweed, rusting beer cans flung from speeding car windows, dilapidated billboards with posters peeling in jagged strips where they've been left to wither in the sun. Beneath one of the billboards, a desert hare stops, standing on its hind legs to gaze up at us as we pass, its clownishly large ears erect and twitching, before hopping for cover. Tears begin to burn my eyes, but I swallow down the emotion before they can form.

That's how Joshua died. Chasing a stupid fucking hare.

The overnight trip was something his new school did every year: they took the students to camp out and study the stars. We'd only been in the US for a few months, and it felt inherently wrong to let him go away for the night so soon. It was Tobias who calmed me down, who reminded me how important it was for Joshua to make new friends and fit in. Even though I understood the logic, my gut wouldn't stop screaming. I lay awake all of that night, crying confusing tears. It's like I knew. I lay awake trying to make sense of the sudden grief I felt and couldn't understand, while my baby lay dead on a desert road.

Joshua had wanted a rabbit the entire year leading up to the move, to the point of fixation: drawing them, dreaming about them, only wanting toys with fur and pointy ears. It was something we'd promised him once we'd settled in San Diego, and the weekend he was away on the trip, Tobias and I had gone out and bought one. Its white fur was so soft it rivalled silk, and it had pink, bulbous eyes. We'd chosen the hutch, bought the sawdust to fill it, stocked up on vegetables and picked out a small food bowl to put them in. We didn't give the rabbit a name; we wanted Joshua to choose one. Only, he never got to meet it.

Joshua wandered away from the campsite. That's what the teachers said. He'd been far more interested in the wildlife than the stars. There was a desert hare near where they'd camped, a constant presence hopping in the distance. The teachers had reprimanded him for lying awake, peering through the flap of the tent and out into the dark, searching for the hare instead of sleeping. They think he finally spotted it in the night and followed it out towards the open road. The hare was found dead too. The police couldn't figure out if it had been hit by one car, and Joshua by another, or if they were both killed in one fell swoop.

I spent a whole month in bed after the funeral, listening to the rabbit we'd bought for him hopping around in its hutch on the other side of the window. The rustling of the sawdust. The chomping and crunching of the vegetables. I lay there for a month loathing it, its mere existence feeding my rage until it was a living, breathing thing, far bigger and stronger than me. When I finally got out of bed, the first thing I did was stride towards that hutch and snap the rabbit's neck. It never did get a name.

If it had been leukaemia, or a brain tumour, or a heart defect, I'd have something physiological to hate. I could loathe the mistakes our own cells make for taking my son away. Maybe I wouldn't have become who I am now. But Joshua didn't have any of those. He was hit by a car and left for dead, and by a man who is still breathing. A man who has been given a second chance – something my son will never get.

I look at Tobias from the corner of my eye, listening to his soft, nasal breaths and watching the constant nervous tremor in his hands where they rest on the wheel. He doesn't understand why I need to do this. He doesn't understand that my grief and pain will destroy me if I don't. It already is and has, I'm not blind to that. But another year, maybe two, and it'll kill me. I can't bear another second of this agony. Another day of walking around with this weight on my chest, or another night of hearing the same haunting *crack*, and I'll be driven completely mad.

I look at the clock on the dashboard and add up the number of hours it'll be before I reach the man who killed my baby. Before I get to stare him in the eyes and drain the life out of them.

Soon Aaron Alexander will be dead, and I will finally be free.

3

Tobias

The motel off Route 95 is bleak and Hitchcockian: a one-storey, wood-panelled building weathered by the desert heat. The sun has peeled the paint from the boards and cracked the doors where they've swelled in their frames; the porch roof doesn't look safe to stand beneath in order to reach the rooms. If it weren't for the lone car parked outside, I'd have assumed the place was abandoned.

'Someone was murdered here once.'

I look across at Evelyn in the passenger seat. She's reading something on her phone.

'Who?'

'Some guy. Reported as a drug deal gone wrong; says here he was shot twelve times.'

'Christ.' I look towards the motel office, the vacancy sign flickering green in the window. 'Do we really want to stay here?'

'Says they have free Wi-Fi.'

'Can't imagine they get a good signal.'

'Ice machine too,' she says, reading on.

'I don't think I want us staying somewhere where a guy was shot. It doesn't sound safe.'

Evelyn sighs, locking her phone and slipping it into her pocket. I wonder what I've done wrong, what I've said to disappoint her. She pulls her bag strap over her shoulder and reaches for the door.

'We're not the guy who was shot in this situation, Tobias.' She gets out of the car, turns back. 'We're the guy with the gun.'

Shutting the door behind her, she slowly heads towards the office. I hurry to unbuckle my seatbelt and follow.

She's just stepping inside when I catch up with her. The room is hot and cramped, lined from wall to wall with old wood panelling slathered with fresh varnish; I can taste its sharp, bitter tang at the back of my throat. Behind the counter sits a woman with grey, straggly hair that needs a brush and faint scratches on the lenses of her glasses.

'Afternoon,' she says, dog-earring a Connelly novel before slipping it out of view. Her attention goes directly to my wife. 'You after a room?'

People used to look to me before Joshua's death. However old-fashioned, people assumed I was the man of the house, the one in charge. Now it takes a while for people to even realize I'm there.

'Yes,' Evelyn replies.

'How many nights?'

'Just one.'

'It's a hundred dollars a night. You can pay up when you leave.'

I assume she's added an extra twenty dollars to the going rate. Maybe more. No one would pay a hundred dollars to stay in this shitheap.

'I'd rather pay now.'

The woman shrugs. 'Cash or card?'

'Cash.'

Watching Evelyn take out her purse and retrieve the money, I realize how much forward planning she has put into this. My wife never carries cash. I can't remember the last time I saw her hold a dollar. She'll have withdrawn this money so as not to leave a trace during our journey through the desert; that's why she'd told me to pay cash at the diner. I wonder what else she's planned in advance, what else she's keeping from me.

'Just need to show some ID and fill out this form, and the room's yours.'

The woman slips a clipboard over the desk. Evelyn stares down at the blank form. We stand in silence, listening to the hum of the fan purring behind the woman, groaning on its hinges as it turns.

'How much do we have to pay to keep these details private?'

The woman looks at Evelyn – a long, contemplative look. Then she glances at me for the first time, her eyes drifting up and down. I wonder what she thinks of us. Whether we're two lovers having an extramarital affair, or a couple of white-collar criminals on the run from the law. It's unlikely that she's got to the truth: that we've driven across state lines to murder a man.

Her upturned mouth curls into a smile.

'Pay double and you can put down any names you like.'

Evelyn places the money on the desk before scribbling lies onto the page.

'You're a long away from King's country, ain't ya?' the woman says with a raised brow.

A rush of heat sweeps through me. I'd said that our accents would be memorable. Evelyn, however, doesn't bat an eye.

'I'm not much of a royalist,' she replies, not looking up from the clipboard. 'Ever been?'

I stare at her, perplexed. My wife doesn't do small talk. Perhaps she's keeping the woman onside for later, for when our crime inevitably hits the news. A trial witness that could help us in the end. More forward thinking.

'I've never been outta the state, let alone the country. I've got all I need right here.'

Evelyn puts down the pen as the woman picks up a half-smoked cigarette from the ashtray on the desk and relights it, then re-trieves a key from one of the hooks lining the back wall. 'Room five, at the end,' she says, smoke escaping with each word. 'Check out is at eleven.'

'Thanks.'

Evelyn slips an extra twenty dollars into the tip pot and heads for the door as the woman picks up the form.

'Enjoy your stay, Mr and Mrs . . .' She looks down at the paper. 'Smith.'

She grins to herself and takes a drag of the cigarette. When she realizes I'm still standing there, her smile vanishes.

'You need something else?' she asks.

'I'm fine. Thanks.' I watch her smoke, her tar-stained fingers as orange as the shale on the other side of the door. 'You can smoke in the motel?'

'We make up our own rules out here. Got a problem with that?'

'No, ma'am.'

When I don't move, she scowls at me.

'Aren't you concerned about the fires?' I ask.

'It happens every year; don't see why this year should be any different.'

'Right. Well, thank you ma'am.'

I head back towards the door.

'Ma'am,' she repeats, mocking my English accent. She laughs under her breath before coughing up smoke.

Evelyn is standing outside, lighting a cigarette of her own. We head down the side of the motel building towards room five, listening to the crackling ember of her cigarette and the faint whistle of the breeze.

The motel sits alone in the desert. Everywhere I look, miles of dirt and rock stare back at me, wisps of dust following the wind before falling back to the ground. Even the mountains look the same as one another; the same jagged peaks and rocky falls. The smell of smoke from the wildfires is stronger out here, making the air taste burnt with each breath.

I think of the woman behind the reception desk; she'd said she'd never been anywhere else, that she had everything she needed here. How could that be true? How could she not wonder what lies beyond these mountains? What life might have in store for her if she only followed the road that so many others take as they pass through? Her outlook reminds me of grief. No wonder or lust for life. No hope. No view beyond the mountains walling us in. Each day a repeat of the one before.

A sharp pain stabs at my arm, and I look down to see a mosquito sucking up my blood. I slap at it but it's too fast and vanishes before my palm smacks the skin. I rub the flesh until it's red-hot. The bite mark immediately begins to swell.

'I should've packed the mozzie spray,' I mutter, spitting on my finger and rubbing it on the bite.

'It's that sweet blood of yours,' Evelyn replies.

I wonder what hidden meaning might lurk within that statement. Whether she's saying I'm too sweet, too soft. I'm always doing that, trying to understand the deeper meaning of her words, her small expressions, her silence. She says so little that I have to pull apart each utterance like I'm deciphering a riddle.

We reach the end of the motel and stop outside room five. Evelyn stamps the cigarette beneath her shoe, grinding it into the desert floor, and steps up onto the porch with the key jangling in her hand.

'I'm going to have a shower,' she says as she twists it in the lock. 'Will you get the bags?'

I'm so used to falling into step beside her, waiting to be needed at a second's notice, that I'd forgotten them. I don't have time to reply before she steps inside the room, leaving the door ajar behind her. I turn back and head for the car.

Beyond the motel grounds, I look out at the sky on the horizon as I walk, at the setting sun's rays ever so slowly bleeding into the blue. A couple more hours and the day will be gone, and all that will stand between us and murdering a man will be a single passing of the moon before the sun rises again. When I reach the car, my quivering hands fumble with the keys to open the trunk. We don't call it a boot anymore, not even between ourselves. Another of those little pieces of our British identities that we've traded in to belong. The hatch lifts open and my eyes immediately fall on Evelyn's holdall.

I stand there for a long time, listening to the pounding of my heart, my eyes never once leaving the bag.

I've not looked inside. I watched her pack the gun in there, saw her printing her notes on Aaron Alexander for the journey. But the thought of the unknown and all of the secrets she keeps calls to me tauntingly.

I look over my shoulder towards room five. The door is still open, drifting with the desert breeze. I turn back and snatch the zip of the bag, pulling it along the metal track with trembling fingers.

My wife has always packed light. Whenever we would go away on trips, she only ever packed what she needed. An outfit a day, one pair of shoes for the daytime, and another for the night. Minimal toiletries. She's never been a woman of excess. But what I see now isn't a case of excess. It's obsession.

It only takes one bullet to kill a man, but she's packed enough ammo to shoot up a whole town. There's the gun, the taser, a Stanley knife, a coil of rope and a roll of duct tape. I trace my fingers over each item, trying to connect them with the woman I've known and loved for almost thirty years, but I cannot mesh the two. The woman I married who wouldn't hurt a fly, versus the woman she is now; the woman with a holdall of weapons for inflicting torture.

I pull out the file she'd been putting together this morning, checking over my shoulder again before flipping the cover. Upon Aaron Alexander's release last month, Evelyn had employed a private investigator to follow him wherever he went, so she would know where to find him. I flick through the pages, seeing photos of him working at a gas station in Beatty, a picture of a tired-looking woman with similar eyes to his, who I assume is his mother. There's a three-page document on his older brother Chris, including his home address in Reno where he lives with his wife. I've not seen any of this before – Evelyn kept these things to herself, as if she didn't trust me with her findings. She's not just hunting Aaron, she's mapping out his entire life, so that if he runs, she'll know where to head next. I slip the file back into the bag and spot something else.

Tucked into the side of the holdall is a large, black wrap, coiled up tight. I pull it out and untie it, rolling out the material until the contents gleam up at me. It's a row of knives, varying in size, sharpness and means of use. Blades to slice, and gut, and gouge. I wrap them up again tightly with shaking hands and zip the bag shut.

What are you going to do, Evelyn? What the hell are you going to do?

*

I get out of the shower and return to the bedroom.

Evelyn is sitting on the bed, freshly showered herself and gazing at the wall where she has pinned up the photos and documents detailing our target, a carbon copy of the display above her desk back home. Images of Aaron Alexander stare at me, but I can't bring myself to look back at him and keep my eyes on my wife.

Her skin is dewy, a wet shimmer to the exposed areas around her white vest, but her hair is bone dry. She avoids washing it for as long as she can; it takes too long to settle into place again, she says. Grief is a lot like that. Years of waiting for our worlds to settle. A wait that takes far too long.

The motel room dates back to the Seventies. Wooden head-board and bedside cabinets, a chest of drawers with a drawer face missing. The lampshades don't seem to have been dusted in as long, and the old wiring of the place makes the bulbs flicker. Everywhere I look, the room holds memories of the guests before us, from the questionable stains in the fibres of the carpet, to the scratches and indentations scarring the walls like acne pits. I only have to glance at the bed to know I won't sleep well tonight, imagining the worn, rusty mattress springs beneath the moth-eaten sheets and thinking of all the sleazy motel sex they'll have seen. The thought of strangers' sweat and other fluids makes me feel dirty enough to want to shower again.

Evelyn's eyes don't leave the wall.

Loving my wife makes me despise myself; the ferocity of my neediness while she remains so aloof. We used to share with each other and work through things in tandem. Now her thoughts are a mystery to me. She sits on the end of the bed with a cigarette burning in one hand and a glass of liquor in the other, staring up at the mass of papers and photographs on the wall without even a sideways glance in my direction. I wish I could tell what she's thinking.

'You got any more of that?' I ask. My voice sounds too loud, cutting through the silence.

She nods to the bottle on top of the chest next to the TV, which is so old it still has an antenna. There's a film of dust on the screen that I could write my name in.

I take the bottle and sit beside her, taking a quick swig of the lukewarm brandy. Immediately, I sense her freeze up at the close proximity and hear her teeth begin to grind. I don't think she realizes she does it.

'Can I have a drag?'

She frowns. 'You don't smoke.'

'I used to.'

'That was years ago.'

'I know. Just fancy it.'

She passes the cigarette to me with a slow reluctance. The pillar of ash that had grown between her fingers falls silently to the carpet. I put the filter between my lips and inhale. The smoke is hot on my tongue and scorches the back of my throat. I loathe the taste, but I love the thought of sharing something with her, even if it'll kill me.

I blow the fumes from my nostrils and pass the cigarette back, watching as she stubs it out in the ashtray on the bed, as if she cannot bear to place her lips on something mine have touched. She gets up and opens the door, letting in the dry desert air and the lingering smell of smoke carried on the breeze, stepping onto the porch to watch the sun as it slowly sinks over the mountains. She leans against the post with her arms crossed in a self-soothing embrace.

Loneliness crushes me. We stand a mere twelve feet apart, and yet I have never felt more alone. I wish she wasn't so repelled by me; I wish I hadn't become so needy, so repulsed by myself. I turn and look at my dusty reflection in the television screen, staring into the eyes of the person I've become. A desperate, clawing whisper of a man. I wouldn't want to be near me either.

I stare at my wife's back, at the new, narrow waist I haven't touched, at the definition in her toned arms and shoulders. The only reason I can fathom for her not telling me about the plan, for not including me in the actions that are set to change our lives forever, is that she doesn't trust me.

What are you planning? I think, gazing at the back of her head, wishing I could rattle the secrets free. *What don't you want me to know?*

While her back is turned, I look at the wall, trying to see what she sees.

'I'm going for a walk,' she says abruptly, heading into the room again. I jump, like a child caught doing something he shouldn't. It's probably the only time I've felt grateful that she cannot bear to look at me. I watch as she heads towards her holdall and removes the handgun.

'It'll be dark soon,' I say.

'I won't go far.'

I don't ask her about the gun. I don't ask what she plans to do with it. Of all the things I could say, I tell her it'll be dark soon. I silently spiral into self-hatred and shame. If only I weren't such a coward.

I watch as she slips bullets from the ammo box and fills the chamber, loads one into the barrel by pulling back the slide. She checks the safety is on before holstering the gun in the back of her trousers and takes the bottle of brandy from the counter as she heads out, leaving the door yawning open behind her. I listen to the crickets dancing, smell the approaching night.

Lying back on the bed, I close my eyes and try to quieten my anxiety. But all I can think about are the weapons in the holdall. The arsenal of knives and torture devices. I feel tears itching to escape from behind my closed lids, as I long for the wife I used to know.

BANG.

I bolt upright. The gunshot echoes repeatedly over the mountains as though more rounds are being fired. Sweat breaks out all over my body as the hot rush of panic pummels me.

I run out of the room, my blood surging with adrenaline and my eyes darting in search of her. The sky is ablaze, the clouds red as blood, the horizon burning with the setting sun. I hear another shot and jolt to a stop. My heart jumps so violently that a wave of nausea rips up my throat. The sound came from behind the motel.

I sprint around the building, near blind with panic, and almost run straight into a decrepit phone booth attached to the side of the motel, the phone dangling on its cord. I swerve and stumble over a rock, kicking it so hard that I'm sure I've dislodged a toenail, but keep going. The entire time, I imagine the scene I'm about to find: my wife on the ground, her face blown away by her own hand, with the gun I watched her load. Had she missed the first time? Did she raise her blood-splattered hand to her temple and fire a second bullet? I turn the corner, hold my breath, and see her.

She is standing with her arms raised and the gun in her grip, aiming into the barren landscape. In the distance, I see them: desert hares scattering across the plains, the white pigment on their rears flashing up and down like furry pantaloons. Evelyn holds the gun steady, homes in on one of them, and fires again.

She edges the gun towards the next, but her finger freezes on the trigger. She's noticed me, feeling my presence behind her. I watch as she turns her head, not quite looking at me. Her grip on the gun grows tighter as she squeezes the blood from her knuckles, turning her attention back to her targets. They're too far now; I've distracted her and she's lost them, and even from here I can see her jaw pull taut as she grits her teeth together. She picks up the brandy bottle from the ground and heads off into the distance without a word.

I turn back towards room five and see the woman from the front desk burst from the reception with wide, frantic eyes, her gaze blurry from being woken from a nap. She has a cigarette burning between her fingers; I wonder if she ever takes a breath without filling her lungs with smoke.

'What the hell was that?'

I spot the panic in her eyes, remembering what Evelyn had said about the shooting that happened here. Maybe she was the one who found the body.

'A truck backfired.' I point over my shoulder at the open road.

'Oh,' she says, recovering herself, looking into the distance for it before tucking a wisp of grey hair behind her ear and returning to the office.

I head back to the room, trying to calm my racing heart as the fear and the shame close in, stuck in the truth I had yet to honestly acknowledge to myself before I'd heard that shot.

I'm not just afraid for my wife.

I'm afraid *of* my wife.

*

We never did talk about the death of Joshua's rabbit.

Evelyn had chosen it. I'd wanted the brown rabbit with floppy ears, but she was insistent on the white one – Joshua was always drawing white rabbits, she'd said.

The morning I found it dead in its hutch, there was nothing especially untoward about the scene. It looked to be sleeping peacefully among the sawdust, its pink eyes closed, before I noticed the foam around its furry white mouth. I assumed a coyote had given it a fright in the night, or maybe it'd had an illness we hadn't spotted when we'd bought it. *They're probably all inbred, poor mites.* That's what I'd thought to myself as I pulled on the rubber gloves to move the body into the garden to bury. It was only when I picked up the rabbit and its little head lolled that I realized its neck was broken. No nocturnal animal could have done that. Not unless it had the manners to lock the hutch back up again before scurrying off.

After I'd buried it, I returned to the house to find Evelyn out of bed for the first time in a month, sitting at the breakfast table with a thin line of smoke drifting from the cigarette between her fingers. We held each other's gaze until I gave in and looked away.

Lying in the motel bed, I replay the scene over and over. I hadn't been able to imagine her doing something like that back then, and I'd refused to let myself think of it again. I certainly wouldn't put it past her now.

I flick on the lamp and get out of bed, reaching for my jeans and pulling out my wallet. I've always kept a photo of Joshua tucked inside in case I forget what colour his eyes were, or what his smile looked like; it's amazing what you can forget when someone's gone, even if there isn't a moment that goes by when you're not thinking of them.

I chuck the wallet on the side and lie back again, staring at the photo. At his angelic features, the dimples in his cheeks that appeared when he laughed. I look at him until the pain grows too great, then I slip the photo inside the copy of the Bible in the bedside drawer for safe keeping, switch off the lamp and roll over to try to sleep.

It's gone ten when she returns.

The room is dark, and the mattress releases the faint scent of piss whenever I move, echoes of past guests escaping the fibres with each toss and turn. I'd sleep on the floor if the carpet weren't in even worse shape.

I lie there, listening to her move quietly around the room. She places the gun back in the bag, takes her toiletries and night clothes from inside, and shuts herself in the bathroom. I hear the lock click behind her, and wonder how many of those hares she tracked and killed.

When the bathroom door opens, I close my eyes again, feigning sleep, and continue listening to her moving around; the zipping and unzipping of the bag, the glug of brandy leaving the bottle. I wonder if she plans to finish the whole thing before we hit the road again. I hear her feet pad across the carpet and sense her standing close to me.

'I know you're awake.'

She knows I can't sleep without her beside me. I open my eyes and see her above me, her face hidden in the dark; all I see is her silhouette, distinguished by the curtained window at her back, lit by the moon.

'We need to be rested for tomorrow. Drink this.'

I take the tumbler from her, getting a strong whiff of brandy that turns my stomach. She towers over me in silence, waiting for me to do as I'm told. I knock it back in one, and cough as the booze hits the back of my throat.

'Now sleep.'

She pads around the bed and gets in beside me, her melancholic breaths smelling of toothpaste and brandy. I don't need to look to know she has her back to me, that she's white-knuckling the edge of the bed to keep us from touching.

My throat is still burning, but I'm not sure if it's from the brandy, or from holding back everything I wish I could say to her. All of the questions I'm dying to ask. I should ask her what she plans to do. If I were brave enough, I would beg her not to go through with it. I would hide her weapons, drive off into the desert with them. I would do *something*.

I try to swallow, but my mouth and throat have been sapped dry.

'I love you,' I whisper. The only words I can find within myself to say.

She doesn't say anything in return.

*

When I open my eyes, the room is bright with the new day.

The curtains have been pulled back, letting in the hot sun. My head feels fuzzy, as if I've drunk too much, but I only had a swig of brandy when we arrived and then a tumbler of the stuff before closing my eyes. My aching, languid body and fuzzy mind make it seem as though I had the bottle. I lie listening to a slow, persistent drip from the bathroom tap. The dread I've carried all these months has grown overnight. What was once a seed within me has grown into a weed, its bristles and thorns cutting into my insides.

I hold my breath, not ready to face what I already know. The truth that is ripping through me like a blade. I close my eyes and try to hold on to the memory of the woman she was before, but the truth keeps knocking.

I know without even turning over that she's gone.

II

ANGER

London, summer 2004

The hospital room is small, too small for the number of people in it. Evelyn and I are at one end of the bed, where she grits her teeth through the pain and crushes my hand in hers, and the midwife is stationed at the other, her focus squarely between my wife's legs quivering in the stirrups. I watch her thigh muscles clenching with each spasm, the tendons from her groin to her kneecaps pulled as tight as harp strings, extending to the sharp line of her calves and down to her toes, which are curled like hairs shrivelling before a flame.

'You're doing so well,' I whisper, trying not to look down at my fingers. They'd been white at first, the blood squeezed out of them. Now they look purple and bruised.

I don't know what to say to her. Is there even a right thing to say? I wonder if other fathers feel guilt like I do. For putting my wife through this pain, for feeling so utterly useless. I kiss the back of her hand as the nurse appears on the other side of the bed and nods for me to continue. I must be doing something right.

'You've got this, baby. You've got this.'

The room smells of birth; each breath is laced with the metallic tang of my wife's blood and sweat. Her face is scrunched up with the pain, sweat shimmering all over her, beading and dripping down her temples, cheeks and neck. I blot her face with a strip of gauze, watching a tear slip from the corner of her eye. I mop it up and kiss her sodden forehead.

'Keep going, Evelyn,' the midwife says. 'One more push and it's all over.'

The midwife's words linger against the backdrop of my wife's scream. The life we had before this moment is about to end. The days when we only had ourselves to care for, the nights we slept soundly. One last push and our lives will be thrust down an entirely different path. A sudden bout of fear hits me as I think of our freedom being torn away with each hissing exhale through Evelyn's teeth, of the responsibility about to be rested upon our shoulders, of all the mistakes we are bound to make and how unprepared I feel to fill the role I need to fill, before an entirely new sound breaks through the room.

A baby's cry.

With a brief snip of the cord, the bundle of writhing flesh is taken to the other end of the room. I turn to my wife and stroke her damp hair as she cranes her neck to follow the midwife.

When she turns back towards us, we both hold one, shared breath. All of my focus is on the blanketed bundle in her arms.

'A beautiful baby boy.'

A sob escapes from Evelyn's lips as he is placed on her chest, and we both get in close, so close we can smell the newness of him.

'Joshua,' Evelyn whispers.

We look at one another, smiling through tears and snot, through a love so intense that I feel dizzy, before peering back down at our son.

Our baby boy. Our beautiful, perfect baby boy.

4

Evelyn

Crack.

I shake my head to rid myself of the intrusive thought; the internal torment that never stops plaguing me. I grip the wheel in my hands and focus on the open road.

I thought I'd feel guilty for what I did to Tobias. Lying to him. Drugging him. Abandoning him in the middle of the Death Valley desert without any means of escape. But as I speed through the mountains with the hot, smoky breeze billowing through the open window and all of his belongings on the back seat, I don't feel any guilt at all, not a drop. I feel free.

When Joshua died, Tobias became my rock, but not in the way one might think. He was a boulder crushing down upon my chest, keeping me close, keeping me down, keeping me stuck. I couldn't turn my head without him noticing, couldn't form a thought without him trying to read it. I couldn't breathe. Tobias hasn't been able to trust the world around him since our son's murder; he needs to control everything in his vicinity, even if he doesn't know he's doing it, even if that control is cloaked in love. Joshua's death was out of Tobias's control, so to feel safe, to feel secure, he has tried to control my grief, keeping me caged up for years, smothering me with his attention and his need to treat a wound that can never be healed. I feel the binds between us snapping with each mile I drive, breathing in the fresh taste of independence.

There are two things that could happen now. Tobias could admit defeat and find his way home, waiting for me to return. Or he could try to stop me. The wise thing would be the former. If he does the latter, I'll do everything I can to cut every last bind once and for all.

I wonder what Aaron Alexander is doing now. I imagine him standing behind the counter at the gas station, greeting people with a smile he doesn't deserve to wear. Does he feel free now that he's out of jail? Does he feel hope for the future he believes he has before him? My heart flutters at the thought of bleeding any semblance of hope from him; taking his future and ripping it to shreds right before his eyes.

I've been planning this journey for so long that I can hardly remember how I spent my days before all of this; there's only a dark, empty void between my life with Joshua and my life now. From the moment I left my bed after that first month, I've crossed off the days on my calendar, waiting for this day. I'd buy a new one each year and look at the blank white pages: the remaining days I had yet to survive before I could finally claim justice. There was never a moment that I thought of changing my mind, of letting Aaron Alexander live. Never a second's doubt.

I don't expect anyone to understand me or my thinking. To fathom the totalitarian rage I have towards him for what he's done. No one can imagine the agony of losing one's child until it happens to them. There is no rationality with grief like this, no seeing the situation from both sides. It's like living in a nightmare from which I can never wake, all while being bombarded by reminders of the past and visions of the future that was stolen from us all. I will never see my child smile again. I will never hear his laugh. I will never breathe in the smell of him when he would wrap his arms around me upon waking. I will never get to meet the man he was to become, watch him grow into his own person outside of myself. Be loved beyond a parent's love, have children of his own and learn of the capacity of the human heart to adore every fibre of another being. And the blame lies entirely at Aaron Alexander's feet.

When I'm not thinking of killing him, I sometimes think of killing myself. Turning the gun inwards instead of out. Pressing the muzzle to the roof of my mouth and pulling the trigger until my pain paints the ceiling. It's not a want, it's more of a compulsion. A voice in my head I don't want to hear, words I don't wish to think. But still they come, creeping in as I lay my head on the pillow, every time I let my mind stray from the man I live to hate. I wonder if Tobias has thought of doing the same; using a bullet as a ticket out of this hell we've found ourselves in. Sometimes I'm convinced he knows when I'm thinking of ending it all. I'll imagine slipping the gun between my teeth, tasting the cold metal, and he'll look at me, reach for me, say something to break my chain of thought. Keeping me anchored in the pain with him. I'm not sure whether I'm grateful for those moments or resent him for them.

You're going into this like a suicide bomber.

Maybe he's right. Maybe I am.

I know what I would have thought of this behaviour before Joshua died. As a psychiatrist, I saw many people trapped within their grief. I'd recommend in-depth therapy, prescribe medication to numb the depression as they worked through it, poke holes in their thinking so the truth could shine through. But now I realize how wrong I was. I didn't know how all-encompassing grief could be. How tyrannical the rage against injustice would be on my thinking. They talk of grief having stages. *Denial. Anger. Bargaining. Depression. Acceptance.* They speak of it as a journey, one in which you'll linearly hit stage after stage, as if there's an end in sight. I always scoff at that last one. *Acceptance.* There is no accepting pain like this. The callous murder of my child, leaving him on a dark, desert highway to die alone. No amount of therapy or love or time could ever bring me to accept that. It must be so easy to see each side of something like this when you're not dying from the inside out.

Crack.

The grief swells in my chest, pushing apart my lungs as it grows. I clamp my eyes shut, shake my head again. I see him hit the road, the rear lights of the car bathing the scene red as it screeches to a halt, before the sound of the squealing tyres screams into the night, and my baby is left in the dark.

A shooting pain travels up my jaw, snapping me out of the thought. I'd been clenching my teeth to get through the memory. I have one bad tooth that gives me trouble; I must have exposed a nerve with my grinding, and it's got worse recently, the anxious tic becoming more frequent as Aaron Alexander's release crept closer. I fix my eyes back on the open road.

Why do you do that?

I hear his voice in my mind, calling from the past. I brace myself before the memory comes.

We'd been driving to Joshua Tree National Park. I was behind the wheel as I am now, with Joshua in the passenger seat, looking up at me in confused wonder. We'd only been in America for a week or two. He'd felt lonely and lost – we all had – and while Tobias had dived straight into his work, Joshua and I were left to our own devices until school began and I joined my new practice to begin my US residency program. I'd got him out of the house by telling him there was a park named after him that we had to see.

Do what, honey?

Chew your teeth.

I'd smiled, my love for him flushing through me.

It's just something I do when I'm stressed sometimes.

I remember seeing his little hand reaching out to my thigh, patting it tenderly with his soft, delicate palm, his short fingers.

Don't be stressed. We're going to be okay.

I'd told him that a lot in the lead up to the move, that we were all going to be okay, and there he was mirroring it back to me.

The memory vanishes and it's just me, the empty passenger seat and the highway again.

I'm sorry I was so wrong, baby. I'm sorry nothing turned out okay. But I'm going to make it right.

I blink back tears, reach for the map and glance at the route before setting my eyes back on the road.

I don't have much further to go.

5

Tobias

I don't know how long I've been lying here. Twenty or thirty minutes, maybe longer. All I know is that the moment I leave this bed, the facts of the matter will become inescapable. Evelyn slipped sleeping pills into that brandy. She did it to make sure I wouldn't wake up while she packed up her things and left me behind.

Left me behind. I repeat the words in my mind and a physical jolt of pain stabs at my abdomen.

I imagine her pouring the crushed pills in with the alcohol and swirling the mixture with her finger so as not to make a sound, wiping it dry on her thigh before coming to my bedside and ordering me to drink. The part that hurts the most, I think, is how desperately willing I was to play along. I'd been so hungry for a morsel of affection from her that I didn't question it when it came. I didn't see or hear her crushing the pills, which means she must have done it premeditatively and brought the powder with her; something I failed to spot when I looked inside the holdall. Another part of the plan she kept from me. Now I know why: I was never in on this with her. I was merely a problem she needed to solve before heading out on the journey that she had always planned to take alone.

I think of her creeping around the room as I slept, peeling the photos and documents off the wall. Maybe she paused with a held breath as I turned over in my sleep and waited for me to settle again before continuing with the task. Then she would have picked up her bag and headed out the door, looking back over her shoulder one final time before shutting it behind her and walking across the dusty forecourt to the car. Maybe that's too optimistic of me; she might not have looked back at all.

Then it dawns on me.

The car.

I throw back the sheets and go to the window, standing before it in nothing but briefs and a T-shirt. The sun seems brighter today, bouncing off the mountainsides and radiating off the dry land, with no sign of a breeze to ease the incessant heat. I stand at the window in silence, staring at the spot where our car had been until my anxious breaths fog the glass.

Evelyn hasn't just left me behind. She's left me here with no means to follow her.

As the details of her plan settle into place, I ball up my hands to stop them shaking, trying to bat each realization away as it comes, refusing to believe that she would go so far, that she would betray me so skilfully and without hesitation. I squirm at the memory of how good it felt for her to care for me last night.

Despite the mounting evidence of her indifference towards me, I can't fight the hope that she might have left a note and begin looking frantically around the room. There is no note on the dresser, nor on her pillow or nightstand. There is no note on mine. In fact, there is nothing on my nightstand at all.

My phone is gone.

I stride over and yank open the drawer harder than I should, hearing a splintering crack from inside, but the only thing I see within is a copy of the Bible and several balls of dust.

I go to my jeans dangling on the back of the chair by the dresser and rummage through the pockets. My wallet has gone too.

No. She wouldn't do this to me.

But no matter how many times I repeat the lie, I can't seem to make it ring true.

I move about the motel room hunting for the missing items, the list growing the longer I look: my bag has gone from the closet; my toiletries are no longer above the sink. My shoes are missing from beside the door. After minutes of searching every inch of the room, the truth hits me like a fist to my gut.

My wife has abandoned me in the middle of the desert, leaving me with only the clothes on my back. I have no phone, no money, no means to follow her. Not even a pair of shoes. Not even my fucking toothbrush.

The photo.

I'd slipped my photo of Joshua inside the copy of the Bible. I pull out the drawer again and flip open the cover: it's still there. I sigh with relief and kiss it before sinking down onto the end of the bed, crushed by the reality I've woken to.

She's left me.

The sense of loneliness is overwhelming. I am all alone, surrounded by miles and miles of desert with no way to cross it. What is Evelyn going to do? What doesn't she want me to see? How far is she going to go? These questions hound me, swarming in my mind until I feel dizzy.

The sound of a key turning in the lock on the door to the room jolts me out of my thoughts.

The door opens, and I see the woman from behind the reception desk standing there with a trolley of cleaning supplies behind her. Her eyes are glazed with her own thoughts, her face etched with tiredness or sadness, or an amalgamation of the two. You can always tell the truth about someone by the expression they wear when they don't think anyone is looking. When she spots me sitting on the end of the bed, her expression falls.

'Thought you checked out?' she asks. 'Your wife came by this morning and gave me the key back . . .'

So, she really has left. Even with all the evidence before me, hearing the woman confirm it makes it all the more real. I suddenly feel too exposed, dressed in just a T-shirt and underwear. I feel the hot outside air kissing the skin on my legs and feet as it creeps in from the desert. The smoke smells stronger today, which means the wildfires are getting closer.

'What time is it?' I ask.

'Noon. Check out was eleven – I told you that yesterday.'

'What time did my wife leave?'

'Not sure. Nine, maybe ten.'

'Right.'

I remain at the end of the bed, staring at the floor. I don't know what to say, what to tell her. I don't know what to tell myself. For the moment I say the words aloud, it will all become too real. There's no going back once a truth has been uttered, even under one's own breath.

'If you want another night, I'll give you another night,' she says, shifting her weight onto her right hip with a sigh, her hand nestling in the flesh at her waist. 'But you gotta come to the office and pay.'

I don't have the money to pay you with. I don't have any way of leaving, either.

Behind her, the barren land taunts me with its vastness. I imagine walking along Route 95 under the belting sun, the hot earth melting the skin clean off my feet.

'I'll be with you in a minute. That all right?'

She shrugs and reaches for the door handle.

'Mrs Smith not staying on with you?'

'Who?'

'Your wife?'

I say nothing, looking down at the stained carpet.

'Only it's a cheaper rate if you're staying on your own. But it'll still be double, unless you want to write down your real name on the form.'

My head is swimming. She's asking too many questions, wanting to know too much, too soon; I haven't even got to grips with this myself. This must be how Evelyn felt in the beam of my constant attention; I was too incessant, too available. Too goddamn annoying. I try to shake off the shame.

'I'll be with you in a minute.'

'Whatever you say, Mr Smith.'

She emphasizes my false surname, letting on that she knows I'm full of shit, and pulls the door shut.

I sit in the hot, stuffy room, listening to the drip from the bathroom as I stare at my dusty reflection in the TV.

What the hell am I going to do?

I rest my head in my hands, my pulse throbbing in the flesh of my palms.

I've got to do what I was afraid to do before. I've got to try and stop her before it's too late.

If Evelyn takes a life, then the wife I loved, the woman she was before, will be gone forever. I try to think of how I might stop her. Could I track her down, try to talk sense into her? What would I do then, when that inevitably failed? How could I stop her from doing the one thing she is hell-bent on achieving?

When the thought comes to me, my stomach churns.

I could get to Aaron Alexander first.

The idea of being near the man brings on a wave of nausea. How could I possibly put aside my hatred for him to protect him, even if the sole reason was to save my wife?

I think of my son, dead in the ground because of him. Would Joshua understand why I protected the man who hurt him, if it meant saving his mother? I rub the tears from my eyes as soon as they begin to appear.

My wife has left me in the middle of the desert so I can't stop her from murdering the man who killed our son.

My head spins as I realize that this is my life now. I used to be a father, a husband. I had a career. I was once a young boy who had dreams of a future that looked nothing like this. Now I'm just a tired old man alone in the desert. Loneliness fills me up again, so heavy and dark that for a moment I consider letting it devour me whole, lying back on the bed and never getting up again.

I need to call someone. I'll call my bank and see how I can get some money from my account and get the hell out of here. But how can I, when Evelyn's taken my phone? I don't know the right number to call, and I can't look it up. My head spins and more *what if*s follow. There's an old, dusty rotary phone on the bedside table, but when I pick up the receiver and place it to my ear, the line is dead.

There's got to be one at the motel I can use. But what if I'm forced to use the phone at the front desk, with the old woman listening in? And if she refuses, what will I do then? Then I remember the phone booth I saw round the side of the motel. I could use that if I had the money, but I don't even have loose change to my name.

Every time I think I have an idea, it's quickly shot down by the fact that I have no means to execute it. Round and round in hopeless circles, all while Evelyn gets closer to Aaron Alexander.

I look at the wall where her mind map had been. All that's left are small puncture marks where pushpins held all the pieces in place. Something glints in the corner of my eye. A photo of Aaron Alexander is poking out from between the side of the chest and the wall, revealing just a slip of hair and one piercing blue eye; it must have slipped off in the night.

I reach down and pick it up, blowing away the dust that has stuck to it, and stare into his eyes. I used to daydream about choking this man. Beating him with my fists until he was nothing but bone and fleshy pulp. So many lives destroyed. So many futures stolen, including his own.

How can I possibly keep this man safe, after all he's done?

I chuck the photo in the trash and pull on my jeans.

With no toothbrush to freshen my breath, and no other belongings to take with me, I head out of the motel room and into the heat. The wildfire smoke is strong; the sky is clouded by it in the distance. The hot earth burns my bare feet in seconds, my pace quickening with every step. There's a truck parked up where our car had been, with an Alsatian in the back that's barking at me from behind the window and lathering the glass in its slobber. I cross the dusty forecourt as fast as I can, practically feeling the blisters forming in real time. The dog is still barking when I reach the door.

I all but jump into the office, looking down at my feet to check if they're smoking. The woman behind the counter stares at me in bewilderment. A man wearing a Dodgers baseball cap, a checked shirt over a rock band tee, camo trousers and heavy-duty boots stands where Evelyn and I had been just yesterday, signing the form to rent one of the rooms. He's staring at me too. I watch their eyes travel down to my bare feet.

'Where the hell are your shoes?' the woman asks.

'Long story,' I reply. 'Can I use the payphone?'

'I don't decide who uses it. You put in the change and dial a number. Don't need my say so.'

'I haven't got any change.'

'I can break a note.'

'I . . . haven't got any notes either.'

They both stare at me in silence.

'It's a *pay*phone sir. Clue's in the name: you gotta pay.'

'I know, but . . . I'm in a bit of a situation, and I really need to call someone.'

'I've got a phone here—'

'It's private, you see . . .'

'She said you gotta pay,' the man barks, looking at me as if I'm vermin that has scurried its way in. 'You deaf or something? Need me to tell you it in fucking sign language?'

My cheeks flush and I turn back towards the door. The embarrassment must have shown on my face, because as I reach for the handle, I hear the woman sigh and call out.

'Wait,' she says. 'I got the change. Your wife left a good tip yesterday. Hang on.'

'Thanks. I really appreciate it.'

The man in the baseball cap continues looking me up and down while the woman breaks the note.

'You English or something?' he asks.

'Yeah,' I say. 'Part of the long story.'

'Well, what's the short version?'

'The short version is I'm English.'

His eyes narrow as the woman fumbles behind the desk.

'Here you go,' she says, dropping the change onto the surface.

'Thanks. Is it possible for you to look up a number up for me? I need to call my bank.'

'You gotta be kiddin' me,' the man spits.

The woman sighs as she returns to her seat, turning her attention to a computer that looks older than I am. The screen lights up the scratches on her glasses.

'Which bank?'

'Wells Fargo.'

She makes a few clicks, scribbles down a number on a Post-it, the digits so small and packed together that I can barely make them out, and sticks it on the surface of the desk. The whole time, the man in the baseball cap is watching me. I feel myself burning up under his gaze but refuse to look his way.

'Any other favours you need, Mr Smith? Or we done here?'

'We're done. Thank you.'

'You sure you don't wanna ask her to come out there and dial the numbers for you, pal?' the man says.

I head back out without another word, sprinting across the hot ground under the baking sun. The dog barks at me again as I pass, jumping into the front of the truck and shoving its snout through the crack in the driver's window to growl some more.

The phone booth couldn't be in a worse state; if the woman hadn't spoken of it working, I'd have assumed it was nothing more than a relic of the past. The glass has been smashed clean out of the frame, which has turned brown with rust. I open the door, half-convinced that it'll come off in my hand, and step inside, holding my breath as soon as I catch a distinct whiff of piss. I pick up the phone where it dangles on the cord.

Reading the number on the Post-it shaking in my grip, I dial and listen to the automated message, selecting the correct lines via the rusted numbers on the payphone until I'm listening to hold music.

'Christian speaking,' a man says upon answering. 'How can I help you today?'

'My name is Tobias Moore. I need access to my account but I've lost my card and I'm stuck in a motel on the side of Route 95. Can you help?'

'Let's see what we can do, sir,' Christian replies, in a cheery, robotic tone. I could tell him that I'd just run over my dog and shat my pants and I'm sure he'd respond with the same mindless chirp.

As we go through the security details, I answer as quickly as I can, anticipating the money for the call running out with each question he asks me. How do these things work? Does it just cut you off? I tap my foot in the well of the booth, trying to slow my racing heart. My empty stomach is churning, sending acid up my throat again.

'I need to be quick, okay, Christian? I'm in a phone booth and I don't have much money.'

'Of course, sir. I'm now in your account. What service can I provide for you today?'

'I need access to my funds but I don't have my card.'

'We can send out a new card in three to five business days, sir.'

'Well, that's not much help, is it? I need the money now. I'm stranded.'

'Hmm. Let me see what I can do. One moment.'

'But I don't have much time—'

I sigh as I hear the jingle back in my ear and begin tapping my foot again; it's only now that I realize how much I'm bursting for a piss. A brief breeze picks up, blowing sand into my back. I squint as it darts over my shoulders and into my eyes, then jump as I hear the loud, urgent voice on the line.

'*One minute remaining. To continue your call, please enter the correct fee.*'

'*Shit*,' I hiss, and fumble for the change in my pocket with the phone in the crook of my neck. I'm feeding in the coins when the holding music stops.

'Hello, sir,' Christian says.

I jump again, almost dropping the phone. If Evelyn saw me like this – a bumbling, sweating mess – she'd tell me to get my shit together. I close my eyes and take a deep breath.

'I haven't got much time, Christian, so if you could please just—'

'I'm sorry, sir, but I can't release funds from your account.'

My heart plummets.

'What? What the hell do you mean you can't release the funds? It's my money, for Christ's sake.'

'It's not that, sir—'

'Then what is it?' I snap. The breeze intensifies, flinging sand at me again. I try to huddle away from it and scrunch my eyes tighter. 'Huh? Tell me. What could possibly justify you leaving a man out in the middle of the desert without a penny to his name? This country is so screwed up. It's my goddamn money!'

'It's not that, sir—' he repeats.

'*Then what the hell is it?*'

'You have no funds in your account, Mr Moore.'

The wind falls. Silence creeps in.

'I don't understand.'

'I can see here that the funds were withdrawn by Mrs Evelyn Moore.'

Evelyn?

Around the front of the motel, the dog starts barking again until I can barely hear myself think.

'How is that allowed?'

'Well, it's a joint account sir.'

'No, no. You're misunderstanding. We have a joint account, but I want the money from my personal current account. You're looking at the wrong one.'

'I can see here that your current account was transferred into a second joint account last month, sir.'

I listen to the words, but I can't seem to make them sink in. The dog keeps barking and barking. I plug my free ear with my finger. I don't remember approving that and I certainly didn't arrange it myself. Evelyn couldn't have done this without my say-so. But then I remember, and my heart sinks.

Last month, Evelyn had given me a bunch of forms to sign; we were sorting the funds we had in our savings accounts, speaking to a financial advisor to see how much longer we could make the money last. She must have slipped the joint account form into the pile. And of course, like the idiot I am, the idiot Evelyn knew me to be, I signed them all without reading them. I had no reason not to trust my wife.

The Post-it note scrunches loudly in my clenched fist.

'*You have one minute remaining. To continue the call, please enter the correct fee.*'

'Thank you,' I mutter into the receiver. It's all I can think to say before hanging up.

The dog has finally fallen quiet, but the silence is almost worse. I turn around and look out of the phone booth and across the sprawling desert until tears blur my vision. I've never felt so lost and alone in all my life.

Thankfully, the dog starts up again, snapping me out of my self-pity. I dash the tears from my eyes and take a deep, shuddering breath. Sulking won't help me stop my wife from destroying what little we have left.

I need help, but who can I call? Evelyn and I have spent the last eleven years severing every relationship we had. Family and friends back in England heard from us less and less until we stopped answering their calls and opening their emails altogether; eventually they stopped calling, and the only emails we got were bills and mailing list junk. We pushed everyone away to make way for our grief, and now Evelyn has finally pushed me away too. I'm stranded in every sense of the word.

Even if I did call someone back in England, what could they do? We're thousands of miles apart. They can't wire me money to help me get out of here because I don't have my bank card to withdraw it. They could maybe pay for another night here over the phone, but that doesn't help me escape, and it would give Evelyn a day's head start.

I step out of the booth, leaving the receiver to dangle and sway on its rusty cord.

Now what?

I still need to get the hell out of here with nothing to my name, and the first thing I'm going to do once I'm clear of this place is find the money for some goddamn shoes.

I stop to piss against the side of the motel and think. I could ask for a cab, but God knows how long that would take or how much it would cost. I can hardly skip the fare without any shoes to run in. I zip up my flies and walk around to the front of the building. The dog is still in the truck, and the man who'd given me grief in the office is carrying cases through to the motel room next to mine with a phone wedged between his ear and his shoulder.

'Miles, I told you we'll sort it,' I hear him say. I step closer, listening to the thud of the cases on the floor, followed by a banging sound. 'I'll be with you by the morning and it'll be done with. No . . . no . . . I told you I'm not paying a man to do the job when we can sort it ourselves.' I hear the banging again. 'Fuck. Miles, hold on, all right? I need to go ask for a fan or move rooms or somethin'. The AC is shot and it's hot as hell in here.'

He steps back out onto the porch, failing to see me in his periphery as he heads in the opposite direction towards the office. The dog barks at him behind the glass.

'Lexy! Quiet!'

The dog keeps barking, and the man keeps walking. I wait until the office door swings shut behind him before looking back at the truck, my heart thumping wildly in my chest.

I'm going to have to steal that truck.

My empty stomach keeps churning. I haven't even had a drink of water; I try to moisten my lips but my tongue is as dry as the dirt beneath my feet.

Would he have left the keys in there? Who'd steal a truck in the middle of the desert with an Alsatian inside?

A man who's got nothing to lose, that's who.

I glance towards the door to room five. I've got nothing to take with me, only the T-shirt I slept in and these old jeans, and Joshua's photo in my pocket. There's nothing stopping me leaving right now.

I look towards the office, wondering how long it takes to ask for a fan and bring it back. If I'm going to do this, I need to do it now. Right now. Adrenaline is surging through my body so fast that my head starts to spin.

Before I can stop myself, I'm running, my bare feet slapping against the hot ground, my heart lodged in my throat. I reach the driver's side and come face to face with the dog snarling at me behind the glass.

'Hey!' the man shouts. I turn to see him standing outside the swinging office door holding on to an old white fan. 'Stop getting her worked up, asshole!'

It's now or never.

I snatch open the door, grabbing Lexy by her collar and dragging her out in one swoop, narrowly missing a bite on the arm. I just manage to jump up inside the truck before she leaps towards me with her teeth bared. I knock her down with my foot, watching a swipe of her drool flick across my jean leg as she falls back, then reach for the door and slam it shut. The man is shouting. I hear the *thunk* of the fan he was carrying being dropped on the ground, the cage breaking open and spitting the blades across the forecourt, followed by the pounding of his feet as he sprints towards the truck. The adrenaline is pumping so wildly now that I feel blind with it and move on instinct. I slam my palm down on the lock as he approaches, not daring to look at him, then open the visor, praying the key will fall into my lap and snatching it up when it does. I struggle to get it into the ignition and flinch as the man punches the glass from the outside. His gold ring bangs against it like a bullet hitting metal. I turn the key, hear the engine grumbling and a cracking sound when he throws a second punch. The engine turns over and I stick it in reverse and swing out widely, so wide that the man has to jump out of the way. Lexy is barking loudly and foaming at the mouth.

I change gear and slam my bare foot on the accelerator, the tyres spinning dust as I steer towards the road. In the rear-view mirror, I see the man race after me on foot with Lexy howling beside him, and the woman from behind the counter standing at the office door, watching me go.

I press the pedal to the floor until they're nothing but dots in the distance and then finally out of sight.

Hunched behind the wheel, I try to catch my breath.

'What am I doing?' I ask myself, as I look around the stranger's truck. It's caked in dog hair and there are cigarette ends crushed in the tray on the dashboard. 'What the fuck am I doing?'

Guilt creeps through the adrenaline, more for kicking the dog than stealing that bastard's truck, mixed with the age-old fear of doing something wrong. I've always been a rule-follower and disobeying the law like this has me ready to break out in hives.

I look down at the dashboard to check the gas: I need enough to make the fifty miles to Beatty, and I don't have any money to fill the tank. But I should have just enough to get there, even if I have to drive at a crawl for the last mile or two.

I stare at the highway cutting through the Death Valley desert, my hands quivering in their tight grip on the wheel, trying to decide what the hell I'm going to do.

All I know is that I've got to find Aaron Alexander before my wife does. If she gets there first, he won't know what hit him.

6

Aaron

Some people understand life better than others, don't they? I don't mean capitalism or politics or corruption, that sort of thing. They understand life in that they know how to live it: they know how to love, how to trust, how to get by relatively unscathed. Standing behind the counter, I see it all the time. Those people who have a spark in their eyes, a gleaming secret the rest of us have yet to uncover. I see the people who haven't, too: the broken ones, the quietly hopeful ones, the dangerous ones. You meet all kinds of folk at a gas station.

In the short month I've been free, I've noticed that it doesn't matter how well off someone looks; some of the most miserable people I see come through here appear to have it all, and yet that knowing spark is missing. I look through the glass partition separating me and the customers at the register and see the mess of them; the internal wounds and the fears and the hopelessness. Then the next customer could pull up in a battered old Ford with mud on their boots and beam. I watch them walk back to their cars and back to their lives, wishing I was one of them.

'Aaron, you in there?'

Jim clicks his fingers in front of my eyes, and I come round with a jolt. He's almost as wide as he is tall, with grey teeth from smoking and piss-yellow eyes from drinking. He has a comb-over that he always forgets to gel down, walking around the store with his few strands of hair waving about like flags at full mast.

'Sorry, Jim.'

'There's a puddle of gas out there. Woman came in huffin' and puffin' about us spoiling her fancy shoes. You didn't hear her?'

'Sorry. I was thinking.'

'That's your problem, dear boy.' He claps me on the back with a sigh. 'Always thinking.'

I head out back for the buckets and broom and take them to the spill by the pumps.

My mom used to say that too. *Away with the goddamn fairies* is how she put it. It's tough when you're the quiet kid. When you're soft and scared and the world is loud and angry. It was always safer to shrink down a size, keep my mouth shut. I was like this even before I went to jail. That's one good thing about growing up in a trailer park, where your mom's boyfriends beat the living shit out of you; you learn to be invisible. If you're quiet enough they might not notice you. You can't be knocked down if they don't see you.

I sift sawdust from the bucket over the spill, watching the black fuel disappear beneath the mess, and move the broom back and forth to soak it all up. Then all there is to do is wait.

I look out at Beatty from the forecourt. It's a small town, far out in the desert. Some people know it as the gateway to Death Valley, but I just know it as home, or as hell, depending on the day. A place where everyone knows everyone, and everyone knows your business. You could sneeze and someone across town would bless you. And if you didn't feel trapped already, the towering mountains walling us in would do it. At dusk, the sun sets behind them, casting a shadow across the town, revealing the height of the rocky perimeter that keeps us in and everyone else out. The only time I left this place was to go to jail, and the only reason I came back was because I didn't know any better. Sometimes you need the familiar, even if the only home you've ever known is somewhere you've always wanted to flee.

I shake my head.

That's your problem, dear boy. Always thinking.

I scrape the mess into the other bucket, a mixture of swollen sawdust dark with fuel that's as thick as oatmeal, and head back into the store.

'What're these doing back here?' Jim asks when I come back from putting the broom and buckets out back. He holds up the bouquet of flowers I'd picked out.

'I'm thinking of going to see my mom later. I've paid for 'em. Cash is in the register.'

'I don't doubt that,' he says. We both know he'll be checking later, just to be sure. 'She still not seen you? Your mom?'

I shrug.

'Maybe today she will.'

I catch the pity in his eyes.

'Maybe, son.' He claps me on the shoulder. 'Hold the fort, would you? I gotta take a leak.'

He's only been gone for a moment when the bell above the door chimes. I snap out of my thoughts and look to see who's entered: whether it's one of the happy folks with the gleam in their eye, or one of the lost ones. There's always more of those. But instead, the person I see walking up towards the counter is Sheriff Kincade.

Sturdy walk. A heavy, stern brow. Dead in the eyes, or at least that's how they seem when he's looking at me. I feel myself growing smaller and smaller as he approaches.

'Gas,' he grunts.

'Yes, sir.'

I look out to the cop car by the pumps and begin ringing up the sale.

He drums his fingers against the counter as I work, watching how my hands are shaking through the partition. Sheriff Kincade and I never cross paths without him saying something untoward. I've been a stain on their department ever since I crossed the state line into California and did what I did. They'd had all the time in the world to deal with me when I was a good-for-nothing junkie, running round town committing petty crimes to pay for my next fix, and they failed. Over the years, I've found that the only thing more dangerous than a cop is a humiliated cop.

He slides the cash beneath the partition, revealing a flash of his fingernails. They're neat and clean; mine are mere stubs, bitten to the quick.

'You kill any more kids since I last saw you?' he asks.

I feel myself flush, shame hitting me in the chest like a fist.

'No, sir.'

I slide the cash from the counter and begin sorting his change.

'You back on the pipe yet?'

'No, sir.'

'Because if you were, I'd send you straight back to jail. You know that right?'

'Yes, sir.'

I slide the change back under the partition. I'm just about to withdraw my hand when he grabs it firmly, so firmly that my fingers turn white.

'Look at me when I'm talking to you.'

I raise my head. He's staring at me like I'm the lowest of the low: lower than vermin, lower than dog shit.

'So, if I sent my boys round to raid your place, we wouldn't find drugs there?'

'You'd need a warrant for that.'

He grips my hand harder.

'Don't be smart with me, boy.'

'Sorry, sir.'

I want to look down, look away. but Kincade has the sort of

eyes that grab onto you and don't let you go. I feel my knees shaking beneath the counter.

'There's not a moment that goes by that we're not watching you, kid. The second you screw up, which you will, we're gonna be there to take you back to where you belong.'

'Everything good here, Sheriff?'

Kincade releases my hand the second he hears Jim's voice.

'Keep the change,' he says, and turns back towards the door. Jim is standing with his arms crossed. 'Things would be better if you didn't hire kid-killers, Jim.'

'I hire people who've done their time and are ready to give back to society. That's how rehabilitation works, ain't it? That's what prisons are for.'

'I guess we don't see eye to eye on that.'

'Yeah, I figure we don't.'

They stand a while, staring each other down. The tension is so thick that I can feel it charging the air.

'I guess you'll be going then,' Jim says.

Jim may be a kind-hearted man, but he was also a Marine back in the day. A man who knows how to be tough when it counts. They stand there, both men of uniform, sizing each other up.

'You have a good day,' Kincade says, then heads out the door. He sits awhile in his cop car to stare me down, to remind me that they'll be watching, before finally driving off. Only then do I take a breath.

'You better head on home, Aaron,' Jim says, breaking the silence.

I don't have the voice to thank him. I just nod, my eyes on the floor, and step out from behind the counter. We cross paths, Jim patting me on the back as I go. I'm halfway towards the door when he calls me back.

'Hey, son.' I turn to see him holding up the flowers. 'Don't forget these.'

He hands them over with a sad reluctance, as if by doing so he will add to my hurt if my mom rejects them.

'Maybe she'll see me,' I tell him.

'Maybe, son.'

I feel his eyes burning into my back as I go, and just about make it around the corner before stopping. I look down at the flowers, already drooping from the heat.

Then I chuck them in the trash and keep on walking.

7

Evelyn

I pass the welcome sign for Beatty and feel my heart jump a little.

WELCOME TO BEATTY
GATEWAY TO DEATH VALLEY

The town is just as I'd expected: a sleepy, dusty cluster of buildings with wide roads and mountains around the lip, only differing slightly from the version I'd conjured in my dreams. Not that I'm able to take much of it in. I'm staring at the faces on the sidewalks, at the drivers behind the wheels of the cars passing on the other side of the street, looking for him, my heart rate spiking with each false sighting.

When I reach a stop light, I snatch the map from the passenger seat and eye the route I've highlighted which leads to the gas station. I'm mere minutes from looking Aaron Alexander in the eye.

The light turns green, and I head off again.

I wonder what he's doing right now. What he's thinking. I imagine him closely, picturing each inhale and exhale, every blink, every twitch of emotion on his face. All the things that he took away from my son; the things that I'll take away from him in return. I think of how he'll look when he's dead. His complexion musky white, his eyes dull and unblinking. His mouth slack and his chest still.

I push my foot down on the accelerator a little harder.

When the gas station comes into view, adrenaline sucks the moisture from my mouth. I lick my dry lips as I pull to a stop at the closest pump.

The stifling air hits me the moment I step out of the car. There's a fresh-looking fuel spill at my feet, nothing more than a stain in the asphalt now, with the odd grain of sawdust left behind from an attempt to clean it up. I step around it and attach the pump to the fuel tank, staring over the roof of the car towards the store.

There's a man behind the counter, but it's not him. This guy is much too round and much too old. I glance around the store through the windows, but fail to spot anyone else inside. According to the private investigator I'd hired, who'd worked out Aaron Alexander's shift schedule, he should be here today until close.

Where are you, Aaron?

I shake the last few drops from the pump and return it to the stand. I was sure he'd be here; now I've got to determine where else he might be. I duck back into the car and pick up my files on him, clutching them to my chest before heading over to pay.

The bell rings above my head as I walk inside. The man behind the counter is tallying up dollar bills at the register. He looks up at me briefly.

'Anything else, ma'am? Or just the gas?'

'Marlboro Lights,' I say as I approach the desk, using Tobias's tactic and speaking with an American twang. 'And these.'

I pick up some M&M's from the display and throw them on the counter. I often forget to eat when I'm thinking about Aaron. Every other need seems to fade out. But M&M's were Joshua's favourite. The memory reminded me of my hunger.

'Fifty-three dollars and twenty-three cents.'

I hand over sixty and watch him feed the notes into the register. He goes to pass me the change, but I wave it away.

'I'm not just here for gas.'

He looks at me properly then, scrunching his eyes slightly to bring me into focus.

'Oh yeah?'

'I'm Aaron's probation officer. He was supposed to meet me at midday, but there was no sign of him. Has he been attending work?'

His eyes widen at this, the whites a dull yellow, and glances at my folder. I wonder how long he's been a drunk, how long his liver has been on the brink. He stands straighter.

'Oh yes, ma'am, he's on time every day. Never misses a shift. Are you sure he was meant to meet you today? He's a good lad who's true to his word.'

A good lad.

Anger flushes through me. There is nothing good about that man. The files tremble in my strained grip.

'Well, truthfully, this is my first meeting with him. I'm taking over from a colleague today—'

'Andrea, yeah. I've met her. What happened to her then?'

'Sick,' I lie, wondering what this Andrea looks like, sounds like. Whether she thinks Aaron is a *good lad* too. 'I'm worried I might've gone to the wrong address. Is this the right one?'

I slip a piece of paper from the files, the one detailing Aaron's mother's home address, and press it to the transparent partition.

'Ah, no ... That's his mom's place. He's just gone there in fact, you might catch him. Otherwise, he lives above one of the delis on Main Street. But now that I think of it, I can't remember which one.'

At least I'm closer than I was before. As I wonder how many delis there could be on one street, I make a plan for my next visit: **I need to see Aaron's mother.**

'I must have picked up the wrong file when I left the office. Thank you so much, Mr . . .'

'Arnold,' he says, with a tar-stained grin. 'Jim Arnold.'

'Thank you, Mr Arnold.'

'It's a pleasure to help a pretty lady such as yourself.'

I grit my teeth behind a smile and grab the cigarettes and candy; another Americanism that's forced its way into my vocabulary. I head for the door with Jim Arnold's eyes glued to my rear.

The smoke from the wildfires has followed me here. The burnt, acrid taste of it lingers in the air, but the people of Beatty are carrying on without so much as a double take.

I head back to my car, smiling farewell over my shoulder to the man who has just signed Aaron Alexander's death warrant. He gives me a wave, his grey-toothed grin set as wide as it'll go.

I get behind the wheel, tear open the pack of M&M's, and pour a few into my mouth as I drive away. The red ones were Joshua's favourites.

*

I park on the street and enter the trailer park on foot; it's as dilapidated as you'd expect, and I think of how this world and mine were never meant to meet.

I stop outside Annie Alexander's trailer; she seems to have as much love for trash bags in place of foliage outside her home as she does for alliteration. I watch the run-down trailer tremble with a person's footsteps. That's one good thing, I suppose. They can't pretend they aren't home. I wonder what I'll do about his mother. What I'll do if she tries to stop me.

I knock on the screen door, noticing the scuffs and dirt, the dead bugs mummified within a spider's web in the corner, and take a step back. The footsteps head towards me, the trailer rocking again underfoot.

Annie Alexander opens the door, smoking a cigarette as she looks me up and down.

'What?' she snaps.

'I'm looking for Aaron.'

'Well, you won't find him here.'

'His boss, Jim, said I would.'

'Well, Jim was wrong. He ain't here.'

'Jim seemed pretty convinced.'

'Well, Jim's thicker than a plank of wood. I haven't seen Aaron in over ten years.' She drags on the cigarette. Ash falls to the concrete step beneath her.

'Where might I find him?'

'Lord if I know.' She frowns, looking me up and down again. 'Who are you?'

I consider lying to her as I had to Jim. It's easy to lie to a man, they're generally too busy staring at my breasts or my ass to notice. But Annie doesn't seem like the type to fall for a woman's charm. She's seen far too much in her life; I can tell that from her sharp, suspicious glare. Nor do I want to lie to her: I want her to know who I am. I want her to look deep into my eyes and know how much pain her son has caused.

'I'm Joshua Moore's mother.'

I see it immediately – the flash of fear on her face. Ash falls silently from the cigarette again. She goes to reach for something inside, but I'm faster. I yank the handgun from the back of my jeans and point it between her eyes.

'One more step and I'll blow your fucking head off.'

She freezes on the spot, looking down the eye of the gun. I can almost see her heart beating in her chest, her off-white T-shirt fluttering with her pulse.

'What d'you want Aaron for?' she asks, her voice suddenly hoarse.

'I'm here to kill him.'

She flinches, before quickly steeling herself again.

'You think I'm going to tell you where my son is so you can shoot him?'

'I'm going to find and kill him either way.'

'What kind of mom would I be if I let you do that?'

'What kind of mother kicks her kid out of the house for being gay?'

The private investigator had shared this with me, explaining the relationships or lack thereof in Aaron's life; who he would and wouldn't go to if he were to run. Turns out, he hasn't got many people to turn to: his biological father has been serving a life sentence since 1996 after shooting a hostage in a liquor store hold-up, and his stepfather is probably the nastiest man in Beatty. His older brother did the wise thing and got clear of them a long time ago.

A flicker of shame crosses Annie's face.

'Yeah. I know all about that,' I say.

'What d'you care? You're here to kill him.'

'Because I'm a mother too.' A slice of pain cuts into my chest. 'I *was* a mother. And I would have loved my child for whoever he grew up to be. But because of your son, and because of *you*, he didn't get that chance.'

'What goes on between me and my son is none of your damn business, is it? And you can save wasting a bullet; I don't have anything to tell you. Even if I did, I wouldn't tell you shit.'

I watch her closely and my heart sinks. Maybe she really doesn't know where Aaron is. I click the safety on and slip the gun into the back of my waistband.

'I've made mistakes,' she says, her face ashen now. The hard bravado has slipped; all that's left is a mournful mother. 'Mistakes I wish I could take back. But life don't work that way. We have to reap what we sow.'

Yes, we do. And it's time for Aaron to reap what he has sown.

'It's your bed to lie in,' I say, turning to head back the way I came.

'What kind of mother lets her kid wander off into the desert and onto an open road?'

I stop dead.

'Yeah, I know all about you too, bitch.'

I think of taking the gun from my waist and pulling the trigger. I imagine the back of her head exploding, her brains spattering against the kitchen cupboards behind her and the hotplate on the counter, painting the trailer walls with skull shards and blood.

'What? You can judge me for my failures, but can't face your own?'

I stand shaking on the spot, before forcing one foot in front of the other. It isn't long before I hear a scuffle from inside the trailer, followed by the heavy thud of footsteps behind me.

I turn around and stare down the barrel of Annie's shotgun, unsteady in her grip. We look at one another, mother to mother. I almost wish she'd pull the trigger and end all of this pain. I'm not afraid of death, not anymore. If I die, I'll be with Joshua. But I can't see him again until Aaron has paid for what he has done.

Annie isn't a killer. I can see that from the fear in her eyes. Her breaths are short and ragged. She licks her dry lips, fixing her finger around the trigger until it's white at the knuckle.

'Do it,' I say, staring into her eyes. 'Because I'm going to kill your son if you don't.'

She continues to glare at me from the other end of the gun, but her tough exterior is slowly waning. A single tear slips down her cheek.

'Please don't do this,' she says, almost in a whisper.

'What would you do, if you were me?'

I watch her think it over, the push and pull evident in her eyes. She wants to kill me, she really does. But she's not got it in her. The gun wavers.

'I'll call the cops,' she says.

'No, you won't. I know all about your partner. The one you let beat your son as soon as he could walk. He'd go to prison for a long time for what I have on him. If you call the police, I'll tell them everything.'

'You don't know shit.'

'I know he supplies half the town with Oxy. Would be a shame if you lost your son and your partner all in one day, wouldn't it? Then you'd really be left with nothing.'

I've hit a nerve. I watch the fear rattle through her, willing her to give Aaron up while also trying to fathom how she could possibly consider trading her son's life for that of her lover, what dynamic they could possibly share that would make her value him over her own flesh and blood. I watch her lick her lips again and notice how dry her tongue is, how dilated her pupils are.

She's high.

Annie isn't considering trading her son for her partner. She's considering trading her son for her dealer.

Sweat has broken out on her forehead; it beads the skin above her top lip.

'I'm starting to think you do know where Aaron lives, and you're just not telling me,' I say. 'Maybe I should go and tell the cops what your boyfriend's been up to.'

The fight returns to her eyes, her brow creasing.

'Fuck you for this. For all of this.'

But still she stands, her finger on the trigger, not finding the courage to pull. I watch the tears fall silently.

'Above the sandwich deli,' she says finally. 'First apartment. I went there once when he first got out, thought about knocking on the door but . . . I was too chickenshit.'

I watch as she sniffs back snot and see the depth of the sadness in her eyes. I almost pity her. We only have one life, and this is what she's chosen to do with hers.

'You've just made another mistake you can't take back – you know that, right? What kind of mother sends her son to his death to save her own hide?'

'Go to hell,' she spits, gripping the gun tighter.

'If you're going to shoot me, do it now. Get it over with. Because once I'm gone, there's no going back. I'll kill him.'

The gun shakes and shakes, as more tears fall from her eyes and slither to her jaw. She's holding her breath, willing herself to pull the trigger. Her cheeks flush a violent red. A whimper claws up her throat. Then she lowers the gun and sobs.

'You should have loved him when you had the chance,' I mutter, before walking on down the track, listening to the sound of her cries until I turn the corner.

8

Tobias

I pull up outside the nearest store on the shoulder of the highway and turn off the engine. It's in the middle of nowhere, surrounded by nothing but desert and mountains, as if I've managed to conjure it from my own desperate will. I'd had to divert from my course along Route 95 to reach it; I couldn't be sure there'd be stops up ahead. Only problem is, I don't have a nickel to my name. But I long for a cold drink to wet my mouth, to keep my tongue from sticking to the back of my teeth. I'll steal one if I have to. I can't drive another mile without quenching this thirst.

I was a wreck on the drive here. Every car that appeared behind me on the highway was a cop car about to pull me over and book me for stealing the truck. But every time it was just another civilian driving through the desert. The paranoia will give me a heart attack if I keep this up.

When I was a good three miles out from the motel and could finally get my bearings, I noticed the large bag in the passenger footwell. I tried to imagine what might be in it as I drove, but now I've stopped I'm reluctant to look inside. It's one thing stealing a man's truck. It's quite another rummaging through his clothes and underwear looking for something worthwhile.

I go to pick it up and drop it on the seat, but it's too heavy and awkward from where I'm sitting.

What the hell is in this thing?

There are some old boots in the footwell beside the bag, poking out from under the seat. Worn brown leather, dry mud caked to the soles. I reach for them and pull them on, holding my breath to avoid the stench.

I get out of the truck and head round to the passenger side to lug the bag up onto the seat. It must weigh at least sixty pounds. Tugging on the zip, I drag it until the bag lies gaping open, and I stare down at the contents with my breath caught in my throat.

Shit. Shit, shit, shit, shit, shit.

Stacks of money and brown, brick-like packages. I've seen enough movies to know what'll be in them. Cocaine or heroin or something equally valuable. Something you'd definitely not want to lose to a stranger stealing your truck and tailing off into the desert.

'*Fuck!*'

I pace the dusty ground with my hands on my head. I can't take the bag back and drop it at the man's feet; he'd shoot me straight between the eyes. But I can't ditch it, because if he does find me and I don't have it on me, he'll shoot me straight between the eyes. If I take it, and he catches up with me . . . Every scenario I can think of ends with me being shot between the bloody eyes.

I return to the bag, looking at the cash and the packages again. There must be hundreds of thousands of dollars in here, maybe more. I pick up a stack and strum the ends through my fingers. Each one is made up of one-hundred-dollar bills. I couldn't say how much the drugs are worth, but by the number of packages in the bag, I'd say the street value is a hell of a lot more than the cash.

I peer around me at the miles of dirt, at the horizon that seems a world away. I rub my tired eyes and let them settle back on the bag.

If he's going to kill me for this no matter what I do, it wouldn't hurt to skim a little off the top.

*

I walk out of the convenience store barely able to keep the stranger's boots on my feet, which squeak from sweat with every step; his, mine, a mixture of the two, I'm not sure. The boots are so old and worn that I was sure the laces would snap as I tied them. I practically have to drag my feet back to the truck to keep them on, almost losing one clean off my foot as I hike myself back up behind the wheel, my bag of junk food rustling as it hits the passenger seat beside me.

The sun has lessened its beating, but instead of relief, all I feel is dread. I've been watching it edge closer towards the horizon all day, reflecting the hours that have passed without my knowing where Evelyn is or what she has done; the hours I have failed to stop her.

It's around three. I've not eaten all day, not even had a sip of water. My mouth is as dry as the dirt on the ground and my stomach is seizing with hunger. I pull the bag towards me and rip open the wrapper on a chocolate bar, practically shoving the entire thing into my mouth whole. I'd been so hungry prowling the aisles that I'd not even checked what I was grabbing, lured by the colourful packaging and promises of high energy and glucose syrup. Thankfully, I'd had the presence of mind to pick up a toothbrush and a pre-paid cell from a stand beside the counter before leaving. I swallow down the chocolate too fast and try to guzzle down a soda too, choking on the concoction as it desperately tries to work its way down my throat.

Calm down. Take a second.

It's Evelyn's voice that I hear. The voice that's always been able to soothe me when I'm getting myself into a flap. But instead of the usual calm it brings me, hearing her makes my mouth dryer, my throat tighter. I wonder if she's found him yet. He shouldn't be hard to find. He won't be expecting her.

The last time I was stuck out in a desert like this, Evelyn and I were in Australia. We'd taken a gap year together to see some of the world before she began her master's and I joined the rat race. We'd travelled for three months, from Thailand to Vietnam, New Zealand to Australia, before finishing off with a drive along the latter's coast until we ran out of gas money and finally flew home. Life had been so different then. Before the pain and the grief, we were such different people. I can see her now in my mind's eye, sitting beside me in the car all those years ago, her hair blowing in the hot breeze and a beaming smile permanently on her face, always looking to find a quiet place to park up and screw because we couldn't keep our hands off one another.

And now we're here. Travelling through another desert, in another lifetime.

Even the thought of what I'm planning makes my stomach churn. I still don't know how I'll manage to look Aaron Alexander in the eye if I reach him, how I'll be able to be near him without wanting to wring his neck. But I'll do it if it means getting Evelyn back. What I wouldn't do to see that beaming smile sweep across her face again, to hear her laugh.

Another thought plagues me. The very thought I haven't wanted to confront but can no longer ignore. What will I do if I can't stop her? What then?

The memory of her beside me in the car comes back to me again: the flash of her smile, the way she threw her head back as she laughed, the gleam in her eyes. That's the Evelyn I know. And to save the woman I know and love, I have to stop the very woman she has become.

I rub my eyes until I see stars.

I will do what's right if the time comes. I'll call the police on my own wife if there is nothing I can do to stop her. But that must be the last resort. I can't let her down, not again.

But even as I make the vow, I'm not sure I wholly believe the words.

I shove another chocolate bar into my mouth and turn the key in the ignition, plugging the cell phone into the lighter socket on the dash to charge before heading onto the road to get back to Route 95.

My hands trembling from the sudden dose of sugar, I drive for a good five minutes before spotting the car tailing me. My mind immediately jumps to the same fear I'd had before: it's a cop car, come to pull me over and arrest me for stealing the truck. Or maybe it's the man himself, come to get his bag of drugs and money and to shoot me in the head. I try to calm myself down, reminding myself it's just the exhaustion and paranoia.

Only this time, it really is a cop car.

I've instinctively slowed down in fear of being pulled over, and the cop car has caught up. It's so close now that I can see it's a local ranger, the metal of his badge shining in the sun's rays. He catches my eye in the rear-view mirror, and I quickly look away. Too quickly.

There are no side roads off the highway. It's just me and the ranger driving in the same direction for one long stretch. I imagine the cop reading the plate on the truck. Will he look it up, just in case? Will my looking away like that have made him suspicious enough to check? The truck has to have been reported stolen by now. I could be stopped in my tracks before I even reach Beatty. All of this would have been for nothing. And I'll do a lot more time if the cop pulls me over and finds the drugs and the cash on me.

When I drive a little faster, the cruiser matches my speed. Sweat breaks out across my forehead, speckling my top lip until I can taste the salt. I glance in the rear-view and see him staring back at me. I drum my thumbs against the wheel, urging the next junction to appear. I'd had to turn off at Amargosa Valley for the 373 to reach the store, and I better start praying now that he turns in the opposite direction to me at the upcoming junction. I want to glance in the rear-view again, but I stop myself, gripping the wheel until the leather creaks.

When the junction appears, I have to fight to keep my foot from hitting the gas too hard in my desperation. I watch the desert crawling by the windows, listen to my heart pounding. I pull to a stop; the cop car slows behind me. I check the highway before pulling left for Beatty. It's only when I see the cop car turning right that I realize I've been holding my breath.

I sigh with relief, rubbing the sweat from my face with a hand that smells of dirty cash, and grip the wheel once more.

I'm almost there.

9

Evelyn

I walk down the back road parallel to Main Street, staring up at the rear of Aaron Alexander's apartment building. The living quarters sit above a line of cheap restaurants, from delis to burger joints and pizza houses, the different kinds of food mixing into one, indistinguishable stench.

I reach the back of the sandwich deli, which is walled off from the street, and look up at the building. A long pipe trails the brickwork to the fire escape leading up to his apartment. I walk through the back gate; the yard is derelict, filled with trash bags and rubble.

I've never been hunting, which feels strange, having lived in America for so long. It feels like a compulsory pastime, something everyone here experiences at least once, or they know someone who has. I imagine this is the part that enthrals them. Not the kill itself, but the anticipation: their heart rates climbing, their hands shaking with excitement and adrenaline. The hyperfocus on every sight and sound.

I cross to the fire escape and stand beneath the rusted ladder. It doesn't look strong enough to take my weight after so many years of being left to wither. Tentatively, I find my footing on the pipe, placing my boot on the bracket holding it to the wall, and hike myself up towards the bottom of the ladder, snatching the first rung and pulling it down to the ground with my weight as I jump, then rubbing my hands clean on my trousers to dislodge the flecks of rust. I spot a brick among the rubble and pick it up, testing the weight of it in my grip until my palm is coated in orange dust, before climbing onto the first rung. It takes my weight without breaking. I climb the rest of the way cautiously, glancing over my shoulder to check for anyone on the back road, until I'm up on the walkway and crouched before Aaron's window. I try it and find it locked.

The brick shatters the pane, littering the bathtub below with glass. I drop it on the fire escape with a clang and take out my gun, imagining him following the sound and darting through the open doorway.

Silence.

I climb through the broken window, glass crunching beneath my shoes as I make my way to the other side of the room and flatten myself against the wall beside the door in wait. But all I can hear are my short, fast breaths.

I whip around the doorframe, gun raised.

He's not here.

It's a studio apartment, with a futon in one corner and a sink in the other, a hotplate propped on a lone pair of kitchen cupboards along the back wall. Above it is a shelf, storing enough crockery for one: one plate, one bowl, one mug, one glass.

For a small space, it's surprisingly clean. I suppose he hasn't lived here long enough to make a mess of it yet. There's an ancient TV sitting on top of a moving box that's beginning to sag beneath the weight, and the walls are bare but for a few cracks in the plaster.

I sit down on the pulled-out futon and sigh.

It feels strange, breathing the same air he's breathed, sitting in the spot where he sleeps, witnessing his way of life before I take it all away. I'd pity him if I didn't loathe him. This can't be the freedom he dreamt of while he was locked up. Although I suppose it must feel like a luxury compared to the cell he was rotting in, and it looks far better than the trailer he grew up in with his drugged-up mother. I look around the room, wondering who'll empty the place once he's dead. What will they do with the old TV, the hotplate, the futon? That's when I see the corner of a laptop poking out from under the pillow.

I slip it out and open it: there's no security password. You'd think he'd be more paranoid after being in prison; I'm sure he had to hide the few belongings he had in there to keep them from being stolen. Maybe he feels safe enough to let his guard down now, having a home of his own. He'll come to see this as his first mistake.

I click through the files and spot his newly written résumé, which uses his work in the prison kitchen as a way to block out his stretch in jail. Under the list of personal skills, he's written 'people person'. The man who doesn't have a second glass to offer a guest, the man who killed a child in cold blood, considers himself a *people person*. My fingers quiver above the keys, the familiar rage bubbling up. I click away and go to his emails.

I see messages from Craigslist dating back a month, confirming his responses to listings for the futon and the hotplate. An email from his probation officer, Andrea, confirming the date and location of their next meeting: a café close to the gas station next Monday. Neither of them knows yet that he won't be alive to keep that appointment.

I stumble across another email and pause. It's from a florist, confirming his order of twelve red roses. I scroll down to the note he added with the order.

Thank you for dinner. Next one is on me. A x

My hands shake harder. He's been out for a mere month, and not only has he found a place to live and secured a job, but he's found someone to love him. He thinks he can destroy our lives, spend a little time in jail, and then all will be redeemed. I scroll down further and stop when I see the recipient's details: the name Kyle Atkins, followed by an address. I think of the map of Beatty I've stared at a hundred times, memorizing every road he might run down, every potential route of escape. It's only seven blocks away.

I remove my phone and take a photo of the address on the screen, close the laptop and head back towards the broken window. If Aaron isn't here, and he's not with his mother, there's only one other place he would be.

10

Aaron

'What was prison like?'

I lie with my head on Kyle's chest, listening to the smoke from the joint crackle in his lungs before he exhales. The smell of weed will always remind me of him and these moments. The mix of marijuana, sex and Cherry Coke. I shouldn't be smoking; the drug tests my parole officer makes me do each month will flash like a damn Christmas tree. But like most people in town, I know a guy. He pisses in a cup and sells it on. Kyle told me about him after I went to my first Narcotics Anonymous meeting with him; I have to go as part of my parole, and Kyle was made to go by his mother when he got clean while I was locked up. The weed is cheaper than Big John's piss, but I don't mind; I'd do anything to feel close to someone like this after so many years alone in jail, even if it means risking being sent right back.

'I know you don't like to talk about it,' he says when I don't reply, and passes me the joint. I take it between my fingers, watching the ember glow as it burns. 'But it feels like I don't really know you anymore. There's this whole life you've lived that I know nothing about.'

In truth, we don't know each other anymore. Not really. You can't get to know a person again in a few weeks after so much time apart. You might say you can never truly know a person at all; how can we, when so many of us never even truly know ourselves? Kyle has been in my life since we were teenagers. Two lonely people who stuck out by a mile and gravitated towards one another to get by. He was my first kiss, my first sexual partner. We were probably best friends, until crystal meth tore us apart, and the only thing we cared about was the pipe.

I take a drag and feel the smoke hit the back of my throat, holding it in my chest until my eyes water.

'What do you want to know about it?'

'Anything,' he replies. 'Do convicts really drink toilet wine?'

I laugh, a sound that's still foreign to me after so many years without it; so long that I'm having to teach myself again, trying out different kinds to see which one fits. My lungs burn from the smoke, and I cough into my fist.

'I didn't,' I reply.

'Did you have sex in there?'

Even through the marijuana haze, I feel myself tense against him, all the memories I've sworn to keep buried clawing their way out.

'I'd rather not talk about it.'

I run my finger along the trail of hair leading from his chest to his belly button. Soft, velvety, getting curlier as it heads towards his groin, hidden beneath the sheets.

'Didn't you go to jail?' I ask.

He takes the joint back and drags.

'Yeah, overnight jail, not prison. Not long enough to learn how to make toilet wine.'

Even with the sun setting on the other side of the window, the room is as hot as a furnace. The floor is covered in clothes and junk and empty soda cans; Kyle seems blind to the mess, his feet never touching the floor for all the trash covering it. It's more of a shack than a bungalow. The walls are paper-thin and rattle whenever the wind howls over the plains where he lives on the edge of town. The windowpanes are caked in sand and dust, cobwebs decorating the frames and fluttering in the warm draught.

'Damn it's hot in here.'

Kyle gets up and bangs on the rusty AC unit sitting on the windowsill. I stare at his naked body: his slender back, the soft skin over the juts of his spine, the golden hairs on his buttocks.

He turns, the joint burning between his lips. I still blush when I look at him naked like this, but he doesn't seem to notice. He falls back into bed, and I hold on to him again. We've never given our relationship a name; sometimes it feels like we're just close friends without boundaries – some sort of transaction we've agreed on to stave off loneliness, one we picked up again the moment I got back. I've never been in love, not the true love people talk about, and sometimes I fear I'm one of those people who'll never find it; who goes through life waiting, and waiting, and waiting, only to realize I'm too late – that all of those hopes and dreams were in vain. That maybe I'm just not the lovable kind.

'Tell me we'll be rich one day,' Kyle says, breaking through my thoughts. 'Even if it don't happen, tell me we will.'

Kyle works in an abattoir for eight dollars an hour. He can never quite get all of the blood out from under his nails, and sometimes he screams in the night from the same recurring nightmare about drowning in the blood that flows down into the grates on the factory floor. And then there's me, who spends all day at the gas station, cleaning up spills with sawdust and pressing keys on a cash register. There's zero chance of either of us getting rich, but I want to dream with him anyway, desperate for the delusion we paint together to be true.

'We'll be rich,' I say, and take the joint. 'So rich we'll be able to wipe our asses with President Grant's face.'

'Only fifties?' he replies with a smirk.

'Benjamin Franklin then.'

'That's more like it. Where will we live?'

'Wherever you want.'

Kyle shakes his head and looks at me in a way I can't totally pin down; pitying me or frustrated with me, I can't tell which.

'You always do that.'

'Do what?'

'Do what everyone else wants.' He takes the spliff from me and takes a drag. 'What do *you* want?'

The room falls quiet but for the faint rattle of the useless AC unit. I don't think anyone has ever asked me that before.

I want to be loved.

'You've got to want something,' he says when I struggle to reply.

'I want to live on a beach somewhere,' I say finally. 'Right up by the shore. We could learn to surf. Drink from coconuts, shit like that.' It's a cliché but it's true. I used to dream of a place like that when I was in my cell; I got so good at picturing it that I could practically smell the ocean. 'What do you want?'

'Well, what I really wanted was some cigarettes . . .'

'Shit, I totally forgot.'

He laughs and rubs my hair until it frizzes.

'It's fine.'

'No, I said I'd bring you some and I didn't.'

I climb out of the bed, stumbling over the junk on the floor and trying to find my footing. My jeans are somewhere in the mess. I spot my tee and pull it over my head. It smells at the pits and is damp in places.

'Don't be too long,' he says, and slaps my ass while the tee is still halfway over my head, making me laugh again. That one didn't sound quite right either.

I jump into my jeans and take one last look at him. Lying there in all his naked glory, golden hairs shimmering all over him, a mischievous sparkle in his bloodshot eyes, the joint burning between his fingers. I feel myself growing hard.

'What?' he asks, knowing exactly what.

'Nothing.' I'm blushing and look away. 'I'll be twenty minutes.'

'And grab me another Cherry Coke from the store, would you?' he calls, as I leave the room and head down the hall, dragging on my shoes at the door before I go.

Last words – they're infamous, aren't they? I think about them a lot. People often say you should tell people you love them as much as you can, because you never know when the last time will be. When I part ways with people, their last words always linger as I wonder if they were the words they would have used if they knew they'd be their last. If something were to happen, and I never saw him again, Kyle's would have been asking for a Cherry Coke.

11

Tobias

I pull up at the gas station and sit for a moment, gathering myself. Driving past the signs for Beatty, it had hit me that this is a real place, with real people, real consequences. To think Evelyn drove these same streets, perhaps parked in this very same spot. So close, yet worlds away. I feel a pang of both fear and longing. It surprises me just how untethered I feel without her, how lost. I've got so used to being by her side through our grief that I've forgotten how to stand alone.

I tuck the bag of cash and drugs under the passenger seat and climb down from behind the wheel of the truck before filling it up with gas and heading for the store, flinching as the bell rings above my head. I spot my reflection in the glass of the refrigerators lining the wall and see how wired and feral I look: messy pepper hair that's slick with sweat, my eyes puffy and bloodshot.

'Fifty dollars exactly,' the man behind the counter says.

I slip the hundred-dollar note beneath the partition and wait for the change.

'I was hoping to see Aaron,' I say.

The man pauses at the register and looks at me with a frown.

'You're the second person to tell me that. The boy's never been so popular.'

My heart drops.

Evelyn.

'So, he's not here?'

'No. He went home early. Who should I say stopped by?'

'I'm afraid it's more urgent than that.'

The man stares at me, his brow furrowed again, looking me up and down with a new, curious glare. He slides my change to me and I shove it into my pocket.

'The person who came before me, who asked after Aaron . . . I'm guessing it was a woman, about five-nine, dark hair.'

'Yeah. His new probation officer.'

I have to admire her tactics. I bet she charmed the socks off him. My wife can have a way with people, when she wants to.

'That wasn't Aaron's new probation officer, sir.'

I watch his face fall. His Adam's apple bounces in his throat.

'That was my wife, Evelyn Moore.'

The man slowly connects the dots, his eyes shifting until it clicks.

'Yeah,' I say. 'The mother of the boy Aaron killed.'

His face has grown ashen, and his hands are shaking on the counter. He notices me staring and crosses his arms over his chest.

'How long ago was she here?'

He thinks back.

'Erm . . . About two, or just before. Yeah, round about then.'

I can only imagine what sort of mayhem Evelyn has caused since then. Perhaps she's already found him. Perhaps I'm too late, and there's already a hole between his eyes and a bullet in his skull.

'Where can I find him, sir? I need to warn him. To get to him before she does.'

'Warn him about what? What does she want with him?'

I don't say anything. I don't need to: the silence speaks for itself. The man sighs and rubs his eyes.

'For the love of Christ.'

'I'm going to stop her. But I need to know where he is. She won't stop until she finds him; I need to get to him before then.'

'He said he was going to his mom's, but he won't be there now. She wouldn't have seen him for long, that's if she let him see her at all. He lives off Main Street, above the sandwich deli.'

'Are you sure that's where he'll be?'

The man is thinking, nervously drumming his fingers on the counter. His brow has started to sweat.

'Either that, or he'll be at his friend's place. They've grown real close again since he's been out, if you know what I'm saying.'

'I know what you're saying.'

'They go to NA together. The boy's been clean ever since he went to jail. Ever since . . .'

He trails off.

'Ever since he killed my child.'

His cheeks flush and he struggles to meet my eyes.

'Yeah. Round about then.'

'Where's his friend's place?'

The man looks up at me sharply.

'How do I know you aren't looking to hurt him too?'

'You'll just have to take me at my word.'

'I trusted your wife, and look where that got me.'

We're not alone in that.

I can see how conflicted he is just by looking at him. He seems like the trusting kind; he has to be, to have believed Evelyn's lies. But now he's doubting the very person he should trust.

'You called the cops?' he asks.

I've thought about it, of course I have. But the moment I do, my wife could well be sent off to prison, and there'll be no saving her then. If I can intervene, I can save her from herself before it has to come to anything drastic. If I send the police after her, she'll never speak to me again.

'It won't come to that. I'm going to find her and put an end to this. But I can't do that without your help. She's not a monster; you'd know that if you'd met her before.'

'She's just innocently driving through to find and kill a guy.'

'She's in pain,' I reply sternly. 'And I'll stop her.'

The man watches me as if he'll be able to tell my true intentions if he looks for long enough. He rubs his balding head and sighs.

'Don't make me regret this.' He writes down the name of the street. 'You'll find him here. It's a little way off the road, the bungalow right at the end. You can't miss it.'

'Thanks,' I say. 'You got his phone number? If I can call him, I can warn him; make sure he's safe.'

The man looks me up and down.

'Why do you want to keep him safe? He killed your boy.'

This is exactly what Evelyn would ask. She doesn't understand my loyalty to right and wrong, my inability to tip the scales of morality to fit my own needs, however great. She doesn't know it, but my stance will save her in the end. I just have to find her and get that through to her; make her fully understand what's at stake.

The man waits for my reply, watching every flicker of emotion on my face.

'My wife, she's . . . not well. Grief changed her, and if she finds Aaron . . .' I feel my throat closing up. 'I'll lose her for good.'

I glance at my watch, trying to avoid the pity in the man's eyes. I've wasted too much time talking; I need to get back on the road if I'm going to find Aaron before she does.

'Are you going to call the cops?' I ask.

I see him thinking it over, looking at the phone on the counter. He glances back at me, sees my pleading eyes, and sighs.

'The police don't like Aaron. No one likes Aaron. He's only got me and that close friend of his . . . well, and you now, I guess.'

My heart jolts at that, but I bite my lip, say nothing.

'You've all been to hell and back. I guess if you stop her before she does anything stupid, no one's life has to get any worse, right?'

I exhale a quiet sigh of relief.

'Right. Thank you.'

'I hope you find him,' he says, jotting down Aaron's number on the slip of paper before sliding it towards me. 'And I hope you stick to your word, about protecting him.'

'I'm protecting my wife.'

'Sure you are.'

I pick up the slip and head for the door, my pace quickening when I see how the sun has edged lower in the sky during my short time in the store, the day slipping away from me whenever I dare to turn my back. I stop when I hear him speak.

'Some people don't want to be saved. You know that, right?'

I pause at the door, my heart racing. He doesn't know it, but he has just spoken my greatest fear aloud.

'That won't stop me from trying.'

I head out to the truck without looking back, the slip of paper trembling in my grip.

12

Evelyn

I park the car by the kerb and walk towards Kyle Atkins's address, remembering all of the nights I've lain awake thinking of this moment. My heart is beating so fast that I can almost taste the bloody meatiness of it.

The street is in the more undesirable part of town: the buildings are weather-worn and dilapidated. The house to my right is in desperate need of a wrecking ball, and the bungalow on the other side of the street has filled its yard with unwanted furniture: a leather couch that has faded beneath the beating sun, an old barbecue set left to rust. The address I'm after is a little way off the road, a bungalow with a torn shutter on the door and windows so dirty that at first glance I fear they've been boarded up, before I get closer and see the film of grime. I remove the gun from the back of my jeans and head round to the rear.

I wonder what Kyle Atkins is like. Not just what he looks like or sounds like, but the man who lies beneath; I wonder how he sleeps at night, as someone who is able to look past a killer's crimes and be intimate with him. How he can be so close with someone who has caused so much pain. I wonder if he is the kind of man who will pull a gun on me when he sees mine. I notice my teeth grinding and try to stop, but my jaw remains clenched, like the fangs of a bear trap sinking into flesh.

The backyard is an ugly sight. Trash bags have been torn open by some opportunistic critter, their innards scattered across the long-dead lawn that's cratered with holes, only the odd patch of dried grass left among the dirt. I step over a crushed Coke can, walking through flies that dance languidly in the air, drunk from the heat. I open the screen door and knock twice.

'It's open, dumbass,' I hear from the other side.

Adrenaline hits me all at once. I feel it rushing to my heart, taste it in my spit. I raise a quivering hand to turn the handle, and step inside.

The kitchen is a mess: the sink is full of dirty dishes, with a pile of used pots on the counter beside it, indistinguishable scraps of charred food seared to the metal. The soles of my boots stick to the lino floor, and the flies have worked their way in here too, buzzing in lost, dizzying circles. The air reeks of marijuana.

'Hurry up and get your ass to bed,' a male voice calls from down the hall. 'I need a smoke.'

My grip on the gun is moist with sweat. I can feel my pulse drumming against the handle through my palm, strumming the trigger as it echoes down my finger. I feel sick with anticipation, lightheaded from the mess of thoughts knotting in my brain. But despite the nausea, the dizziness and the sweat, I feel ready.

Eleven years.

I edge slowly towards the open doorway leading to the hall, the gun held in both hands and aimed down, ready to raise it at any moment. It's messy in the hallway too. There are worn clothes discarded on the floor, underwear someone slipped down and stepped out of. An old tee left in a dusty, scrunched-up ball.

'Did you get my soda?' the voice calls.

I creep closer, stepping around the clutter on the floor, and slowly peer into the room. A man lies naked on a bed, with only a thin, sweaty sheet covering his lower half. He is propped up against the wall where a headboard should be, picking tobacco out of the cigarette butts in an ashtray and emptying the shreds into a slip of rolling paper, his fingertips black from the ash. My heart sinks: it isn't Aaron in the bed, but a man who I assume must be Kyle. I watch as he runs his tongue across the paper and rolls it shut. He's just lighting it between his lips when he notices me in the doorway. He freezes, his eyes wide, before reaching down the side of the bed in a flash.

When he returns his gaze to me, he is pointing a Glock directly at my head. Mine is already pointed at his heart.

The smoke from the roll-up curls upwards from his mouth.

'Who the *fuck* are you?' he asks around the cigarette, gun trembling. He narrows one eye against the smoke, but the other is fixed on me. My attention flicks between him and the gun. 'I asked *who the fuck are you?*'

'I'm here for Aaron. Tell me where I can find him, and I'll go.'

'Lady, are you deaf? Tell me who you are, or I'll fire this thing. You're trespassing and I have every right. I could shoot you dead right now—'

'It's not going to come to that.'

'You broke into my house waving a *goddamn gun*!'

His eyes shift about the room, always returning to me. I try to decipher what he's thinking, what he might do next. Whether there's something in the room that he's thinking of lunging for. If there's something other than the gun that he could use to hurt me. There's nothing more unpredictable than a scared man; you never know what their ego will have them do.

'Tell me where he is, Kyle. Then I'll go.'

I watch his bare chest rising and falling quickly, can see the drum of his heart pounding beneath the skin. His face has turned pale. The way his words are clotting together with nerves as he talks tells me his mouth is as dry as mine.

'What do you want with him?' He grips the gun tighter and focuses his aim. '*Who the fuck are you?*'

A sliver of sweat slinks down my temple.

'I'm Evelyn Moore.'

I watch his scattered mind connect the dots. When he figures it out, his eyes flash with fear. His finger tenses on the trigger.

'You get the hell out of here before I blow a hole clean through your head. Aaron did his time. There's no business you can have with him that's right or fair.'

'You don't get to decide what's fair and what's not.'

'What, and you do?'

'He killed my *son*.'

'And he did his time for that.'

'You think eleven years in jail makes up for killing a nine-year-old boy who had his whole life ahead of him? Do you?'

'The court decided—'

'*Fuck the court!*'

The words spray out of my mouth. I feel the anger surging through me, shaking the gun in my grip. The tiniest pull on the trigger and it would fire.

'Look, Evelyn . . . he ain't here. It's just you and me and these two guns, so I suggest you get the fuck out of here before this gets out of hand. I'm not dying today, and I don't think you want to either.'

Sweat starts to bead above my lip. I can feel heavy drops teetering on my forehead, threatening to fall. I fight the urge to wipe them away, keeping my eyes on him.

'Tell me where to find him and I'll leave.'

'That's never gonna happen and you know it.'

Tears of desperation sting my eyes. Eleven years of waiting, and it's all going wrong. I can't go back to the pain tearing me up each day while Joshua haunts me every time I dare to close my eyes. I may not have found Aaron like I'd planned, but I'll get him. I won't stop until I get him.

'Tell Aaron that I'm coming for him, and that I won't stop until I find him.'

Kyle stares at me along the length of his outstretched arms, his gun shaking violently as he waits for me to leave. He's sweating too; I watch him lick the sheen from his top lip.

I slowly release the breath I'd been holding and take a tentative step back, when my foot tangles in something on the floor. I feel my weight shift and my knee give out from under me. The gun fires in my hand the second I hit the floor.

I flatten myself against the wall and gulp for air; I've knocked the wind out of myself and can't draw breath. I stare up at the bed as I gasp, my ears ringing from the shot.

Nothing happens at first. A taunting silence beyond the ringing. It feels like there's a foot crushing down on my abdomen to keep me from breathing. I pull myself up using the doorframe and slowly peer into the room.

Kyle is even paler than before. He stares at me as I stand in the doorway. I look into his eyes, see the fear in them, then down at the blood slowly appearing from the hole in his gut. It blooms out of him, teetering on the edge of the wound at first. But it isn't long before it begins to flow, and flow, and flow. Rivers of blood streaming down his sides and soaking into the off-white sheets. The cigarette must have fallen from his mouth with the jolt of the bullet hitting him: it's burning a black hole into the fabric.

As Kyle's eyes sheen with tears, I realize how young he still is. How despite the gun, and the drugs, and the company he keeps, he's just a boy who's lost his way. I wonder if the tears are from the pain he's feeling, or the fear, as it dawns on him that he probably is going to die today. He clamps his free hand over the wound. Blood seeps between his fingers.

'*Fuck you!*' he shouts.

He raises his gun and fires a shot; the bullet clips the doorframe, which explodes into splinters beside my head. I flatten myself against the wall again and watch another shot hit the plaster on the other side of the hall, followed by another, and another, clouds of dust billowing into the air as he continues to shout '*Fuck you, fuck you, fuck you, fuck you*' at the woman who's just cut his life short. He fumbles the gun in his hand, and there's a bang as it falls to the floor. I look down at my feet, trying to make sense of it all.

I'd got tangled in the mess. I stare at the piece of fabric snagged around my foot – a pair of crumpled underpants – and wonder what kind of parents Kyle has, if they'd taught him to clean up after himself. What might have happened today if they had.

I can hear him breathing fast and heavy from inside the room.

I peer in again: he's staring down at the bleeding wound, tears falling silently towards his jaw. His chest is heaving abnormally fast, and his breaths are short and strained. The dirty white bed-sheets are red now.

I look at the dying man, then down at the gun I shot him with, but I can't seem to connect the two. My heart is jumping in my chest with the adrenaline. It was an accident; the gun I brought wasn't meant for him. But there he lies, with one of its bullets lodged in his gut.

This would never have happened if it weren't for Aaron Alexander.

I slip the gun back into my waistband, not even wincing as the hot metal sears my skin, and stand frozen to the spot, unsure what to do. Do I run? Do I stay? I hear a sharp intake of breath from inside the room and a thick wave of guilt crashes through me.

Don't. He's no better than Aaron. We are the company we keep.

But still it grows, pooling in my eyes and tugging at my insides in an agonizing push and pull. I want to leave, to make him suffer like Joshua did. But I can't stop thinking of the look he'd given me after the shot, how his eyes had been as wide and terrified as a boy's. I stand with my back against the wall, my thoughts tugging me in so many directions, before I finally sigh with defeat, cursing under my breath before stepping into the room.

'Don't fucking come near me!'

He reaches for the ashtray on the bedside table and throws it in my direction. Glass explodes against the wall, ash and cigarette ends littering the floor.

His eyes are already starting to glaze over, as if the lids are too heavy to keep up. I wonder what the bullet tore through when it entered him: his intestines, a kidney, one of the arteries carrying blood to his heart.

A childlike whimper escapes him, and before I realize what I'm doing, I'm sitting on the bed beside him and holding my shaking hands above the wound, trying to find the courage to press down. I clamp them onto his abdomen and he screams, his warm blood immediately creeping through my fingers.

'Get the fuck away from me!'

He shouts it with as much venom as he can muster, spit flying from his mouth and stringing between his teeth as tears leak from his eyes.

'I'm sorry.' It escapes in a whisper. I stare down at my hands, slick with his blood, and watch as it drips silently down my wrists in dark, winding trails.

He coughs violently. I watch through his open mouth as the blood jumps up his throat and speckles his tongue while he struggles for breath. His Adam's apple bobs up and down with each nervous swallow. Tears stream from his eyes, then from mine. He looks so young, so scared.

I instinctively reach for his hand. He tries to free himself, but I grip harder, and eventually he gives in. Something shifts then, and his face twists with a sob, pink drool webbed between his lips.

'I don't want to die,' he whispers.

I try to speak, but the words clog in my throat. Is this how

Joshua felt, dying alone on the highway? Did he speak those same words into the night, only with no one there to hear them? I blink furiously to see through the tears that just keep coming. The blood is flowing out of him so fast; there's no way paramedics would make it in time to save him.

He grips my hand until my flesh turns white and winces with a sudden shock of pain, before his eyes widen and he takes one last ragged breath. His head lolls to one side and the room falls silent.

His eyes are vacant now. There is no pain left in them, no fear. Just one final tear slinking down his cheek. I reach for his neck with a quivering hand and press two fingers to it to check for a pulse. I move them around, searching for a beat. But all I've done is dirty his pale skin with blood-red smears.

I sit silently in the aftermath, numb.

The ringing in my ears fades away, and the room is so quiet. That's when I hear a dog barking outside. I dash the tears from my eyes and look towards the window. Every neighbour on the block would have heard those shots, which means the police won't be far behind.

I look back to Kyle on the bed, his lax, dead eyes boring into me, and slowly slip my hand from his. The cigarette he'd been smoking that had started burning holes in the sheet has rolled to the floor. I pick it up, take a drag, and stub it out on the bedside table. I spot his cell phone on the surface and slip it into my back pocket. The dog barks again and I jolt, snapping out of the shock that had me sitting holding a dead man's hand. I have to get out of here.

I head for the door, stumbling through the clutter and the mess, not daring to turn around and look back in fear of the sight never leaving me.

I bound down the hallway, out of the back door and into the yard, the shutter banging closed behind me. I'd hoped for a rush of air, but the day is too humid and I'm met by a wall of heat instead. I run out of the yard and back towards the road with the gun digging into my skin where it judders in my waistband. Sweat soaks through my shirt.

I jump behind the wheel of the car and turn over the engine, blood staining the leather and wetting the keys. It's too hot in here and there's not enough air. I hit the accelerator so hard that the wheels spin and squeal.

I killed him, I think as I head for the main road. *I killed that boy.*

I come to a stop at the end of the street, listening to the grumble of the engine, and consider the paths I have before me.

Life is full of choices, and with each comes a consequence. I weigh up my options, thinking of the innocence I had seen in the boy's eyes as he lay dying; the vulnerability and the fear. I could turn back, own up to what I've done before anyone else gets hurt.

I look into the rear-view mirror at the house at the end of the street and catch sight of myself. Tears have started to dry on my cheeks in silver trails. My eyes are bloodshot, and the terror in my expression has twisted my appearance. I don't recognize the woman in the mirror.

I look to the right at the junction, then to the left, from where I can hear the faint call of police sirens.

Then I push my foot down on the accelerator and speed away.

As Kyle lay bleeding, I'd wondered if Joshua had felt the same way as he did, dying on the highway alone. It's that thought that haunts me the most and keeps me going. Aaron left my baby in the dark while he was calling out for me – for anyone – to help him, only to die alone. But even as I remind myself why I'm doing this, I can't help but wonder if what I have done has made me as bad as the man I'm dead set on finding.

13

Tobias

I take the corner too fast and speed to the end of the road towards the bungalow. I've called Aaron, I've called Evelyn. The first call went straight to voicemail, and the second kept ringing, and ringing, and ringing.

I check the address Aaron's boss had written down, the paper still shaking violently in my grip, and look at the unsightly house sitting at the end of a track just off the road. I get out and walk fast. The wildfires are close; I can smell the smoke in the air, feel the sting of it in my eyes. The cul-de-sac is strangely quiet. There are no birds singing, no sign of life but for a single dog barking from a neighbouring yard and the odd twitch of a curtain as I pass the other houses on the street.

I hurry down the track and head for the front door while trying Aaron's cell one last time. The call goes straight to the answering machine again.

'*Shit.*'

The phone trembles in my hand. I'm tired. So, so tired. My body has been in fight or flight mode for so long that I feel sick from the stress, and my head is pounding. Even my bones feel like they're throbbing. I'm too old for this shit.

I knock on the door and listen out for signs of life on the other side, but all I can hear is the buzz of flies and the thump of my pulse in my ears. I head round the back of the bungalow, checking the windows as I go.

The screen door is shut, but the back door itself has been left yawning open, providing a glimpse of the kitchen on the other side: the counter is covered in dirty pots and crockery, and the floor is covered in grime. But the thing that disturbs me the most is the silence.

Anticipation sucks every bit of moisture from my mouth, and I have that instinctive, hair-raising feeling: I may not know what has happened or what I'm about to find, but I know it's something bad. The air of the place has sent goosebumps rising up my arms and back.

I stand on the spot and stare through the screen door as my heart squeezes in my chest. I don't have a gun to protect myself, should there be danger beyond the threshold. But something tells me I need to go inside.

I push open the screen door, listening as it creaks on its hinges. 'Hello?' I call.

No answer.

I step into the kitchen. Flies buzz tirelessly above my head and against the dirty window above the sink. There's something rotting in here; food caught in the drains, or a trash can that needs emptying. Maybe it's something worse; a dead rat decomposing beneath the floorboards. There's a small camping table where a breakfast table should be, covered in dirty clothes and bills and junk. A rusty hammer sticks out of a plastic bag filled with odd screws. I take it by the handle and take a step towards the hallway.

'Hello?'

Still no answer.

My grip on the hammer is slick with sweat. I try to lick my lips, but my tongue is as rough as a cat's.

I head down the hall, and notice there are splinters on the floor;

then I see the chunk of wood missing from the doorframe on my right, the bullet holes in the wall to my left. My stomach drops.

Evelyn.

I don't have proof, just that same gut feeling: Evelyn was here.

My heart is pounding. I know that I'm about to find something neither of us can undo.

I edge round the door, eyeing the messy floor of the room, the foot of the bed, the AC unit on the windowsill that's dark with rust. Then I see the blood on the sheets and freeze.

A man is lying on the bed, his lifeless eyes staring upwards towards the ceiling. There's a gunshot wound to his torso.

I stand frozen in the doorway, listening to the beat of my heart and the rush of blood in my ears.

Evelyn, what have you done?

I bolt into the room, almost slipping on the blood that's found its way to the floor, and stumble against the bed. The man's lifeless body jolts under my weight. His eyes remain vacant and unblinking. I'm so scared I could vomit.

I thrust a shaking hand to his neck and check for a pulse. I hold it there for what feels like a lifetime, silently begging for a faint, distant echo from his long-cold heart, but I feel nothing. A gurgle of blood slips out of the wound, but not much: most of it has already left him, soaking into the sheets and the mattress beneath his body and dripping onto the floor. This must be Kyle. The close friend of Aaron's that his boss talked about.

Evelyn wouldn't do this. She couldn't.

I slip my shaking arms under Kyle's body – one beneath his shoulder blades and the other beneath his thighs – and try to lift him to the floor. The weight of him makes me buckle and we both fall; I feel something give in my back and groan, but I push on, frantically clearing the mess from around him. My sweat drips down onto his bare, bloody chest as I begin pumping my hands against it.

One, two, three, four, five . . .

I bend over him and breathe through his lips, tasting blood and death, then return to the compressions.

One, two, three, four, five . . .

His head lolls against the floorboards while his vacant eyes stare up at me, watching me as I try in vain to save a dead man. Blood oozes out of the wound with each compression, but still I keep pushing.

I do this for a minute, maybe two, until I'm breathless and soaked with sweat. Then I sit back and slump against the windowsill behind me, knocking into the rusty old AC unit. My eyes never leave the body.

I'm forty-seven years old, but in this moment I feel like a child. A terrified, confused child. I know I should get up, get the hell out of here, but I find myself frozen to the spot, covered in a stranger's blood.

Then I hear the sirens. Once I hear them, I can't hear anything else, and by the sound of them they're only four or five blocks away.

I force myself up, stumbling to my feet as I try to think of what Evelyn might have touched, what I might have touched, and work manically to remove any trace of us. I take a rag from the floor and rub the dead man's lips where mine had been, dash it over his bloody chest where I had placed my hands, then wipe down the handle of the hammer. But now my DNA will be on the rag.

The sirens are getting closer. They're maybe three blocks away now. This is a crime scene, and I've just put my DNA all over it. I catch my reflection in the mirror on the wall and see a swipe of red across my forehead where I'd tried to mop my brow. I look down at the dead man.

'I'm sorry,' I whisper. I'm about to run for the door when I spot something: a gun lying on the floor beside the bed. I slip it into the back of my jeans.

I rush out of the room and along the hall, back into the dirty kitchen and through the buzzing flies, then out of the screen door into the yard. I take a deep breath and cough through the smell of wildfire smoke sitting in the air, coming in from the west across the plains, before I start to run back down the track. The blood on me looks so bright out here against my pale skin. I reach the truck and clamber inside, leaving a swipe of red on the door handle, and then more smears all over the cabin, staining the clutch as I lift it.

I turn in the road, stones and dust spraying beneath the wheels, and speed down the street, lowering the windows as I stop at the junction to listen for the direction of the sirens. They're coming from the left, and they'll be here any second. I turn right and slam my foot down on the accelerator.

14

Aaron

As I walk down Main Street towards my apartment, I notice the buoyancy of my steps and the faint smile pulling at the corners of my mouth. It could be from the joints Kyle and I have smoked, but it feels like there's more to it. I think this is the closest I've ever been to happiness. For as long as I can remember, I've walked with my head down and my eyes locked on the ground, my shoulders rounded to make myself smaller. An apologetic stance begging to go unnoticed. It was the same before the accident. When I spot another queer person about town, I often see them doing the same thing: all of us avoiding eye contact in fear of what we might find staring back at us.

I'm still pretty high, and for a moment I forget why I'm heading home, before it suddenly comes back to me: I told Kyle I'd bring him some cigarettes. Jim gave me a large carton of Camels when I first started working at the gas station. He'd watched me closely during my first day, and I'd thought he was looking at me in the same way the rest of the town did. I'm not wanted or welcome in Beatty; I'm a stain on their community, a convict and kid-killer they wish they could forget. But at the end of the shift, when I'd plucked up the courage to ask to bum a cigarette off him, he'd asked me how much money I had since leaving jail. I told him the figure. Twelve dollars, give or take a cent. The rest had gone on the house stuff I'd bought off Craigslist: the hotplate with dodgy wiring that you have to bang two or three times before it'll work; the TV that's older than I am. Jim had told me to wait a moment, gone inside, and returned with a large box of cigarettes. And along with an advance on my pay check, he'd invited me back to his and given me my first home-cooked meal in over a decade. I went to bed and cried that night. Hate I understand, but kindness still feels so new.

I've reached my doorway beside the deli with the spring still in my step when I hear my name. The sound of the man's voice knocks the smile clean off my face.

Sheriff Kincade is leaning on his cruiser, which is parked up by the kerb. He heads towards me with the same confident stride he had earlier, the same smirk pulling at the corners of his mouth. He keeps walking until he's right in front of me. Even then, he gets closer still, until I have to press myself up against my front door and he's breathing down on me. His nose is mere inches from mine and I can feel his crotch pushing up against me. He must have been waiting outside my place for hours.

'We didn't get to finish our little chat earlier,' he says.

'I got the message loud and clear.'

'No, I don't think you did.'

He takes in every bit of my expression, his eyes dancing round and his grin widening as he notices every twitch of anxiety, the nervous bobs of my throat as I swallow. He glances along either side of the street to check we're alone.

'I went and paid a visit to Big John after seeing you earlier, and I picked you up a little gift.'

My heart is pounding so aggressively that I feel sick. I don't know where to rest my eyes: on his mouth, over his shoulder. He tilts my chin so I'm staring straight at him.

'Don't you want to see it?'

I shake my head violently.

'We both know that's a lie.'

I grimace as he reaches down into his pocket, knowing what's coming, and flinch as he slips the bag of meth into mine. When he laughs, I catch the smell of beer on his breath; a sheriff who drink-drives and buys drugs from one addict to force upon another. Luckily, he seems too buzzed by the booze to notice the smell of pot on me.

'Well, aren't you going to thank me?'

'I don't do that anymore, I told you.'

'Well, that doesn't really work for me. I need a reason to lock you back up, and I'm an impatient man. I know you want it – I can see it in your eyes. You don't stop being a thieving little meth rat just because you put down the pipe, boy. That lying, conniving, ruthless addict inside of you will always be there, waiting for you to break. I bet there's nothing more you'd love to do right now than throw open that door, hide away in your little den, and smoke the whole bag. I'm right, aren't I?'

My heart is pounding so hard now that I'm feeling dizzy and starting to sweat. I will myself to try and figure out a way out of this, to find the right thing to say, but my mind is dominated by a single thought: the baggie of meth inside my pocket.

'I—I—I need to go inside.'

Kincade laughs under his breath.

'Yeah, I bet you do. That shit won't smoke itself.' He grins and slaps me on the ass. 'See you soon.'

He steps back and returns to his car, greeting a straight couple as they pass him by, all smiles and none the wiser.

I've fought the key into the lock before he's even got behind the wheel, and race up the stairs to my apartment with the meth burning into my thigh.

I slam the door shut behind me and rest against it, trying to catch my breath. It's like my lungs are on fire and my throat has swollen shut. I reach into my pocket and throw the baggie to the floor. The white crystals twinkle up at me, promising an escape from all the fear, all the pain. I stare down at it until tears block my view.

I cross the room to sit down on the futon and cry over how weak I am; about how right that bastard Kincade is. It's been over a decade that I've been clean, and yet all I want to do right now is to open up that baggie and smoke the lot. To no longer feel the way I feel. To put an end to the pain and the loneliness. To *forget*.

Time passes, I'm not sure how much, and all the while a violent tug of war goes on inside my head.

Flush it. Flush the lot of it. Don't let Kincade win.

Finally, I dash the tears from my eyes, sweep the baggie up from the floor, and stride towards the bathroom, only stopping when I see the mess.

There's shattered glass all over the floor, reflecting the sun on the other side of the broken window, looking like little pockets of fire. The tub is filled with it, along with scuffs from a stranger's shoes. Someone climbed up the ladder and smashed in my window.

My first thought is Kincade, but I force it away. He wouldn't need to do that; he's just proved he feels perfectly safe harassing me outside my own front door.

I head back into the main room, trying to see if anything has been touched. There's not much to steal from this place; it's all second-hand and not worth a dime. That's when I spot something I hadn't before, while all of my attention had been on the baggie: my laptop is on the futon in plain view.

That was another thing Jim gave me; I'd told him over dinner that I wanted to write someday, but I didn't know where to start. He'd left the table and come back with his late wife's laptop. It's almost as old as I am, and she'd not used it for a long time before her passing due to going blind in first one eye, then the other, but if it worked, he said, it was mine. It's probably my most prized possession. And here it is, lying out in the open, in a place I know I didn't leave it.

The air in the apartment has changed. I can't explain it, but the space no longer feels like mine. I slip the laptop back beneath the pillow.

If it was someone trying to scare me off, they'd have trashed the place. Kincade had threatened to send his boys round, but this isn't their work – he'd want to make a show of it, humiliate me in front of the neighbours in the same way he believes I humiliated him. This was someone who came with a purpose.

It wouldn't be to steal anything because nothing I have is worth taking. Maybe they came to hurt me and left as soon as they realized I wasn't home. I stand in the room, listening to the whistle of the wind slipping in through the broken window behind me.

Someone else might call the cops and report a break-in, but it doesn't even cross my mind. I've never trusted the police – being poor and queer, I learnt fast that they're never on our side. Kincade is proof of that. So, if I plan on getting through this, I'll have to look out for myself like I always have.

I pull out my phone to text Kyle, to tell him I'll be a little later than planned, but the battery's dead.

I head back towards the futon and pick up the charging lead plugged in at the wall to hook it up. The wait is unbearably long, and my apartment feels more and more hostile and unwelcoming by the minute. The air is getting cooler, creeping in through the broken window in the bathroom. A shard of glass falls from the frame and hits the tub with a loud crack.

My phone fires up and immediately starts flashing with notifications. I sit down on the futon and check through them: multiple missed calls from Jim, and a couple more from a number I don't recognize. I'm just about to call Jim back when the phone starts vibrating in my hand. The unknown number is calling.

I look down at the flashing screen. When I find the courage to answer, I raise the phone to my ear without saying a word.

'Hello?' a man says.

I listen to him on the other end of the line, breathing heavily as though he's been running. Beyond that, I hear the grumble of an engine.

'Is this Aaron?' he asks.

'Who's this?' I ask in return. My voice gives me away; if I can hear the tremble in my words, he will too.

I listen to the engine, and I'm sure I hear the distant wail of a police siren calling in the distance.

'Don't hang up,' he says. 'My name is Tobias.'

He says this as if it's meant to provoke a reaction; fear perhaps, or trepidation. I swallow down the bile that has slowly crept up my throat. My heart is racing, and I wonder if something has happened to my mother; if Tony has beaten her to death this time, or if she finally took one pill too many and never woke up.

'Tobias Moore.'

I can't breathe – that's the first thing I can think of. I can't breathe and my chest is on fire. The second thing I think of is my own stupidity. I'd dared to feel happiness just now as I walked down the street towards my door. I learnt a long time ago that happiness is the most dangerous emotion a person can feel. Sadness and fear, I'm used to them. But happiness can be ripped from you, beaten from you. I've always felt like someone is watching me – God, fate, I don't know – waiting for the moment I dare to acknowledge joy, only to send me back to where I belong.

'I don't want to scare you,' Tobias says. 'I don't want to hurt you. I'm calling to warn you.'

A reel of questions fires in my mind, leapfrogging one another before I can try to fathom the answers.

'My wife,' he says. 'She's coming for you.'

'C-coming for me?' I stutter.

'To hurt you,' he says, in case I didn't understand before. I did. 'My wife, she's a determined woman. When she wants to do something, she won't stop until she achieves it. She's going to keep hunting you until she finds you.'

I look towards the bathroom door, quivering with the breeze rolling in through the window. She's been here, in my home. Did she perch right here? Take in the room as I'm doing now? I try to make sense of what's happening, but all I can do is sit on the futon and shake.

'I want to protect you,' he says. 'But you have to trust me.'

'W-why would you want to help me?'

I listen to his breaths and the purr of the engine on the other end of the line.

'Because I'll lose her forever if I don't.'

I wonder where she is now. Where she's been already, looking for me around town. I wonder how much time I have before she comes back here. The man is quiet on the other end of the line, as if he's trying to muster the courage to say whatever's coming next.

'You've done your time, Aaron. Whether we like it or not, you got the sentence you got, and you saw it through.'

'You don't sound like you believe what you're saying.'

'Well, it's a bit fucking hard talking to the man who mowed down my son and left him for dead,' Tobias spits down the phone. He takes a deep breath, sighs it out. Trying to calm himself down. 'Look, none of this will be easy. For any of us. But whatever you think of me, and whatever I think of you, we need each other right now.'

I can't remember what this man looks like. I should remember the face of the man whose child I killed, shouldn't I? But there had been so many people in the courthouse the day I was sentenced. A hundred faces blending into one; a sea of eyes burning into me with such ferocity that it's a miracle I didn't go up in flames right there before the judge. But the one face I do remember, beyond the lawyers and the guards, is that of Evelyn Moore.

I hadn't wanted to look at her, as cowardly and selfish as that is. I couldn't face looking into the eyes of the woman whose child I'd killed in fear of never forgetting it, but just before I was dismissed and led out of the room in cuffs, her eyes caught mine, and I almost stopped in my tracks. The saying goes, *if looks could kill*, and if they truly could, I'd have been dead right then and there. Her eyes were two pools of hatred. I can still remember the unbearable heat of them, the intensity of her focus, as if she were mentally wrapping her hands around my neck and wringing the life out of me.

From the brief moment she and I shared in the courtroom, I know Tobias isn't lying: if she is hunting me, she won't stop until it's done.

Until I'm dead.

'Aaron,' he says down the phone. 'Are you there?'

'Yes,' I say, almost in a whisper.

'I want to help you, but you'll have to trust me. Do you trust me?'

I don't think I've ever trusted someone completely, not even myself. To mistrust others was probably one of the first life lessons I was ever taught: I couldn't trust my mother, whose poor judgement consistently led us into harm's way. I couldn't trust my stepfather, who'd made it his life's mission to beat the gay out of me. I couldn't trust my brother, who said he would always be there for me, only to run the first chance he got and leave me behind. I knew not to try to make friends, because I always became their punching bag, the runt of the litter the group always turned on. I had learnt not to trust people before I had even learnt to walk.

'Aaron?' Tobias says. 'Do you trust me?'

I take a deep breath, steeling myself.

'No.'

I hang up the phone and sit in the silence, shivering as the coming night breezes in through the broken window. That's when I notice the baggie is still in my hand. I unfurl my fingers, revealing the glinting crystals in my palm; my mouth is sapped dry at the mere sight of them.

I need to get the hell out of here, I tell myself as I reach under the futon for my backpack. *Then I need to get the hell out of Beatty.*

I try to call Kyle, to tell him that I'll be gone for a while, but there's no answer.

Then I shove the baggie back into my pocket.

15

Tobias

The boy's blood fills the sink as I rub at the dried flecks with soap, watching it liquidize again beneath the water, turning it pink.

The gas station toilet is as grotty as you'd imagine. It stinks of trucker piss, shit, cigarette smoke and body odour; the sort of musk you'd never want caught at the back of your throat like it is mine. But the most horrible part of the room isn't the stained toilet, or the filthy tiled floor, or the graffiti on the walls, or the stench, but the reflection in the mirror.

I look like death. Despite the odd patch of sunburnt skin, my face is pale and sickly, and my stubbled cheeks are gaunt; dark circles sit like shadows under my eyes. At first glance, I appear more skull than man.

Kyle's blood has soaked into my T-shirt. I peel it off, the fabric bonded to me with sweat, and pull on the scrunched-up black tee I'd found in the back of the truck; it's covered in dog hair and smells of another man's pits, but it's better than blood.

I head back out, shading my eyes against the last remaining sunlight. It'll be dark soon; the sun is just beyond the horizon at the other end of the desert. A whole day passed without catching up to Evelyn; another night of not knowing what the next day will bring lies ahead.

I'm exhausted. Bone-tired, as my father would say. Every one of my joints aches, and my feet are throbbing and covered in blisters from the stranger's old boots and the hours I spent barefoot, running across motel grounds and pushing my bare soles to the pedals of the stolen truck as I sped towards Beatty.

I wonder if the man I stole from is hunting me. Of course he is; he isn't going to let a stranger run off with his stash. How might he find me, and what will he do if he does? I can't imagine he'd be thrilled to know I've taken some of the money and spent it as my own. Then there's the question of what the hell I'm going to do with a massive bag of drugs and cash. If I'm caught carrying this, I'll go to jail for a good twenty-five years or more. The police are unlikely to believe me if I tell them the gear isn't mine. But I can't ditch the bag either. If the man does catch up with me and I don't have it, I'm guessing he'll be a lot angrier than if the stash were only a few hundred dollars short.

I get back inside the truck and sit behind the wheel, unsure where to go or what to do. It's a sense of loss that brings a surge of panic the moment I dare to let it in.

Where are you going to go, Aaron?

Wherever he goes, Evelyn will follow. That's the only thing I know for sure. I think back to how young he sounded on the phone, even after all those years in jail. He sounded lost, frightened, as if he were a boy alone in the world rather than a grown man, as if he remained stunted at the age of twenty, the age he went to jail. He certainly didn't sound like the sort of killer one would expect. There was no defensiveness in his tone, no threats to try to scare me off. Just a scared little boy stuttering on the other end of the line. Even so, I can't stop myself from loathing him. Just the thought of him breathing on the other end of the line makes me feel sick.

I wonder what Evelyn is doing right now: if she's stopped for the night or if she'll continue her hunt. My wife is the sort of person who decides upon a goal and doesn't let up until the deed is done. I'm not sure how I thought this was going to go when we set off from San Diego yesterday morning, but I never would have imagined that my wife would kill anyone other than Aaron Alexander. To think that the woman I loved and married raised a gun and fired a bullet into the gut of an innocent man is incomprehensible. But the proof was right there before me, bled out onto the once-white sheets, his lifeless eyes staring up at me from the floor before I turned and bolted. I remember the feel of his cool, wet flesh beneath my palms as I tried to revive him, the blood bubbling out of the wound with each thrust and the faint metallic taste of it on his lips. Evelyn didn't just shoot that man. It looks like she left him there to die alone too.

I could call the cops. Have them stop her before she causes any more harm. But the thought of losing her for good makes it impossible to consider. We were always extremely close, and by that I mean I was dependent on her, which I'm ashamed to admit. She was always the strong one, the wise one, the one who knew what to do and what to say. But after our move across the pond, I became even more reliant on her strength. And then when Joshua died, well, she became my world. To hand her in to the police wouldn't just mean losing her; it would mean losing my whole sense of self. After almost thirty years together, I have no idea who I am without her. It would be the end of the road for the both of us.

I can fix this. I just need to stop her before she causes any more harm.

But still, fear chips away at me. Evelyn has taken a life now. She has changed the game from threats to actual murder. It's clear to me in this moment, more than ever before: this wasn't just a fantastical desire that would fade when she was faced with the reality of it. This is a quest that will continue on and on, with blood shed by those who dare to get in her way. Am I still her husband, in her eyes? The father of the child we lost? Or am I just another man standing in her path?

I look at my hands trembling on the wheel and spot the boy's blood trapped beneath my fingernails. I try to scrape it out, digging violently at the red crescent moons glaring up at me from the end of each nail. My wife isn't the only one with blood on her hands. I had the chance to call the cops before she took a life; I could still do it now and prevent her from hurting anyone else. And yet I just can't bring myself to betray her; to give up on her after everything we've been through and all the years we've spent together. I have to know that all is lost before I give up; I'm the only person left in this world who gives a damn about her.

My wife used to be the kindest person I have ever known. I guess it's the most sensitive souls who are hurt the most. When Joshua was taken from us the pain was just too great for her, and she built a wall around her heart to keep that pain away, only to keep it locked within her with no place else to go. The woman I know and love is trapped behind that wall, and I won't stop trying to reach her. She has saved so many others in her life through her work, now it's time someone saved her in return.

I take the photo of Joshua out of my pocket, admiring the grooves of his face where the camera caught him mid-laugh, the sparkle in his eye and the milky white baby teeth flashing in his smile. The reason for Evelyn's pain, and mine. Thinking of him like this is both agonizing and a gift. I get to remember how beautiful he was, how kind his heart was, just like his mother's was before grief changed her; but then the pain comes, ripping through me like a knife cutting me open from hip to sternum.

Desperate to keep moving, I slip the photo back into my pocket and turn on the engine. I stare out at the open road for a spell, then turn it off again. I have no idea what to do or where to go, and I don't have Evelyn to set me straight. I feel the loneliness and the fear bubbling up again, silently wrapping themselves around my throat.

I pick up the burner phone and think for a while. I said I would call the police if she went too far, if I didn't think I would be able to stop her. Is this not the very moment I've been dreading? I stare down at the phone, trying to pluck up the courage to do the right thing, my pulse pounding in my ears. But however hard I try, hitting the keys for 911 with a quivering thumb, I can't bring myself to follow through.

I take the coward's way out and tap her number instead, desperate to try to get through to her one last time. The call rings and rings until, to my surprise, she answers.

16

Evelyn

The motel I've checked into is fifteen miles outside Beatty, on another deserted road that looks just like the one before. I've put enough distance between me and the crime scene, but still in the right direction to head to where Aaron will be going next: Reno. If Aaron is going to run to anyone, it'll be his brother.

I stand at the basin in the small, grotty bathroom, scrubbing at the blood beneath my fingernails and obsessively planning my next steps. If I keep focused on my goal, I won't have to think about what I've done. But however many times I try to banish the thought from my mind, the sight of the blood swirling around the drain keeps dragging me back. The memories resurface in flashes: the bang of the gun, the boy's blood seeping between my fingers, his dead, glassy stare. I splash my face with cold water and drink some from my cupped palm before wiping it across the nape of my neck, but I still feel tense, my entire body like a taut fist that I can't unfurl.

I head back into the bedroom, dark from the pulled drapes, and sit on the end of the bed, my jaw moving from side to side. The grinding is getting worse. My teeth are clenched constantly and feel brittle from the pressure. Most of the time, I don't even know I'm doing it. Whether I'm awake or asleep, concentrating or dazed, sober or drunk, my jaw works away at itself, each tooth slowly whittling another one down. I rub my fingers against my temples, feeling the pressure travel through the muscles towards the top of my head. The one tooth that hurts more than the rest is throbbing after such a long day, to the point where I can feel my pulse in the nerve and my face feels hot. I pour myself a brandy from the bottle in my bag, in the hope that it'll keep my jaw still for a while.

I had been numb with shock after leaving Kyle's house, but the adrenaline is wearing off now; my entire body is aching and my eyelids have grown heavy. Grief is a weighty burden to carry, and pairing that with a man's blood on my hands, I'm ready to collapse. But something tells me that thoughts of Kyle's lifeless body are going to keep me up all night.

I rub my eyes and sigh, letting my face rest in my hands awhile, only to think of Kyle, dead on the bed: violent flashes of him staring back at me, his blood seeping through the sheets and soaking into my jeans as I sat beside him. I look down at my hip: there's a dark maroon patch sodden into my buttock and thigh. I'd gone into the motel reception like this, crossed the parking lot to my room. I try to remember how many people might have seen me as I unbuckle my belt and wriggle out of the jeans, chucking them into the corner of the room too hard. The buckle clangs against the wall before dropping to the floor.

I take the brandy by the neck of the bottle and swig, trying to fight the emotions that are set on working their way to the surface. I usually face things like this in the same way I was raised: the British trait of bottling it all up, pushing the lid down whenever the emotions try to froth over, despite my career being spent trying to get people to open up. No one can keep their emotions locked within forever; they all come bursting out in the end.

I can't stop thinking about Kyle after the bullet hit him: the pure, childlike fear that filled his eyes. It was the same fear I'd seen in my mother's before she passed. It's the look people give you when they know they're going to die.

I'd only meant to scare him; to make him tell me what I needed to know. But all it took was a slip and fall for the gun to go off in my hand, and suddenly he was gone. I furiously swipe the tears away as they come, hating my own softness.

Does this make me as bad as Aaron Alexander?

I pinch my leg until the pain overtakes the guilt. I need to be stronger, harder. But when I open my eyes again, I spot the skin on my thigh is tinged red where the blood soaked through my jeans. It's stained my underwear too. I march back to the bathroom and run the tap too fast, water hissing out and splashing back at me as I scrub my bloody flesh until water runs down my legs in pink trails and my skin hums from the vigour. I only stop and dry off when I hear a phone ping from the other room.

The alert wasn't from my phone, but Kyle's; the phone I'd swiped from the bedside table before bolting. I pick it up and squint at the screen through the dark.

Aaron

Hey, I tried to call but you must have fallen asleep. I'm heading to my brother's place in Reno for a while. I can explain over the phone. If a woman called Evelyn Moore comes looking for me, tell her you don't know me, okay?

That's my element of surprise gone. I wonder how he found out about me. That guy Jim was far too clueless to put two and two together. But clearly, Aaron doesn't know about Kyle yet; I wonder what will happen when he does. I sit down on the end of the bed and begin thinking of a reply, scrolling through the message chain to make sure I get Kyle's tone just right, making note of the typos he used to make.

Kyle

What's going on? Keep texting me so I know
ur okay

I'll dodge the call when the time comes, but for now I need Aaron to keep telling me where he is and where he's headed.

I see the ellipses that tell me he's typing appear at the bottom of the chat box, and excitement fizzes in my stomach. I wonder what he's saying, what he's thinking, and as I sit holding my breath and watching the dots flashing on the screen, I remember all that's at stake. My son is dead in the ground, while the man who killed him is right here, living and breathing, so close to me that I feel I could reach out and grab him.

Aaron

I'm okay, just need to lay low. I'll call you soon
and explain everything

I watch the ellipses dance at the bottom of the screen again. My lungs are tight, waiting to exhale, but all I can focus on are those flashing dots. Finally, another message pings through.

Aaron

Remember what I said. If anyone asks after
me – you say you don't know me. I care about
you and I don't want you getting hurt

It's a bit late for that, I think, and swig more brandy from the bottle. I feel the liquid burn down my throat until my eyes water. I let the phone screen fade until the room is dark, and it's just me and the sound of my brandy-scented breaths and the methodical thudding of my heart. I'm rubbing my temples when the light of a screen flashes again, only this time it's not Kyle's phone that's ringing. It's mine.

I pick it up from the dresser and watch the unknown number flashing back at me. I can't explain it, but I know in my bones that the person on the other end of the line is my husband.

Clearly, I've underestimated his dedication to stopping me. I left him without his phone, his wallet, even swiping his shoes on the way out, all while he slept in the motel bed behind me, his brow wrinkled in his sleep. I wonder how he did it, escaping the desert without any means. What wrongs has he committed to get to this point? Even self-proclaimed good men like my husband can't get through something like this without stepping on someone else's toes. But however far he's willing to go, he must know that I'll go further. I feel a shiver of anger ripple up my spine; he can never just leave things alone. He has to keep coming, and coming, and coming. That incessant, buzzing fly I can never seem to catch and crush.

I accept the call and raise the phone to my ear.

'Evelyn, it's me.'

He's exhausted. I can tell by his tone; the sleepy rasp his voice takes on. I sit at the other end of the line, listening to him breathe in and out.

'You left me,' he says when he speaks again.

I almost want to laugh. Of all the things to mention first. I've set off to kill a man, and this is the first thing he says.

'What did you expect?'

'I don't know. But not that.'

'You weren't going to help me. You would have only dragged me down.'

'That's just it. I do want to help you.'

'No, you want to stop me. There's a difference.'

'I want to help you see that you don't need to do this. That killing a man isn't the way to go. Look at the harm you've already caused.' He sighs deeply. 'Why did you do it? Why did you kill that kid?'

Tobias has got further than I thought. Kyle's death won't have been reported by the media yet, if they'll mention it at all; even Aaron doesn't know. Which means Tobias had to have gone to that same house and seen the body for himself. I've underestimated him. I mustn't do that again.

'You know why I'm doing this. And if you were stronger, if you weren't so self-righteous, you'd be doing it with me.'

'No, Evelyn. I wouldn't.'

I feel the guilt writhing within me again, the shame draping over me.

'Because you're a better person than I am? That's your MO isn't it? You're better than everybody else.'

'No, it's not. It's because I don't believe that killing someone will take your pain away. You're still going to be angry when he's dead, Evelyn. Whatever you do, whoever you kill, it's never going to be enough. And deep down, you know that too.'

Another wave of anger courses up my spine. My jaw is clenched tight again, my bad tooth humming. He makes it sound so easy, as if I could merely snap my fingers and all of this pain would disappear. He must have called to bring us closer together, to try and make me see what we once were to each other. But all he has done is push us further apart.

'Is this why you called? To preach down the phone at me, all holier-than-thou?'

'Come home with me. It's not too late.'

I can feel the love in his voice, can hear how he believes every word he says. He truly thinks that we can turn back for San Diego and accept our son's fate, put all of this behind us. But now I realize the truth: my husband doesn't know me at all.

'You'll never understand,' I say.

'Then help me try.'

'Don't talk down to me.'

'I'm not, Evelyn. I'm trying to get through to you. I'm trying to stop you from hurting anyone else before it's too late.' He falls quiet for a moment, and I think back to when we were at the diner, how his face had flushed red as he tried to keep his thoughts at bay. 'Maybe you're right, maybe I'll never understand. Because I certainly don't get how you can kill someone and simply walk away. How could you do that? Shoot that kid?'

I feel the guilt working its way through me: my throat tightening, heart racing. I think of how I held his hand as he lay dying, how he sobbed and told me he didn't want to die.

'I didn't mean to,' I hear myself say, and it's only then that I realize I'm crying, as my voice croaks with emotion and tears burn my eyes. I thought I was stronger than this, harder than this.

'What do you mean you didn't *mean* to? You shot him, Evelyn. You left him to die—'

'I slipped and the gun went off, all right? I only meant to scare him. Stop trying to make me out to be the devil just because you're too weak to do what needs to be done.'

He doesn't say anything, but even by the sound of his breathing I can hear the hope in him. As if all of this is a mistake that can still be taken back; that because I'm crying it's proof that I'm not the woman he feared I'd become. I scold myself for giving in to his ploys. I'd started to soften at the familiar sound of his voice, forgetting whose side he's on. I wipe my tears away and force myself to harden.

'Evelyn—'

'If you try and stop me, I'll kill you,' I say. 'But I think you know that already.'

I can hear cars passing on a nearby road and his quick nasal breaths. He must be pulled up somewhere; God knows how he got a car without a dime to his name. If I weren't so angry at him, I'd be impressed.

'Well, I'm still going to try,' he says.

'You'll regret it.'

I hang up the phone and sit in the dark, silently scolding myself for unravelling. I've planned this for so long, trying to anticipate who and what might get in my way, but I didn't consider that my own weakness might be a problem I'd have to overcome, not even for a moment. I dig my fingernails into my thigh.

Stop this right now. I'm the only one who cares what happened to Joshua; I'm the only one who's set on making things right. I can't let him down now at the first hurdle.

I go to the window, pulling the curtains open and sliding back the pane to light a cigarette. I stand watching the vacancy sign flicker from a weak fuse, thinking of my sanctimonious husband, then of the man I'm hell-bent on killing. The former believes he's above us all, while the latter must consider himself a victim. But they're both wrong. The only victim in all of this is Joshua. The one person this is truly about.

I flick the end of the cigarette, close the window and the curtains, and head back to the bed to sleep, lying on my back and staring up at the water stains on the ceiling. When I close my eyes, Kyle's are waiting, staring back at me behind my closed lids: those two wet ovals shimmering with fear of the death he knew was coming.

I shake my head roughly until the image goes away. If I want to get to Aaron, I need to stay focused. No more thoughts of Kyle Atkins. No more calls with my husband.

I open my eyes again when I feel something on my arm; the pitter-patter of small, spindly legs. I turn on the lamp: it's a bed bug biting down on my arm. I splat it dead, smear the bug's blood and shell on the pillow beside mine, and roll over.

There was a time when I would have bolted out of this room at the sight of a bed bug. I'd have had to leave or I wouldn't have been able to sleep a wink, scratching at insects that weren't there, convinced they were all over me.

I close my eyes, bracing myself to see Joshua again in my dreams. Half of me longs to see him, to remember his smile, the softness of his skin, the sweetness of his breath. I remember every detail of him in my dreams. But the other half of me dreads the pain that will inevitably follow. I can't count how many times I've woken in tears after spending the night with him, only to wake up and lose him all over again.

I take one last swig of brandy from the bottle on the bedside table, turn over, and pray for sleep.

17

Aaron

I take another bite of scrambled eggs and feel a piece of shell crack between my teeth.

'Good?' Jim asks, with childlike hope gleaming in his eyes.

I nod with a smile and a mouthful of shell. 'Good.'

'I'll top up your OJ,' he says, and picks up my glass.

Jim lives a simple life. His house is to the west of Beatty, a two-bed place where he's lived for the last twenty-five years ever since he left the Marines. The only signs of his time in the forces are the odd scar and the tattoos on his forearms, which have faded to a botanical jade-green.

The house isn't tidy, but it isn't a dive either. It's lived in, and by a man who's been on his own for a decade ever since the loss of his wife to cancer. Pancreatic, I think. And even though Jim seems content enough, I can't help but wonder if he's ever dreamt of more. He's told me in the past about how he saw the world while on active duty, but wandering through desert battle grounds isn't what I'd call seeing the world.

One of Jim's cats jumps up onto the table and sniffs near my plate, its big amber eyes peering hungrily at my eggs. That's when I'm able to name the other thing I can feel nestled among the eggs: cat hair.

'Hey, hey, hey!' Jim says, flapping his hand at the cat to make it scarper. 'You watch your plate; she'll nab that bacon quicker than you can blink.'

He places the glass of juice on the table and sits down opposite me.

I'd called Jim last night, after I spoke to Tobias Moore. It's easy enough to decide to make a run for it, but if you don't have the means, you're stuck. Jim told me to come to his and lay low for the night before setting off; Kyle would have already left for his night shift at the abattoir, shuffled onto a bus with the other workers and ferried out of town, which left Jim as my only option. I certainly wasn't going to lie in wait at my place for Evelyn Moore to bust in another window. It feels too strange to call her by her first name, too intimate; aside from my crime, we're nothing more than strangers to one another. But then, when I think about it, the only thing that's as intimate as having a child with someone is being the person to take that child away.

'You seen about these fires?' Jim asks.

'Heard it on the radio in the store yesterday. Sounds like it's gonna be bad.'

'Yep. Getting worse too. They burned through the night, spread from San Bernadino to Sequoia. There're new fires up by Gold Point too.'

'Jesus. Hell in a handbasket, or however the saying goes.'

'That sounds about right.'

I force the rest of the food down me, trying not to let it show on my face every time I feel a bit of eggshell scratching down my throat.

'So,' Jim says after we've eaten. My stomach gurgles, unsettled by the eggs and bacon, the shell and cat hair. 'What're you gonna do?'

'I don't know.'

'She means business, this woman. Her husband seemed scared of her. I say you should be too.'

'Maybe it's all part of the act, and they're in on it together,' I reply, and take a gulp of OJ. 'Good cop, bad cop.'

Jim falls quiet, seeming to consider this. 'I don't know,' he says finally. 'I believed him.'

'Well, maybe he's really good at it.'

'I still think you should talk to the Sheriff—'

'You know the cops in this town want me dead just as much as she does.'

'What if I come with you? Maybe I can talk to Kincade, get him to see sense.'

'You think a small-town cop wants to see sense, and not what they already know to be true?'

Again, he seems to consider this.

'Well, it's an option.'

'An option for other people maybe, but not me. I can look after myself.'

I think back to Kincade waiting for me when I got home last night and slipping the meth into my pocket. To know someone has paid for their crimes and fought tooth and nail to get clean, only to try to mess it all up; it's pure evil. He was right though, about the addict always being a part of me. After all, the meth is still in my pocket, dominating every damn thought that enters my head. He saw his chance to get me while keeping his hands clean. He doesn't need to destroy me, not when he can simply sit back and wait for me to destroy myself. I'd lain awake half the night in Jim's spare room, fighting the urge to smoke myself into oblivion.

'So, what *are* you going to do?' he asks again.

I look down at my plate, as if the answer might be lying there before me, but all I see is the yellow smear of egg and the drops of oil that had followed the bacon from the pan.

'I'll go to my brother in Reno, and then take it from there.'

'And what, keep running all your life? If you don't want the cops stopping this woman, who else is going to do it? And what's your probation officer going to do when you don't turn up to your next meeting—'

'I don't know, all right? All I know is that I need to get the hell out of Beatty. I can think better on it then.'

I only know Chris lives in Reno because, after years of sending him letters from jail, they were all sent back to me in a bundle from the new tenant that had taken the place over from him: he'd left them behind, unopened. Along with the letters, the tenant had written down my brother's new address in case I wanted to try to get in touch. I never did write to him again.

Another of Jim's cats starts rubbing against my leg; more likely for a scrap of food than to bring me comfort, but it still manages to calm me down a little.

'Sorry.'

'Hey, if you're not allowed to snap when you've got a psycho chasing after you, when are you, huh?' He gives me a wink. 'I guess I gotta trust you know what you're doing. And I'll do everything I can to help you get you on your way. Come with me.'

I follow him over to the door leading to the garage, three cats weaving around our feet, and step inside. I wait for the light flickering overhead to calm before asking what we're doing in here. Jim rips off a sheet cover to reveal an old motorbike parked in the centre of the garage.

I stare at it a while, unsure what to say or do next.

'It's old, but it used to be a real good ride.'

'This is yours?'

'Hey, I used to be cool before I fucked my hip and gained all this weight.'

'Just didn't take you for the motorbike kind. It's pretty cool. Why are you showing it to me?'

'I'm lending it to you,' he says. 'To help you get on your way.'

Acts of kindness frighten me, have done all my life. Cruelty

I get; lots of people find it easy, and they're usually transparent about it. But when someone does something nice, I can't help but wonder what they're trying to gain, always looking for ways they might benefit from the act in the long run. But by the look on Jim's face, he means it. His eyes shimmer with both worry and hope.

I stare at the bike, unsure what to say.

'I've never ridden a motorbike before,' I mutter.

'You ridden a bicycle?'

'Well, yeah, but—'

'Basically the same thing.'

I doubt that's true, but I stare at the bike in wonder anyway. It's either this or a bus ticket. I can't afford anything else.

'I'll show you how to use it. Real easy once you get the idea.'

He heads to the garage door and pulls it upward with a succession of metal whines and creaks.

'Why are you being nice to me?'

The question slips out before I can stop it, quick as vomit. I watch Jim turn, his expression etched with confusion.

'Why shouldn't I be?' he replies.

Because I don't deserve it, I hear myself think.

Before jail, when I was nothing but a junkie, I'd have robbed this poor man blind. If he'd taken me in then, he would have woken up to find all of his valuables missing. I would have stolen the bike, the notes in his wallet, his late wife's jewellery. Anything valuable that wasn't nailed down that I could pawn for cash to get my next fix. I'm not that guy anymore, but I still don't understand why he's so trusting of me. Why he's taking me under his wing like this after everything I've done. Hell, with the meth in my pocket, I don't even trust myself.

I look down at the floor, wishing I hadn't asked. I can't remember the last time someone was nice to me like this, especially a man. Now I come to think of it, this might be the very first time.

'Thanks, Jim,' I reply, dragging my eyes up to meet his.
He shrugs with a soft smile.
'What're friends for?'

*

After Jim has shown me how to work the bike, it's time to say goodbye. I can't escape the feeling that this parting of ways seems final, that there'll be no coming back from the journey I'm about to take. By Jim's demeanour and the lost look in his eyes, it's clear he feels this way too.

'You'll be all right?' he asks.

We both know I have no way of knowing how all of this will turn out, but I reply with the answer he wants to hear.

'I'll be okay.'

I wonder when we might see each other again. There's a chance I could be dead by the end of the week, if Evelyn Moore gets her way. I wonder who'll tell Jim. Will the cops call the gas station to let him know? Or will he wait to see if someone else lets my studio apartment above the deli, after I don't return to work? Maybe it'll make the news like the trial did, and he'll find out by lining up the day's papers by the counter and seeing my mugshot staring back at him, under a headline proclaiming my death. Or maybe the mention will be so small in the paper that he won't spot it at first, and only see the write-up when he's clearing out the cat litter tray and spots the grainy photo of me staring up from the muck. Jim is probably the closest thing I've got to a next of kin, but there's no time to do anything about that now.

I fit the helmet he gave me over my head, inhaling the smell of my own nervous breaths.

'Hang on,' he says. 'I've got something else for you.'

He heads back towards the open garage and into the house, and I sit on the bike, enjoying the secrecy of the helmet, like a buffer between me and the world. I try not to focus on my hands shaking where they grip the handlebars, or think about the drugs calling out to me from inside my pocket, and flip up the visor when my anxious breaths start to fog the glass.

Jim walks back towards me holding a black fabric bag. When he reaches me, he opens it: a gun, and a box of bullets. He unzips my backpack and tucks it inside.

'I think you're gonna need it,' he says.

The realization hits me then, about what kind of journey I'm about to embark on, and suddenly I feel like a little boy sitting atop a man's bike with a gun in his backpack. None of it feels right or real. I don't feel like myself; it's as if I'm in a limbo state between who I used to be and who I'm set to become.

I hate guns, but I'm a good shot; my brother made me practise on the track at the trailer park, shooting the cans he'd lined up in a row; I preferred it when he taught me, rather than my stepdad, who'd smack the back of my head every time I missed. I became really good at dodging those hits. But just because I'm a good shot doesn't mean I like guns.

I look out at the road, trying to prepare for the journey I'm about to take.

'Can you not watch me go?' I ask, without looking at Jim. 'It'll be easier if I don't have someone waving me off.'

'You take your time,' he says, and pats me on the back. 'Godspeed, dear boy.'

I wait until he's back inside the house and the lump has left my throat before turning the ignition and heading down the road.

18

Tobias

I wake to a hot, stuffy room and the sound of a dog barking. I've never liked leaving windows open when sleeping on the ground floor – you never know who might see it as a way in – but I should've left one open last night. The air's hot enough to boil the fur off a cat's back, and I'm sopping with sweat from head to toe. The dog is still barking. I turn to the curtained window with a vexed frown. I slept like shit, only catching about three hours of shut-eye, and my temper is particularly short.

I peel away the sheets and head to the bathroom to take a leak. Only a trickle comes out, and the spit in my mouth has all dried up. I try to remember the last time I had a drink of water, and lean down to gulp from the tap at the sink. That's another thing I miss about home; the water tastes like shit here, so much so that most people don't drink it. I probably shouldn't either, but beggars can't be choosers.

The dog is still barking, and barking, and barking.

Someone needs to shut that dog up.

But when it does fall quiet for a moment I almost will it to start up again, to distract me from the loneliness that sets in the moment the silence descends. I feel just as lost as I did yesterday, stranded out in the middle of the Death Valley desert. At least then I had a destination to reach. All I have now is a bag filled with more cash and drugs than I know what to do with, a stolen truck, a stranger's boots, and no knowing where the hell I'm meant to go next.

If you try and stop me, I'll kill you.

It was like talking to a stranger, rather than my own wife. But there was a brief moment when the old her had crept through. She'd wanted me to know she hadn't meant to kill that boy. I heard the guilt in her voice, the quiet tremble of fear following the words. In the same way I creep down the stairs in the mornings to catch a glimpse of her before she notices me, I witnessed another vulnerable piece of her on the phone. The part of herself that she only reveals when she's alone and she can drop her guard. She may have a man's blood on her hands now, but she's still in there somewhere, deep down. Something in my heart tells me the woman I love can still be saved.

Or maybe that's just what I desperately want to be true.

Trying to track her down is going to be harder now than it was yesterday. Now Aaron knows she's on his tail, he'll have bolted and left Beatty if he knows what's good for him, and Evelyn will no doubt know where he's headed.

I sit down on the lid of the toilet and bury my face in my hands. I think back to the files I flipped through when I went to collect the bags from the trunk back at the motel in Death Valley. Aaron's brother lives in Reno, over three hundred miles and a five-hour drive from here. Is that where he would head? I've still got the drugs and cash with me, like a ball and chain I can't outrun. As long as I have that bag, I'll have someone after me, and I'll be forever looking over my shoulder in the same way Evelyn and Aaron will be looking over theirs.

The dog begins its barking again, even louder than before, and my thoughts stop dead. I'm so stressed that every joint in my body aches: my shoulders, my elbows, my wrists and my hips. It fascinates me what stress can do to the body, how quickly it can make us fall apart.

I head back into the bedroom, following the sound of the excited dog to the window, and throw open the curtains.

What I see makes me dart out of view and flatten myself against the wall beside the pane.

The man whose truck I stole is standing directly on the other side of the glass.

He's looking at the truck parked outside my room with his back to the window, but he's wearing the same Dodgers cap as yesterday, the same checked shirt and camo pants. It's the same dog too. The man and his mutt are standing with another man, both looking into the truck and speaking gruffly, the anger evident in their voices.

'Go to the office and find out which room he's in, and if they don't tell you, you beat it out of 'em,' he says. 'We'll get the bag back and then sling this fucker up. I swear to God, when we find him I'm gonna let Lexy tear his goddamn balls off.'

Lexy whines, as if excited at the thought of castrating a man. A trail of sweat snakes down my temple.

As his friend heads towards the office, the man I stole from peers through the window into my room, cupping his hands around his eyes and leaving fog on the glass from his breath before turning away. I look at the closet where I slung the bag of drugs before I crashed last night. Thankfully, I thought to shut the door.

I've got to get the hell out of here.

I crouch down and snatch up my clothes and boots from the floor, then my phone and Kyle's gun from the side of the bed, and hurry at a low crouch towards the bathroom. I get dressed as fast as I can, assessing the situation and what the hell I'm going to do next. I check the wad of cash is still in my pocket from the day before: I've got about a grand on me, which should be more than enough to last. I assess the bathroom window. It's small, maybe too small, but it's the only way out I have. It's either that or walk out the front door and straight into them.

I shut the toilet lid and stand on it to reach the sill, pushing the window open and looking out from side to side. The coast is clear.

I holster the gun in the back of my jeans and clamber up, my face dripping with sweat, salty trails running into my eyes and soaking into my T-shirt. I have one leg out of the window when I hear a bang on the door. Not from a fist, but a foot. The kind of bang that has someone's entire weight behind it.

They're going to kick their way in here.

I slide through the narrow window, edging further and further out until I fall and hit the ground in a cloud of dirt, at the exact same moment I hear the door fly off its hinges, crashing inside with a succession of bangs and cracks, the frame on the wall smashing to the floor where it's knocked from its nails.

I reach up and quietly close the window as the men trash the room in search of the bag, before scrambling along the back of the motel: one straight line with nowhere to hide. I'm halfway down the side of the building when I hear a man's voice behind me.

'There he is!'

I skid to a stop, dry earth rising like smoke at my feet. The man has his head out the window, calling over his shoulder.

'Get 'em girl!'

I just about get a glimpse of Lexy jumping down from the window as I turn and sprint.

The end of the motel building is about fifty feet ahead. I run towards it with all my might, until my eyes jar in their sockets and my feet pound against the ground so violently that my legs threaten to buckle at the knees. But however fast I run, Lexy is faster. I can hear the quick, light pad of her paws and her hot, excited breaths. I'm just about to reach the corner of the building when I feel her teeth sink into me.

I scream in pain and hit the ground, dust clouding around

us as Lexy begins tugging at my forearm, saliva foaming at her mouth. I can feel my flesh ripping, my nerves zinging as her teeth sink deeper, and I punch wildly. My fist connects with her ribs, her snout, the top of her skull. I hear a whine, and as soon as I feel her teeth give, I reach around for the gun in the back of my jeans and aim between her eyes, before bottling it and firing a shot above my head. The sound cracks like thunder through the air; the bullet hits the edge of the motel roof, showering debris down onto us both. Lexy is crouched in fear, her hackles high and my blood dripping from the fur around her mouth. I fire again and watch as she scarpers back the way she came with her ears flat to her head and her tail between her legs.

I try to assess my wounds but all I can see is blood. I follow the flow and spot distinct puncture marks where she sank her fangs into me and tugged. I watch the blood pour out of me in shock, my hand shaking wildly as warm trails slink silently down my arm and patter on the dirt below.

The men will be here any second. They'll be too bulky to fit through the window like I did; they'll have to run round the motel building to get to me. I let my bloody arm hang – I need my gun out and ready – and stagger to my feet, trying to ignore the throbbing pain. I head for the corner of the motel, blinking furiously to see through the sweat trickling into my eyes, and flatten myself against the wall. I draw in a deep breath and peer round the corner.

One of the men is heading straight towards me, holding a crowbar in both hands, ready to swing. I lean against the wall again and try to focus, listening to his approaching steps and the racing thud of my heart.

I jump into view just as he appears and point the gun at his forehead.

We stare at each other, standing so close that I can see the crust in the corners of his eyes and smell the excitement on his breath. We can both smell my blood. I watch his nostrils flare as the metallic tang hits him. I don't need to look to know it's slowly pooling at my feet.

'Drop it,' I say.

I watch him swallow nervously. He flinches as the hot barrel of the gun kisses his forehead, and I press it into him harder. The crowbar clangs to the ground.

'On your knees.'

He stares at me, trying to work out if I have the balls. The same balls they'd planned to let the dog rip clean off me.

'Don't think I won't shoot you, because I will,' I lie. 'Get on your fucking knees.'

With his brow creased with anger, he slowly concedes and kneels at my feet. Some of my blood drips onto his trouser leg from where it is streaming steadily off my arm.

'If I see you again, you won't get a second chance. I'll put a bullet between your eyes. Got that?'

He nods slowly, his eyes widening as I flip the gun around, holding the barrel to expose the handle, and smack it violently against his temple. I watch as his eyes roll back into his head and his body slumps to the ground.

Wedging the gun between my thighs, I reach down to wrestle the navy shirt from the man's back, struggling one-handed against his muscly weight before finally tugging it free. It smells of sour sweat and cigarette smoke, but I'm in no position to be turning my nose up. I tear it into long pieces and wrap a strip tightly around my arm to stop the bleeding, gritting my teeth through the pain and looking about me as I go, anticipating another burly man racing round the corner at any minute. I finish wrapping the fabric round and round and tuck it in on itself, before shoving the rest in my waistband to fashion a sling out of later if I need it.

My teeth are chattering from the adrenaline and I'm starting to feel cold, even with the sun belting down and the sweat dripping off me. I run in the direction the man came from, pressing myself to the wall to check for signs of his companion and their blood-hungry dog, before stumbling through the maze of the parking lot.

I need to steal a car and hit the road. But first, I need to know which way to go. If I'm going to find out where Chris Alexander lives in Reno, I'm going to need to find Aaron's mother.

19

Evelyn

I sit in my car beside the gas station and watch the normal people come and go, wondering where they're headed. What they'd be capable of, if they had a gun and a vendetta like mine.

I slept lightly – so lightly that I might as well not have slept at all; the only way to know I did is by the dreams I had and the pain in my jaw after a night of grinding. My cheek looked swollen this morning when I peered into the bathroom mirror first thing. Not enough for a stranger to notice, but enough for me to clock the puffiness on one side, the odd asymmetry. My bad tooth is throbbing more than the day before. The aches come in waves, pulsing with my heart. I pop a painkiller. Then another. Only Advil; I can't afford to be drowsy. I need to be focused on my target and get through the day ahead. If I play my cards right, all of this will be over before it gets dark.

I woke this morning hardened again. My dreams of Joshua last night have set me on the right path. The guilt I feel for killing a man is nothing compared to the guilt I have for not protecting my son when he needed me most. For not being there to save him, or to come when he called for me in the dark. For letting him be in harm's way in the first place. Each time I think of Kyle, I force myself to remember what's at stake. Who the real victim is in all of this.

I didn't hang around the motel for long; I can't afford to be remembered. I stuffed the blood-sodden jeans in my bag and vacated the room at 7 a.m. sharp, left the key in the drop box and hit the road, only now stopping for gas. I should eat, but I feel more focused when I'm empty.

I pick up Kyle's phone and read Aaron's last text.

Aaron

I crashed at Jim's last night and he let me borrow a bike. It's not so fast, but it works. I'll call you when I get to Reno. Are you okay?

I'd messaged him before hitting the road asking for an update, using Kyle's usual tone. I wonder which of us will get to Reno first.

I check the map on the passenger seat. He'll have taken Route 95, which he'll be on all the way to Silver Springs before joining the 439. We're on the same strip of highway with not many miles between us. If I keep my foot down, I should be able to catch up with him in an hour or two. I heard on the radio that there were more wildfires at Gold Point; hopefully we'll get past them in time, before they spread too far and we're both diverted, possibly sending us in two different directions. He's bound to know these roads better than me, having lived in the desert for so long.

I put down the map and pick up my binder for the details on Chris Alexander. The private investigator was expensive, but it pays to stay one step ahead. Chris is four years older than Aaron. He joined the army at twenty-two and seemingly only came home to visit and marry his high school sweetheart between postings; he got out five years ago and became a mechanic up in Reno. He wasn't there when Aaron got behind the wheel of a car high out of his mind and killed Joshua. He wasn't there for the sentencing. He doesn't get to be here for this and play the hero.

I dial the phone number from the open binder and listen to the call ring through. I need to try to get to Aaron without crossing paths with his brother. It's one thing to hunt and kill a waif, but it's quite another to overpower a soldier. A good person to run to when you have someone on your tail.

'Harry's Motors,' a man says.

'Hi, I was wondering how long you're open today.'

'Till seven, ma'am.'

'Can I book my car in with Chris?'

'He's booked up till close today. You want me to check for another day?'

'No, no. That's fine, thank you.'

I hang up, close the binder, and check the time. I have at least three more hours until I reach Reno, then a couple more to get this done and get the hell out of there before Chris leaves work. As long as I'm in and out, it'll be over before he's even started thinking about his dinner. I fire up the engine and pull out onto Route 95 in determined silence, thinking of Aaron, of Joshua, of Tobias.

Come home with me. It's not too late.

The more I think about Tobias's betrayal, the more I hate the man I once loved. I remember the look on his face as he sat on the other side of the table in the diner. Pitying me and my grief like one might pity a dog with a limp. He'd got to me last night; caught me in a moment of weakness and made me slip. But that won't happen again.

I've been stewing in thoughts of my husband for fifteen minutes when I hear the sirens.

The cop car signals, instructing me to pull over. A rush of panic scores through me. There could be so many asinine reasons for pulling me over: I was driving a little over the speed limit, or maybe one of my brake lights is out. It doesn't have to be connected to what I've done. But something tells me I won't be so lucky.

I pull the car to a stop on the side of the highway and reach for my gun and my taser, rummaging around in the holdall on the passenger seat. I slip them into the door compartment with the gun barrel-down, ready to grab if I need it.

The officer steps out of his vehicle and heads towards me, eyeing the car through his dark shades. I keep my hands at the ten-two position until he motions for me to lower the window from the other side of the glass.

'Good morning, ma'am.'

'Is everything all right? I wasn't speeding, was I?'

'No, ma'am. We've got a call out for green sedans. Just need to run a few checks.'

I'd parked the green sedan on the street outside Kyle's place before going in and firing a bullet into his gut. Maybe one of the neighbours called it in; the cops will have found his body by now, left to bleed out on the bed with my bullet inside him. I thought I'd had time to put distance between us, and the deed would be done before my actions caught up with me. That's the thing with luck, you never know which way it's going to turn. I wonder how my luck will fare now.

'Oh? Why's that?' I ask.

'Relating to an investigation, ma'am, but that's all I'm at liberty to say. If you could show me your licence and registration, I'll do the checks and then you can be on your way.'

Or you'll try and take me away in cuffs.

I pause, my pulse hammering in my grip on the wheel.

'I'm in a bit of a rush. Is this going to take long?'

He peers over his shades at me, his expression neutral but his eyes stern.

'It'll take as long as it takes, ma'am. Licence and registration.'

I try to think of ways to buy time but come up short. Do they only have the visual description of the car, or do they have the registration plate too? If they do, it's all over, and all of this will have been for nothing. It will mean Aaron walks free.

I think of my gun in the door compartment, then glance at the officer's weapon fastened in his holster. I reckon I could grab mine and fire faster than he could.

'Is there a problem?' he asks, staring at me as I sit deep in thought behind the wheel.

Yes.

'No,' I reply with a forced smile. 'No problem. May I reach into my glove compartment?'

'Yes, ma'am, just keep your hands slow and where I can see 'em.'

I take my time, slowly moving through the paperwork in the glove compartment, listening to the police officer's quiet sighs of impatience and the pounding of my heart. There's no way he'll leave without seeing the documents. I'll have to do what he says and deal with what comes next.

I slip my licence from my purse and hand it over with the forms.

'Thanks, ma'am. I won't be a moment.'

He walks back towards his car, stopping at the rear of my vehicle to check the plate as I tap the wheel and watch him in the rear-view mirror. He frowns as he corroborates the details he has on his system with the information I've given him. Is it mere concentration? Or has he found something? I slowly reach down into the door compartment and take hold of the gun, switching off the safety with a fast flick.

He heads back towards me with the same slow stride, my licence and registration in hand.

It's only when he reaches the window again that I see he's unfastened the clip keeping his gun strapped in its holster.

I keep my hand on mine, my finger resting an inch from the trigger.

'Thank you, ma'am.'

I take the licence and registration from him with my free hand. 'So, I can go?'

'Just a question or two,' he says. 'Keep your hands on the wheel please, ma'am.' He checks his notes. I keep my hand on the gun. 'Where were you coming from? And where are you headed now?'

'Why?'

'Because I asked you.' He looks at the wheel. 'Ma'am, I said keep your hands where I can see 'em.'

'I don't understand why you need to know where I've been—'

'Ma'am, I am not going to tell you again.' He places his hand on his gun. 'Put both hands on the wheel. Now.'

We stare at each other. I'm sweating from the tension and the heat, while the cop watches me intently from behind his shades. He's just about to speak again when his radio crackles to life.

'Wait right there.'

He steps back and responds into the radio, as I switch my grip from the gun to the taser, easier to conceal if I need it. I slowly tease it up my sleeve before putting my hands on the wheel.

He steps back towards the window.

'Step out of the car please, ma'am.'

There's only one reason why he'd want me to do that: to thrust me over the bonnet and cuff me. Whatever his checks told him, he's got enough of a reason to bring me in. Did he just radio for back-up, in case I don't comply? My pulse is hammering and I can feel sweat prickling all over me. We stare into each other's eyes, the silence dragging out.

'Why?' I ask.

'Because I told you to. Now I won't tell you again: step out of the car.'

I look into the rear-view mirror, eyeing the cruiser behind us. I'd bet money it has a dashcam recording this entire thing.

I unbuckle my belt and slowly reach for the door with a held breath. I'm watching him peripherally the entire time, and I've just stepped out of the car when I see him reaching for his cuffs. That's when I let the taser drop down from my sleeve and into my palm, flick the switch, and ram it into his neck.

The officer jolts, standing ramrod straight as the electricity bursts through him. He convulses so hard that his shades judder down the bridge of his nose and I can see his eyes bulging and the veins and ligaments on his neck swelling to the surface. I flick the switch off and watch him fall to the road. There's a dark patch on his pants where he's pissed himself, and spittle foams at his mouth. He blindly pats for his gun, drunk from the shock, so I reach down and tase him again, straight in the chest this time. I hold it there until a strange sound crawls up his throat and the foam at his lips turns red where he bites down on his tongue. When I finally stop, he slumps against the tarmac, out for the count.

It's quiet now, but for the hot, whistling breeze. I stand there, panting for breath and shaking from the adrenaline, then wipe the sweat from my brow as I turn back to the car and slip my gun back into my waistband, my bad tooth throbbing. That was a close call. Too close.

I look along the highway in each direction to determine we're alone before snatching the radio from the cop's waist and stamping on it until it's nothing but shards of black plastic and wires. Then I reach down to grab him by the ankles and drag him towards his cruiser, watching as his head juts against the rough road. I'll hide him in his own trunk. By the time he comes to, I'll be gone.

I can't let that happen again, I tell myself as I reach the rear of the vehicle. Because as I scramble for his keys and struggle with the weight of him, folding him inside before slamming the trunk shut, I think of how wrong this could have gone. If he'd had the chance to overpower me, I would have gone to jail while Aaron Alexander continued to walk free.

I reach into the cruiser and inspect the dash. The camera is built into it, with nothing to rip out and destroy. I reach back for my gun, click off the safety and pull back the slide, and then fire a round of bullets into the electronics.

As soon as I'm back behind the wheel, I light a cigarette and exhale slowly, grateful for the choice I made. Because had I not switched the gun for the taser before getting out of the car, I know I would have shot that officer to keep him from getting in my way.

*

I had many dreams of Joshua last night, but one has lingered long after waking: I dreamt of him as a teenager, of the young man he was set to grow into before that chance was taken away. I imagined him with a voice that was a few octaves lower, a protruding Adam's apple that danced up and down his throat as he laughed, and a fluffy line of hair above his lip that he called a moustache, proud to be growing into a man.

My dreams have been so vivid ever since he died, and seeing him for what he was bound to have become made me sob upon waking; it felt like my chest had been cracked in two and I was spilling out of myself. I snatched up a pillow and howled into it until my tears and drool soaked into the fabric, holding it as if it were him and rocking back and forth. But once I pulled myself together, I felt my strength returning to what it had been. The dreams of him are a reminder of what I've set out to do, of everything we've lost because of one man.

According to the map, it's only two miles on foot to the nearest town, and another half a mile to the car rental place I need to reach before hitting the road again for Reno. But first I need to get rid of the sedan. The officer will wake up soon, and it won't take long for back-up to arrive to find out why he isn't answering his radio. If I keep driving our car, I'll be stopped again, and I doubt I'll luck out a second time.

I stop at the next gas station and fill up the canister from the trunk. The station is in the middle of nowhere; it's just me and the mountainous terrain along Route 95. I pay for the gas and get back in the car, driving down the highway for a mile or two. I check there are no other vehicles in sight before turning off the road and driving cross-country over the dirt, cutting through the desert in a cloud of dust with the steering wheel shuddering beneath my hands.

When Route 95 is a whisper in the distance, I pull to a stop and step out with the canister. The heat hits me like a gang of fists and sweat breaks above my brow. I remove my belongings and place them at a safe distance, then unscrew the lid of the canister and chuck the cap inside the car before beginning the job at hand. I splash the petrol over the bonnet, the roof and the wheels, before clambering inside and soaking the seats and the dash, then the floormats; healthy sloshes on every pane of glass and every one of Tobias's belongings that I'd taken from him at the motel.

I stumble out, dizzy from the fumes, and place the canister inside the trunk to let its contents leak out, before shutting it and taking a few steps back to survey my work. I light a cigarette and inhale it hungrily, squinting into the sun.

I drag on the cigarette until it's almost burnt away, before flinging it onto the driver's seat.

The flames appear in a violent, hot *whoosh*. I watch them crawl and grow, enveloping the seats, the dash, then curling out from the open door around the lip of the roof, as hot black smoke trails up towards the sky.

I slip my arms through the handles of the holdall to wear it as a backpack and set off in a fast jog, the weapons and blades inside knocking into my spine with each stride. I'm a good five hundred feet from the car when it explodes, the ground rumbling beneath my feet from the blow. I don't turn back; I head on with my eyes fixed on the journey ahead and my mind on the man I'm set to kill, my teeth still grinding quietly in my mouth.

20

Aaron

The midday sun is beating down mercilessly as I pull to a stop at the gas station to take a leak. I wriggle out of the helmet, my hair slick from the heat and the fear of riding myself off the road. It wasn't just like riding a bike, like Jim said. I've been revving the engine too hard or too soft; my instinct was to grip onto the handlebars for dear life, but it would only send me speeding forwards, terrified that I might fly off at any moment. But somehow, I'm still here, and about halfway to Reno.

The last time I spoke to my brother, he told me he never wanted to see or speak to me again. I'd called him from jail the night after the accident, crying as I told him what I'd done and shaking from withdrawals after spending so long in a cell without my next fix. I can still remember begging him to help me, like a little boy crying out for his mom. He had tried to help a few times over the years, buying me lunch when he could afford it, giving me a place to stay when I was at a dead end, but it always felt like I was a part of his past he couldn't shake. I didn't exactly help myself either; I'd always end up betraying his trust by stealing from him to get my next hit. I couldn't tell you how many times I emptied his wallet when his back was turned. When he hung up on me that day, he was true to his word: he never spoke to me again.

Chris seemed to ride out our upbringing as if he were born for it. He didn't just take the beatings, he beat back. He didn't just live in a trailer park, he thrived in it. He walked around Beatty as if it was the very place he wanted to be. He was that guy: six-two, naturally broad, captain of the football team. His high school sweetheart, Nikki, was head cheerleader. The stars seemed to align for him, except for having a queer brother.

That didn't stop him looking out for me; I'd say I was raised by my brother more than my mother. While she was comatose from pills, Chris would fix me my meals, make sure I was ready for school and clean up Mom's puke when she'd accidentally OD'd, all while telling me everything would be all right, even if he didn't believe the words himself.

He tried to make me tougher, teaching me to shoot our step-dad's gun and trying to get me to box with him to get ready to throw a punch when I needed to. But he also didn't punish me for being soft. He accepted it was my nature and kicked the shit out of anyone who tried to hurt me for it. But the older we got, the harder our home life became. Chris and Mom's boyfriend, Tony, would get into full-blown fights by the time he turned sixteen, and eventually he was thrown out to fend for himself, and I had to fend for myself too. It was my turn to take Tony's beatings, to clean up Mom's vomit when she took one pill too many, to tell myself everything would be all right. By the time I was turfed out four years later, Chris had moved on, made a life for himself, and I learned that the brother I'd adored, the brother who had been my whole life, had only seen me as a small part of his.

I climb off the bike and cross the dusty forecourt, heading round the back of the gas station for the bathroom, my bladder clenched like a fist.

I turn the corner and sigh at the sight of the little wooden out-house with 'Toilet' sprayed on the door in white aerosol paint.

Even from here, I can see the flies hovering around it, the sound of their languid buzzing slowly creeping across the plain.

I wander into the desert instead and piss onto the parched earth. An ant slowly crawls up from a crack in the ground and begins to drink it, followed by another, then another, until the pool is too big and they start to drown.

I zip my fly and head back, wondering if I have enough money to spare for a bottle of water or a can of Coke, before deciding to go without. I don't know how long I'm going to be running for; I need to make every cent last, even if it feels like my tongue is made of sandpaper, scraping the roof of my mouth.

The thought of a chilled can of soda makes me think of Kyle, and I pull out my phone again to check if he's messaged.

Kyle

How things going? Where are you now?

I would have been a couple of hours out of Beatty when he sent it. I stop by the bike and peer at the screen; the battery has lost half its juice already. But still, I call him. I want to hear a familiar voice, to keep me going on this crazy journey that I'm still not convinced was the right call to make.

I pace back and forth, kicking rocks across the dusty ground, listening to his phone ring. Maybe he's sleeping after his shift, or he took on some extra hours. He's always said time stops in the slaughterhouse: the abattoir is dark, allowing no sense of time. He once told me you can't even count how many kills you've made in a day; there are just too many, and the blood and pelts and whines soon become one and the same. I'm just about to hang up when I hear him pick up on the other end of the line.

'Hey,' I say. 'I've not got much phone battery; I've just stopped off at a gas station off Route 95. Are you okay?'

He doesn't say anything. Just pants for air down the other end of the line.

'I'm sorry I ran off. It was for a good reason, and I promise I'll explain everything soon.'

Still, he doesn't speak. Just the same hungry breaths crackling down the line. He's going to hold a grudge until I explain.

'You know that thing that happened, that got me sent down? Well, the mother of the boy is looking for me. She broke into my apartment, and she's been asking for me all over town, so it's better I lay low for a while. Do you understand?'

I wonder if he's cut out and check the screen: the call is still connected.

'Are you still there?'

I screw my eyes up against the glaring sun, pacing and listening for him on the other end of the line.

'Yes, Aaron, I'm here.'

I stop in my tracks.

'Who is this?'

'You know who it is.'

I listen to her breaths while holding my own, my lungs squirming for air behind my ribs.

I'm talking to Evelyn Moore.

'See you soon,' she says, before the line goes dead, the one-note tone cutting through me.

I go to put my phone away and drop it from shaking so hard. My head is light as I bend to snatch it up again.

How the hell did she get hold of Kyle's phone?

I frantically wrestle the keys out of my pocket, my whole body trembling as I clamber onto the bike, so hard that I can barely get the key into the ignition.

I fix my helmet over my head and try to turn over the engine, but I'm met with nothing but a pathetic grumble. I turn the key again. And again.

The bike is dead.

'*Fuck!*'

I stumble off it, kick it hard until it falls on its side with a crash. I stagger across the dusty forecourt with my hands on my head and no clue what to do next, crying silently in the safety of the helmet with my frantic exhales fogging the visor. I rip it off, letting it roll across the desert floor as I check my phone: I've only got thirty per cent battery left now.

I pull out the note the new tenant had sent me along with all of my letters, and dial the number for my brother's house. I listen to the phone ring, and ring, and ring, but no answer comes.

I'm stuck in the desert with no way out, and Evelyn Moore not far behind.

21

Tobias

I stand across the street from the bar where I'm told Annie Alexander will be, huddled in a doorway to catch some shade as I watch the shadow of a person moving around inside. The shelter I'm coveting is meaningless; I'm dripping with sweat and my feet have swollen in my boots; I figure I'll have to cut my way out of them when the time comes to take them off.

I'd walked three miles to the trailer park Jim had mentioned the day before, only to find Aaron's mother wasn't home. I stood outside, willing the door to open, when I heard a voice call to me: a neighbour sat on a deckchair outside a trailer on the other side of the dirt path hollering to tell me Annie wasn't in. I was careful not to approach her, so as not to reveal the blood on me and scare her out of talking, and yelled back to ask where I could find her. The neighbour told me Annie would be cleaning the tavern on Main Street; that she cleans the bar twice a week, then an office building, before hitting the school to clean it after hours.

That's the problem with small towns: people know too much about each other. I couldn't tell you the first names of half the neighbours in our cul-de-sac back in San Diego; as for our time in London, I couldn't even give you one. But here in Beatty, they seem to know everything about one another.

Before I left, the woman offered me some lemonade from the pitcher beside her, her skin shimmering from suntan oil, the kind that comes in a brown glass bottle and stinks of something on the turn. She spotted the blood on me on my approach and tensed up.

'What do you want with Annie anyhow?'

I left without drinking the lemonade and have thought about it every step I've taken since.

The tavern looks hard and unwelcoming, with a wooden frontage in need of a good paint job and dark windows with dirt on the panes. I continue to watch the figure moving around inside and will it to be her. She's my only hope of finding the address in Reno and reaching Aaron in time.

A woman passes by, faltering in her stride when she catches sight of me, her eyes widening before she walks faster up the street. I look down at myself: blood is dripping from the make-shift bandage and turning the sidewalk red. I wonder how long it takes for infection to set in; how long I have before I need to stop my chase and find a doctor.

I stagger out from the doorway and into the street, squinting against the belting sun. I try to ignore the gun wedged into my waistband, gnawing into the base of my spine with each step. Though at least it's a distraction from the throbbing of my arm.

The sign on the door reads 'Closed'. I push it open anyway and step inside.

The tavern is dark and dingy. The air smells of cigarette smoke despite the ban, and of stale sweat and beer. I can't say much for Annie's cleaning; my boots stick to the floor with each step. I stand at the empty bar and wait.

The swing door in the far wall edges open and a woman appears, pushing the door with her back as she drags out a bucket and mop, another bucket filled with cleaning supplies in her other hand. She stops when she sees me, the door swinging back and forth behind her until it finally comes to a stop. This is Aaron's mother. They have the same eyes.

'We're closed,' she snaps. 'Says so on the sign.'

'I'm not here to drink,' I say, and take a step closer.

Annie takes a step back.

'Well, whatever it is you want, you'll have to wait until we're open.'

It's only then that I remember how I look: sweaty, bloody, practically slurring from thirst. I look down and see the drops of blood at my feet.

'I'm here to see you,' I say to her, and take another step. 'My name is Tobias Moore.'

I watch my name register in her eyes. Her face drains completely white.

'Bill?' she shouts to the floor above, while edging back towards the door. '*Bill!*'

'I'm not here to cause trouble, all right? I need your help.'

Annie is halfway through the swinging door.

'Why the hell would I help you or your crazy wife?'

So, Evelyn has been to see her. Judging by the fear in her eyes, my wife didn't make a great first impression.

'I'm trying to stop my wife, not help her. If you know about her, I'm sure you know what she's planning to do. I need to keep that from happening.'

Annie looks at me long and hard, gnawing at her bottom lip as she thinks. I can almost see the tug of war going on in her mind. Above us, I hear someone moving around on creaking floorboards, then coming down a set of stairs on the other side of the wall, getting louder and louder the longer our silence drags on.

'Please,' I say.

Another door opens beside the bar, revealing a large man in a dirty wife beater with old, faded tattoos inked up his arms. By the look of him, he's just woken up – and by the smell of him, he's hungover as hell.

'What the hell are you hollering about? There better be a fire. I told you not to wake me up unless there was a goddamn fire.'

Annie is staring at me, still trying to figure me out. I look back at her and silently beg her to believe me. The man notices me and steps forward.

'Who the hell are—'

'I need more bleach,' Annie says quickly.

The man stops in his tracks.

'What?'

'Bleach. I need more.'

'You woke me up for *bleach*?'

'I can't clean the place without it.'

'You gotta be kidding me.' He heads round the bar, muttering gruffly to himself, cursing Annie and the bleach. He opens the cash register and chucks a five-dollar bill on the counter. 'If you wake me up again, and there ain't a fire ripping this place apart, I'm gonna lose my shit.'

'Got it,' Annie replies, her eyes never leaving mine.

The man trundles back towards the swinging door. I listen to the heavy thuds of his steps on the stairs.

The tavern falls silent.

'What happened to your arm?' she asks.

'A dog bit me.'

'You'll need shots.'

'I know.'

'It could get infected.'

'I know.'

She looks me up and down, her face softening at the state I'm in, before she meets my eye again.

'You want to stop your wife from hurting my son?' she asks.

'Yes. Evelyn is headed to see Chris in Reno. She thinks Aaron is on his way there.'

'He won't be, he and Chris don't talk.'

'It sounds like Aaron hasn't got many other options.'

Her face softens again, a flash of guilt in her eyes. She looks down at my arm, at the blood dripping on the floor, and snatches the five-dollar bill from the surface of the bar.

'You got money?'

'A little. Why?'

She puts out her hand for the cash. 'You'll need proper bandages for that bite.'

I rifle in my pocket and hand her a twenty-dollar bill. 'Sit in the booth in the corner over there,' she says. 'Bill won't wake up again, but if anyone asks, tell them you're with me.'

She heads out the door and into the street before I can reply.

*

I grit my teeth as Annie bathes my arm in a bowl of warm water, the sterilizer she'd poured in stinging the wounds. The kitchen behind the swing door where she'd first appeared is a maze of stainless-steel counters and cupboard doors.

I'm dressed in a fresh T-shirt and jeans that she swiped from Bill's laundry, which he makes her do for an extra two dollars an hour. They're far too big: the tee drowns me, and the jeans won't stop slipping at my waist, but they're better than nothing. I'm still stuck with the same old boots.

I look at the items she bought: generic painkillers, a bottle of sterilizer, a pack of bandages and strip stitches, a tube of ointment.

'It's to prevent infection,' she says, when she catches me looking. 'Why'd the dog bite you?'

'I was running away.'

'From what?'

'From the dog that was trying to bite me.'

She gives me a look. Despite the pain and exhaustion, I smirk.

'From a man I stole a truck from. My wife left me stranded in Death Valley to stop me from following her. It was the only way I could get to Beatty.'

She dries my wounds off with a towel, delicately blotting at them before running down my hand and drying each finger. I haven't been touched tenderly by another person like this in so long that I feel a tug of desire, followed quickly by loneliness.

'Don't they have cabs where you come from?' she asks.

'I didn't have any money then. My wife took it all.'

A flicker of fear crosses her eyes, and she looks down at the strip of adhesive stitches, rotating them round and round between her fingers as she thinks.

'She really isn't going to stop until she gets him, is she?'

She gazes at me again. The fear is still there, shimmering.

'Not unless I get to him first.'

'And do what?'

Good question, I think to myself. Annie is still staring at me.

'I don't really know.'

I watch as she blots the sterilizer onto a piece of gauze and dabs at my arm. It stings, but it's bearable.

'I'm leaving it to dry for a minute,' she says, my hand resting in hers. We both notice it shaking. 'Then I'll apply the stitches.'

'Okay.'

We fall silent for a while, but the whole time I can see her thinking, fear glinting in her eyes.

'What I don't get is why you'd want to protect Aaron after what he did. I can't decide who's crazier, you or your wife.'

There aren't many people who would understand Evelyn and me. Hell, we don't even understand each other, or ourselves. I let out a heavy sigh.

'I've already lost my son. I can't lose my wife too.'

Annie looks away, removing my hand from hers to open the packet of stitches. I catch myself wondering if she's thinking of all she has lost too.

'How'd you learn to do this?' I ask, as she peels the strips and begins pressing the wounds together.

'A lotta practice.'

I wonder about the abuse she must have suffered. I can see scars on her face now I'm up close: a white, faded line above her eyebrow from a blow, the slight disfigurement of her nose from past breaks. Her hands are rough and worn from her work. Once the stitches are in place, she dabs them lightly with the sterilizer again.

'Now it's time for me to tell you what I don't get,' I say. 'If you know what Evelyn plans to do, why haven't you called the police?'

It's Annie's turn to fall quiet. I watch her wrestling with her thoughts as she tears open the packaging of the bandages and begins to unwind the white gauze.

'My boyfriend would go to jail if I did. And if he didn't, he'd sure as hell make me pay for putting us on the sheriff's radar.'

'You're protecting him over your own son?'

She gives me a look. The same look I get from Evelyn when I question her motives. It's that territorial, instinctive stare of a mother protecting her young. She begins wrapping the wound, tighter and tighter in her anger. By the time the bandage is half-way up my forearm, my fingers feel swollen and tight from the pressure.

'I'm not saying I don't have regrets,' she says. Her face softens then, and her pace with the bandage slows until she comes to a stop, lost in thought.

'Aaron is . . .' She glances towards the ceiling as the tears come, as if to try to stop them from falling. 'He's a sweet boy. No, he's the *sweetest* boy.'

I watch one tear fall, then another, listening to her talk about how the man who killed my child is *sweet*. Her voice cracks when she speaks again.

'The second that boy was born, I knew he was different, and ... I was scared. For him, for me. For both of us. You can't be sweet and a boy, not around here. They'll beat that out of you the first chance they get, and boy, did he get beat. That kid came home with a new cut or bruise every day, only to get more rained on him by his stepfather.'

She wipes the tears away with a violent flick of her fingers, giving me a flash of fingernails that have been bitten to the quick. Fresh trails of tears immediately fall in their place.

'I didn't know what to do with him. I didn't know how to protect him. I was a bad mother – I'm not going to pretend I was anything other than that. When he told me he was queer at sixteen, I kicked him out. I thought he'd make a better life out of this town, away from everyone, even me. But broken people are going to continue breaking things, and that's exactly what he did when he ...'

She stops talking mid-sentence.

'When he killed my son.'

She clears her throat, her cheeks flushed red.

'He wasn't himself,' she says. 'He'd fallen in with the wrong crowd, although I suppose they were the only ones who would take him in. He got hooked on meth, and once you're on that, there's no going back. He was robbing people all over town for his next fix, and he was running around with some man, or so I heard. He put Aaron up to most of it. Plied him with drugs and then made him do his dirty work. He saw the sweetness and naivety in him and manipulated them to his advantage.

'I couldn't sleep for a week when I learned Aaron had come back to Beatty when he got outta jail. I couldn't understand why he'd return to the place that was so evil to him. I kept him at arm's length to keep him safe from his stepdad. You probably won't understand, but I did it because I love him. Even if he thinks I hate him for what he's done. All I've ever wanted for him was to get the hell out of here and become who he needed to be. Having me in his life was only going to slow him down. He was too sweet-natured; he'd have stayed for me, even if it meant sacrificing his own happiness. I couldn't stand idly by and watch him do that, even if it meant he hated me for pushing him away. I'm probably making no sense.'

She sighs and sets about finishing the bandage, unclipping a safety pin and fastening it in place.

'I saw him at the gas station once as I was walking across town towards the school,' she says. 'The first time I'd seen him in over eleven years. And despite all he's been through, I could see that he was still that little boy I always knew. Stood there with an open heart in a world that hurts him over and over again. How can a person go through all that pain, all that violence, and still come out as sweet as he went in? I don't know whether that's a miracle or a curse. Life will keep hurting that boy until he fights for himself. But he just keeps on taking it.'

I watch her silently, trying to figure her out. How can she sit here professing her love for a child she cast out? When I think of all of my regrets – not stopping my wife sooner, not telling my son how much I loved him every second of every day, not hugging him for a second longer each time – they're things I can't fix. She still has a chance to set things right, but she's here instead, cleaning a dingy bar rather than keeping her son safe, or at least letting him know he's loved, even if it's from afar.

I look at Annie and see nothing but regret. Her skin has grown ashen, slack with the weight of her guilt, and I can see that, deep down, she believes her life wasn't meant to turn out this way. I wonder who she wanted to be when she was a child. I wonder what she wanted to do with her life, and how she might have done things differently had she been given a glimpse of the future that was to come.

'I have regrets too, Annie. We all do. But they won't go away until you make things right. You can still see your son – that's something Evelyn and I will never be able to do. Don't waste your chance. Because I promise you, it will be the biggest regret of your life.'

She looks away. I can't say I believe she will change. Some people don't seem capable of it. They keep their heads down, soldiering on along the same old track, and then reach the end of the line and wonder how they got there.

'Maybe with Evelyn after him, Aaron will finally put up that fight,' I tell her.

She doesn't say anything more, but I know my words have got to her. I just hope she plucks up the courage to right the wrongs that so clearly haunt her. I may not be able to help my wife, but maybe I've helped Annie.

'You'll want to hit the road soon,' she says. 'Word is if the fires from Gold Point travel any further east, Beatty'll be evacuated and the road north will be cut off.'

I watch her retrieve her bag and root around inside, pulling free a small notepad and pen. She scribbles something down while sniffing back tears.

'This is where Chris lives,' she says. 'Don't let her hurt them, Tobias. I don't want to have come to my senses too late.'

22

Aaron

A real man would have jumped into action by now. But all I've done is stand by the overturned bike beneath the sizzling sun. A little boy dressed up in a grown man's skin, waiting for someone to come along and tell him what to do. To take him by the hand and lead him to where he needs to go.

I can't stop thinking about Kyle and what might have happened to him. Did Evelyn steal his phone from him while he was none the wiser, as a way to contact me, or did something more sinister happen? Did she hurt him, like she is evidently set on hurting me? I wish there was another way to contact him, just to hear his voice. A shiver runs down my spine when I wonder: was it her messaging me, pretending to be him the whole time?

My phone is dying, and the bike is long dead. The tank is half full, which means the problem is something a mechanic would need to fix. It isn't surprising, when I think about how long it was left in Jim's garage. But to get a mechanic you need money to pay them, a phone to call them and time to waste while the work is done. I have none of those things, time being the thing I have least of. With each moment that passes by, I feel Evelyn getting closer to me, gaining ground.

I've got to get the hell out of here.

I head towards the entrance to the store. There's a man on a bench outside by the door, smoking a cigarette just a few metres from the gas pump, an empty beer bottle at his feet. I'd seen him pull in and hadn't thought to watch out for him leaving. Shades cover his eyes, and a cap shields his face from the sun, but I can feel him looking at me, assessing my size, my power, or lack thereof. Another man might steel up and raise his chin, walk with a confident swagger. I keep my head down.

The bell rings above my head as I step inside. It's no 7-Eleven. More of a dilapidated outhouse with a few aisles of food products and a lone refrigerator at the back, buzzing with an electrical hum.

There's a man behind the counter, his teeth brown from chewing tobacco. He sees me coming but doesn't say a word, just spits brown drool into a cup. I guess you don't need to welcome customers with a smile when they've got no place else to go.

'Hey. My bike's broken down. Have you got a phone I could use?'

'Yeah, we got a phone.'

He stares me down from behind the counter, spitting more brown drool into the cup.

'Great. So, could I—'

'We got a phone, but we ain't got one for you.'

He continues to stare. The store is silent but for the humming refrigerator.

'Please, I really need some help—'

'So did that boy who you left for dead. Yeah, I know who you are.' He spits in the cup again. 'I ain't helpin' no kid-killer. Get the fuck outta here.'

My cheeks blaze red as the shame scorches through me. I turn towards the door with my eyes on the floor. The bell rings above my head on my way out, and then I'm back where I started on the dusty forecourt. I've never felt so useless or alone. You'd think I'd have learned to fend for myself, given my childhood and everything that followed. But every time something goes wrong, I feel at a loss as to what to do or where to go, never trusting my own instincts.

'You need a ride?'

It's the man on the bench.

I can't see much of his face under his hat and shades; can't make out the look in his eyes. My gut screams no, but I can't think of any other option I could take instead. I need to keep the distance between Evelyn and me while I still have time. I weigh up who might be more of a danger: the woman hell-bent on killing me, or the strange man offering me a ride.

'Where you headed?' he asks when I don't reply, getting up from the bench.

He's taller than I thought he'd be. He's wearing a black polo shirt with a logo emblazoned over his heart, one I recognize but can't seem to place. I met a dozen men like him in jail and avoided all of them like the plague. No one makes a gesture like this out of the goodness of their heart; there always has to be something they're after in return. I try to figure out what his price will be as he approaches.

'Reno,' I say.

'I'm passing through Reno.'

He's lying, I'm sure of it. I look at the road cutting through the desert, at the nothingness of the terrain around us and the mountains beyond. I've got no choice.

'Okay.'

'That's my truck over there.'

I notice the gun at his hip. It's not an unusual sight to see on an American man out in the desert, but it unsettles me all the same.

I follow the man to his truck, a flatbed covered in dirt.

'You want the bike in the back?' he asks.

I shake my head. 'It's dead. I'll only have to leave it at the other end.'

I climb into the truck and sit in silence as he gets behind the wheel and pulls out onto the highway, his breath smelling of the beer he drank and the cigarettes he smoked. I look out of the window at the broken-down bike as we drive away, watching in the rear-view mirror as it gets smaller and smaller in the distance.

'What brings you out here?' he asks.

'It's a long story.'

'It's a long drive.'

I don't know what it is, but I don't like him. I don't like the smell of beer and cigarettes on him; I don't like his questions. My gut churns and churns.

'I'm going to see my brother. The bike was a friend's.'

'You sounded like you were in a hurry,' he says. 'I heard you in the store before.'

I know I've seen the emblem on his shirt before, and I wrack my brains to try to place it. It's like a distant warning calling from the back of my mind; one I can't get close enough to hear.

'Just need to get to my brother, is all. What about you?'

'I'm meeting up with my boys. We've got a job to do.'

'What do you do?'

He shakes his head.

'Not that kinda job.'

My mouth is so dry I can barely swallow. I notice my hands shaking in my lap and hide them between my thighs.

'Why wouldn't the cashier let you use the phone?' he asks.

Before I'd got in the truck, my instincts had told me something wasn't right. Now they're goddamn screaming. I feel trapped, in a way I should have seen coming. I guess I did, but I was so desperate that I'd ignored it.

There's no escaping it now.

'You'd have to ask him,' I reply.

'He said something to you. Gave you a reason. What was the reason?'

'I don't remember.'

'Sure you do.'

I look in the side mirror, not sure what I'm hoping to see. The only thing reflected back at me is the empty highway and the desert beyond it. It's the same sight ahead. No way out.

I look at the man's gun on his hip. Then down at my bag by my feet in the footwell, thinking of the gun that Jim had given me, tucked away inside. Is it even loaded?

'He called you a kid-killer,' the man says. 'Why would he call you that?'

I'm shaking all over now, there's no hiding it. He's going to come out with his true intentions soon, whether with his words, or his fists, or the weapon at his side. I stare at the bag between my feet, trying to gauge how long it might take me to remove Jim's gun to protect myself. Longer than it would take for him to reach for his.

I look at the emblem on his shirt again, trying to think back, and I finally remember where I know it from. A wreath of yellow leaves forming an open circle, with two letters inside in the same blazing yellow. *PB*.

The answer comes to me like a blow.

Proud Boys.

The far-right nationalist group who use violence and aggression to get what they want. Racist, homophobic, misogynistic men who dare to call themselves patriots.

'Come on, Aaron. Why'd he call you that?'

The silence between us stretches out until it feels as long as the highway ahead. My whole body is trembling, every muscle tightening. I look at him out of the corner of my eye, seeing the acne pits on his cheeks, the faded tattoo on his sunburnt neck.

'I never told you my name.'

I instinctively lunge for my bag, but a strong, rough hand snags my face and thrusts me sideways, slamming my head into the window. My eyes blur from the blow and my head won't stop spinning. He holds me there, his other hand on the wheel, as I huff for air and mist the glass. He releases me suddenly and I brace myself with a faint gasp: he's snatched up his gun and is pressing it into my groin.

'Make one more move and I'll blow your fucking balls off.'

I can taste blood in my mouth from being slammed against the window, and search for the source with my tongue: I've bitten the inside of my cheek. I wait with bated breath until he removes the gun from my crotch.

I need to get out of this truck, but even if I do, there's nowhere to run. It's just me and him and the desert. I eye the weapon in his grip at the wheel, and then glance around the cab as subtly as I can. I catch sight of the cigarette lighter integrated into the bed of the dash between our seats.

I can't keep letting life happen to me. If I don't do something now, I'm dead. I've got to defend myself for once. Otherwise, it won't just be my head buried in the sand.

I slowly edge my fingers towards the button on the lighter and press it down.

'What do you want from me?' I ask.

'We're just going for a little drive.'

I watch the lighter out of the corner of my eye, waiting for it to pop up. Will it make a sound? Will he hear it? As soon as it's ignited, I need to act. No second guessing. No chickening out. No freezing with fear, like I've always done.

'Are you going to kill me?' I ask.

He doesn't answer, just keeps on driving.

The lighter pops up and I reach for it, feeling it dance clumsily between my fingers like a hot piece of coal. He turns to look at me and I thrust it directly into his eye. He yells the second the hot metal singes him, and the truck swerves violently, throwing us both to the left. He drops the gun to reach for his eye and I lunge to pick it up. The truck has crossed to the other side of the road, jolting as it drifts off the highway. He swings the wheel to the right, throwing us both in the same direction. His eyelid looks like wax from a melting candle, tears oozing out of the slit.

I snatch up the gun and hold it to his head.

'Pull over!'

'*Fuck you!*'

I press the gun into his temple.

'*I said pull over!*'

The man pants for air, liquid still streaming from his eye and down his cheek.

'*Fuck.*'

He pulls to a sudden stop, the brakes squealing, throwing me into the dash. Dust billows around the truck.

I snatch up my backpack and fumble blindly for the door handle.

'I'm going to get out, and you're going to drive away. If you try anything I'll shoot you. I swear to God, I will.'

'Like hell you will, fag.'

'You wanna find out?'

The silence swells inside the truck. I pull the handle until I hear the door click open and clamber out, never once letting my eyes or the gun stray from him.

'Now *drive*,' I shout, and pull back the slide on the gun. Sand blows into my eyes, and the weapon trembles in my grip. He stares daggers at me from behind the wheel with his one good eye, the other red and swelling shut. I aim the gun overhead, praying to God that it's loaded. He jerks in his seat with the sound of the shot and I aim it back between his eyes. '*I said drive!*'

'We're gonna come for you, you fucking kid-killer,' he yells. 'Don't think we won't.'

He slams his foot on the accelerator, so fast that the door bangs shut on its own, and speeds off down the highway, leaving me in a cloud of dirt in the truck's wake.

I stand swaying for a moment to get my bearings, before turning and running into the desert to get away from the road. The truck is long gone, but still I keep running, until my lungs are on fire and I double over to vomit. Eggs and bacon and cat hair empty out onto the cracked earth.

What the hell am I going to do?

I shove my hand into my pocket and pull out my phone. I only have thirteen per cent battery now, and one bar of signal.

I slump to the ground, sitting in my own sweat and sick, and call my brother's house again.

When I hear Nikki at the other end of the phone, I burst into tears.

23

Evelyn

I head out of the car rental place in Hawthorne with the keys to a navy Buick. I'd chosen it after seeing a same-coloured Buick parked up across the street outside a diner, and as I cross the forecourt I'm glad to see it's still there. If I'm going to switch the plates without being seen, I need to act fast.

I put my bags in the trunk, get behind the wheel, and cross the road towards the diner, parking in the space beside the second Buick.

There'll be a paper trail between me and the rental. When the police find their colleague passed out in his own boot, they'll come looking for me, and it'll be this registration they'll be keeping an eye out for. Switching it will buy me some time, keep me under the radar for a little while longer. The run-in with the cop has changed things: now I've not only got Tobias on my tail and Aaron on the run, but law enforcement will be hunting me down too. I need to get control of the situation, and fast.

I get out of the car, grabbing a screwdriver from the holdall and crouching down by the rear bumper to get to work.

After jogging through the desert beneath the afternoon sun, I'd stopped at a bar on the outskirts of town to wash away my sweat in the cramped bathroom and change into clothes that weren't drenched. I'd run for so long that my thighs were chafed from the friction and the underwire of my bra had cut into me until it had drawn blood. My feet are nothing but blisters and welts now, stinging and weeping with each step.

After I've switched the plates, I head into the diner. It's cramped and reeks of oil and fat from the fryers on the other side of the kitchen hatch. Most of the booths are empty but for a few truckers down the far end; a couple of lone men perch on stools at the counter, watching the old TV protruding from the wall.

I can't remember the last time I ate. My stomach feels like it's slowly gnawing away at itself, but I can't imagine keeping anything down. Even if I could, I'd have to get it past my aching teeth.

I order a black coffee to go and drum my fingers on the counter. It's more of a trick to keep myself focused rather than a sign of impatience. My attention drifts towards the television. The wildfires are getting worse.

Having started in Spring Valley and San Bernardino National Forest, the fires burned through the night with embers starting new blazes in Sequoia and Gold Point. Towns in the surrounding areas are being warned that they may have to evacuate due to drifting smoke and the risk of further spreading.

I'm just about to turn my attention away when the anchor cuts to the next story, about another fire in the desert. The shell of my burnt car fills the screen, still being devoured by flames. An aerial shot from a press helicopter takes in the charred earth and the black smoke rising through the air.

The car was said to have exploded along Route 95, blowing debris up to three hundred feet in each direction. A reporter close to the scene confirms that the fire appears to have been started deliberately and that no one was in the vehicle at the time. Firefighters are at the scene working to stop the flames from spreading and the police say they have a suspect, with a press conference to be held later today. It's safe to say that firefighting services are being pushed to the brink here in Nevada.

I stand with my sights set firmly on the TV, my heart pounding as everything seems to close in around me.

There's only one reason why they'd be holding a press conference. It means they know what I look like, from a photo they've found or CCTV footage showing me on the run. Maybe the dashcams transmit footage wirelessly to an external server and they saw me tasing that cop, or he radioed in my registration plate when he stepped away from the vehicle. As soon as they show America what I look like, it won't just be the cops I'll need to be wary of. Everyone I cross paths with will be a threat.

'I got one just like it. The best, right?'

I break from my thoughts and look at the man beside me at the counter. He has sauce around his mouth from the half-eaten burger in his hand. He nods down to the key in my hand, then out the window to where our two Buicks are parked side by side. I force myself to smile at the man I've clearly stolen the registration plate from.

'The best,' I reply.

The woman appears with my coffee, and I lay down some cash before heading out the door and back into the heat.

I need to get to Reno, and quickly.

24

Aaron

I sit on a bench outside the bus station in Reno shaking like a dog left out in the cold. The adrenaline that had kept me going has waned, and my phone died before I'd even reached the bus station in Yerington. I ran and stumbled across miles of desert, staying away from the road and following the mountain edge in fear of Evelyn passing me on the highway, or the man in the truck coming back for me. I was so thirsty that I kept snagging the sweat-soaked rim of my tee and bringing it to my mouth to suck on, my dry tongue scraping at it like sandpaper.

I lean my head back against the wall, thinking about how wrong things have gone. I shouldn't have got into that truck. My instincts told me not to, and I did it anyway. It's like cornering a growling dog and then being shocked when you get bitten. I've got to stay alert to everything now, and trust my gut every time. If I don't, I'll die. The brush with harm I had today was far too close for comfort. I look around for Evelyn, convinced she'll appear at any moment. Every passer-by's face is hers, until I double-take, finding a stranger staring straight back at me.

A car has pulled up on the other side of the street. A blue hatch-back that's at least ten years old but gleams like it's brand new. I watch the driver's side door open and a woman step out: she is six or seven months pregnant by the size of her belly, and her face is clear of make-up, her naturally blonde hair tied back.

Nikki.

We stare at each other for a moment from opposite sides of the street, each waiting for the other to make the first move. She smiles slightly and slowly raises her hand to wave me over, before getting back behind the wheel.

*

We drive for a full ten minutes in silence, neither of us knowing what to say to bridge the gap. So many years have passed since we last spoke. Even the baby in the back is quiet, gurgling bubbles of spit and shaking its rattle. It had frightened the life out of me when I'd got into the car and heard a sound from the back; my fried nerves had me imagining Evelyn sat in the seat behind mine, ready to reach round and snatch me by the throat.

Chris and Nikki have a kid. Not just one kid, but another on the way by the look of her protruding belly. I guess that makes me an uncle. But can you be considered an uncle if you never even knew the kid existed? Chris and I both grew up in the same trailer park, destined for nothing, and while I followed our parents' path – a drug-addicted mother, a father serving time – my brother did something with his life. He found love, got out of Beatty and created a family of his own. But I can't bring myself to be happy for him, not just yet. He chose to cut ties with the family he had, for the family he wanted. Which is all well and good unless you're the one left behind.

'Robbie,' Nikki says. 'The baby's name is Robbie.'

I nod silently and keep looking out of the window, watching Reno pass us by.

The last time I saw Nikki I was eighteen years old, and she would have been twenty-two. They'd let me stay for the night when I had no place else to go. They were renting a small apart-ment above the tavern where Mom worked. I think I stole from her and Chris, but I can't remember what I took. My years as an addict are hazy. All I remember is the desperation I felt between each hit: the euphoria of the first inhale, followed by the withdrawals when it finally wore off. I don't remember what I stole from Nikki because I used to steal from everyone. Not because I wanted to, but because it felt like I would die if I didn't get my next fix. Sometimes I'd really try to be good, until the withdrawals had me practically clawing my own skin off, scratching and scratching until I bled. I always surrendered to it in the end, double-crossing everyone who happened to be in my path.

'It's good to see you,' she says finally, but I can tell by her nerves that it isn't strictly true. Nikki's the kind of person who's been raised to do and say the right thing. 'Are you okay?'

I shake my head.

'You said on the phone that someone was after you. Is it someone from jail?'

'Evelyn Moore.'

'What about her?'

'She's the person who's after me.'

Silence fills the car, but for the baby's gurgling. I can practically hear her thoughts, her regret at letting me back into her life and worry about all the trouble I may well have brought with me.

'I see.'

'She's going to kill me.'

'I don't think she would do that, Ron, not after all this time—'

'I think she's killed my boyfriend.' It's the first time I've said it out loud, the first time I've even allowed myself to accept it. It's very likely that Kyle is dead. I don't know any other reason why she'd have his phone, and why he wouldn't have got in touch with me another way to warn me. Tears spring to my eyes as I think of him.

Nikki is quiet for some time, listening to me sniff back tears while driving the streets towards East Reno.

'Have you talked to the police?'

'We both know the cops won't do shit to help me.'

'Maybe not in Beatty, but here in Reno—'

'I can't. By running I've broken the terms of my probation. I'm meant to meet my parole officer on Monday, and the second she realizes I'm not coming, they'll send someone after me to bring me back and lock me up again.'

'All the better reason to talk to them now. They'll understand, you won't be blamed.'

'You know they aren't going to protect someone like me in the same way they'd protect someone like you. I don't trust them, Nikki. I've been on the other side of them for years and they're just as terrifying to me as she is.'

'So, you're just going to keep running?'

'What else is there to do?'

'You could face it.'

'You're telling me to stand at the other end of her gun and hope she won't shoot?'

'What would your brother do?'

I sit with my hands in my lap, picking at my nails.

'I don't know what he'd do. I don't even know the man.'

She sighs behind the wheel, the leather rasping in her grip.

'I'm sorry, Ron.'

'Are you? Because I was in jail for eleven years, a stone's throw away from here, and I never saw or heard from either of you. Not once.'

'I tried to get him to visit you, but you know what he's like. Stubborn as a mule.' She glances in the rear-view mirror at the baby. 'It was a hard thing for us to process.'

'It was hard for *you*?'

'For all of us, I meant. Sorry, I'm not handling this well. This was all pretty sudden.'

We drive along in silence, the city slowly being stripped away as we move further east, into the suburbs and the mountains.

'Did you go to your mom? Did she not take you in?'

I bite my bottom lip.

I was too scared she'd turn me away.

'We both know how that would've gone if I had.'

I can feel the tears coming, feel my throat tightening. I look into the wing mirror, back the way we came. My mom, my brother, they want nothing to do with me. Even Nikki, as kind as she is, doesn't want me here, screwing up her life. I've known all along that I don't have anyone to turn to, but the thought of having lost Kyle and seeing Nikki's reluctance in the flesh is enough to break me.

I don't have anyone to turn to.

The baby begins crying in the back. Grumbling at first, before his whole face turns red and he's screaming so loud that my ears ring, scrambling my brain.

'Just drop me back at the bus station,' I say over the screams.

'What?'

'I'm tired of being the shit people have to scrape off their shoes. I'll find somewhere else to go.'

'No,' she says, with a force that shocks her as much as it does me. 'We'll think of something.'

I look down at my lap again and pick at my fingernails some more, until strips of keratin litter my jeans. Nikki is trying to soothe the baby, looking at him through the rear-view mirror.

'Chris is going to chuck me out as soon as he lays eyes on me, isn't he?' I ask.

She signals to make a left-hand turn and clears her throat.

'I'll talk to him.'

*

The suburb is nice, or at least it's nicer than the trailer park we grew up in. Houses of the same size and look frame the street, the design like a poor man's villa; they're all mirror images of each other, even down to the drought-stricken lawns; the only differences are the cars on the driveways and the drapes at the windows.

Nikki takes the baby from the car seat and leads me inside with him in her arms. He looks back at me over her shoulder with a confused frown. Robbie has no idea who I am to him; until twenty minutes ago, I didn't know he existed either.

We step straight into the living room. One tatty sofa, a TV in the corner and toys all over the rug. There aren't any pictures on the walls, no personal touches to bring the place to life. Just rooms with furniture that could be anyone's. Maybe they don't have the money to spruce them up, and everything they earn goes towards keeping the roof over their heads.

Nikki drops the key into a dish on the sideboard and walks through a doorway into the small kitchen–diner, which has a narrow set of doors leading to a dusty yard, the lawn as dead out back as it is out front. A slim staircase sits in the gap between the kitchen and the dining nook.

Robbie starts up his crying again; the sound slices straight through me and my already rattled nerves.

'I need to change him,' she says. 'I'll be five minutes.'

She heads to the stairs, then stops. She turns back with a worried look on her face, glancing at her bag where she'd placed it on the counter. All these years have passed, and she hasn't forgotten how I used to be: stealing from people's wallets when they dared to turn their backs, taking anything of value that wasn't nailed down to pawn for my next hit.

'I'm not going to steal anything,' I tell her. 'But you can take it with you if it would make you feel better.'

She blushes. 'It's fine. Wait here.'

I stand in the kitchen, listening to her talk to the baby as they head upstairs, then the sound of her footsteps creaking on the floorboards from the storey above.

I wander into the dining nook. There's a couple more things

in here to make it theirs: a mirror above the sideboard against the wall, and a framed photograph on the surface. I step forward and pick it up.

It's a photo of Chris, Nikki, the baby and Mom.

I stare down at the photo in the frame with a lump in my throat. Chris didn't abandon his whole family, he only abandoned me. It hurts to see how easy it seemed to be for them to carry on with their lives after I was gone. How can you be family to someone one minute, and strangers the next? And if it's so easy to cut ties with someone, can you really say you ever loved them at all?

I hear Nikki behind me and put down the frame before turning. She's looking at the picture, a guilty glint in her eyes.

'He just needed a nap,' she says.

'Right.'

She shuffles awkwardly on the spot.

'I tried calling Chris. I can't get him on his cell or at the garage. I was thinking maybe you could go over there and see him.'

'Alone?'

'I can't, not with Robbie upstairs. We're trying to save on gas so I drove him to work this morning and he'll carpool it back with his boss later. I just think it would be better for him to see you there, one on one, rather than here. We don't want to catch him by surprise or there'll be no getting through to him.'

'Yeah, I'm sure he'd love seeing me turn up at his work after all these years.'

'There's no easy way to enter someone's life again.'

'Not when you're cast out there ain't.'

I'm acting like a child, I know I am, but seeing how happy they are without me makes me want to hurt her feelings, twist the knife a little. I don't want this to be easy for her. None of it has been easy for me.

'He's your brother and he loves you. He just has to remember that.'

All these years, I've thought of them every single day. Wasted so much of my life wishing that things could have been different. And the whole time, my family wilfully forgot me.

'You can take my car,' she says, and pauses again. A familiar wariness crosses her face. 'You're sober now, right?'

'I've been off that stuff for eleven years, Nikki.'

You'd know that if you'd visited or called.

'Of course,' she replies, blushing again.

I'm glad she's embarrassed. After the shame I've had to carry all this time, it feels good to share the burden. But I can already feel the guilt building up within me. I know that I'm going to feel like such an asshole when I head out of here. It's not like she's far off the mark; I've still not ditched the meth Kincade forced upon me, which is still burning a hole in my pocket, silently begging to be smoked. But right now, I can't seem to stop the cutting jabs.

'Right, well . . . I'll get you the address.'

She takes a card from a small stack on the side and hands it to me along with the key. It's a business card for the garage.

'This is a good thing that's happening,' she says as we head for the door, as if she's trying to convince herself as much as she is me. She opens the door and places her hand on my arm. 'He'll see that. But give him a minute or two to realize it, okay?'

It's not her fault, but I resent her anyway. I shouldn't have to be told how to handle my own brother; I should know him well enough all on my own. But truthfully, I barely know the man at all.

I nod silently and walk out onto the driveway.

Nikki watches me get behind the wheel, and I wonder if she saw how hard I was shaking as I walked away, my legs quivering like a fawn's. She's still watching as I put the car in drive, reverse out, and head back the way we came.

I never made it to Mom's trailer with those flowers because I was convinced she'd turn me away. My family cast me out and washed their hands of me so many times I didn't think I could take another knock. But now I finally have to eat my words, and hope that my big brother will see me for who I am now, rather than who I was before.

You're still the same old junkie, a voice whispers in my head. *At least while you've got that baggie in your pocket.*

I reach the junction at the end of the road and take a deep breath, giving way to a navy-blue Buick as it turns in, before sighing and pulling out onto the main road, fighting the urge to pat my thigh and make sure the baggie is still there.

25

Evelyn

I pull up outside the house and watch for signs of life on the other side of the windows. There's no obvious sign that Aaron has been here: there's no car on the drive, no bike. It seems like no one's home at all. But I know he'll be here soon enough; he has nowhere else to turn.

The street is long but quiet. There are no kids playing in the yards, no one delivering mail, no dog walkers. I get out of the car and head up the garden path towards the front door to ring the bell.

After a brief moment, the door opens.

'Can I help you?' the woman asks over the security chain.

Nikki, Chris's partner. I recognize her from the file.

I lift my top and reveal the handle of the gun in my waistband.

'You're going to invite me in now.'

We fall silent, staring at each other over the security chain. Her heart will be racing as fast as mine.

She goes to slam the door, but it bounces off my foot in the jamb, and I thrust my shoulder into it so fast and hard that the security chain breaks clean off. The door smacks her straight in the nose, and I barge my way through to the sound of her cries.

Blood streams from her nostrils; it's painted the white door with violent red streaks. I watch it pour down her mouth to her chin, down to where she has a protective hand on her abdomen, and I see the swell of pregnancy for the first time. Six months along, maybe a bit more. The private investigator said nothing about her being pregnant, and the only photos I saw of her were of her face. I think of carrying Joshua within me, and how I would have done anything to protect him.

'You know why I'm here,' I say, closing the door behind me. 'Tell me where he is, and you'll never see me again.'

She backs through a doorway and into the kitchen, stopping only when the corner of a unit juts into her lower back.

'I don't know what you're talking about.'

I slip the gun from my waistband and pull back the slide. A bullet clicks into place. I raise the barrel towards her head.

'Yes, you do.'

She licks her lips nervously, grimacing when she tastes blood. I watch her closely. People are at their most dangerous when they're backed into a corner. Reckless. Unpredictable. She never once takes her hand from her bump, and I silently scold myself for envying her. For wishing I could turn back time and be pregnant with Joshua again, that I could do everything differently.

'Aaron's not here.'

'Funny, that. You don't know what I'm talking about, and yet you know who I am and who I've come for.'

Blood drips from her nostrils and falls onto the laminate floor as we stare at one another through the silence.

'If someone killed your baby,' I nod to her stomach, 'how many years in prison would be enough for you?'

I watch the thoughts flit across her eyes. The doubts. The fear.

'How far along are you?' I ask.

She blinks back tears and sniffs violently.

'Twenty-eight weeks.'

'Is Aaron worth putting your baby in danger? Are you going to protect him or your child?'

She bites down on her lip so hard that I'm sure she'll break the skin. The tears continue to flow.

'You need to put your child first, Nikki. And you will, from the moment it arrives. Nothing else will matter, and nothing – and I mean nothing – will stand in your way to do right by them. Now, where is he?'

'I'm sorry, but he's gone.'

I step closer, until I can smell the metallic tang of her blood, feel the heat of her fast, anxious breaths against my face.

'Think of your baby, Nikki.'

'Not liking my answer won't make it any less true,' she says. 'He was here, and now he's gone, and I don't know where he's headed.'

I listen to the house, waiting for the creak of a floorboard from upstairs, or any other sign that we aren't alone. My eyes rest on a doorway by the stairs.

'What's through there?'

'A closet,' she says.

I wave the gun towards it.

'Get inside.'

'I'm not going to—'

'I said get inside.'

She stares me down; her eyes flitting towards the stairs nervously before returning to mine; an unconscious tell. Someone's up there. Someone she doesn't want me to find.

I slowly raise the gun and place it against her belly.

'Okay, okay!' she shouts. Her face is a wet mess of blood and tears and snot. 'But then you need to go. Please.'

She backs slowly towards the closet and fumbles with the handle. The door creaks open and she tentatively gets inside.

'Don't come out until I'm gone.' I look down at her abdomen and I feel that splicing pain again, guilt and envy cutting through me like a knife, before I shut her in the dark. I take a chair from the dining table and fix it under the door handle, then I head for the stairs, hearing a sob from inside the closet as I go.

'*Please don't hurt him!*' she shouts from behind the door.

I ignore her and keep on walking up the stairs until I reach the top. There are three doorways on the small landing: a bathroom directly in front of me, and two other doors, one off to the right, the other to the left. Both of these are closed. I pause and listen for any sounds before ducking into the bathroom, my gun poised in front of me. It's empty.

I listen at the door on the right. My pulse is thrumming in my ears, covering any sounds I might hear from within. I reach down for the handle and let the door swing open with a creak.

I step into the main bedroom, peering around and under the bed, before checking the closet. I expect to see Aaron cowering in a corner like the coward he is. But the closet is empty.

I step back out onto the landing and head for the last door. Nikki had looked at the stairs with fear in her eyes. There has to be something or someone up here that she doesn't want me to find. I reach for the handle, raising my gun as the door drifts open.

On the other side is a baby's room.

The gun quivers in my hand. There's nowhere to hide in here: just a cot, a changing table, a rocking chair in the corner, a chest of drawers for baby clothes and a shelf for toys and books. No closet to hide in, no corner to skulk into. I slowly lower my gun. Aaron isn't here; it's just the room they've decorated for the baby.

I remember how excited Tobias and I had been, doing up Joshua's room. He'd been kicking away inside me as we painted the walls with non-toxic paint. I remember how we'd planned to go and pick out the furnishings together; when the day had arrived I'd been laid up with backache, and yet somehow Tobias still came back with everything I'd hoped he would. I think back to each kick, remember how young Tobias had looked, how happy we'd been. I come to, brought round by the sound of a baby. A cruel memory from the past.

Then I hear another gurgle from the cot on the other side of the room.

I close my eyes, longing for it to be just a cruel trick my mind is playing on me; a sound I'm remembering from before, when Joshua was small. But I hear it again, clear as day.

I tentatively step closer and peek over the side of the cot. A baby stares up at me, bubbles popping on his lips. He's gripping his feet in his chubby little hands and rocking lightly.

Please don't hurt him!

Nikki hadn't been talking about Aaron. She'd been talking about her baby.

I stand before the cot, transfixed by the little life inside. I admire his soft, puffy cheeks, the wisps of blond curls, long eyelashes that flick with every blink. The tears come and I let them fall. I'm too busy remembering every detail of Joshua when he was this age, with the same chubby wrists and bubbles popping on his lips, his tiny, pink tongue wiggling in his mouth.

The baby begins to grumble. I should smile, ease its worry, but my heart is breaking. I jump as he begins to scream and hide my gun away.

'Okay, okay. I'm sorry, sweetheart.' I instinctively reach in and sweep him up in my arms. 'I didn't mean to frighten you.'

The smell of him, the warmth of him, the comical wriggle of his legs and the soft grip of his fingers; it's like having Joshua back in my arms. I loved him so much that my chest ached with it, and I feel it all flooding back. I stand in the middle of the room, soothing the baby by bobbing up and down, his breath warm on my ear and his cheek pressed against mine, while I whisper sweet nothings to him with tears sliding down my face. It isn't long before his grumbling turns into contented babble, and I close my eyes, remembering.

I can't bring myself to let go, but the reminder is too painful. My heart feels ready to crack in two. I give him a kiss on the head, breathing in the scent of him, and place him back inside the cot.

I back away slowly, smiling as the tears continue to flow and flow, stumbling into the doorframe as I turn towards the stairs.

In the kitchen, I yank the chair out from under the closet handle and throw open the door. Nikki is sitting on the floor, peering up at me with blood still streaming down her face.

'Your son—' A strangled sound creeps up my throat. I dry my face with the back of my hand. 'He's beautiful.'

She is looking up at me with terror in her eyes, too stunned to say a word.

'Tell Aaron to meet me at Sunset Motel outside Reno, room nine. I'll be waiting.'

I head for the door without another word, listening to Nikki rush out of the closet and up the stairs as I step outside and down the path, unable to shake the sound of the baby's cries, the warmth and the scent of him when he had been in my arms.

26

Tobias

I stop in the shade beneath an oak tree in front of the convenience store to catch my breath.

I need to go to a hospital. I need to get a car. I need to find Evelyn.

I can't rent a car without my licence, and I can hardly keep up with Evelyn and Aaron hopping buses. I'm going to have to steal one of these cars. It's not lost on me that in trying to stop my wife becoming someone she isn't, I too am becoming someone I'm not.

It's almost three; Aaron and Evelyn will have already headed out of Beatty by now, and yet I'm still here, running around in circles.

I never thought I'd see the day I'd steal one car, let alone two. I managed the first one in an opportune moment, but I don't know how I'll pull it off again. I don't know how to shimmy open a door or hotwire a vehicle like they do in the movies. Essentially, I can only steal a car if the keys fall into my lap while the owner's back is turned, which doesn't bode well.

I wait beneath the tree for twenty minutes, trying to ignore the throbbing of my arm beneath the bandages, and watch the cars coming in and out of the lot. Finally, I spot a mother and two young children heading out of the shop with a cart of groceries, and see my chance. The kids are unruly, ignoring her calls to stay close to her and running around tagging each other among the cars. The woman keeps shouting after them until she's in red in the face, but still they run wild. She pulls the cart up beside a black SUV and opens the trunk manually.

The kids are still running loops around the lot when the woman loses her patience and slams the trunk shut before marching after them. I watch her set of keys sway where they dangle in the lock.

As the woman wrangles her pack, I sneak onto the lot and swipe the keys, sidling round the SUV to the driver's door and letting myself in. The inside smells of baby powder and a sharp, artificial scent coming from the air freshener shaped like a round, yellow face that's dangling from the rear-view mirror. It smiles at me from where it hangs. I snatch it off and throw it in the footwell.

The woman has just got the boys by the scruffs of their necks when I start the engine and pull out of the spot.

'*My car! Help! Someone's stealing my car!*'

I push my foot down on the pedal and speed out of the lot, swinging round corners until the produce in the trunk crashes against the sides and spills out of its bags, cans and bottles rollling, chips crunching in their packets. I instinctively clench both hands around the wheel, and as I pull out onto the main road and floor it, I look down at the bandage to see it turning red on my arm.

I can deal with all of it later. First, I need to get to Reno.

I need to stop Evelyn before it's too late.

27

Aaron

I pull up at the garage and sit behind the wheel with the engine still running. The doors to the building are rolled up, revealing the men working on the cars inside, covered in swipes of oil and dirt. I scan from face to face, looking for him.

There's still time to turn back. I could drive on, keep heading north. Find somewhere safe before Evelyn gets too close. That way, I don't have to face the rejection that waits for me should I get out of the car.

I'm still thinking of leaving when a man climbs out of a pit beneath one of the cars, wiping perspiration and grease from his brow. He looks out and spots Nikki's car.

My brother.

He's larger than he was. I can see where he built muscle during his time in the army, and how it's turned soft over the years but still follows the contours of how his body used to be. He no longer looks like a teenager, but a man, with lines on his forehead and around his eyes that are black with dirt, and a thin, receding hairline. He's peering out at the car with a curious smile, no doubt expecting to see Nikki behind the wheel. His smile falls the moment he recognizes me. He drops the rag and strides towards the car.

As he approaches, I turn off the engine with a shaking hand

and climb out. I can taste the contents of my stomach, the acid climbing up my throat and burning at the back of my mouth. I've not even shut the door behind me before he grabs me and slams me against the car.

'What the *hell* are you doing in Nikki's car?'

I'm shaking in his grip, unable to pull the words out. His face is so close I can smell his breath. He pulls me forward roughly before slamming me against the car again. My head ricochets off the edge of the roof and sends my mind spinning.

'*Answer me.*'

'She sent me here!'

'Bullshit,' he spits.

I push at him as hard as I can, but he's too strong, pinning me down as I struggle.

'She tried calling you, asshole!'

He assesses my face, looking for a lie, before pulling his phone from his pocket. He sees the missed calls on the screen and his grip on my chest eases up. He lets go, but I stay where I am, pressed against the side of the car and panting.

'Why would she send you here?'

'I need your help.'

He scoffs. 'You haven't changed a bit.'

'It's not about that. I've been off meth since before I went to prison. Not that you'd know.'

He paces back and forth on the forecourt, rubbing his balding head and leaving smudges of oil in his wake.

'You're meant to be in jail.'

'I made parole. Sorry to disappoint.'

'Stop your whining,' he says. 'I've got the right to be shocked that you're on the outside and driving my damn car.' He stops pacing and looks at me, as if for the first time. Taking in all the ways I've grown up, the way I did with him. 'Why do you need help? If it ain't for money or for drugs, then what is it?'

'Evelyn Moore is after me.'

His brow creases. He rests his hands on his hips.

'What do you mean "after you"?'

'She's been waiting for me to get out of jail. Now she's hunting me down.'

'You can't defend yourself against a middle-aged woman?'

'You know what? Forget it. I'll deal with this myself. It's not like I haven't had the practice.'

I go to get back inside the car, but he slams the door shut just as I open it. He spins me around until we're nose to nose again.

'You brought your problems to us? Put my family in danger?'

'Last time I checked, I was your family too. By blood, at least.'

We stare at one another for some time, and the pain I was scared to feel begins to surge up. How can he not have missed me the way I've missed him all these years? How can he not love me? I feel the tears burning in my eyes, my throat, my chest. I won't cry in front of him. I won't let him see I care.

'I knew this was a mistake,' I croak, and push him away from me as hard as I can. I climb inside the car and go to shut the door when he grabs it.

'Wait—'

'*What?*' I shout. 'What more could you possibly have to say to me that you've not already said? You don't want me here, I get it, now let me go.'

There's a sob brewing in my chest. I hate him so much for not loving me; for cutting me out so easily when all I've wanted these past eleven years was to see him again. I want to hit his chest over and over and make him tell me why. I want to know how our childhood years meant so little to him that he could cast them aside. I hated my childhood; I hated the drugs, the trailer, the beatings. But I always loved him.

He stares down at me crying silently behind the wheel. His eyes never stray from me, and when I look at him I see the anger fading.

'Shit,' he says with a sigh, before turning to the garage. 'Jerry, I've gotta go.'

'What you mean, you gotta go?' the man calls back. 'We got customers.'

'Emergency.' Chris turns back to me. 'Move over. I'm driving my own damn car.'

I stumble over into the passenger seat as he swings in, slamming the door shut behind him.

*

The smell of him has filled the car. He rummages around in his pocket for a pack of cigarettes and teases one out with his teeth before chucking the box onto the dash.

'Have one,' he says, before lighting his own and blowing smoke out the window.

I slip one out, taking the lighter from him. Chris gave me my first cigarette back at the trailer park when I was eight. He made me smoke it all the way down like a man, even when I told him I felt sick. He laughed his ass off when I finally puked.

I'd thought I'd fear him after all these years. Fear his rejection, his disapproval. But now I'm with him, remembering how much I'd loved him, how much I'd needed him, I'm filled with anger; the suppressed rage and resentment that I've not yet allowed myself to feel. I'd buried it so far down that it couldn't reach me, until now.

'You didn't come to see me once,' I say.

'I was in the army, what was I supposed to do?'

'And after that? When you moved here, a stone's throw from where I was locked up?'

'Too much time had passed by then.'

'*Pussy*,' I mutter under my breath.

'What did you say?'

'I called you a *fucking pussy*. It was easier to leave me behind than own up to being a shitty brother, right? You abandoned me

long before the accident. I guess I hoped that after all these years,
you'd be man enough to admit it.'

'You can quit that uppity bullshit right now, kid, or I'll knock
you silly.'

'You abandoned me, then Mom threw me out. And we all
know why you both did it.'

'We didn't like the choices you were making.'

'Being gay isn't a fucking choice!'

'I know that now, all right? But I didn't then. I was young and
stupid and I didn't know any better.'

'That's supposed to make me feel better, is it? You leaving me
behind for something I could never change but, ah – don't worry!
It was just my brother being a dumb kid who didn't know any
better! If that's an apology, it's a fucking shit one.'

He's wringing his hands on the wheel. I wonder if his heart is
racing as fast as mine.

'I'm sorry, all right?' he shouts. 'I'm fucking sorry. Mom was a
junkie and we lived in a shitty trailer park in a shitty town and my
baby brother was a queer, and I didn't know how to handle any
of it. Then you turned out just like Mom, but worse; you hit that
pipe so hard, so fast, and then you ran around town with those
dirty meth heads. I couldn't watch you kill yourself like that, it
made me sick. I took Nikki and I ran. The army gave us a chance
for a clean break. I'm not proud of it, but it was what I had to do.'

He flings the cigarette out the window.

'But you had so many years to put it right,' I say. My voice
croaks with fresh tears. I feel them wetting my lips and my
cheeks, but I don't care. 'You don't get to play the innocent
kid who needed to get out of a bad place now that you're a
grown man.'

'For all we knew, you were still a good-for-nothing junkie, in
jail for killing a goddamn *kid*.'

'Why do you think I was a junkie in the first place? I didn't have anyone to turn to or anyone to lead me right. You all fucking left me to rot!'

'*You ain't blaming that shit on me!*'

He shouts so loud that my heart skips. But instead of shrinking, instead of becoming smaller, I shout right back. My anger won't stop coming, crashing through me in waves that'll drown me if I don't get it out.

'So what, you don't have any doing in it? You think I still would have got hooked if I had just one person in the world who fucking loved me?'

'What do you wanna hear, huh?' he shouts, smacking the dash with his fist. 'You wanna hear how much of a failure I am? *We're all fucking failures.* Mom's a waste of breath, Dad's banged up and we barely know him anyway, I'm a washed-up soldier with no education and no skills except for knowing how to hold a gun, and you're a queer kid-killer. We're *all* fucking failures. We took our lives and we pissed them up the wall, and we're all too fucked up to fix it.' He sighs and rubs angrily at his eyes. 'Give me another goddamn cigarette.'

I chuck mine out the window, the one I'd been too angry to smoke, and light another from the pack. I pass it to him without a word, my hands shaking violently from the adrenaline coursing through me. When I look at him, I notice he's crying. He glances at me through the tears before setting his sights back on the road.

'I'm sorry, all right?' he says. 'I didn't know what to do. You think that because I'm the older one, I'm always meant to know what to do. But I don't, Ron. I don't know what I'm doing now, and I didn't know back then neither. I was just five years old when I learnt to stick my fingers down Mom's throat to make her throw up and stop her overdosing; I was seven when Tony gave me my first black eye. I was ten when that fucking perv Frank from the trailer next door touched me for the first time, and I knew I couldn't tell no one because if it got back to Tony he'd have thought I was queer and beaten me dead. I was sixteen when they turned me out, and I was twenty-two when I finally got the fuck out of that hell of a town. I found my ticket outta there and I fucking took it. I left you behind and I'm sorry, I'll always be sorry about that. But broken people can't fix other broken people. I just . . . I didn't know what to do.'

I cry silently in the passenger seat. I've not cried like this in a long time, not since the holding cell after I killed Joshua Moore. It feels like it's been building up over the years; all the years I've had to stay strong and vigilant; all the years I've spent surviving, not daring to let down my guard in case I couldn't clean myself back up again. All the years of not saying what needed to be said. I'm crying for all the wasted years of my life spent on drugs and in jail, all of my mistakes. I'm crying for Kyle, for my brother and the life he's had that I never stopped to fully understand, for being angry at him for not saving me when the whole time he needed saving too. I'm crying because I miss my mom.

'You could say sorry too, y'know,' he says.

'What?'

'You don't think you betrayed me by hitting the pipe? You were meant to be the good one, the special one, the one that was going to *do* something with his life. Life was hell when we were kids, but whenever I saw you writing down those stories in that little book you had, dreaming up some other life someplace else, I thought to myself, "He's going to be okay". But then you fucked it all up. You became a junkie like Mom and stole from everyone around town; you stole from *me* every time I tried to let you back into my life until I couldn't stand it anymore. You don't think I was terrified you'd wind up dead? That the cops would find your body out in the desert somewhere with the coyotes picking at you? Or in some smack house after OD-ing just like Mom did so many times when we were kids? You had such a big future ahead of you and all you did was destroy it, over and over again.'

I don't think I've seen my brother cry since he was nine years old. But he's really crying now. Tears streaming down his face and snot glistening in his nostrils.

'I had to push you away to keep from being so fucking scared all the time. When you killed that kid, I hated myself for feeling a small bit of relief. I was relieved you'd be locked away where you couldn't keep hurting yourself. I was relieved that I could finally go to sleep at night without fearing the call, telling me you were dead. I didn't push you away because I didn't love you. I pushed you away because I do.'

We drive the rest of the way in silence. I sit sniffing back the tears, trying to figure out how I got it so wrong. I thought he'd abandoned me because he didn't love me. I never stopped to think for a second that it was because he did.

I long to be home again, back in Kyle's bed, lying together naked after kissing and fucking each other, passing a joint back and forth as we imagine wild futures for ourselves, beyond the confines of the paths that were set for us. I long to hold him and be held by him, to feel safe again.

Chris turns onto his street, taking one last drag on the cigarette before flinging it out the window. When the car pulls up on the drive, we sit a while, lost for what to say.

'I'm sorry,' I whisper.

He pulls me into a hug, so suddenly and aggressively that I flinch. He holds me so tight that I can barely breathe, but I cherish it, inhaling the smell of him: the sweat, the oil, the cigarette smoke, all of it. I hold him tighter than I've ever held anyone.

'Do you forgive me?' he asks.

I nod into his neck, tears and snot soiling his shoulder.

'Do you forgive me?' I ask.

''Course I do.'

He pulls back, cups my face in his hands. I look down and he gives me a brief shake.

'Look at me,' he says. 'I love you, all right? Don't ever think I never loved you.'

I nod, trying to stop the tears from coming. I've wanted to be loved for so long that I don't know what to do it with it now that I am.

'Let's go inside,' he says.

We get out of the car, wiping our faces. I feel lightheaded, but I'm light in my body too, like a weight has been lifted; a weight I didn't even know I was carrying all this time.

'Nikki,' he calls, as we step through the door.

She's leaning against the counter in the kitchen, dried blood on her face and her nose swollen, holding a knife in one hand and the crying baby in the other.

'Oh, thank God,' she says. She drops the knife and rushes to Chris. 'I'm okay. We're okay.'

'What the hell happened to you?'

I can feel the anger rippling off him like heat. He takes in the scene: the blood on his wife's face, on the floor. He puts a hand on her pregnant belly.

'Evelyn Moore. The mother of—'

'I know who she's the mother of.'

I look down at the floor, listening to the silence ring through the room but for my brother's angry breaths. This is all because of me.

'Where is she?' he asks.

'She said she was staying at the Sunset Motel, in room nine.'

'Ron,' he says. I look up and meet his eyes. 'Take Nikki's car. Drive as far north as you can get.'

'What are you going to do?' she asks him, as he heads for the door, tugging at his T-shirt. 'Chris—'

'I'm dealing with this. Get me the keys to my truck.'

He passes me at the door and heads out. Nikki and I follow him into the blinding path of the sun as it begins to edge closer to the mountains. He's headed for the garage, swinging open the door. 'Move that damn car,' he shouts, and throws me the key.

I get into the driver's seat and swing out until I'm by the sidewalk. Inside the garage, Chris unlocks a cabinet and pulls out a shotgun. I watch him get behind the wheel of a truck, turn over the engine, and speed out down the drive, reversing out into the street before flooring it without another word.

Nikki watches from the driveway until he's out of sight, her arms wrapped around herself in a soothing embrace. She approaches and I wind down the window.

'Listen to your brother,' she says. 'Head north and get as far away as you can.'

'I should stay, this is all my fault—'

'Your brother would do anything for you,' she says, biting back tears. 'And that terrifies me. He's probably going to go and get himself arrested or worse. He's got a son now, Ron, and another on the way. I can't let you jeopardize that.'

A tear slides down her cheek. She dashes it away.

'Drive north,' she says. 'Drive north and don't come back.'

I sit in silence behind the wheel as Nikki heads back up the drive, crying as she goes.

28

Evelyn

The Sunset Motel off the highway outside Reno is as run-down as all the rest. I step out of my room and onto the boardwalk with the rusty ice bucket. The day is morphing into evening, and yet it's still too hot; the kind of heat that could sizzle the white lines off a highway. The air smells of smoke and destruction from the relentless wildfires eating away at the desert from the east, carried on the wind with the sand and the dirt. I look to the blazing horizon and wonder if it's from the setting sun or the burning earth. I can't see the smoke, but I know that if I blew my nose the snot would come out black.

I trundle towards the ice machine, my eyes heavy and my limbs lethargic. I need a cold shower or a slap, but I settle for ice; I'll lie on the bed and place it on me until the cubes melt away.

'Return the ice pick after use,' reads the sign on the wall above the icebox. I'm so exhausted that the words squirm in front of me and refuse to settle. The pick looks as old as the motel: the long metal spike is rusting in places, and the white handle has turned brown from copious hands. I take it from the top of the machine and open the lid, stabbing at the contents to break the cubes free, but only managing to dislodge clumps the size of fists. I stab and stab until I've had enough and transfer the ice to the bucket before slamming the lid shut.

It's already started to melt by the time I'm back in my room, and it's only when I kick the door shut behind me that I notice I'm still holding the pick. I sigh heavily and chuck it onto the side table; I'll return it later, once I've cooled down a bit.

My tooth is pulsing in my mouth. The pain comes in waves, zinging down the nerve. The swelling around my jaw is getting worse. I'll have a drink, numb the pain. I just have to plough through.

I lie on the bed and run ice shards up and down my neck, round to the nape, then along my chest and down each arm, water dribbling over me in slow, cold trails. I break a cube off and pop it into my mouth to suck on, but it begins to melt as soon as it rests on my tongue.

The motel room hasn't been decorated in a good forty years. There are cracks in the walls that have been left to worsen, and peeling, psychedelic wallpaper, the glue on the underside exposed and oxidized to a dirty brown. The first time I laid eyes on the bathroom, a roach as long as my finger scurried across the cracked tiled floor. I lunged forward without thinking and crushed it beneath my bare foot; I had to wash it off in the bath, its crooked, broken legs swirling around the drain.

I stay motionless on the bed, grappling to keep a hold of myself. But no matter how hard I try, I can't stop thinking of the baby. His chortling cries, the delicate wriggle of his limbs, the fresh, clean smell of him. I can remember Joshua being that small like it was yesterday; I can even remember thinking how fast it was going back then, how little time I had to enjoy him before he grew. It shocks me how many memories I have of him that small. The seemingly minor things that wouldn't have been significant to anyone else. How he would hold his feet on the changing table, giggling away. The sound he made when he fed and the tiny burps that broke at the back of his throat immediately after he was done. Holding Nikki's baby has brought them all back. When I feel the tears approaching again, I clear my throat and sit up.

Pull yourself together. Stop being so damn weak.

I get up from the bed, pick up my gun, and sit at the dressing table across the room. I begin pulling the weapon apart to clean it and give myself something to do, to distract me from the heat and the sound of that baby's cries echoing in my mind. But no matter what I do, I keep hearing them, and the memories keep coming no matter how hard I try to push them away.

I'm tired, that's all. Nothing has changed. My goal is still the same as it was.

But the baby keeps screaming and screaming.

I remove the bullet from the chamber and slip the magazine free before removing the slide. I'm about to remove the barrel when the ice rolling around in my mouth touches my bad tooth. The pain is immediate and blinding. I drop the gun parts to the surface of the desk and cup my face, spitting out the cube before trying to breathe through the sudden agony. I sit with my elbows on my knees and my eyes closed, doubled over and dripping from where the ice had melted on my skin.

I'm just coming round from the pain when I hear a knock at the door. I glance at the ice pick on the side.

'I'll return it in a minute,' I shout. A whimper of pain follows the words, and I clench my eyes shut, breathing in deeply before sighing it away. It feels like the nerve is being yanked and yanked.

The fist bangs again.

'I said in a minute!'

I'm sitting in the silence, trying to gather myself, when I hear a sound that makes my eyes fly open. My line of sight rests on the ice cube melting into the stained carpet, and I slowly look up towards the door.

That was the cocking of a shotgun I heard.

The hole in the door appears in a flash, blasting the lock across the room. Splinters fly in all directions. The door swings open with a violent kick and slams into the wall.

Chris Alexander stands in the doorway. I recognize him instantly from the photos: he's tall with thin dark hair and a protruding gut, the same cold eyes as his brother. I watch as the barrel of the shotgun swings through the air towards me, and just manage to lunge behind the side of the bed before the shell blasts the back of the chair clean off.

'You thought you could come after my baby brother, huh?'

I scramble across the floor, twisting onto my back as the sound of his boots thuds towards me. I look at my gun, picked apart over on the table. The only things I have to defend myself with are my fists and luck. He appears fast, the shotgun cocked and aimed at me with his finger firmly on the trigger. His eyes never once leave mine.

'You thought you could hurt my pregnant *wife*?'

He swings his foot back and drives the tip of his boot directly into my stomach. I double over in pain, spit flying from my mouth with the force.

When I open my eyes, I blink back the tears that came with the blow and look up at him: the shotgun is now aimed directly at my head.

'Think of this as a mercy,' he says. 'Now you get to be with your son, right?'

The mere mention of Joshua coming from his lips makes my blood boil. I raise my own foot, kicking him swiftly in the groin, and don't wait for him to double over before thrusting myself upwards, barging him with my shoulder so we land against the dresser with a loud crash in a mess of flailing limbs. His elbow launches straight into my face during the struggle, hitting my jaw first, before ricocheting off the bone and swiping the end of my nose.

I'm not sure which comes first, the pain or the blood, but I see white sparks from the blow at the same time I taste the blood trickling into my mouth, streaming from my nostrils and down the back of my throat. I spit it at him, seeing the hot, red wad hit him in the eye and run down his cheek, before lunging forwards and sinking my teeth into the side of his neck. He yells out in pain, but I don't stop biting, grimacing from the metallic taste of him. I only let go when his fist meets my head, punching and punching until everything spins and I bolt for the open door. I just about reach the threshold when I'm swiftly yanked back by my hair. The room whirls, my stomach somersaults. I slam down hard onto the floor, smacking my head on impact.

Crack.

I think of Joshua hitting the road.

Crack.

I think of Aaron Alexander driving away, leaving my baby all alone.

Crack.

I try to sit up, but I can't see straight; my vision is swirling and swirling, and I can taste vomit in my mouth. I try to draw breath and can't. Chris staggers around me, blocking my path to the door, and peers down from his great height. Hot sweat drips onto me as he crouches down and straddles my hips. I groan with the weight of him and watch blood trickling from the teeth marks I left in his neck. He drops the gun and, without another word, silently wraps his hands around my neck.

I stare up at him and gasp for air as he turns red from the strain. Spittle hisses out from between his gritted teeth.

Sparks flash each way I look. He squeezes tighter. I feel like my eyes are going to pop from their sockets; my tongue flails uselessly in my mouth and a strange sound rattles up my throat. I swipe at him with my hands, scratching at his eyes, his neck. I grip onto the gold chain he wears and snatch it off in my panic, the metal loops cutting into the fleshy pads of my fingers. I kick wildly beneath him, my legs knocking the end of the bed, the chest of drawers.

My head feels set to explode and all I can taste is blood. Then I spot the gleam of the ice pick poking over the edge of the dresser above us, knocked into view by our struggle.

Chris squeezes harder and harder, hissing and spraying saliva over my face. I kick at the dresser. The ice pick jolts forward an inch. I kick again, and again. The sparks in my eyes are so thick that I can barely see anything at all now. I desperately kick and thrash, knowing I have mere seconds left before I fall unconscious, when the ice pick lands on the floor beside me with a soft thud. My hand flails across the carpet, dust jamming under my fingernails. As soon as I feel the handle, I snatch it up with all my remaining strength and thrust upwards. I hit something. Like a pin breaking through a cushion.

Tense, confusing seconds tick by. I hear a choking sound that's not my own and yank the pick free. Hot blood cascades down upon me. My hand lands on the floor with a thump; the ice pick falls out of reach.

As soon as he lets go of me, I gasp for air and kick my way out from under him, hacking onto the carpet as I try to crawl away. My heart is pounding and I collapse on my back, heaving and coughing. I lie there a while, trying to force air past my swollen throat until the sparks in my eyes slowly begin to clear.

I drag myself up to a sitting position, squinting against the sunlight creeping through the open doorway, and look around the room.

That's when I see Chris slumped against the dresser, quietly choking on his own blood.

The ice pick had punctured one side of his throat and sliced straight through to the other.

*

I sit on the floor with my back pressed against the end of the bed and my eyes on the dying man in front of me.

Chris Alexander is going to die, there's no question about that. It's only a matter of how long it will take. He's heaving for air and his skin is the palest I've ever seen. He cannot speak. He can hardly move. All he can do is stare, and wait.

'Do you know the sex of the baby?' I ask, my voice a low, demonic rasp from where he'd choked me.

He nods.

'Girl?' I ask.

He shakes his head.

'Boy ...'

He nods.

'Your sons are going to grow up without a father. You have your brother to thank for that.'

Anger flickers in his eyes, but he is too incapacitated to say anything in return. All he can do is stare, and blink, and cry silent tears. The blood is still trickling down, soaking into his T-shirt. It's on the carpet too: a dark maroon stain growing steadily beneath him.

'Imagine how it would feel if the shoe were on the other foot,' I tell him. 'If your child was the one who died today, and all you could do was try and survive it. Do you think you could? Do you?'

He simply gazes back at me with the same rage I'd seen when he'd pointed the shotgun at my head. I bet he wishes he'd pulled the trigger now.

'If you think I feel sorry for you, I don't. Actually, I envy you. You'll never have to feel the way I feel. You get to die without knowing the agony of having your child go before you. You'll never have to go through life just making it through the day, every day, longing for peace that never comes.'

He tries to talk and coughs up blood. Tears stream down his face from the pain. Even so, he is set on talking. He looks at me intensely, forcing the words up his mangled throat.

'Go ... to ... hell.'

I smile at the fight still in him. I'd be the same, I think; fighting till the last breath.

'Your brother and I will see you there.'

His eyes roll back and then return to me, but without the focus they'd had before. His pupils flit drunkenly around the room, unable to settle. We sit this way through his last moments, listening to the wheezing of his breath, the violent, bloody coughs, and even after he is gone, his head lolled against the dresser, I stay there on the floor, watching him.

I come to with a gust of wind slipping through the open door. I'm not sure how long I've been here, sitting before a dead man. Could be mere minutes. Could be an hour. Chris's eyes are glassy and blood has finally stopped leaking out of him. I try to stand, stumbling to my feet and swaying on the spot. My head is still pounding from when I'd hit the floor, and I quickly lose my balance as I turn towards the bathroom. It's as if I've got water trapped inside my skull, sloshing around and sending me in the wrong direction with each step. I grit my teeth as I knock into the door jamb and hear a splintering *crack*.

I yelp from the immediate onslaught of pain. It wasn't the crack I hear in my head. It was a very real sound, coming from inside my mouth.

My tooth.

I stumble into the bathroom, blinking back tears, and grip onto the sink. The pain is red-hot and searing through my jaw. I stare into the mirror: my eyes are bloodshot from Chris choking me, and I can already see bruises starting to form on my neck. I raise a shaking hand towards my mouth, curl my finger behind my cheek like a fishhook, and pull it away to peer inside.

My tooth has cracked in two, clean down the middle. Air hits it and makes me cry out.

I grip the sink for a while longer, trying to stomach the agony, but it only gets worse. Each breath aggravates the nerve and my pulse throbs within the broken tooth.

I head back into the bedroom, tripping over Chris's leg as I go. Over-the-counter meds won't do; I need the strong stuff. But I won't be able to get it without a prescription or leaving a paper trail. Which only leaves one other option.

I look at the hole blown in the door by the shotgun. Then the dead body propped against the dresser, legs splayed out. The debris on the floor where the back of the chair was blown clean off. Someone would have heard those shots.

I reach down for my holdall, sweeping the gun parts inside and zipping it shut. Then I pick up the dead man's shotgun from the floor and head back out into the desert.

The blue sky is gone. It's filled with smoke from the approaching wildfires. I cough the fumes from my lungs and head towards the car, Chris's truck still parked beside it. He'd left the windows down. I blink away my tears and spot a bag of tools on the passenger seat. I reach in and grab it, struggling to pull the weight over the lip of the window before putting it in the back of my car.

I sit behind the wheel practically feral from the pain, breathing in and out through my nostrils, and start the engine with my sights set on the highway.

29

Tobias

I pull up at the address in Reno just as the sun is setting. It's taken me too long to get here, too long to stop whatever chain of events is unfolding. I don't know this for sure, but my gut tells me so. An intense instinct that whatever happened here was bad.

I walk up the empty driveway and knock on the door. When it opens, a woman sporting two black eyes stares back at me.

'Who are you?' she asks.

'Tobias Moore – I'm not looking to cause trouble.'

She goes to slam the door; I wedge my foot between it and the frame.

'I'm trying to stop my wife,' I say quickly. 'I'm trying to put an end to all this.'

She stares at me through the gap, her eyes scanning me distrustfully.

'Well, you're too late. Now leave me alone—'

'Was she here? Did she . . . ?' I look at her swollen nose and black eyes.

'She's at the Sunset Motel. My husband's gone after her. If you want to put a stop to this, go now. Stop them both from doing something they'll regret.' It's then that I see she's cradling her pregnant stomach.

'I'm sorry, I didn't mean to frighten you.'

She looks down at my foot. I remove it from the jamb.

'Go,' she replies. 'And don't ever come back here again.'

She slams the door shut.

*

I see the lights of the cop cars flashing outside the motel first. Then I see the ambulance. A hundred scenarios shoot through my mind as my heart rate spikes.

Evelyn, what have you done?

I slow the SUV and turn onto the forecourt, passing the open doorway to a room as I go. The police are inside, filling it like maggots in a wound. I jump out of the car and instinctively stride towards it.

'Hey, you!' a man shouts.

I turn. It's an old fella, pale as a sheet and shaking like someone has him by the shoulders.

'What's happened here?'

'You after a room?' the man jitters.

'No, I—'

'I'll give you the room half price. No, a full free night, and if you stay for more than one, the second night'll be half price. This ain't never happened before, I swear.'

'*What happened?*'

'There's a body in the room. A woman checked in earlier today, and now—'

My legs threaten to buckle.

She's dead. I was too late.

'She's gone,' he says. 'She's gone, and there's a dead man in the room.'

'She's gone,' I repeat. I feel the blood slowly trickle back into my legs as the guilt settles in: I am grateful for Chris Alexander's death. Grateful the dead body isn't my wife's.

'This is gonna send my business under, I'm tellin' you,' the man says. 'If you need a room, I'll give it to you for free, like I said.'

'I don't want a room.'

I turn and feel him grab my arm.

'Please don't tell no one about this. I shouldn't have told you. I just want to run my business, you understand?'

I pull away from the man, unable to speak another word, and head back towards the car, unsteady on my feet.

30

Evelyn

I drive down the highway blinded by tears and head back into Reno. It doesn't matter how many times I blink them away; with each wave of pain, a new set form, drying on my face in silver trails.

I pull up at the first pharmacy I see, and rest my head in my hands with my eyes closed to try to breathe through it. Hot, thick dribble eases out from between my lips and into my lap. It feels like someone has taken a penknife and jammed it straight through the crack in my tooth and into the nerve. When I open my eyes, I see I'm still covered in Chris's blood: it's on my hands, dried in splashes up my forearms and stained into my clothes. I grab the rear-view mirror and point it towards my face. His blood is there too, flecks of it dried on my cheeks, the bridge of my nose, the corner of my mouth.

Another shock hits the nerve and I almost double over.

I wipe the tears from my face and yank open the holdall, teasing out the pair of pantyhose I'd packed. I pull them over my head before reaching for the shotgun resting in the footwell.

Outside, the sun is still beating down. My hot, sour breaths dampen my face beneath the makeshift mask, each exhale escaping with a low groan. I cock the shotgun, kick open the door of the pharmacy, and fire a shot at the ceiling.

The strip lights crash down onto the floor amidst the sound of strangers' screams.

'Get down on the *fucking ground*!' I yell across the store. Through the black fabric, I can just about see a few scared faces staring back at me from where they're crouched for cover. 'Anyone who makes a run for that door gets shot.'

I head down the aisle towards the register, swaying as I go. I snatch up a tote bag from a display and throw it onto the counter, aiming the gun at the first face I see.

'I need the strongest painkillers you've got. Oxy, codeine, morphine. Put them all in the bag.'

The gun wavers in my grip. The pain is so bad that I almost lose my balance.

The man at the other end of the shotgun is staring at me in terrified silence. A dark patch has formed at the crotch of his khaki pants.

'*Now!*'

He jolts into action, skidding on the urine pooling at his feet, and takes the bag from the counter. Another pharmacy worker helps him, all the while sobbing quietly, and I turn to survey the store. The customers are lying on the floor with their hands over their heads. That is, all except for one.

A young boy is nestled in the crook of his mother's arm, staring right at me.

I look back at the boy while swaying on the spot.

'Ma'am,' the man says from behind me.

I spin around with the shotgun aimed ahead of me. The end of the gun narrowly misses the tip of his nose.

'No, no, no, please! I did what you asked!'

The shotgun dances through the air as I check the contents of the bag. They've given me enough painkillers to kill a horse.

'Put some bottled water and gauze in the bag too. Then wait ten minutes until you call the police. If I find out you called them

sooner, I'll come back and shoot you both between the eyes.
Got it?'

The man nods as he does what I asked. I can't see too well, but
I can hear that he's crying. I snatch the bag from the counter and
turn around to head for the door.

The child is still looking at me.

I stop before him in the aisle.

'Look away, boy.'

He keeps on staring, his eyes wide with both wonder and fear.

'*I said look away!*'

'*No! Please!*'

His mother throws herself over him, sobbing as she holds him
to the floor.

I look down and realize what I've done: the shotgun is pointed
right at the child.

Tears blur my eyes again, and I stagger down the aisle, waver-
ing from side to side and knocking products off the shelves as I
take the corner too close. I tumble out of the store and into the
street.

The tears are still coming. I can't stop them. I can feel them
sticking to the pantyhose over my head, hear the rattling sob
crawling up my throat. It was the boy that did it. Those wide,
doe-like eyes. The curious wonder behind them, despite the
danger. He looked just like Joshua. Or maybe he didn't; maybe
I'm going crazy.

I just about make it inside the car when the sob erupts out of
me. I yank the pantyhose from my head and wail into my hands.

I don't know who I am anymore.

*

I stumble into the first motel I see, shivering from the pain and
already lightheaded from the pills I've thrown back.

'I need a room.'

The man behind the counter stares back at me.

'You don't look too good, lady. Maybe it's a doctor you need.'

I'd cleaned myself up before stepping inside, washing the blood away with the bottled water and pulling on clean clothes from my bag, but my face is still swollen and my eyes and neck are turning black with bruises.

I glare at the man and a shiver visibly runs down his spine. He sorts me a room without another word, and I swipe the key off the counter and head back outside.

I let myself in, drop my things, and grab what I'll need before heading to the bathroom. I put the bag of supplies on the toilet cistern and hold up the pliers I'd spotted in Chris's tool bag. They're dirty, spoiled with rust in places, but it's my only way of dealing with this tooth. I wash them under the tap before emptying the rest of the bag contents into the basin and placing the bottles of booze I'd bought at a liquor store en route on the windowsill.

Pliers, gauze, an array of pain medications rattling in their bottles. I sway before the mirror and take some more meds without checking their name, before pushing the end of the pliers into my mouth towards the tooth. The crack looks bloody now, faint red bubbles escaping from within. I place the metal pincers on either side and howl as the metal knocks against it. The pain is blinding. I hunch over, gripping the side of the basin, and watch as my tears fall into it. I down some more booze and wait a few minutes for the pills to kick in, thinking of the boy who had stared at me in the store. Those wide, haunting eyes.

When I'm struggling to keep myself standing, I know it's the best the drugs will do. I've got to do this before I pass out. I reach in with the pliers again, and clamp the pincers down onto the tooth. Feral sounds escape my prised-open lips. My tongue is lolled over to make room, wiggling helplessly out of the side of my mouth.

I grip the pliers as hard as I can and pull.

My eyes flash white. I hear metal clatter to the tiles at my feet, and the sound of someone crying. Me. I'm crying. My vision clears and I'm bent over the basin, my forehead resting on the tap where I'd completely doubled over.

I try again. My eyes flash and I retch, hunched over with strings of bile slinking from my mouth like webs.

I stumble into the hotel room and rummage through Chris's tools for something else. Anything that will stop this onslaught of pain. I settle on a hammer and chisel and return to the bathroom. I take up the bottle of brandy and sit on the floor with my back to the tub. I swig some, swilling it around my mouth and gulping it down until I'm seeing double: I have two pairs of hands rather than one, and there are two bottles wavering in my grip. I wrap a hand towel into a coil and use the good side of my mouth to bite down on the end of it. Then I hold the chisel to my tooth with one hand, and shakily raise the hammer in the other, bracing my feet against the opposite wall and pushing my weight into the back of the tub.

Whack.

A flash of blinding light.

Whack.

I scream behind the towel, tears streaming down my face.

Whack. Whack. Whack.

Half of my tooth pings across the floor with the last blow. I yank out the towel to retch onto the tiles, staring down at the shard of tooth gleaming in the bloody vomit. I swig more alcohol, droplets of tears dancing on the edge of my jaw, before raising the chisel and the hammer again. I drop the chisel, pawing at the floor for it as my vision blurs and splits. I finally manage to grab it, put it in place, pull back the hammer, and strike with all my might.

A fractured scream rips up my throat and I slump over, my face hitting the cold floor with the last half of the tooth rolling free in my mouth. I spit it across the tiles as my eyes roll back. Then everything goes dark.

31

Aaron

I drive for mile after mile with no clear destination, only a goal: to get the hell away from Reno as fast as I can. I drive until I'm out of town and back in the desert, keep driving as the mountains get bigger and the sky gets darker. But I didn't drive north when I left my brother's; that's what Evelyn will be expecting. I headed south instead, back the way I came, praying it'll put a long distance between us before she realizes what I've done.

The whole time, I'm thinking of my brother. Of how many years we've wasted. I'm thinking of Nikki telling me to never come back, losing his love just as I finally found it again. My stomach is grumbling and my mouth is parched. I'm thinking of the meth in my pocket, of numbing the pain the only way I know how. But still, I keep driving.

Evelyn Moore had been so close to finding me. I don't know what Chris could possibly do to stop someone like that. Her life seems to depend on ending mine. I try not to think about what he might be saying to her or doing to her to make her stop; every time I think of them meeting up at the Sunset Motel I start to shake. I steel myself and focus on the road.

Just keep heading south. That's all I've got to do.

Darkness falls slowly across the land, creeping and creeping until the dashboard lights up and I turn on the headlights. Flying bugs glow before the beams as I head into the night to nowhere. I drive until I can see Walker Lake, the smell of its salty water seeping through the vents. Miles long and miles wide, a weird phenomenon of water in the middle of the desert.

The wheel begins to tremble in my hands. I watch it stutter as the headlights dim and the road grows dark. I look down at the dash.

The tank is empty.

'No!'

The engine is winding to a stop, no matter how hard I slam my foot on the accelerator, pumping it repeatedly to no avail. The headlights are fading. I steer the car towards the side of the highway, letting it crawl to a stop in the dirt, and pull up the handbrake as everything goes black.

I sit in the dark car, in the even darker desert, feeling more alone than I have ever felt in my life. The tears build, and with them the fury, a scream swelling within me until it works its way up my throat and roars out in a bellow of rage and spit. I yell and yell, pounding my fists into the dash and the wheel.

I throw open the door and run across the dark, dead ground, right up to the lip of Walker Lake, still screaming as I go. Screaming at the desert. At the water and the mountains. Screaming at the sky, at God. Screaming for years of pain that's built up in me for so long.

I scream until my voice grows hoarse and the tears dry up. The salty taste of the air over the lake has stuck to the back of my throat. I try to spit it back up as I turn to look at the dead car. There are no other drivers on the road; the only sign of life around me is the dancing crickets. I'm miles from another living soul.

It's just me and the mountains and the crickets.

I take the meth from my pocket, watching the crystals twinkle through the bag beneath the full moon. I want to hunt around inside Nikki's car for items that I can fashion a pipe out of so bad, so that I can smoke the lot. To numb the emotions building in my chest, to stop the tears from falling. I've made pipes out of the craziest things in my time; the wildest items I used in a jam were a hollowed out lightbulb and an empty pen tube. There's always something an addict can use; they just have to look hard enough.

As the need grows, I try to think of what life was like when this stuff controlled me. The sickness, the pains, the agonizing withdrawal that made me want to peel my skin clean off my body. All of the evil and immoral things I did to get my next fix. I think back to the sores I would get in my mouth from the smoke, and the burns I'd get on my hands. But it's so easy to look past all these things when the drug comes calling.

I hold my breath and open the baggie, watching the contents shimmer from the tremor in my hands.

Then I pour them into the lake, watching the crystals vanish into the dark water.

I'm not that man anymore.

I wipe my face dry and take my phone from my pocket. There is one last person I can call. It's the only path I have left to take.

III

BARGAINING

London, autumn 2005

I'm in the shower when I hear Evelyn scream my name.

'Tobias! Oh my God, Tobias!'

A million fears rush through my mind as I stumble out of the shower with shampoo still frothing in my hair, pawing blindly for a towel from the rack as the suds run into my eyes. Every thought that comes to me is about Joshua. He's not waking up from his nap despite her trying to rouse him. He's hit his head. He's swallowed something he shouldn't have, like a paperclip from my office, something Evelyn has warned me to keep out of reach a thousand times.

'Tobias! Come quickly!'

'I'm coming!' I rush out of the en suite with my eyes scrunched up against the suds, slipping on the hardwood floor as I turn from the bedroom onto the landing. My heart is thumping and my breaths are short from panic. She calls my name again as I reach the living room, stopping in the doorway and looking for the source.

Evelyn is sitting on the floor, holding Joshua upright where he stands before her with his chubby little hands gripping her thumbs.

'He walked!'

'He what?'

'Walked! Get the camera!'

'The camera!' I go for the door and turn back. 'Where is—'

'The study! Quick!'

I rush into the study and scan the desk.

'Where?'

'Top drawer!' she calls back.

'Top drawer, top drawer,' I mutter under my breath, yanking it open and finding what I'm looking for. I bolt back into the hall, feeling the towel slipping at my hips, and run into the living room while turning on the camera.

Joshua is giggling from all the excitement, looking between us with a smile.

'Are you ready?' she asks me, her eyes on our son's beaming face.

'Ready.'

'Go, baby, go!' she says.

She lets go of his hands, allowing him to find his balance before taking one step, then another, and another, until he reaches the sofa, gripping onto the fabric of the seat and looking back at us with a smile so adorable that I well up.

'You are such a clever boy!' Evelyn says, swooping him up and kissing him all over. I leave the camera running, capturing their love. I could watch them together for hours.

She turns to me with the widest smile I've ever seen. It falters briefly when she looks at me, before it returns in a flash and a burst of laughter.

'What?'

Joshua is giggling with her. She points below the camera.

I look down and find I'm butt-naked. I laugh too, laugh until I'm crying with her, and approach them both. I kiss her, then him, and we sit in a knot of limbs in the bizarre, euphoric moment.

'What is Daddy like, hey?' Evelyn says, before stroking my face tenderly and giving me that look. The look of pure, unadulterated love.

I would stay in this moment forever if I could.

32

Tobias

Despite the unbearable heat of the day, the desert feels cold to-night. The sort of cold that works its way into your bones. I can feel it pressing against the windows of the car as I drive, smell the earthy scent of the air coming through the vents. Or maybe it's me, and I'm in shock, and it isn't cold at all. I grip the wheel and drive on, set to meet the man who killed my child.

There is nothing that can prepare a man for this moment. I've wanted this all along: to get to Aaron and keep him from my wife. But now the opportunity has arrived, so has the stark reality of having to stand before the person who left my son for dead. I have to look him in the eyes, watch his chest rise and fall, breathing the same life into his lungs that he'd ripped from Joshua. I have to store up all of my anger, my pain and my sadness, and put on a brave face.

I'm doing this for my wife.

He called not long after I left the motel. I'd waited there a while, sitting in my car to watch them wheel out the body bag. The cops got suspicious of me after a while. An officer strode over to the car and told me there was nothing to see and no comment would be made, thinking I was the press. Better that than the hus-band of the person who put that body in the bag to begin with. I drove away wondering how she did it. Did she shoot him? Strangle him? Maul him with one of the many weapons she'd brought with her? I didn't want to know, but my mind kept creeping back to the thought.

I'd told myself I would report her if I thought she was too far gone. If it was the only way to keep anyone else from dying. But instead of telling that officer what I knew, I drove off, too scared to lose my wife for good; too selfish to go through this grief alone, even if it means her putting other people in danger. On the highway I thought about turning around and heading back to the motel to tell the officers what I know so many times. But I never did. I was still fighting this internal battle when my phone rang.

'It's Aaron,' he said, before I could utter a word. I held my breath, not sure what would come out of my mouth if I spoke. Before, it had been me contacting him; psyching myself up, planning what I was going to say and not say. But hearing his voice, being caught unawares by it, felt like a rug being tugged out from under my feet.

'You said you'd help me. Did you mean it?'

'Yes,' I heard myself say. 'I'll help you. Just tell me where you are.'

Silence followed. So complete that I wondered where he could be, to be surrounded by quiet like that.

'How can I trust you?'

He sounded like a scared little boy, so different from the man I had pictured all these years. I gripped the wheel to centre myself. To remind myself of the goal.

Get Evelyn home.

'You can't. You can't trust anyone fully, and anyone who tells you that you can is lying. You can only trust yourself, and your gut told you to call me. Listen to it.'

Another long silence followed, but for the sound of anxious breaths, both his and mine.

'I'm broken down,' he said finally. 'Off Route 95 by Walker Lake.'

'I'm coming for you right now,' I replied, slowing down before looping back round on the highway to head south.

That was hours ago. Hours that I've spent trying to gather myself, to plan what I should say to him to keep him onside. Thinking of ways to keep my hatred for him buried out of sight while trying to keep my foot on the gas pedal. As I drive towards the man who destroyed our lives, every muscle in my body grows tense, as if my entire being is repelled by the thought. My heart skips every time I pass a road sign telling me how many more miles I have left to go. Whether I feel ready or not, the decision is made for me the moment I smell the salt drifting in from Walker Lake. Then I see the mountains bordering the water, and the full moon shimmering in its reflection. I spot a car parked on the side of the highway, then the shadowy figure beside it.

I pull over on the opposite side of the road and turn off the engine, my body anchored to the seat. I unfurl my hands from the wheel and watch the blood seep back into my knuckles. A mess of emotions brews within me; I want to vomit and cry all at once. Instead, I get out of the car.

Crickets dance in the dark as the chill and the salt hit me, making me shake harder. I stand in the shadows and look towards the broken-down car.

The last time I saw Aaron Alexander, he was just a boy, standing in cuffs before the judge, awaiting his sentence. He'd kept his head low, with his voice so quiet that the judge had told him to speak up several times. But now he's all grown up.

He is a tall man who seems intent on making himself small. His head is kept low, as before, but now his shoulders curve inwards. Even through the dark I can sense the fear in his eyes as they meet mine. There are no other cars on the road. No headlights in the distance, no lit buildings or towns resting on the horizon. It's just him and me, the desert and the dark.

I am doing this for Evelyn.

I step out with the intent to cross the road when I see the gun in his hand and dart back behind the car, putting metal between me and a bullet.

'Put that goddamn thing away!'

'No,' he says. 'Not until I know I can trust you.'

'You see me holding a gun?'

'Doesn't mean to say you won't pull one the second I put mine away.'

'I'll leave my gun in the car if you put yours away right now.'

'No. You first.'

We stare at each other across the divide in loaded silence. Evelyn would think me a fool for losing control of the situation so fast. This man killed our child and came to me for help, and yet it's him calling the shots. I open the car door.

'I'm going to reach for my gun now and place it inside. Don't mistake it for anything else.'

I watch him tighten his hold on his weapon, ready to raise it at a second's notice.

'Okay?' I ask.

'Yeah, okay.'

I slowly reach for mine and slide it out from my waistband, watching him over the roof then through the glass as I crouch down and place it in the glove compartment. I stand back up and raise my hands.

'Now you.'

He pauses, eyeing me from afar.

'Look, you called me because you have no one else to call. You can either put your gun away and get in the car or you can stay out here and wait for my wife to find you. Your choice.'

I get inside and start the engine, watching him through the

window as he reaches down and picks up his backpack. He places the gun inside before slipping the straps over his shoulders. He hesitates a few seconds longer, analysing the threat I might pose, the danger I could put him in, before he finally crosses the road.

He sits in the seat beside me and shuts the door behind him.

I breathe in the stale sweat and fear emanating from him, and wonder how long he's been out here. The smell and warmth of him disgust me, his scent filling my nostrils. I feel the same rush of conflicting emotions I had when I pulled up. I want to strike him and choke him for what he did to my son. To my wife. To all of us. I want to vomit and break down crying.

'Where are we going?' he asks quietly.

I put the car in drive and slowly pull back onto the highway.

'I don't know.'

33

Aaron

Tobias opens the door to the motel room and throws the key onto the sideboard.

He couldn't afford two rooms. That's what he'd said as he came back out from the clerk's desk. I stare down at the two beds side by side, with only a small table keeping them apart. I don't know how I'm going to sleep next to him. I should be used to it after sleeping next to cellmates over the years, but the thought still fills me with dread. Ever since I was a boy, I've learnt to sleep lightly, always ready to dodge a fist or a kick should they come when I let down my guard, and I can do it again. If only I wasn't so tired.

'Which one do you want?' he asks, signalling to the beds.

'I don't mind,' I reply, wanting the one furthest from the door.

'Okay.'

He empties his pockets on the bed nearest the door as if I'd spoken my wish aloud. 'I'm going to take a shower. Don't leave the room until I get back.'

I nod silently, but he's already shutting the bathroom door behind him.

I stand in the quiet space and fight the overwhelming urge to cry. I always feel loneliest when the chaos stops. It forces me to face everything I've lost, without any distractions to keep my mind off it all. It makes me want to keep running, to try to out-manoeuvre the loneliness, but it always catches up with me in the end.

I sit on the bed, listening to the sound of running water from the bathroom and the mumbling of the TV in the room next door. I think of Kyle, and what might have happened to him. I think of my brother. I think of how many brushes with death I've had in the last twenty-four hours. When I feel tears of exhaustion scratching at my eyes, I blink furiously and walk to the window. The desert stares back at me.

I eye the dark silhouettes of the mountains, the horizon in the distance where the shadowy land meets the night sky. It would be tough for anyone to find us out here, but I don't doubt that Evelyn could. She has every time up to now. There seems to be no place she won't find me. I wonder how long we have here before she comes knocking.

Tobias looks much older than I remember. His hair has thinned over the years and his skin has wrinkled. Age didn't do this to him, not alone anyway. It's grief that's responsible for his dull complexion and the droop of his eyelids; the sag of his cheeks and mouth. I put some of those wrinkles there myself.

How can he bear to be in the same room as me, after everything I've done? How can he look me in the eye, or face the thought of lying next to me? He must have the same sense of dread that I have. He seems to have a better handle on his hatred for me than his wife, but I catch myself wondering how long he can keep a grip on it. If at some point he'll lose control and turn.

The bathroom door opens, and I jump.

Tobias steps into the room, looking anywhere but at me. He's got dressed back into the same clothes. I wonder why he doesn't have anything else to change into, and notice the bandage on his arm. He must have kept it away from the spray, because it's still dry.

'You gonna shower?' he asks.

I need to, but I don't want to move or turn my back. I shake my head.

'We need to sleep. To be ready for tomorrow.'

'What's tomorrow?' I ask.

'Tomorrow, we run.'

He gets into bed. I kick off my shoes and reluctantly get into mine. I stay clothed, not wanting to be too vulnerable, to keep a layer between him and me; to be able to wake and run at a moment's notice. He turns off the light and rolls over with his back to me.

I lie in the dark staring up at the ceiling, listening to the crickets outside and the TV through the wall.

Tobias rolls onto his back suddenly with a frustrated sigh.

'I need a drink.'

*

We sit on the walkway of the motel, smoking the joint I'd found crumpled and dried out in the bottom of my backpack, and swigging from bottles of Bud he got from the fridge in the clerk's office. The night is cool and quiet except for the crickets and the odd car driving along Route 95. The weed makes me feel more relaxed, to the point where I occasionally forget who we are to one another and ask questions I would never have asked before.

'Why did you come here? To America?'

He takes a swig of beer.

'For new beginnings,' he says.

And all I brought them were endings.

I take a drag and pass him the joint.

'We'd lived in London our whole lives,' he says, raising it to his lips. 'I was offered a job in San Diego, and it felt like the right decision at the time.'

'You never thought of going back?'

'Too much happened,' he says, his voice tight from holding the smoke in before finally breathing out. 'If we left America, we'd be leaving him too. It's complicated.'

Him. He doesn't say Joshua's name, as if he daren't mention it aloud around me. He passes the joint back and I inhale, hold the smoke in my lungs until they're bucking inside my chest.

'And I think my wife wanted to stay to be close to you, for when the time came.'

He's picking at a crack in the wooden walkway, pulling out splinters one by one.

'How long has she been planning this?'

'Longer than I've known about it.'

'You think she's been waiting for my release this whole time?'

'Yeah, I think so.'

I take one more drag and offer him the joint. He shakes his head. I flick it over the railing of the walkway and watch it drop.

'And you don't feel the same way?' I ask.

He's quiet for a long time, or at least it feels that way. My mind is floating from the weed, but my heart is beating fast, waiting for the answer. From his expression, he looks torn.

'It's complicated,' he replies finally.

He picks at the splinters some more, stopping when one digs into the pad of his finger. He pulls it out and puts his fingertip in his mouth, sucking to get rid of the blood before wiping it on his jeans.

'Grief has destroyed my wife – she wasn't like this before. She was a psychotherapist. Her job was to help other people through their pain, but when she was met with her own, she couldn't take it. She thinks if she rights your wrong, if she takes a life for a life, it will subside, but it won't. If she gets to you, the woman she was will be gone and there'll be no going back. I can't let that happen.'

When he speaks of his wife he seems to age a good five years, misery and pain flooding his face at the thought of her. His eyes are glassy as he looks out at the desert, the full moon reflected in them.

'You're willing to put your own pain aside to protect me.'

He straightens up.

'I'm protecting my wife.'

He swigs the last of his beer and then starts picking at the label, peeling it off in strips.

'I think she's killed my boyfriend,' I say.

I've got to know, but I don't know how I'll deal with it when I do. I hold my breath; I can't seem to look at him in case he's about to confirm my darkest fears. He sighs and glances over. Something has come over him. A melancholic thought or memory.

'Yes, she did.'

My heart jolts. There's no apology. No attempt to verbally right that wrong. Not to me, at least. I suppose he's right not to, after all I've taken from him. There must be a part of him deep inside that's glad to see me lose someone too. An eye for an eye. Tit for tat. I feel the grief surging up, the tears stinging my eyes, and harden myself. I'll cry about this, but not yet. Not in front of him.

'We should sleep.'

He gets up and heads into the room, leaving the door ajar behind him, as I sit wondering how my life came to this. Sharing a joint and drinking a beer with the father of the boy I killed. Losing everyone I've come to love.

I think of Kyle and the tears finally come, and I bite down on my lip to keep from making a sound. I press the heels of my hands into my eye sockets to try to hold them back.

I'll never hear his voice again, never hear him laugh again. I'll never see his smile or the dimples in his cheeks. I'll never kiss his lips that always tasted of Cherry Coke and cigarettes. We'll never lie together, come together. We'll never talk of the future, now that his has been cut so short. I can't stop thinking of all the things I'll never get the chance to hear, or see, or say again. All of the *next times* that have been ripped away. I don't know if I was in love with him, but I know he was the man I loved the longest, and losing him – and the chance to see if that love could have grown into something more, into the love that it would likely always have bloomed into – breaks my heart in two. And it's all because of me.

I wipe my eyes and stagger to my feet, trying not to think about how this might end. Tobias thinks he can stop Evelyn, but I don't know how that can be true. If she's been stewing on this for eleven years, if she's taken a life – the life of someone I loved – and is still pursuing me, then I can't see there being any humanity left in her at all.

When I step back into the room, Tobias is lying on his side with his back to the door. Conversation over. I head to my bed and wriggle out of my jeans, my head floating from the grass. I climb in and try to morph the lumpy mattress to the shape of my body.

The room falls quiet, and we lie in the dark. The TV in the next room has been switched off.

'Do you know what happened to my brother?' I ask, speaking into the shadows.

He is silent for a while. I wonder if he's fallen asleep until he rolls onto his back and finally speaks.

'He's gone.'

Tobias turns over again, this time facing the door with his back to me. I sink my face into the pillow and sob silently.

34

Evelyn

The first thing I see when I open my eyes is my tooth lying in a dried pool of blood on the tiled floor. That is, until my eyes begin to water as the pain rushes in, as if it has been waiting patiently for me to wake.

It's insurmountable: a deep, relentless throbbing in my mouth where the tooth used to be. My jaw feels swollen shut. The pain isn't localized, it's everywhere. I feel it in each row of teeth, in my eyes and the cheekbone on the right side of my face, trailing down the nerves and tendons of my neck to my shoulder.

I try to rise from the floor and stumble. My neck has stiffened from lying on the cold tiles all night. I'd passed out, twisting my back and pinning my shoulders the wrong way.

I spot a bottle of meds nearby and tear off the lid. My mouth tastes of blood and brandy and medication and cigarettes. I swallow a handful of pills and swig more booze, feeling the warm alcohol seeping into every crevice of my mouth and into the crater where my tooth used to be.

The room starts to spin. I sit against the side of the tub and try to breathe through the pain until the pills take hold, bubbling in my otherwise empty gut. The sun pours in through the window, blinding me. I paw for the pack of smokes in my pocket and raise a shaking cigarette to my lips. My hands are covered in dried blood. I'm not sure if it's Chris Alexander's or mine, or a combination of the two. I light the cigarette and inhale.

The pain is still so intense that I can't think straight; I can't remember which motel I'm in, whether Chris Alexander is lying dead in the other room or if I drove off to stay elsewhere. He is dead, that much I remember. I can feel where my neck is bruised from his hands. I know I'm still in the desert from the grains of sand pinging against the bathroom window whenever the wind blows. I only remember holding up the pharmacy when I see the other drug bottles at my feet; the memory of the scared little boy staring up the barrel of the shotgun screams through the pain.

I take another drag on the cigarette and try to rid myself of the thought, but the young boy is waiting there behind my lids, watching me with those wide blue eyes.

Tears blur my vision and I sit blinded, thinking of all that I've done. I thought I was strong enough for this. I had wanted to do it for so many years, dreamt about it, planned every step I'd take, crossed the days off my calendar, but the further I go down this treacherous path, the weaker I seem to get. I think of Kyle, lying dead on his bed. I think of Chris Alexander with the ice pick through his throat. The cop I tasered. That scared little boy staring up at me, past the shotgun pointed at his face.

For so long, this mission of mine has felt like the right thing to do. Paying forward the justice that hadn't been fairly dealt. Aaron Alexander, the child-killing monster, had to be dealt with to tip the balance; to make the world a better, safer place. But instead of hurting Aaron, I've hurt others. I've taken two lives, I've brutalized a young, pregnant mother and terrified her baby. I've pointed a shotgun into an innocent child's face. Aaron Alexander isn't the monster in these instances; to all of the people I've hurt, it's me.

I sit and let the tears fall, listening to a faint drip from one of the taps and the tick of a clock somewhere in the room. I thought this would be enough, but the pain is still ripping through me. Not the tooth; the pain of losing Joshua. I think of him and crumple, crying quietly on the bathroom floor.

Maybe I am a monster, but I can't stop now. Not now I'm so close. I could never live with myself if he walked free.

The cigarette has burnt away into a pillar of ash between my fingers. I let it fall to the floor and take another swig of brandy. The pills have kicked in enough now for me to think of getting up. My head is heavy on my neck and my tongue feels lazy in my mouth. I don't even know what I've taken; I simply grabbed a bottle and chugged. The effects will feel like double that dose with all the alcohol in my system.

I grip the side of the tub and ease myself up, groaning from the stiffness in my joints and the pain echoing from my mouth, tremors shivering up my temple towards my crown. Then I lean on the basin and get shakily to my feet. I look at my reflection in the mirror and freeze: my face has ballooned. The entire right side is swollen, and my neck is dark with bruises.

I stumble into the bedroom. The bed is made and unslept in, and there is no body in sight. I've mixed up the two motel rooms in my drugged-up state.

I put my phone on charge and check the time: it's a little after nine in the morning. I take a towel from the side and head out of the room to find the icebox and fill it with cubes. I inadvertently scatter some on the floor in my medicated daze, before wrapping them up tightly and placing the bundle on my cheek. The sun is burning hot despite the early hour; I can feel it scorching the nape of my neck and I have to squint to see the boardwalk beneath my feet. The fires have followed me through the night and I can smell the smoke in the air.

I return inside and lower myself to sit on the end of the bed as slowly as an old woman might, reaching for the remote to turn on the TV and flicking through the channels for updates on the fires.

I stop when I see my face filling the screen.

The suspect held the pharmacy at gunpoint yesterday evening, shortly after the body of a man was found at the Sunset Motel. In a press conference last night, the Nevada Police Department stated that they believe the two crimes are connected, and released details of the subject: Evelyn Moore, a forty-eight-year-old British woman and the mother of nine-year-old Joshua Moore, who was sadly killed in a hit-and-run that was covered heavily in the news cycle back in 2013. The department has asked the public to remain alert and not to approach the suspect, but to call them with any potential leads. The suspect is still believed to be armed and dangerous.

I turn off the TV and stare at my reflection in the screen. I would have been frightened by something like this before I lost Joshua, back when I was a law-abiding citizen. Now the only fear I have is that someone will stop me before I can do what needs to be done. The shrinking window I have in which to find Aaron has changed things. I force down all of the fears I'd had before. Smother the guilt for the monster I've become. I won't let him get away with it. If I'm caught and Aaron walks free, all of this will have been for nothing.

Guilt is only slowing me down.

I have to find Aaron before the police find me.

He'll have set off somewhere new by now, only this time I don't know where he'll go. I'd familiarized myself with his connections in Beatty, and knew my last best chance to get him was in Reno. Now it's anyone's guess.

I close my eyes to calm myself and take a deep breath.

Crack.

The sound splinters through me as I imagine my baby all alone on the highway. I snap open my eyes and get up, as if the intrusive thought won't be able to get me if I keep moving.

Something's changed within me. I've lost the foresight to cover my tracks, leaving the body for the police to find. I've become reckless, with nothing left to lose. The woman I was and the woman I am now are strangers to one another; one was too kind, too forgiving. Now I'm nothing but a jumble of broken flesh and bone, held together by a vendetta that seems to be slipping from my grasp.

I walk to the window and look out at the desert, at the smoke rolling in over the mountains.

Today is the day.

Today, I will find Aaron Alexander, and this will finally end.

35

Tobias

The first thing I see when I wake is the face of the man who killed my son.

I lie there for a moment, taking in his features, soft with sleep. The way his lips are parted with a slight droop where he lies on one side; the soft rise and fall of his chest as he breathes.

This isn't the man I expected. I'd seen him before his prison sentence, and I've examined the photos of him printed in the newspapers and pinned to the wall in my wife's study so many times. But along the way, Evelyn and I have been guilty of painting a picture of him that wasn't entirely true. In our minds, he was a selfish, reckless monster who destroyed our lives with malice. A worthless drug addict who hurt anyone who dared to get near him. But meeting him now, witnessing his fragility and his stunted, childlike heart, I don't know what to think. Yes, he is the man who killed Joshua. But he isn't the monster that I have believed him to be all these years. When his age and appearance are stripped away, he's nothing but a boy. A frightened, vulnerable little boy.

Joshua would be twenty, if he were alive today. Around about the age Aaron was when he killed him. I wonder what he would look like now. I try to imagine him with strapping shoulders, a square jaw, and can't. The truth is, I struggle to remember him as he was, let alone imagine what he could have been. I reach towards the bedside table and pick up the photo of him, trying to commit his face to memory again. His angelic eyes. The cowlicks on either side of his hairline. His sweet, gap-toothed smile. The picture is creased and dog-eared from being in my pocket these last few days, and I try to smooth out his beautiful face with my thumbs.

I've probably conjured every thought I possibly could when it comes to my son. I've wondered what college he would have gone to; whether he would have stayed close to home or flown to another state. Whether he'd have had a first girlfriend, or a first boyfriend. What kind of career he might have had. Part of the loss of Joshua isn't just losing the boy we knew, but the man we will never get to meet.

I look over at Aaron on the bed and remind myself not to get too close. I can pity him, but I mustn't warm to him. I mustn't forgive him too easily; I have to remember that despite his fragility, he is still the enemy.

Screw the money. If we stay here another night, I'll get the adjoining room and sleep in there.

I place the photo back on the bedside table and sit up, rubbing my dry eyes. Aaron is still asleep; from the dark circles around his eyes, I'm guessing it's the first time he's properly slept in a long time.

I brush my teeth, wash my face, and get changed into the same clothes I'd worn the day before, my T-shirt stinking at the pits.

When Evelyn left me in the desert, she had taken control and left the rest of us running wildly around her. But now I've changed the game. She should have exhausted all of her avenues by now, missing her chance to find Aaron in Beatty, and again in Reno. She won't have foreseen my finding him first. Now I just need to figure out what to do with him and how to keep them apart.

Aaron begins to stir. I head quietly back through the bedroom towards the door and step out onto the boardwalk.

The desert is the same as when I'd left it. Dry, dead, oppressively hot. The sort of heat that instantly sets your head aching.

Evelyn will be lost now. She won't know which way to turn. And as the stakes rise for her, they inevitably rise for me. This will be my last chance to get through to her; to convince her that the tables have turned, that the thing she wants most is the one thing I will never let her have. I look down at my phone and consider my options. Then I press her number.

I listen to the call ringing through and the pounding of my heart. I only realize I'm holding my breath when she answers.

She doesn't speak. I listen to the sound of her rasping breaths. I know she's hurt before she's even spoken a word.

'We need to talk,' I say.

'Then talk,' she croaks.

Her voice doesn't sound like her; it sounds strained and full of pain. Before all this, I would have jumped to ask if she was all right, to do anything to help. But now there seems to be a gulf between us that's impossible to cross.

'Not on the phone. In person.'

'There's nothing you can do or say to stop me, Tobias. I've told you that.'

'I already have.'

She pauses, and I listen out for signs of where she might be from the background of the call. But all I can hear is her breathing and static on the line.

'I have him, Evelyn. Aaron is with me, and I'm going to do everything I can to keep him from you.'

She's quiet a little while longer.

'I told you that if you got in my way, I'd kill you. Remember?'

'If you do that, then you'll never find him.'

I imagine her biting her tongue to keep from saying what she really wants to say. Biding her time until she can take control of the situation again.

'Where should we meet?' she asks.

'I'll send you the location. We'll meet there at midday.'

I hang up before she can say another word.

I stare out at the horizon and try to fathom how different and far apart we have become. It wasn't like I was talking to my wife at all, it was like we were strangers. I silently fear that the woman I knew and loved cannot be saved. Maybe she is already dead, and this monster is the only part of my wife that's left. But in the same way she needs revenge, I need to believe there is a part of her worth saving. Our pursuits keep us both moving forwards, even if we're headed in opposite directions.

In the silence and calm of the desert, I dare myself to consider the truth that has been killing me inside for as long as I can remember. Such an ugly, revealing thought that I've shut it down every time it began to rear its head. But it's a truth I can no longer outrun.

If I truly loved her, I would stop being so selfish. I'd call the police and get her detained so she can get the help she so clearly needs. She isn't herself, and by letting her run rampant like this, I'm enabling her. All because I'm terrified of what I'll do without her, of the kind of man I'll be when I finally have to stand alone.

I stay with the thought, silently scolding and loathing myself. I'm feeling so much stronger than I did before, so much more independent and able to stand on my own two feet, but I can't seem to cut this final tether. Whatever I do, however far this goes, I just can't seem to let her go.

I'm going to get through to her. She sounds broken and exhausted. Maybe this is the day I finally make her see sense.

I head back into the room. Aaron is awake, sitting on the end of his bed with his jeans pulled on. His eyes are puffy from sleep and, awake, his grief makes him look so much older; I have no doubt that last night's revelations have hit him all over again since waking. The deaths of his lover, his brother. I should know: Joshua's death hits me afresh every day, the moment I open my eyes.

Now you know what it's like to experience a sliver of the pain we feel.

'I'm meeting Evelyn,' I say.

I watch his face pale when I speak her name.

'W-why?'

'To try and talk her round.'

He dashes his hand through his hair, which is wild from sleep.

'And you think she'll listen to what you have to say?'

'I've got to try.'

He doesn't seem convinced.

'Where are you meeting her?' he asks.

'I passed an abandoned industrial yard off Route 95 yesterday. I'll have her meet me there. It's far enough away from here for her not to find you.' I reach into my pocket and check for the dwindled wad of money. 'I'm gonna get you some breakfast and then head off. While I'm gone, you're to stay in here: keep the curtains closed, no looking out the window, and under no circumstances do you leave this room, understood?'

'Okay.'

I pick up the key and the gun I stole, the gun I've yet to use. Loaded with bullets that I could never fire at my wife.

'I'm going to get that room next door after all,' I say.

'I thought you didn't have the money.'

'If the meeting goes according to plan, this should all be over soon, and money won't be a problem.'

I watch him through the mirror hanging on the wall. He nods. Maybe he thought we had bonded a little last night. Hell, maybe we did while my guard was down. But now it's back to the matter at hand.

I go to ask him what sort of food he likes, then I remember who we are to one another. I'm not a father, not anymore, and he's certainly not my son. I'm not here to care for him. I make for the door.

'You dropped this, by the way.'

I turn back to see him holding out the photo of Joshua. My son's little face stares up at me, reminding me of everything that's at stake.

I take the photo and am about to thrust it back into my pocket when I see how creased and worn it is, how his gorgeous face is starting to fade. I cross the room and lock it in the safe hidden in the closet instead, before heading out the door.

36

Evelyn

The meeting place is an abandoned industrial yard off Route 95. There's a garage that was once called Roy's, the signage peeling away in jagged, sand-scoured strips and the glass frontage smashed through; from the trash and mess inside, it looks like it was home to squatters for a while. An old gas station sits nearby, the kiosk boarded up and graffitied over, the metal hoses dangling from the pumps and left to rust. By one of the pumps sits a car, its paint worn away by the sun and desert grass growing from the upholstery where seeds were blown through the broken windows. The yard is off the beaten track now that the desert has reclaimed the road, though the highway is only a little way off in the distance. The whole place feels apocalyptic; a brief glimpse of the end of the world.

I underestimated Tobias when I left him behind in Death Valley. I wasn't sure I'd ever see him again; this is a mission I never expected to come back from. I certainly didn't foresee him having the strength or ability to track me down. He was so self-righteous in his morality, and yet so weak in every other way, that I thought he would find his way home and wait for a wife who would never return. But I was wrong, and now he has the one thing I want.

Just the thought of the two of them together makes me feel

nauseous. How can he possibly protect the man who took from us the one person we loved more than anyone in the world? The one thing we loved more than we loved each other? How can he be in such close proximity to him, breathe the same air as him? How can he bring himself to look that man in the eye?

How can my husband live with himself?

I shade my eyes from the hot sun, my head pounding from dehydration. Looking for cover, I step into the shade under the roof of the gas station; each movement is slow and lethargic due to the meds I've taken and the brandy I've drunk. They've taken the edge off the pain, but it's still undeniably there, pulsing in my swollen jaw, my ribs twinging where Chris Alexander had kicked me with his steel-tipped boots. I run my tongue across the groove in my mouth where the tooth used to be. A bloody plug has formed in its place, and it tastes foul, like an infection is setting in. I spit onto the ground: a brown wad, stained with old blood.

In the distance, a car pulls off the highway and onto the track, dirt billowing from beneath the tyres. There's only one person it could be. When it gets close enough, and we recognize each other from either side of the windscreen, I cross the yard and step into Roy's garage.

The worn seats and desk of the waiting area are covered in sand where the outside is working its way in. It's on the floor too, along with animal excrement and the odd reed of grass growing through the cracks.

I head through a swing door and into the garage itself. Everything of value seems to have been stripped when the last inhabitants left the place, but the pit where the engineers would have lain is still there, along with the metal framework they'd have used to hoist cars up off the floor and empty cabinets where they'd once have kept their tools. One area of the floor is black from an old fire when someone clearly squatted here for a night or two and tried to keep warm as the night drew in.

I hear a car door shut and listen as footsteps crunch on the dry ground, followed by the creak of the door. I remove my gun and pull back the slide to load a bullet.

When Tobias steps inside, we stare at each other without a word, taking in everything that has changed between us.

He looks old. That's the first thing I think when I look at him. He's burnt from the sun, and he appears much skinnier than he did before. The whites of his eyes are bloodshot, his lids are puffy, and there's a dirty bandage wrapped around his arm. I have never seen him look so tired.

I watch as he takes in the sight of me: the swelling, the bruises. Pity washes over his face.

'What on earth happened to you?' he asks.

'I could say the same to you.'

'Evie, your face . . .'

'You wanted to talk,' I say. 'So talk.'

I watch him try to harden himself as I have, drawing back his emotions.

'This has gone on long enough,' he says. 'It stops now.'

'It ends when he's dead.'

'So, you're just going to keep killing people until you get to him, are you?'

He looks at me for a long time, and I sense the shame he has for himself, and the disappointment he has in me.

'How can you possibly stand there and judge me?' I ask. 'You're the one protecting the monster who killed our *son*.'

He flinches, and I'm glad my words cut deep. Protecting that man, the person who created all of this pain and destruction; it's the worst betrayal he could have made.

'I'm protecting you,' he replies.

'No, you're protecting yourself. You have to be the good guy, right? Even if it means betraying the ones you love.'

'You want to talk about betrayal? You left me in the desert to rot. After all we've been through, after our whole world crumbled around us, after I spent the last eleven years trying to pick up the pieces, you cast me aside. All I've ever done is love you, and look out for you, and try to do what's right. Not because I want to be the good guy. But because you and Joshua are my world.'

'If that were true, you wouldn't be protecting *him*.'

'I'm doing it for you. But you're so hell-bent on revenge that you can't see it.' Tears have formed in his eyes, and he turns away. 'God, if Joshua could see us now . . .'

The thought hits me in the chest. I imagine him standing between us, seeing what we've become. The cowardice in his father. The monster in me. The bloating of my face and the gauntness of his father's cheeks.

When I tear myself away from the thought of him, I find Tobias staring at me. There's a strength within him that I haven't seen in a very long time.

'It's over, Evelyn. You're never going to get to him. Not while I'm still standing.'

I raise the gun and point it at his head.

He flinches, but he doesn't back away. I don't know where this sudden bout of bravery has come from, but I resent him for it.

'Do it. Take another life. Push away another person who loves you because you can't bear to expose your heart after Joshua's death broke it. But it won't change the fact that all of this anger, all of this rage, is because you cannot accept that he's gone.'

I step closer, the gun rattling from my anger. A single tear slips down my face.

'Give him to me, and then it's over,' I say, almost in a whisper. 'This all stops if you give him to me.'

'No.'

'I told you I would kill you if you got in my way.'

'If you kill me, you'll never find him,' he says. 'The police are looking for you now. Your face is on every news station. You held up that pharmacy, pointed a gun at a *child*. You've left a trail of bodies and destruction in your wake. They're coming to get you, and they'll catch up soon enough. I've just got to keep him out of your reach until then.'

I stride closer, until the gun is mere inches from his face. His throat jumps.

'Go ahead, shoot me. You'll have no hope of finding Aaron if you do.'

A feral sound crawls out of me. I hate him. I hate him with every fibre of my being.

'I don't know what I was thinking,' he says, looking at me in a new, broken way, his eyes drowning in pity. 'There's no hope of getting through to you, is there?'

We stare at each other on either side of the trembling gun. I grit my teeth and a volt of pain zings to the exposed nerve. I wince and step back, blinking away the tears.

'I'm going to go now, and do what's right in the memory of our son,' he says.

As he turns and walks towards the door, a sound erupts from me, caught somewhere between a sob and a scream. I pull the trigger, the window between the garage and the waiting area shattering loudly. The bullet narrowly misses his head, and he crouches as the glass explodes. When he straightens up, he looks back at me through tears before continuing through the waiting room and out the door.

I feel myself breaking, as if my rib cage is going to crack open and all of the pain and grief of the past eleven years is going to surge out. A confusing, spinning mess that I can't cut through to think straight.

Another gunshot sounds from outside. I bolt through the waiting room and out into the desert.

Tobias is driving up the dirt track. I memorize the make and model of his car, and the registration plate, before rushing to my own. That's when I see what he's done. He's shot out my tyre.

I race after him on foot, choking on my tears and coughing up the dust billowing in his wake. I raise my gun and fire blindly. One shot. Then another. I hear the rear windscreen smash. See the car swerve violently off course before righting itself and ploughing down the path, until it eventually turns onto the highway, just as I trip on the dirt track and fall to the ground, blinded by clouds of grit. I hack it up, spit stringing my lips to the ground, and wipe my face.

When I look up, he's gone.

37

Aaron

I lie on the bed, curled into a ball as the TV plays in the background and the hours tick by on the clock on the wall.

Kyle, dead. Chris, dead. It doesn't feel real yet, as if I need to see them for myself, laid out in a morgue somewhere. Their skin blue and their chests still. Or maybe if I at least knew how they'd died, I could process it more then. I haven't cried; I shed enough tears yesterday to last me a lifetime. Instead, I lie here in silence, shaking and numb. I've been like this for what feels like hours, my knees clutched to my chest, thinking of how Chris and I had finally come together, only for Evelyn Moore to rip us apart. Of how I dared to think I might love Kyle someday, or at least, in the best way I know how. I don't know what's worse: crying myself sick over something like this, or feeling deathly, impenetrably numb. It's the first time since I did it that I wish I hadn't chucked the meth into Walker Lake. I could smoke it now and forget all this. Feel a brief wave of euphoria instead of this soul-crushing pain.

The room is dark from the closed drapes, and so hot that sweat has formed all over me. I finished the water Tobias got me an hour ago, and my mouth has already dried up. God knows when he'll get back – *if* he'll be back. There's no saying what will happen when they meet. If Evelyn is set on killing me, and has killed other people already, then who's to say that her estranged husband will escape her wrath? Maybe she's already shot him between the eyes, and I'm waiting for a dead man to return. If he's not back by nightfall, should I assume he's gone, and think of a way out of here?

I unfurl my legs from the foetal position, sit up, and walk to the window, peering out from between a gap in the drapes. A fly is buzzing between the glass and the bug screen. I slide the screen aside and splat it dead. Whether it died slowly from the heat or fast from my hand, it was going to die either way.

Tobias told me not to leave the room, but if he's meeting Evelyn, surely the only person facing any kind of danger is him. Hell, I haven't seen anyone on the forecourt the whole time I've been stood here.

I grab my wallet and the room key and step out into the day, stopping outside the adjoining room Tobias paid for and peering through the window. It's the same as mine, but arranged in reverse: same beds, same furniture, with the bathroom towards the rear. Tobias had seemed frostier this morning, determined to keep me at arm's length. I was surprised by how much it had hurt.

I walk along the boardwalk towards the stairs and peek over the balustrade, but there's still no one to be seen. There's a flatbed truck that's starting to rust with age and a Civic parked in the shade in front of the office, but nothing else. The vending machine is beneath the walkway by the office door. I'll be down and up again before I can so much as blink.

I'm heading down the stairs and straight for the shade beneath the walkway along the front of the building, when a dog barks at me. It's inside the truck, yelping from behind the window, its breath fogging up the glass. I put my head down and keep walking. I've just slipped my last five-dollar bill from my wallet and reached the vending machine when I hear the cocking of a gun.

'Okay, okay. Yeah, he's here. Checked in last night.'

'Which room?' a low voice asks.

'Come on, man. This is my job on the line here.'

I keep myself hidden behind the bulk of the vending machine and chance a look through the open door to the office. Three men are standing in front of the desk. The one holding the gun is dressed in a baseball cap, checked shirt and tee, combat pants and bulky boots. The man beside him is all in black, his bald head pulsing with thick veins; his gun is holstered at his side. The last man I recognize the moment I set eyes on him: it's the man from the truck. His eye has scabbed over where I melted it shut.

Proud Boys.

'You won't have no job to go to if you're dead,' the man in the cap says.

'I'll call the cops,' the clerk replies stupidly.

'You reckon they'll get here in time to stop me? It'll take them an hour to get out here, maybe longer. It'll only take me a second. That motherfucker stole from me, and no one gets away with that – I ain't gonna stop until he's dead in the back of that flatbed out there. You can either save your own ass or I can throw your skinny rump on the back of the truck with him when I'm done.'

I slowly tiptoe away from the vending machine, my heart pounding. The dog starts barking again, its hot saliva spraying against the window. I turn and sprint for the stairs, taking them two at a time until I'm back on the walkway and running towards the room.

I slam the door shut behind me and rest against it. It smells of body odour and breath and mothballs in here. I should have run round the side of the building and hidden. I should have run a mile through the desert in the opposite direction. Instead, I've run back to a room with no way out. But I didn't steal any truck, and Tobias is driving an SUV; the man I burned isn't here for me. With any luck, they'll focus on whoever they're looking for and the guy who tried to kill me won't know how close he got to finding me like he swore he would.

A gunshot rings out.

I jolt at the sound and freeze.

After a minute or two ticks by, I reach down for my bag, fumbling with the zip, and snatch up my gun. I click off the safety and load bullets from the ammo box, which shakes in my hand like a damn rattle.

I pull back the slide and press myself against the door with a held breath.

There are footsteps on the walkway.

I listen hard, standing in the dark room, rooted to the spot. If I concentrate, I can hear the low hum of male voices. Or maybe it's just my fear playing tricks on me.

Then a crash comes from the room next to mine as the door is kicked in.

I drop to the floor and crawl under the bed, shifting the gun into both hands and aiming it up at the connecting door with my heart in my mouth, listening to the men rip through the room on the other side of the wall: the dresser crashing down on its front, beds flipping over, closet doors thrown open and banging against the wall. Dust drifts down from the ceiling and coats the carpet at the foot of the bed.

The handle on the connecting door rattles. I brace myself and grip the gun tighter. My pulse is drumming all over my body and sweat is dripping into my eyes. I listen to the voices on the other side, low and gruff.

Then the door comes crashing into the room.

I cock the gun towards them and watch as two of the men step inside, only their dirty leather boots visible.

'Where the hell is he?'

'You think the guy lied?'

One of the men yanks the drapes straight off the wall and sunlight bursts in. I flinch as the curtain pole prangs down beside the bed. More dust billows from the drapes as they pool on the floor.

'He'll be back. He's left his shit here.'

In silent terror I look over at my bag where it's resting against the dresser. One of the men gives it a swift kick across the room.

'Hey, I know that bag,' a voice says. 'It's that fag's bag who glued my fucking eye shut.'

'Sure it is,' the other man says.

'I'm telling you, that's his goddamn bag.'

'Chuck,' the second man shouts. 'Bring her in.' He speaks in a lower voice to the first man. 'If our guy's been here, Lexy'll sniff him out.'

I watch as the man named Chuck brings the dog I'd seen earlier, stepping in from the boardwalk and through to the adjoining room. Lexy begins sniffing the carpet, following me by scent rather than sight – if she peered up from the floor, she'd see me staring back at her from beneath the bed with my gun aimed right between her eyes.

I watch in silence as she sniffs about the room before tailing back to the bed, looping from one side to the other. When she gets to the foot again, she raises her nose from the floor and sniffs under the bed.

We lock eyes.

The dog starts growling.

'What you got girl?'

The man on the left reaches down, his fingers hooking onto the underside of the bed. Bile lurches up my throat. He's about to flip it over when I shift my aim and fire a shot straight through his ankle. I see the bone shatter in real time, blood bursting from the flesh. The dog scarpers, pulling away from her leash and bolting back through the adjoining room towards the boardwalk, as the man I shot slams down with a cry. His head hits the floor, parallel to mine.

'*No, no, no!*'

I pull the trigger again and watch his eyes roll back, the life leaking out of them and onto the carpet. I flip around and shoot the next ankle I see. Another man falls to the ground just as the third fires a round of bullets into the bed, blasting feathers and springs all around me as I scrunch into a ball and cover my head. When I hear the chamber empty, I raise my gun just as the bed is thrown to the side, exposing me in a flash. I fire a shot at the man peering over me and watch the bullet clip his neck.

The first man is dead. The second, the man I met before, is fumbling to aim his gun. I point mine at his head and shoot him through his one good eye.

The room falls quiet.

I lie on the floor shaking so violently from the adrenaline that my teeth chatter.

Two of the men now lie lifeless: the first is staring right at me with blood leaking out of his skull, while the other – the man with no eyes – is facing me all the same, crying streams of red tears. The final man has slumped down the wall, his blood smearing the wallpaper as he went. It fills his airways and he starts to choke, clamping both of his hands over the wound to try to stop the flow, but it isn't long before they fall to his lap and his head sinks back, his eyes rolling in their sockets.

I scramble up to a seated position and back myself against the wall, trembling silently. My ears are ringing from the shots. I'm not sure how long I stay there, staring at the dead men, but eventually I get up, stumbling to my feet, dizzy with fear.

I need to get out of here. If anyone else is staying at the motel, they'll have called the cops at the sound of the first bullet, before the men even burst their way in. I fish through the pockets of the dead men until I find the keys to their truck and grab my backpack, slinging the strap over my shoulder and staggering out through the adjacent room.

The sun is blinding, and I grip the balustrade as I head down the steps. There are blood splatters on my hands where I'd aimed my gun at the first man's head; he'd been so close that it had splashed right back at me. My legs are shaking so hard that I'm sure they'll buckle.

Down on the forecourt, the dog has retreated back to the truck. She sees me and cowers, slowly making a loop around the vehicle for cover, her leash trailing behind her.

'Get the fuck out of here!' I yell, running down the rest of the steps. 'Go on! Get!'

I walk towards the truck. The dog is crouched beside it with her tail between her legs. I fire a bullet at the ground.

'*GO!*'

The dog flees, running towards the desert. I walk in the same direction, watching the dirt cloud beneath her paws grow smaller the further she gets, and stop when I'm in line with the door to the motel office. There are blood spatters on the wall, and I spot the clerk's boot sticking out from behind the counter. There seem to be bodies everywhere I turn.

I open the door to the truck and clamber up behind the wheel, before shutting myself in and taking my phone from my backpack.

I could drive off alone; leave Tobias to his wife and let them sort out their own mess. Maybe he isn't coming back at all. But something tells me to stick by him. I'm not sure whether it's my conscience or the fear, but every time I decide I'll go it alone, I can't bring myself to turn the key in the ignition and drive. Even so, I've got to get away from here in case the cops show.

I dry my face with the back of my hand and drive out of the lot. When I'm a mile up the road, I take out my phone, click on Tobias's number with my bloody thumb, and hit call.

38

Tobias

I'm driving down Route 95 trying not to pass out when my phone rings.

My eyelids feel heavy; the shock that had been coursing through me at first is starting to wane, and I'm losing too much blood. My T-shirt is soaked in it where one of Evelyn's bullets smashed through the back windscreen and straight through my shoulder.

I reach for the phone on the passenger seat, the car swerving in the same direction before I snap the wheel back to right the course. The phone slides in my hand. It's Aaron.

The car swerves again, drifting from the highway and onto the desert beside it, dirt pinging on the underside and crunching beneath the wheels. I consider pulling up, but I'm almost there now; I can't risk passing out before I get there. I correct the car's path and answer the call.

'Aaron,' I say. I sound drunk.

'I had to go,' he shouts. 'I had to get out of there.'

'Where are you?'

'I left. I'm on the highway driving south.'

The motel is in view now. I push my foot down on the gas. My eyes are growing heavier and heavier.

'Get back here,' I slur.

'You can't go back there, the cops—'

'I've been shot. I won't make it another five minutes.'

He's silent as I pull off the highway for the motel.

'Shit. Okay, but if you hear sirens you gotta hit the road, no matter how bad you feel. You got that?'

The phone slips out of my hand before I can answer, and I let the car roll to a stop, the bonnet bumping into the side of a Civic with a loud crunch of metal. I lift the handbrake and open the door, hitting the ground with a thud. I lie there coughing up dirt as blood drips onto the cracked earth. Then I hear a growl.

Lexy is crouched beneath the staircase, her hackles up and teeth showing.

'You just don't quit, do you?' I spit on the ground, then stumble slowly to my feet. It doesn't even occur to me to wonder why she might be here, or if I'm starting to hallucinate, seeing blood-hungry dogs that aren't even there.

I drift towards the staircase and start to climb, practically hanging off the railing. My head feels light, and I sway as if I'm about to collapse, but I keep going until I reach the top and drag my feet along the walkway. The door to the second room has been kicked in. I lean my weight against the doorframe and peer inside.

The room has been trashed. Furniture lies in pieces, and the beds have been flipped over. The connecting door has been kicked in too. I stumble towards it and find the bodies.

Three men. Two have been shot in the head while the other is sat upright against the wall with a hole in his neck, blood staining his front like a bib. It takes me a moment to focus, but when my head finally stops spinning, I recognize one of the men: it's the guy I stole the truck from. His cap was shot right off his head.

My eyelids flicker. I shake my head to try to keep my focus, looking about the room to get my bearings: I need to get the photo I'd put in the safe before I pass out.

I stagger over the mess, tripping on one of the men's legs, and drag one of the overturned beds aside with the last few morsels of energy I have, desperate to get to the closet. I fall to my knees before the safe and punch in the code. My eyes blur, and I can barely see the keys. I put it in wrong; it won't open. I try again. It still won't open. I wipe my eyes, feeling sweat and blood slick my palms, and concentrate with all my might. The door clicks open, and I reach in for the photo.

Joshua stares back at me through a film of my bloody fingerprints. His smile. His kind, innocent eyes.

I've got about a minute or two before I'm out for the count. I'm not sure if it's police sirens I can hear or tinnitus, but the sound starts up in my ears until they're ringing like bells.

I climb up and stagger out the door, heading along the walkway towards the stairs and practically falling down them like a drunk, stumbling at the bottom and landing on my ass on the second-to-last step. I lean my head against the railing and stare out at the open road, pleading for Aaron to pull into view.

I look down at the photo of Joshua still in my grip. What would he think of us now? Shooting one another, chasing one another through the desert? After seeing her, I fear there's no saving Evelyn now. She's lost that glint in her eyes that I'd held on to for so long; the good part of her hiding deep beneath the surface. I thought it wouldn't be until she got to Aaron that I'd lose her. Now I fear she's already gone.

I shove the photo into my pocket and close my eyes when I hear a whine at my feet.

It's Lexy, wagging her tail.

'You've got to be kidding me,' I slur, and reach out to pet her. She licks my hand, the fur on her head bloody from my palm.

Then everything goes dark.

*

I wake up to the sound of a dog barking. I'm in the back of the SUV I stole, lying across the seats and looking up at the blue sky rolling by the window.

'Lexy, shut it,' a voice warns from the driver's seat.

I imagine the man in the checked shirt, camo pants and steel-capped boots.

He's got me, I think. *He's finally got me.*

But then I remember seeing him dead with a bullet through his skull. I frown and lift my head. My vision swirls and blurs, but I can just make out the man's face.

Aaron.

I try to talk, but the words come out in a long drawl.

'Where . . . are we going . . .'

'You need to go to hospital.'

'No.'

'We've got to stop the bleeding—'

'Find another way. If we go to the hospital . . . a gunshot wound . . . they'll call the cops.'

My vision swirls again. Nausea crawls up my throat.

'No cops,' I hear myself say.

I listen to the rev of the engine and the sound of the tyres spinning on the highway, loud as a drum through the broken rear screen.

'Okay,' he replies. 'No cops.'

I breathe a sigh of relief, and then my eyes drift shut.

39

Evelyn

After Tobias left me in the desert and I discovered the car didn't have a spare tyre stowed away, I hiked back onto the highway and tried to hitch a ride for a good hour until someone finally pulled over to help: a man transporting live chickens headed for slaughter. I waited until I was in the passenger seat before pulling my gun on him. I drove away without looking back, as the chickens squawked in the back of the truck and the man grew smaller in the side mirror, feathers drifting on the wind in my wake. The old me couldn't have done something that cruel, but the woman I am now, with a closing window of opportunity to avenge my son's death, can't feel anything but cold determination.

I drove without any direction, not knowing where to head next, popping pills whenever the pain spiked. I'd exhausted all of my options. It was only when I was halfway there, driving through the growing smoke, that I realized where I was headed: I was driving to the place where I'd started, to find out where I should head next.

I pass the welcome sign for Beatty in a haze of pain. My face is still swelling, and the taste in my mouth grows more and more foul with each hour that passes.

The town is dark with the smoke drifting in from the desert, lit only by the blue lights of cop cars. They're down every road, knocking on every door. I lower the window to hear an officer talking into a megaphone.

'*This is a notice to evacuate. Please congregate in the designated areas to prepare for transportation. Choosing to stay will likely result in loss of life.*'

I raise the window and drive on until I reach the gas station, parking across the street and looking at Jim behind the counter. Cars are lined up waiting to get their gas and drive the hell out of Beatty, each driver pulling in and filling their tanks until the wells run dry and the pumps close.

I wait until his shift ends and the line of cars has dispersed, spitting out of the window as I watch. My saliva had been brown from old blood, but now I'm spitting pus.

Jim heads out of the garage towards his car, a beaten-up Honda, one of the taillights kept in place by duct tape and hope. He pulls away and I start up the engine and follow him all the way home. He lives west of the town, in a shabby house on a nice, quiet street. I watch him park and head to his door, greeting his cats as they congregate around his feet. He steps inside and closes the door behind him.

I step out of the car. The day is growing cooler as the sun sinks in the sky. Shadows are already beginning to creep from beneath the trees lining the road. A pang of hunger hits me, and I can't remember the last time I ingested something that wasn't alcohol or a narcotic.

I knock on the door and retrieve my gun. When Jim opens the door, I aim it directly at his head. I watch the colour drain from his face, before he slowly stands aside without a word, letting me pass.

Then I knock him over the head and close the door behind me.

*

Jim comes to, tied to a dining chair in the middle of the room. His eyes roll in their sockets until he finally has the strength to focus. His temple is bruised where I struck him. I pour myself a sherry from the bottle I found in one of the cupboards while I was looking for supplies to tie him up, but all I taste is rot from my wound.

The cat travel crates are lined up beside him: two on his left, and one on his right. He notices them first, staring down at them with a frown, then he sees me sitting before him and his confusion sinks away. He sits in silence, transfixed by the gun that I'm pointing at his gut.

'Welcome back, Jim.'

He goes to speak and saliva oozes from his lips. He tries to suck it back.

'What do you want?' he asks. His tongue sounds lazy in his mouth, as if he's downed a bottle of Jack.

'I need to find Aaron, and you're going to tell me where he'd go next or direct me to someone who'll know.'

'You look like shit,' he says. 'I've told you everything I know.'

I pull back the slide on my gun. His freezes at the sound.

'Don't lie to me, Jim.'

'It's true. I told you where his mom lives.'

'You know more about him than that.'

'Maybe I do. But I'm not telling you a thing.'

We stare each other down, but he's the first to look away. He sighs against the ropes keeping him upright.

'No one's saying what he did wasn't bad, ma'am. But he did his time for it. He's paid his dues.'

'I doubt you'd be saying that if it was your child he killed.'

'Maybe I wouldn't. But he's a good lad who's had a bad life and made bad decisions. He's caused you a lot of pain. But that doesn't give you the right to take a life in return.'

'And you get to decide this, do you?'

'No ma'am, that's the law who decides that. What he did was an accident. What you're setting out to do is cold-blooded murder. They ain't the same.'

I down another tumbler of sherry in one, enjoying the hot sting.

'Here's how it's going to go, Jim.' I wipe my mouth with the back of my hand. 'I'm going to ask you a question, and every time you fail to answer me, or every time you lie, I'm going to pull the trigger.'

I aim the gun at the first crate.

'You get to decide how this goes.'

He follows the direction of the gun and looks back at me pleadingly.

'Please don't do this.'

'Answer my questions, and I won't.'

'I can't . . .' he whispers.

'You can, you just don't want to. Now . . .' I pour another sherry, knock it back. 'Where would Aaron go next?'

I watch the veins rise on his forehead and his face flush.

'Fuck you,' he spits.

I pull the trigger.

He jumps at the sound, knocking tears from his eyes. His mouth falls open.

'No! Please stop!'

'You're the only one who can make this stop.' I aim the gun towards the next crate. 'Where would he go, Jim?'

'I don't know!'

I pull the trigger. A short sob bursts up his throat.

'*Stop it!*'

'*You are the only one who can make this stop,*' I shout back.

He sits sobbing silently, his shoulders juddering with his cries. Spit spools from between his lips.

I shift my aim to the final crate.

'If you don't know where he'd go, then who does?'

He looks up at me through his tears, drool glistening on his lips and chin.

'Go to hell.'

I fire another bullet. A faint line of smoke creeps out of the crate as Jim continues to cry, the ropes binding him to the chair the only things keeping him upright.

I aim the gun at his head.

'Last chance.'

I stare at him, the gun steady in my grip. A broken man looks back at me. I watch the thoughts flit through his mind. I think of Tobias, how he clings on to his self-righteousness, his view of right and wrong despite the odds, despite what's at stake. These men, they're all the same. It's not a virtue, it's a narcissistic need to be seen as good men. I don't admire them, I pity them. They're the ones who lose in the end.

'Is he worth dying for?' I ask. 'Is being a good man worth your life?'

He blinks back his tears, inhales deeply through chattering teeth.

'His probation officer, Andrea,' he says finally. 'She'll know more about his history and where he might go.' He nods towards a box on the console. 'Her card is in there.'

'Thank you, Jim.'

He looks at me, waiting for me to lower the gun, his expression falling when it remains aimed at his head.

'I told you everything I know.'

'I know,' I reply.

Then I pull the trigger.

I watch as his life flashes before his eyes, hear his breath shudder out of him with relief when he realizes there were no more bullets in the chamber.

A sound comes from the closed door off the living room, and he turns towards it.

Meow.

He looks at the crates, then back at me.

'The crates were empty,' he says. 'The crates were *fucking empty.*'

I get up without a word, collecting Andrea's card and passing him on my way to the door as he sobs with relief. I'm about to step out when he calls to me.

'How did you know the gun was empty when you pulled the trigger?'

I look at the sad excuse of a man tied to the chair, sniffling back tears, his back to me and his eyes fixed on the place where I'd sat.

'I didn't,' I reply, and shut the door behind me.

40

Aaron

I stand in the latest motel room, about thirty miles away from the last, looking down at the supplies I've arranged on the bedside table: a penknife, a blowtorch, a half-drunk bottle of whisky and a first aid kit. Inside are a roll of bandages, tape and a half-used tub of antiseptic ointment.

This is going to hurt like hell.

I look down at Tobias where he's passed out on one of the beds; Lexy is lying on the other, watching me cautiously and wagging her tail whenever I look her way. I try not to look too often; every time I do, I remember us locking eyes when I was hiding beneath the bed. Just before I pulled the trigger and killed three men. I scrunch my eyes shut: I can't think about that yet.

I'm not sure why I took the dog. But when I turned up and found Tobias passed out on the step, she was lying by his feet protectively. She'd growled at me at first. But after I used the last of my money buying a pack of chips from the vending machine and scattered them over the dirt, she ran over to them and ate them all up, giving me time to throw Tobias's arm over my shoulder and lead him to the SUV. The truck I stole was almost out of gas, and the SUV had more room, even if the rear windscreen had been shot out. I'd cleared the glass, so it didn't look so obvious, and gone round to

the front of the car to get inside, when I saw Lexy sitting patiently
by the door, wagging her tail and waiting to be let in.

I guess I have a dog now.

I'd found the blowtorch, the whisky and the penknife in the
dead man's truck, and the first aid kit came from the clerk behind
the counter downstairs. Under Lexy's watchful eye, I remove the
towel from Tobias's gunshot wound, and a fresh load of blood
trickles out. I give him a light shake and call his name, but he's
out cold. His skin is grey from blood loss. I shake him again, a
little harder this time. His eyes move behind their lids.

'Tobias, I need to stop the bleeding.'

He mumbles something in reply.

'It's going to hurt. I need you to open your eyes and listen
to me.'

He comes to and looks up at me as if it's taking all of his
strength.

'I've got to cauterize the wounds, okay?'

He frowns, not understanding. I raise the knife and the blow-
torch for him to see. His face turns completely white.

'Do you trust me?'

He takes a while, but he nods. 'Yeah,' he slurs. 'I trust you.'

It surprises me how much this means, making me feel soft. I
steel myself – I can't be anything but determined for what I'm
about to do.

'Bite down on this.'

I take the fresh towel that I've wound like a rope and put it
between his teeth.

'However much it hurts, you can't scream, okay?'

I splash whisky on the wound; the only thing I have that's
remotely close to disinfectant. He arches up from the bed with
the pain, spittle bubbling round the towel. Lexy's ears shoot up.

'I'm sorry,' I say, as I pick up the knife and the blowtorch. I
heat the tip of the knife until it's glowing like lava. The whole

time, Tobias watches, looking up at the fluorescent blade in silent
horror. Lexy lets out a quiet growl.

'Remember, don't scream. She'll go for my throat if you do.'

He nods slowly. There are tears in his eyes already.

I climb on top of him, pinning his arms down with my knees
and pressing his abdomen beneath me.

'Take a deep breath and hold it.'

I wait until he has heaved in as much air as he can around the
towel before I press the tip of the knife to the wound.

He writhes beneath me, screaming into the towel with tears
running down his face.

'I'm sorry.'

I raise the blade to check the wound then press down again,
keeping a watchful eye on the growling dog as I go. Tobias is
about to pass out by the time I climb off him.

'I need you to turn over so I can do the other side.'

A muffled sob slips from his lips, but he does as he's told, turn-
ing onto his side and flopping over. The bed is soiled with blood.
He lies on his front with his head to the side and bites into the
towel so hard that his lips turn white.

I splash whisky on the second wound and then climb back on
top of him to pin him down again. Only this time he has no fight
left, and merely groans as I cauterize the entry wound. I work fast
while trying not to breathe in the scent of burning flesh.

When it's finally done, he's out cold. I roll him onto his side and
remove the towel from between his teeth, dousing it with whisky
to wipe down the wounds once more. I lather them in ointment
and dress them with the bandages from the first aid kit, before
perching on the edge of the bed with a sigh. I should have enough
supplies left to replace the bandage on his arm too.

'Sleep now,' I say, before swigging whisky straight from the bottle.

*

I sit outside and watch the sun descending in the sky, the bottle of whisky in one hand while I stroke Lexy with the other as she lies beside me with her head in my lap.

The last eleven years of my life have been plagued by killing someone. Now I've killed three more. I sit with that realization, while the memory of the scene plays in a loop in my mind, their heads bucking with the shots, blood bursting out and painting the walls; the life leaving their eyes one by one, and the silence that came afterwards. This whole time, I've been wondering how this journey will end. Whether Evelyn will catch me, or if I can keep running. But now I know that if I'm not killed myself, I'll be sent back to jail for killing three men. Self-defence doesn't sound so good when it's claimed by an ex-convict who's done time for manslaughter. They'll make sure to lock me up and throw away the key this time. But if this is what freedom is like – running for my life, existing on adrenaline and fear, killing people before they can kill me and losing people I love – then perhaps it won't be so bad to be locked away again. That's what I tell myself, to keep the terror at bay.

I think of the clean shots I made, the precision and the focus that feel so foreign to me usually. I pulled the trigger and didn't miss once. The kid who learnt to shoot to make his brother proud, and to keep from being hit. I think of Chris again, then Kyle, and long to feel numb.

The door to the motel room creaks open.

Lexy lifts her head from my lap; her tail wags lightly against the boardwalk when she sees Tobias.

He looks better than he had before he'd slept. He'll have produced more blood while he rested and made up for some of what he lost. But he still looks deathly pale, and walks as if he's asleep on his feet. He sits down on the other side of me with a thump.

'Someone's made a friend,' he says.

'She'll come to you if you feed her,' I reply wryly. 'How're you feeling?'

'Like shit.'

We stare out at the view, the sun slowly setting on the horizon.

'How are you doing?' he asks. 'I went into the room, back at the last motel. I saw what happened.'

After all the pain I've caused him and his wife, he's asking if I'm okay. I don't know how to take it, my body squirming in the face of his compassion. I can't find the words and simply nod.

'Thank you,' he says.

'For what?'

'For coming back. You didn't have to.'

'Sure I did.'

I pass him the bottle and he takes it gladly, gulping from it to numb the pain until there's a trail of liquor slipping from the corner of his mouth. He lowers it and gasps for breath.

'How'd you learn to do that?' he asks. 'Seal a wound?'

I clear my throat, wishing I had some weed to mellow me out and keep me from feeling. Some memories are better off buried, but whether it's from the exhaustion or the whisky, I feel myself opening up.

'My stepdad shot my mom once. She wouldn't call the cops; she said they'd take me and my brother away. My brother was out, so it was me who helped her with it; she told me what to do. I don't know how she learnt to do it, I never thought to ask. Kids think moms know everything at that age, don't they?'

Tobias is looking at me tentatively, as if truly seeing me for the first time. As someone who prefers not to be seen, I feel myself squirm again, and vow not to drink any more. I've drunk too much, said too much already.

'How old were you, when that happened?'

I shrug. 'Seven, maybe eight.'

'Jesus. That's no life for a kid.'

'It was the only one I knew.'

'Is that why you turned to drugs?'

Sadness floods my chest. I hate to think back and try my best to keep it all buried. I want to stay sealed up, keep my secrets close. But I guess he of all people deserves to know.

'I met a guy when I was sixteen. Billy, his name was. Thought he loved me, that old story. But I didn't know what love was; I only knew what pain felt like. When he was mean to me, it felt . . . normal. Anyone else would have left, but I guess I didn't know any different. He was a meth-head, and it wasn't long before he got me on the pipe too. The drugs helped numb that pain for a while, even though it ended up creating more of it along the way, and then I'd have to take more drugs to numb that. An endless cycle of drugs and pain and fear, until I don't really remember all that much. It's just a haze.'

'And the night it happened . . .' he says. 'What was going on?'

I take a deep breath, blinking back the tears as soon as they appear.

'I tried to leave him. I'd found a job in San Diego and saved up for a room of my own. I planned to sweat myself out in there and get clean, then start a normal life. I slipped away in the night, and I really thought I'd done enough for him not to find me, but somehow he did; he always did. He drove to San Diego, dragged me out, and was taking me back. He was too fucked-up to drive, so I had to get behind the wheel and drive us home, all while he shouted at me, punched me. He took the odd break to smoke meth until the whole car was filled with it and I was high as hell from the fumes. I just remember the drive taking forever. Each mile felt like a year. I was fucked-up, he was fucked-up. I just drove while he yelled and hit me. Looking back now, I'm so angry that I didn't think to stop the car. I could've got out and refused to drive any further. But I just did what I was told; I did what I had to do to survive. And then it happened.'

My mind takes me back there. I see a flash of the memory: the bend in the highway, the pitch-black desert, darkness as thick as hands covering my eyes. We took the bend, and there was Joshua in the middle of the road. It happened so fast, quicker than a blink.

'He told me to keep going, but I was frozen, even as he hit me. I always did that as a kid too. I got scared and I froze. That's when he put his gun to my head to make me move. So, I did as I was told and kept driving.'

I come back from the memory and feel the tears itching on my cheeks. I dash them away.

'He would have killed me sooner or later, I can see that now. I guess going to prison saved my life.' Tobias is offering me the bottle again. This time, I take it. 'He's dead now, or so I heard. His meth lab blew, took him and his friends with it.'

I swig from the bottle.

'You never said there was someone else in the car, Aaron.'

'I was behind the wheel and Billy said there was no point two of us going to prison. He made it make sense at the time. I've never really talked about it.'

There's a long, drawn-out silence. Lexy sighs, her hot breath warming my lap.

'What do we do now?' I ask.

I look at Tobias, at the man who finally seems to have softened towards me. Whenever I used to think of the father of the boy I killed, I never expected I'd ever get to know him, and I certainly never dreamt of liking him. Not in a million years.

'I'm going to take you to the one place she won't expect,' he says. 'Home.'

41

Evelyn

I knock on the door to Andrea Martin's office, listening to the shuffle of papers and the click of computer keys before she answers.

'Come in.'

I open the door and shut it behind me without a word.

'Can I help you?' she asks.

'Yes, I believe you can.'

I watch her expression drop as she takes in my swollen, battered face. The room falls quiet but for the clock ticking on the wall.

'Do you have an appointment?' she asks, checking her schedule on the computer screen with a furrowed brow as I sit down on the other side of the desk. I pull the gun on her, and her frown vanishes.

'I'm here about Aaron Alexander. I need his file.'

Her eyes remain glued to the gun. I watch as a thousand thoughts flit behind them and wonder to myself who and what she is thinking of, amidst the fear. It's amazing to watch what happens to a person when a gun is pulled on them. Everything they thought they were is scattered to the wind.

'Well ... I'm afraid that's confidential. I can't just—'

I raise my hand, cutting her short.

'I am so sick of people talking about rules, about right and wrong. I followed the rules all my life, and then my son was killed and my life fell apart. Sticking to the rules didn't do me a damn bit of good.'

We sit in silence. She is still staring at the gun.

'Right and wrong didn't save my child. The rules didn't keep Aaron Alexander in prison where he belonged. The rules aren't designed to protect you, Ms Martin.'

She swallows nervously. Her mouth will be dry, adrenaline sapping all moisture from it.

'You're the woman from the news,' she says. 'The woman who robbed the pharmacy and killed that man in the motel.'

I nod once, matter-of-factly.

'Do you have a child, Andrea?'

It's clear that she does before she utters a word. Tears spring into her eyes the moment she thinks of them.

'A girl, Casey. She's two years old.'

'How would you feel if someone killed her and got away with it?'

'It would break me.' Her chin begins to tremble. She pats the tears on her cheeks as they fall. 'I'm very sorry about what happened to your son, Mrs Moore.'

'Don't be sorry, just do as I ask. Get me his file and answer a few of my questions, and you'll get to go home to Casey.'

She wrestles with the decision in silence, but not for long. She's thinking of her daughter, of life and death rather than right and wrong. A wise woman.

She nods slowly.

'Good. Where's the file?'

She raises a shaking hand to point to the filing cabinet in the corner of the room.

'In there.'

'Go get it.' I shift the gun and aim it at her head. She jolts. 'Keep your hands where I can see them.'

She gets up from her chair with her hands up. When she turns towards the cabinet, I can see how violently her legs are shaking; the fabric of her skirt is quivering at her knees. She flicks nervously through the files and slips one free. I follow her with the gun as she sits back down and places the file on the desk.

'What did you want to ask me?' she says.

I open the file, my gun never leaving her, reading as I talk.

'I need to know where Aaron would feel safe; where he would go if he were on the run.'

'Is he? Running?'

'I wouldn't be here if he wasn't,' I reply, scanning the pages, flipping more and more violently with each dead end.

'He has a . . . friend,' she says.

'Kyle's dead.'

She doesn't say anything for a moment, and I look up from the page. She's crying silently. When she catches me looking, she frantically tries to think of another name.

'He has a brother in Reno.'

'Also dead. Who else?'

'Um . . .' She wipes away the tears. 'I don't know who else. He didn't have many people to turn to. Maybe someone from Narcotics Anonymous.'

'No. He wouldn't go back to Beatty. Where would he run to? Somewhere far? Did he make any friends in prison who've been released?'

'No. He kept to himself. Says so in his file.'

'There isn't shit in here, Andrea.'

She looks down at the file desperately, as if the answers will appear if she longs for them hard enough.

'I'm sorry. I don't know what else I can tell you.'

'So, you're wasting my time.'

I get up and walk around the desk towards her. She looks up at me through her tears. She is shaking so violently that I can hear the chair squeaking.

'Please don't kill me . . . my daughter . . .'

'I'm not going to kill you,' I reply. 'We're just going for a little walk.'

*

I look down at Andrea Martin, gagged and bound in the trunk of her car.

'Wait an hour, then make all the noise you want. But no earlier than an hour.'

She looks up at me, tears slipping down her face and over her taped, gagged mouth. She nods.

I yank the emergency cord from the door of the trunk to keep her from getting out and slam it shut, watching her wide, terrified eyes as they are thrust into darkness.

When I'm a good distance away, I chuck the cord on the ground and head across the lot towards Jim's car. I'd taken it when I'd left his place, leaving the truck full of chickens squawking on his driveway.

I get inside but have no idea where to go next. It's one dead end after another.

I feel the anger bubbling away, building within me until I strike out suddenly and punch the dashboard over and over, the skin peeling from my knuckles. I watch blood bloom out of the cuts before taking a deep breath and turning the key in the ignition.

I pull out of the lot with no idea where I'm headed.

*

I sit at the bar, listening to the other punters around me and knocking back a tumbler of brandy. The tavern has been wood-panelled to within an inch of its life: there's varnished wood on the floor, the ceiling, the walls, the furniture. The other drunks keep to themselves, the only sounds the knock of snooker balls from the table in the corner.

My head is swimming from exhaustion, from all the booze and pills. I should eat, but I'm still not sure I'd be able to keep anything down. I try a handful of salted peanuts from the bar, chewing them on the good side of my mouth, but the pain kicks up again so I order another brandy instead, defeated. The barman nods, avoiding my eyes as he serves it up, charging almost fifteen dollars for the pleasure. He takes a sly glance at my swollen, cut hand, the blood dried on the knuckles. He'd given me that same look when he first saw my swollen face as I walked in.

I gaze down at the tumbler of brandy, trying to ignore the pain thrumming through me, the violent pulsing from my jaw. Sadness keeps bubbling up, wetting my eyes, and sinking back down again. I had it all planned out, and it's gone so spectacularly wrong. But mostly I feel like there's something wrong with me. My strength and hardness comes in waves, allowing me to do cruel, callous things to people, before it recedes again and leaves me with nothing but guilt and doubt.

I taste the infection in my mouth every time I swallow. I have aches and pains all over my body from this journey, but the physical discomfort is nothing compared to the weight in my chest that appears when the next song comes on the jukebox.

Joshua loved this song. I can't even remember the name of it now, I just remember his smile whenever he heard it playing, and the memory of him dancing to the beat, swaying his little hips, the laughter that always followed. Tears run silently down my cheeks.

I come to and find the barman looking at me again.

'*What?*' I snap.

He shrugs and looks away. I hadn't noticed it too much before, but he seems nervous about something. Extremely nervous. That's when I catch the sound of the approaching sirens in the distance, calling over the song on the jukebox.

The barman is trembling now. He's drying a glass with a cloth which is shaking in his grip. As the sirens get louder, he shakes harder.

The cruisers appear outside the bar one by one, their flashing blue lights reflecting off my car out front. I've just lost my ride and everything in it.

I turn to the barman and raise my gun. The fucker who called the cops on me.

'Lead me out back. Now.'

The punters around me had been looking at the cop cars outside, but as soon as they catch sight of my gun, they all begin ducking beneath tables and behind stools. A woman screams. I ignore them all, keeping my eyes on the barman. He nods quickly, going to place the glass on the side of the bar and missing by an inch. It shatters on the floor, making the woman scream again.

He heads towards the door leading out back. I follow behind him, keeping my eyes trained on the cops outside before walking through the doorway with the gun aimed at the back of his head.

'You called the cops on me, huh?' I ask, as he takes me through the kitchen. The workers stop one by one as they see us pass, their mouths hanging open.

'It wasn't me, I swear.'

'Sure it wasn't. Walk faster.'

I prod the back of his head with the barrel; he whimpers before quickening his pace and opening the back door, which leads to an alleyway.

'You're lucky I'm low on bullets.'

I smack the handle of my gun into his crotch as I pass and bolt down the alley.

I've lost my weapons. The car. The pills. The files I had from the private investigator and Andrea Martin. I've lost Aaron to Tobias. I have no way out of here, nor the faintest idea where to go.

The sky is growing dark, and the air has a nip to it as night rolls in. I keep running until I reach the neighbouring block.

A couple in their mid-thirties are headed to a car parked by the sidewalk; an old Lincoln that's more of a relic than something to be admired. I can hear the cops behind me, pouring through the back door of the bar and into the alley. I have mere seconds until they turn the corner and spot me.

When I raise my gun, the woman screams and the man instinctively steps in front of her.

'Keys. Now.'

He throws them to me, and I snatch them from the air.

'Step back. Onto the sidewalk.'

I watch them move, keeping their eyes on me as I head round the car. I clamber in and drive away, the tyres screeching against the tarmac from the force.

The road swirls ahead of me after one too many. It's almost night now. I turn on the headlights as I drive to nowhere with nothing to my name. All I have is my gun, a few remaining bullets and my purse. I don't know where I'm headed or what I'll do when I get there.

All I know is, I've got nothing else to lose.

42

Tobias

We drive in the direction of San Diego in comfortable silence. At least, comfortable in the sense that we've grown used to one another. In every other sense, I couldn't be experiencing more discomfort if I tried. The wound in my shoulder is burning like it's on fire.

Aaron is driving. He's been quiet since the motel. He has killed before, but there's a difference between an accidental killing and intentionally pulling the trigger of a gun. And not just one person this time, but three.

When I used to picture Aaron, before I met him, I'd failed to envisage the softness he has, the fragility. Before, he was made up of hard edges, reckless decisions and remorse only for his own sake, rather than Joshua's and ours. I never could have imagined how compassionate and nuanced he would turn out to be. He cares without having to try; his kindness isn't a choice, it's an integral part of who he is. It's something you can feel emanating from him, this caring for those around him before himself. I almost wish he wasn't this way; that he was evil, someone I could hate freely. But now that I've met him, I cannot escape the truth.

Aaron is a good man who made a terrible mistake.

To think of the death of my son and the fracturing of my life as a mere accident doesn't sit right in my mind; a puzzle piece that won't quite fit whichever way I turn it. But I cannot escape the truth now, even if I can't bear for it to be so.

I watch him as he drives and try to see his mother in him. She had been harder, more selfish, but the kindness she had shown me when she treated the wound to my arm was perhaps a glimpse of who she used to be. Maybe she was as kind as Aaron once, but life wrung it out of her. I wonder how Aaron made it this far without that soft heart of his steeling itself up entirely.

A couple of years before Joshua was born, Evelyn had confided in me how lonely she felt after the death of her parents. She hadn't felt buoyed when I'd told her that she wasn't alone, that I was there for her.

It's a different love. You could leave tomorrow. The love of a good parent means you're never truly alone, because you'll always have someone on your side, someone who will never leave you. That's until they do, and all you're left with are relationships that could end, and people who could leave. Losing an anchor you didn't know you needed until it's gone, and realizing you never got to thank them, or apologize for taking them for granted while you had them.

Looking at Aaron, I know now why he is the way he is, and why his life has turned out like it has. He's never had an anchor. He's in a perpetual state of waiting: waiting for people to leave him, never knowing unconditional love. A large, lonely heart with no one to love and no one to protect it.

I hear a sigh: Lexy is dozing on the back seat, her body vibrating with the car as it barrels down the highway. Anyone else would have left the dog to fend for itself. Another example of Aaron's compassion.

I look out of the window at the desert and the night sky, wondering what Evelyn is doing right now and where she might be. If she could read my thoughts – silently forgiving Aaron, putting our son's death down to a cruel twist of fate – she would never forgive me. Perhaps I even believed these things to be true before I met Aaron, but I was too frightened of losing her to consider them, even within the confines of my own mind.

I think of how she had looked when we met in the desert: her face swollen and the blood of murdered men beneath her fingernails. There is a part of me that knows I have to accept that the woman I knew before we lost Joshua is gone; that she has wandered too far into this wilderness of grief and lost her way. That I must accept that I'm unlikely to ever get all of her back. But however hard I try, I can't shake the glimmer of hope within me. Hope that something within her is still salvageable. That if I just keep pushing, I might be able to save her in the end.

The booze I drank has worn off and the pain is creeping back, as if my wound is waking up from a slumber. I'd close my eyes again if I could, but it'll be too much to sleep through now, and I need to stay awake to tell Aaron where to go.

The thought of home doesn't bring the comfort it used to. Before, I had Joshua and Evelyn waiting for me. I would see Joshua sitting by the window looking out for the car and watch his face light up as he spotted me turning into the cul-de-sac. I'd watch him dart out of view and before I'd even got out, he'd have the front door thrown open. I'd clamber out and drop to my knees to greet him as he ran into my open arms, clamping him in a hug as he practically threw himself into the embrace. Evelyn would stand at the door, laughing to herself. We were happy, and I mean truly happy. That was so long ago now, and sometimes I wonder if the scene is real, or whether it's a beautiful dream I created to make up for the memories of him that I've lost.

Now, the only thing awaiting me at home is emptiness. Empty hallways. Empty rooms. The sort of grief that sinks its teeth into you and doesn't let go.

'Do you think she'll ever come back from this?' Aaron asks,

tugging me away from my thoughts. He glances my way briefly, taking his eyes off the road before returning them to the highway. He'd been thinking of her too. I look out of the window again and into the darkness.

'I don't know.'

Many people would have given up by now; given up trying to see the good in someone who is determined to stamp it out. But I know where the rage comes from. I know that it's merely masking her heartbreak.

'It's difficult to understand when you didn't know her before. But whenever I look at her or think of her, I remember how she was at the hospital when the doctor told us Joshua had died. It wasn't a scream she let out. It wasn't a cry. It was the most agonizing wail I have ever heard.'

I remember watching the pain pummel her in real time. Her legs buckled, but not gracefully like in the movies; the news floored her, suddenly and violently. She hit the ground and wailed for what felt like hours. She wouldn't let me touch her; she just howled and howled.

The doctors finally sedated her, and she didn't fight them. Her eyes begged for the needle as they brought it in, pleading for them to take the pain away. They guided her to a bed, and when she woke up, I watched her heart break all over again as she remembered he was gone. She'd looked at me with the innocence of a child, staring at me in hopeful wonder, silently asking *was it all a dream?* Tears filled my eyes, and she knew. The wailing started up again. She took another needle and passed out.

'That's what I think about, when I see her rage,' I continue. 'Not the monster she appears to be, but all of the pain that's inside of her. The agony she's in. But she's so blind to her own grief, so terrified to feel all of that pain. She's been this way for so long now that she can't let go. She can't let *him* go.'

Aaron is quiet, listening intently.

'You actually remind me a lot of her,' I say. 'You know, before. She had the biggest heart.'

He says nothing, and I look away.

'What will you be like after?' I ask.

'After?' The surprise in his tone makes it seem like he's not thought of a future for himself beyond this.

'What do you want to do with your life when this is over?'

He is silent for a long time, so long that I wonder if he'll reply at all.

'I guess I'll think about that when I get there,' he finally says.

I look outside as we pass a road sign. Over fifty miles to go until we pass Joshua Tree. My son always believed the park was named after him.

'Not too long now,' Aaron says.

I nod before closing my eyes again, and try to sleep.

43

Aaron

'Wait here,' Tobias says, as I pull up outside the house.

I watch him struggle out of the car and limp towards the front door. It's one in the morning, and all of the houses in the cul-de-sac are dark. I'd expected them to live somewhere wealthy, but the real thing is still different from what I'd imagined all these years. Even at night, I can see the manicured front lawns and rosebushes, the expensive-looking drapes shielding the windows, the latest car models parked on the driveways. The Moore household is *Father of the Bride*-type shit. It feels like a whole different world to mine. Lexy stands up on the back seat and watches Tobias through the window, stretching and wagging her tail. I bet it's a whole different world for her too.

Tobias looks through the windows on either side of the front door, before retrieving a spare key from a coded box and letting himself in. Lights go on inside, throwing a golden hue through the downstairs rooms. He reappears at the door and beckons me in.

I step out of the car, calling Lexy to follow. She hops into the front seat, then down onto the driveway. She urinates on the lawn as we pass, then dutifully trots beside me, her tail still wagging.

I freeze before the doorstep, and the dog does too. It feels inherently wrong, my being here. I'm about to step into the house of the family I destroyed. The guilt had been immeasurable before, but now I'm seeing more of their lives I can also see for myself in real time how much pain my actions caused. This house feels like a home. It's not a trailer that shudders with the desert breeze. It's not a studio apartment with only enough cutlery for one. It's a home, made for love and cherished memories and all the things I've never known. Lexy sniffs at the air, creeping towards the open door.

'Come on,' I say quietly, and step inside.

The house smells homely; of furniture polish and something sweet. Oak herringbone flooring runs from the entrance hall through to the rest of the downstairs floor. I only know what it's called because I read a magazine in prison one time when the options were slim. It was then I realized how different the rich and the poor are from one another. We didn't even have floorboards in our trailer, just scuffed lino that was turning black with mould.

I look down the hall, through to the dining room at the end and, beyond that, the kitchen. To my left is the door to the living room; to my right is a downstairs bathroom and the entrance to a study, one wall studded with pins.

Lexy is still standing outside, sniffing at the air and cowering a little.

'Come on,' I say again softly, coaxing her in. She steps inside, one tentative paw at a time, and I shut the door behind her. I see Tobias has taken off his shoes, so I take mine off too.

'Through here,' Tobias calls.

I walk through to the dining room, past a table for eight that sits beneath an elaborate chandelier. The kitchen is bigger than my entire studio apartment. It's got quartz countertops, a large island and a breakfast nook at the other end of the room, nestled in a large bay window overlooking the garden. Lexy's claws tap against the hardwood floor as she follows behind me like a shadow.

Tobias is going through a kitchen cupboard. He retrieves a first aid kit to re-dress his wound and a large Tupperware full of meds. I watch as he finds a glass dish and fills it with water for the dog; Lexy laps it up fast and wets the floor, as I look around and try to imagine how it would feel to call a house like this home.

'We should get clean and then eat something,' Tobias says, placing a glass of water in front of me on the island counter. It's a crystal glass. I don't think I've ever drunk out of crystal before. I stare at the intricate pattern, too afraid to pick it up in case I break it.

I wonder how he feels having me here, if it feels as strange to him as it does to me. I'm too thirsty to resist any longer and lift the glass to down the lot.

'I'll show you to your room. The dog can stay with you for the night, till we figure out what to do with her.'

My room. Not the guest room, but mine.

I follow him up the stairs, a wide staircase with family photos framed on the walls. I can't bring myself to look at them and keep my eyes on my feet. Lexy bounds up the steps and waits for us at the top.

Tobias leads the way along the landing, but as we pass an open doorway I stop in my tracks.

Joshua's room.

I step inside, taking him in. The walls are teal blue. The small bed, unslept in for years, is still dressed in his sheets: the pattern is that of ocean waves rolling over the bedspread. Plush toys that he once would have held in his sleep are arranged at the head of the bed, leaning against the pillows: an octopus, a dolphin. But it's the white rabbit that catches my eye, its fur faded and dull from being handled so often.

There's a low bookshelf against the opposite wall, lined with books that will never be read again. Beside it, an armchair wrapped in a deep teal velvet. I imagine Evelyn and Tobias taking it in turns to sit in the armchair in the evenings with Joshua on their lap, reading the book he'd chosen until he fell asleep in their arms and they carried him to bed.

I wonder what he would look like now; how all of their lives would have turned out if it hadn't been for me. I try to imagine the life I might have made for myself too, had I not gone to prison so young, or never hit the pipe. I try to form the faces of the men I might have met and loved, the cities and countries I'd have explored to find myself. The jobs I might have done. But I fall short every time.

Tobias stands behind me in the doorway, looking in with grief etched on his face. He looks a decade older like this. As if the pain has sapped the life out of him. Lexy sits silently beside him, her tail swishing quietly across the floor when I look her way.

'I'm so sorry,' I hear myself say.

Tobias tears his eyes away from the toy rabbit on the bed.

'I know,' he replies, before heading along the hall, leaving me alone in the room.

Lexy continues staring in at me with her tail swishing across the herringbone floor.

44

Evelyn

The motel rooms all look the same to me now. The same scuffs, the same dust, the same tatty old furniture and ugly bedspreads; lumpy mattresses with springs that feel like knives digging into my back.

I drop the key to the stolen car on the chest of drawers and pull the bottle of brandy I bought from its brown paper bag. The car, the brandy and my gun are practically all I have to my name now. The only clothes I have are the ones on my back, and the only thing I have in the way of medication is the booze. The police will have seized everything inside the last car: the weapons, the pills I stole at gunpoint, the files revealing my plans. It isn't a question of if I'll be arrested anymore, but a matter of when. They have all the evidence and the bodies they need to secure a conviction when the time comes. I won't deny any of it, either. But none of this can happen until Aaron Alexander is dead.

I sit on the end of the bed and drink the brandy straight from the bottle. In just a few days, my plans have fallen apart. I missed my chances to get him in Beatty and Reno, and now Tobias has stepped in and blocked any other paths that I could have taken next. I cut him off financially, geographically, I took the man's fucking shoes, but still he's found a way to stop me in my tracks.

The loneliness hits me suddenly and all at once. I look down at the filthy patterned carpet, wondering how we came to be this way; how fast fate can change our lives in ways that none of us could possibly see coming. When Tobias and I met in that café in London all those years ago, smiling at one another over our copies of *Frankenstein*, or during those blissful hours we spent alone with Joshua at the hospital before family and friends were allowed to visit and it was just us three, neither of us could have imagined the people we would become, or the places we would end up: passing through motel room after motel room, chasing one another through the Nevada desert with blood on our hands. I wonder if he would do it all over again if he were given the chance, or whether he would forgo our having Joshua if it meant avoiding the aftermath of losing him. I'd go through this time and time again, if I had to.

I gulp from the bottle some more, not stopping until a quarter of it has gone and my eyes grow wet from the sting. I hunch over, letting the haze of the booze work its way through me. It won't stop the pain until I've drunk more, but I've got to pace myself. I have to figure out my next move before I pass out. When Aaron is finally dead, I wonder if I'll hand myself in or put the gun in my mouth.

I place the bottle on the side and strip out of my clothes before walking into the bathroom. I need to shower the desert off me, the dirt and grit plastered to my face with old sweat, and scrub away the sharp odour creeping from under my arms.

I run the shower and step under the spray, wincing as I run my hand over each wound: the big ones, the small ones, the cuts and bruises I hadn't spotted until now. I feel broken in every way a woman can: my body, my mind, my heart.

Blood and sand circle the drain at my feet as I stand beneath the spray, tears of frustration seeping out of me. I stay there for as long as I can, until the water runs cold and I begin to shiver.

I wrap myself in a towel and hang my only clothes in the closet, glancing out of the draped window for any sign of police before letting the towel drop at my feet and climbing into bed, swigging from the brandy like a toddler might suck from their bottle to lull themselves to sleep.

Setting the bottle on the side table, I close my eyes, thinking of ways to get back on track as I doze. Jim couldn't think of anywhere else Aaron would go, nor could his probation officer. I've exhausted all the avenues I knew of: Aaron's mother, boyfriend and brother. I've got to find out where he might go next, and how Tobias will help him get there, or the two of them really will win.

My eyes spring open in the dark room, as I suddenly realize the mistake I've made.

All this time, I've been thinking of what Aaron would do next, when I should have been thinking of Tobias; of where he would lead Aaron, rather than the other way around. But my husband has made a mistake too. Because in taking the lead, I know who to follow. I know him far better than Aaron, far better than he knows himself. And I know exactly where they'll go.

I check the time on my phone: it's half one in the morning. If I want to get there by dawn, I need to leave now. I get out of bed and slip my clothes back on, grabbing the last of my belongings and the key to the stolen car from the chest of drawers.

It's time to go home.

45

Tobias

I wake up with a jolt, the sound of my own scream echoing in my mind. I'd been dreaming of Joshua out on the road.

In the dream, I watch him running behind the hare, racing towards the highway. I watch as the car speeds around the bend. Joshua doesn't see the car. The driver doesn't see Joshua. I'm the only person who can see what's about to happen: I scream his name, but he doesn't hear me. I run as fast I can, my heels pounding against the desert floor and my heart thumping in my chest, screaming until my voice grows hoarse. Joshua is almost at the road as I begin to head up the bank behind him, getting closer and closer. He takes his first step out onto the highway. I reach out to grab the neck of his shirt, my fingers grazing the fabric of his collar just as the car drives into him.

And then I wake up.

I'm sitting up in bed where I'd lurched from the collision and broken from the dream, my hand outstretched where I'd been reaching for him. I'm doused in sweat; it's trailing down me in streams and speckled on my chest.

I've had that dream so many times. Running to stop the inevitable, missing him by an inch every single night, only to wake wondering if I could have saved him had I set off running just a second sooner, or if I had run just that little bit faster, shouted that bit louder.

Bang.

My eyes dart to the closed bedroom door.

The sound came from downstairs. Maybe Aaron can't sleep, and he's fixing himself something in the kitchen. Maybe the dog needed to go out to pee. But my heart is racing knowingly – something isn't right.

Bang. Bang. Bang.

I creep out from beneath the sheets and open the door.

The house is still dark, with the sun only just beginning to rise on the other side of the windows. I creep down the stairs and spot the silhouette of a person behind the panels of frosted glass in the front door.

I reach the door as they begin knocking again and open it with a shaking hand.

Two police officers stare back at me, their patrol car parked up behind them on the driveway.

'Mr Tobias Moore?'

'Yes . . .' I croak.

'Step out please.'

'What's this about?' I ask, opening the door wider. The morning breeze carries a cutting chill with it, rustling my nightclothes and sending goosebumps up my arms.

'Mr Moore, you are being charged with the felony of grand theft auto. You have the right to remain silent. Anything you do say can and will be used against you in a court of law.'

I'm spun round as he talks, flinching as I feel the pinch of the cuffs clicking into place around my wrists. I look at the car I stole parked on the driveway.

'You have the right to an attorney,' the officer is saying. 'If you cannot afford an attorney, one will be appointed for you.'

He keeps talking while the other officer shuts the front door;

I'm turned around again in a daze before being led down the garden path, the odd bit of gravel digging into my bare soles. I look back at the house, thinking of Aaron waking up alone, not knowing where I've gone. I shouldn't have answered the door. Why the hell did I answer the door?

I'm led to the cruiser. One officer opens the door, and the other lowers my head beneath the lip and ushers me inside, shutting me in. I stare up at the house, disoriented by shock and sleep.

The officers climb inside and take a turn of the cul-de-sac before heading out the way they came. I stare out of the window in a terrified daze, watching the curtains twitch at my neighbours' windows.

The cruiser drives past a car parked on the side of the road, and I lock eyes with the woman behind the wheel for a mere second before we're driven apart again.

My wife was behind the wheel of that car.

I close my eyes, realizing what she has done.

Now that I'm out of the way, she can finally end this. Kill the boy who trusted me to protect him. I should have known she'd figure out where I'd go. I shouldn't have been so goddamn naive.

This is it, the moment I've been dreading. The moment I have to turn her in to stop her from committing any more despicable acts. I part my lips and try to speak the words.

We keep driving in silence. Driving, and driving, and driving without a word spoken.

Evelyn can't let go of Joshua and, in turn, I can't let go of her. *I'm just as bad as my wife.*

The cruiser drives on, as I sit in the back shedding silent tears. She's won.

46

Aaron

I wake up to a sound. The slamming of a car door out on the street maybe, or an exhaust backfiring in the distance. I'm alert as soon as my eyes open, almost as if I hadn't slept at all.

Lexy is growling at the door.

'Hey, what's got you? You need to pee?'

I get up, suddenly cold, and pull on the sweater Tobias put out for me. I open the door and step out onto the landing.

The house is deathly quiet. No creaks of floorboards or rumbling water pipes. I feel a cold draught tickling my ankles. Lexy doesn't move; she simply stands at the open door and growls towards the stairs.

'What is it girl? Come on.'

I pass Joshua's room and head for the staircase, trying to watch where I step when the treads creak beneath me, in fear of waking Tobias. I'm halfway down the stairs when I stop in my tracks.

The front door has drifted open, groaning on its hinges with the morning breeze.

Lexy reaches the bottom of the stairs before me and walks towards it, sniffing at the air, then the floor. I follow behind her and peer out. The cul-de-sac is silent with the early hour. Drapes still cover the windows of the neighbouring houses. A sprinkler system starts up on the front lawn across the street.

I hear a growl from behind me, louder and meaner than before, and feel what's coming as soon as I begin to turn: the whistle of something cutting the air.

I see a flash of Evelyn Moore's face just before the handle of her gun cracks against my temple.

Everything goes dark before I've even hit the ground.

IV

DEPRESSION

London, spring 2013

'How far away is it from here?' Joshua asks.

We're sitting at the dining table. Joshua is on one side, and I'm on the other, with Evelyn between us at the head, our dinner plates practically wiped clean. We've had Evie's famous tacos, Joshua's favourite. If he's caught on that we chose this meal to try to get him in the right mood for the news, he doesn't show it.

'America is quite a long way away,' Evelyn replies. 'But Americans speak English like we do, and they have nicer weather where we're going.'

'Where are we going?'

'San Diego,' I say. 'It's like summer all year round there.'

'It doesn't get cold?'

'Not like it does here.'

'Does it snow at Christmas?'

'I don't think so,' Evelyn says. 'They don't get a lot of rain either. They have palm trees, like the ones we see when we go on holiday.'

'Like in Spain?'

'Yes, like in Spain.'

He's quiet for a moment, his brow creased as he thinks. I can almost see his little mind working behind his eyes.

'Do they eat tacos?'

I smile. 'They'll have some of the best tacos you've ever had.'

He smiles at this too, before moving on to his next important question, his brow furrowing again.

'Do they have chocolate?'

'They have everything we have here, to a degree,' Evelyn says. 'And if they don't, they have special shops for English people, to buy all the products from home that they like. And when you go to school, you'll hop on one of those big yellow buses like they do on TV.'

His smile grows brighter as he forgets himself, before reining in his enthusiasm. I know my son like the back of my hand, how clever he is. I know what's coming before he even parts his lips to speak.

'If we move to America, can I have a rabbit?'

We look at each other and try to hide our grins.

'Yes. If you're a good boy and make this exciting step with us, you can have a rabbit when we get to San Diego.'

'I'm going to go pack!'

He bolts from the table and down the hall, bounding up the stairs before we have time to recover ourselves from laughing.

'We don't go for another month!' Evelyn calls, but he's already gone.

I'd been nervous about putting the idea to him about moving abroad. It had felt exciting when I'd got the interview, even more exciting when I'd accepted the job, but when things had started to become real – health insurance, school registration, IRS formalities – I'd begun to think of all of the changes we'd have to make, how Joshua would essentially have to say goodbye to everything he'd ever known. We all would.

Evelyn reaches for my hand over the table and squeezes it.

'This is the right decision, isn't it?' I ask, doubt chipping away at me.

'We could go anywhere in the world, and it wouldn't matter,' she replies, getting up and sitting on my lap. 'Because we'd be there together.'

I move my lips to hers and kiss my wise, beautiful wife, who is sacrificing so much to make this daring jump with me, throwing our lives to the wind and seeing where we land. She kisses me back, long and deep, before pushing me away lightly, squeezing my crotch where I've gone hard beneath her.

'Later,' she says with a wink, and begins to clear the table.

47

Tobias

The hospital is bright, too bright, like I've woken with my eyes set directly on the sun. I listen to the low hum of the strip lights buzzing above my head and look around.

The cops brought me in when they saw the gunshot wound; or at least, the gunshot wound beneath the second-degree burns. There's an officer stationed outside my room and another at the end of the hallway. *A detective will be here soon*, the cop at the door had said. According to the sign on the wall in the hallway, I'm at Sharp Memorial Hospital.

I lie here dressed in nothing but an itchy gown with no back and cuffs biting into my wrists, binding me to the railing of the bed. The medicinal scent of the place is stuck at the back of my throat and my lips are dry, but the nurse won't let me eat or drink before I have surgery to fix my shoulder; something about a suspected broken shoulder blade and cleaning the wound. There's nothing to suspect: the bone is visibly deformed, moving in ways it shouldn't.

I watch the day pass me by on the other side of the window, imagining what my wife might have done to Aaron in the time I've been lying here. I barely recognized Evelyn when our eyes met this morning as I was ferried away in the back of the cruiser.

She looked so much older, so much thinner but for her swollen cheek. I think of the woman I loved for so long – the beaming smile she wore as we travelled all those years ago, the bellowing laughter after Joshua's first steps – and try to accept that she's gone. Whoever was behind the wheel of that car this morning, it wasn't my wife.

I tried to save her from herself and failed. Just as I failed to protect Aaron, abandoning him in a town he doesn't know, at the hands of a woman who wants him dead. I practically delivered him to her, behind a door that only she and I held the key to open. Aside from the two of us, who else will know where to look for him? Does he even have any loved ones left who will care to find out?

And I let her go right on in.

I'm not blind to the selfishness of my acts. I wish my need to save my wife was solely to protect her. But every time I think of telling the police what I know, of betraying her in a way she could never forgive, I think of how my life would be without her. She's been a part of my life – no, my entire life – for twenty-nine years. I was just able to grow a full face of stubble when I met her in that coffee shop. Every experience I've had as an adult has been with her, and the thought of stepping away, becoming my own person and not having her to turn to, doesn't seem possible. And deep down, when I really think about it, I'm terrified that when I'm alone, I won't like who I am without her.

If Evelyn is a monster for killing to ease her grief, then I am too, for letting her.

I think of Joshua and the photo I've stared at a thousand times, remembering his sparkling eyes, the gaps in his smile, the soft, plump skin on his cheeks. My throat burns, tears threatening to fall at the thought of him seeing what we've become, so broken and at odds. How can Evelyn not see how horrified Joshua would be by the sight of us now? How heartbroken he'd be knowing what we've done to each other and those around us?

When we'd met in the desert, inside the derelict garage, I'd seen how broken she was, how defeated. Maybe if I'd pushed a little harder, she'd have broken her resolve. I could see how angry she was at herself for the guilt she carried; for not being stronger as she destroyed life after life. If she were the monster I fear, would she feel that guilt? Is there still some part of her left to save? Or perhaps this hopeless, endless cycle I'm running in, hoping she'll one day come back to me, is merely a way to avoid the very thing I must face and letting her go.

The sound of high heels clacking against the hospital floor brings me round. A woman in a black trouser suit is heading up the corridor towards my room, conviction in her stride, locking eyes with me through the open doorway. A suited man follows close behind her. She stops to talk briefly to the officer at the door in hushed tones before stepping inside.

'Mr Moore, my name is Detective Yeoh, and this is my colleague, Detective Collins.'

I don't say a word, and they don't take a seat. They tower over me where I lie in the bed, no doubt to try to intimidate me, to force out the words they want to hear and have me condemn my wife.

'We understand you've been read your rights and have been officially charged. Why did you steal the car, Mr Moore?'

Detectives wouldn't waste their time on a stolen car. They're here because of Evelyn and all she has done. I lie in the bed silently, my eyes on the cuffs at my wrists, then the skin beneath that has chafed red.

'Was it in pursuit of your wife?' Yeoh asks.

I could tell them where she is right now. I could still do the right thing. I've done all I can, but she's too far gone. I have to do the right thing.

But still, I lie in the bed in silence, unable to prise open my lips and say the words.

'Was it your wife who shot you, Mr Moore?'

'I believe I asked your colleague for a lawyer,' I croak, nodding to the officer standing watch at the door. 'I won't be answering any of your questions until I have one present.'

'We are concerned for the welfare of your wife, Mr Moore. Anything you can tell us will help us find her.'

Everyone in the room knows that's a lie. Their concern would quickly lead to them locking her in a cell and throwing away the key.

The detectives watch me intently.

'Is she worth it?' Yeoh asks, after I don't respond. 'How many more people does she have to hurt before you realize you can't protect her from the inevitable? If you know something that you're not telling us, that'll be another crime to add to your charge sheet. Obstruction of justice can carry up to a five-year term, and rest assured that if you don't start talking, I will be pursuing that charge. So, I'll ask you again: is she worth it?'

I feel her watching me while I stare up at a fly hovering around the strip light, buzzing, and buzzing, and buzzing.

Yes, she is.

'I told you, I won't talk until I have a lawyer present. That isn't obstruction of justice, it's exercising my rights. The only person delaying proceedings here is you.' I tear my eyes away from the fly. 'So, I suggest you get me a fucking lawyer.'

She sighs heavily.

'If your wife kills again, Mr Moore, I will hold you equally responsible.' She heads for the door, her partner in tow. 'We'll get you that lawyer. It looks like you'll be needing one.'

I watch them leave the room and close my eyes as I think over what I'm set on doing. I wonder if Aaron is dead yet, and if my silence has been in vain. I wonder what Evelyn plans to do once the deed is done.

I need to get out of here and find her before it's too late.

48

Evelyn

Joshua's room is light with the day, dust dancing in the rays beaming through the window. It still smells of him, this room. How can it still smell of him after eleven years? Maybe it doesn't, and the scent is a memory from before, so believable that I'm sure I'm breathing him into my lungs, holding my breath for as long as I can to keep hold of him.

I'm sitting on his bed, feeling the softness of the unwashed sheets beneath my palms. I take his pillow and bury my face in it, inhaling him. I remember the scent of him as I held him close like this, feeling his soft exhales on my neck as I rocked him in my lap, singing softly in his ear, the gentle tug of his fingers as he held tight. I pull the pillow away before the tears come, to avoid contaminating it.

What would you think of me now, Joshua?

My face is so swollen that I can barely see out of one eye, and my cheek is flaming hot. I can still taste the infection in my mouth, a sharp, sour tang to the saliva that coats my teeth and gums and sits at the back of my tongue. If he saw me now, would he be frightened? Would I look like a monster to fear, rather than the mother he loved?

I check my watch: I still have hours until sundown, to allow me to go through with my plans undisturbed, but after waiting eleven years for this day, I can wait a few more hours.

My eyes fill with tears as my chest begins to ache with an encroaching wave of loneliness at the thought of all of this being over. It had been easier to face the grief when I had my revenge to cling on to. But now that the deed is almost complete, I can feel my insides shifting and the emotions bubbling up, waiting for the moment when Aaron Alexander is dead and I have nothing left to anchor me.

Shouldn't I be happier? All these years, I thought this was the thing to help right myself again. Tip the scales back to the centre. I thought I would feel differently, finding him. I pictured it so many times; I knew what I'd say, what I'd do, toyed with all the ways I could hurt him. But after knocking him unconscious and dragging him down the basement steps and tying him to a chair, I felt none of those things. I felt lost, and scared, and guilty. All these years, he had been a mere thing, a cancerous mass on my brain that controlled everything I did and dominated my every thought; but seeing him tied to the chair, his eyes flicking behind their closed lids, and hearing the pained groans he made as he came round, I realized he was human.

Maybe it's because I'm home; two worlds meshing together that were never meant to meet. Home is meant to be the place we feel safe, but I'd felt better when I was alone in the desert. Now that I've stopped, I can feel all of the emotions rising to the surface. I can't stop thinking of Tobias in the back of the cop car, looking at me with those puppy-dog eyes. I can't stop thinking of Kyle bleeding out, of Chris with the ice pick in his neck. Of the baby crying in my arms and the little boy at the other end of that shotgun.

I'm weak. So fucking weak.

This time the tears fall before I can blink them away, and I take a deep breath as the sobs begin to grow, breathing in the scent of Joshua on the air.

I take the plush rabbit from among the toys on the bed. The white fur is brown in places from where he'd carried it with him everywhere. Loving to death the very thing that would go on to kill him. I can barely see the toy through the tears now. A whimper escapes me, and I take the rabbit's head in my fist and yank it until the fabric rips and the stitching snaps, soft white filling coming out in clouds and decorating the floor until the rabbit is nothing but a flimsy, headless torso in my lap. I sit staring down at it, panting for breath, white fibres stuck beneath my fingernails.

I mustn't unravel. Not now that I'm so close.

I slowly pull myself together and head out into the hallway without looking back, in fear of his memory unspooling me again.

I stop at the top of the stairs, catching sight of my reflection in the mirror on the wall. I barely recognize myself: one eye is completely swollen shut now, my lips have puffed up where the inflammation in my mouth and cheek is beginning to travel.

I walk down the stairs and over to the door to the basement. Beside it is the closet, where I can hear the dog scratching at the door from the inside. I'd had to taser it and drag it inside before it came to, in case it bit me. I open the basement door, pulling on the cord until the bulb flickers to life, and start down the stairs.

Aaron is tied to the chair in the corner, his head hung low in defeat. When he looks up at me, he mumbles through the gag I'd shoved into his mouth and sealed with tape to keep the neighbours from hearing his screams. I wonder how long it will take for him to lose the concept of time down here in the dark.

I drag a free chair in front of him and sit down.

'We have a while yet. We're going to wait until the sun goes down, and then we're going to leave, and I'm going to kill you. If you're a religious man, now would be the time to repent.'

He tries to say something else behind the gag, pleading with me. I slowly shake my head.

'There's nothing you can say. It would be best for you to accept the hand you've been dealt.' I watch him closely, as the hope seeps from his eyes and he drops his gaze back to his lap.

'It's because you left him alone.' I hadn't planned to say anything more, but the words come crawling out of me. He looks up. 'You hit him, and that was awful. But it's because you left him there in the road, that's why we're here. You broke his bones, you terrified him, and then ... you left him to die alone.' The tears flow again before I can stop them. I wipe my eyes with the back of my hand, run it beneath my nostrils. 'Joshua was always so afraid of the dark.'

I head back up the stairs without another word, pull on the cord as I reach the top, and thrust him into darkness before shutting the door behind me.

49

Tobias

The day has passed by too fast. I've seen the sun rise and begin its descent again; watched through the window as the blue sky was slowly enveloped in smoke.

About an hour ago, I heard the nurses talking at their station about the wildfires. How they've started up in San Diego, mere miles from the hospital and the rest of the city. Staff have become more and more frantic as the day has gone on, their strides faster, their attention spans shorter as they prepare for admissions as a result of the fires. There were fearful whispers of an evacuation from the surrounding areas before the head nurse arrived and hurried them all along.

I've been stuck in this bed all day, fighting to stay awake as my eyelids threaten to close from exhaustion and the pain meds. The only time I've been free of the cuffs was when the cop at the door exchanged them for a zip tie strapping my left wrist to the bed, by order of the nurse before my X-rays; whether it was intentional or accidental, the officer didn't put me back in the cuffs again, giving me a glimmer of hope that I might be able to escape. But hours have rolled by since then, and he's not left the doorway once, whittling that hope to a nub.

Is it already over? Am I already too late? The pain is growing as the meds wear off, but my mind is still groggy. I can't ask for more; I need my wits about me if I'm going to find a way out of here.

I'm trying to squeeze my hand out of the zip tie when my nurse enters the room. Her name is Stacey, or Sandy, or something to that effect. I'm too tired for anything to stick. The cop standing guard follows her inside, watching over me as she approaches the bed. My hand is swollen and red from my tugging.

'Right, Mr Moore, I'm going to fit you with a cannula for the IV and then we can get you prepped for surgery. That sound good?'

I nod in response, watching as she pulls on some disposable gloves before squeezing my free hand to find a viable vein.

'I hear around the hospital you're in for grand theft auto,' she says. If this is her attempt to distract me from any discomfort that's about to come, it isn't working.

'That's right.'

She reaches into her pocket and produces a small pair of scissors. She cuts into the packet for the cannula and places it on the equipment tray beside the bed before squeezing my hand again to elevate a vein.

'The cops pull you over?'

'A tip-off.'

'Ouch. Neighbour with a grudge?'

'A wife with a grudge.'

She clears her throat. 'Sharp pinch.'

She slips the needle in and flushes it through with saline to make sure it's in place before taping it down.

'Right, Mr Moore—' She stops speaking suddenly, looking at me sternly. She retrieves a small torch from her pocket.

The scissors are still on the table.

'Follow the light, please.' She moves the torch back and forth a few times. 'Are you feeling dizzy or nauseous?'

'Yeah. Can't seem to keep my eyes open.'

'Have you hit your head recently?'

'Too many blows to count.'

'What's the problem here?' the cop asks from behind her.

'It seems he may have a concussion.'

'He either does or he doesn't, ma'am. We've got a lawyer coming to talk to him—'

'He's concussed, sir,' she says, turning to him.

I reach for the scissors on the table as slowly as I can.

'Nothing he tells you in this state would be admissible in court, right? I'll be sending the doctor in to see him again. It looks like he'll need to be sent up for an MRI before we can consider operating.'

My heart jolts as my fingertips brush the metal blades. I pick them up and slowly retract my hand again, slipping the scissors under the sheets.

'We really need him to talk to his lawyer when they arrive.'

'That's your priority. My priority is his welfare. Sending a concussed man to an operating room to be put under anaesthetic could well kill him. Then he won't be talking to a lawyer at all.'

The cop nods sheepishly before heading back to the door. The nurse turns to me again.

'I'll go and get the doctor now, Mr Moore.'

She reaches for the items from the tray, and I wait with bated breath for her to notice the scissors are missing. My heart is thumping in my chest, and I feel myself perspiring. It's only when she has headed out the door again that I allow myself to breathe.

'Concussion, my ass,' the cop mutters as he stands guard outside.

I slowly remove the scissors from under the sheets and slip the zip tie between the blades.

While I cut away, I eye up the cop, assessing his size, noting the gun holstered at his hip. The other officer is nowhere to be seen; I keep looking out for signs of him out in the corridor as I cut at the tie. The blades are blunt from overuse, but I'm slowly making headway. I cut faster and faster until the plastic finally comes apart with a soft snap.

I remove the cannula from the back of my hand, sending a jet of blood across the sheets, before creeping out of the bed. I wonder how long it would take for the cop to tackle me if I reached for his gun. If I could undo the clasp in time and yank it free before he could get a swing in. I probably only have five minutes or so before the doctor comes to my room and notices I'm gone. Maybe less, if the nurse realizes she left her scissors behind and turns back round. If I don't act now, Evelyn will kill that boy, if she hasn't already.

I tighten my grip on the scissors and lunge for him. I press the blades into his neck and yank his head back with a fistful of hair. My hand is wet with blood, oozing out from where the cannula had been.

'Don't move,' I whisper in his ear. 'Don't make a sound.'

His whole body has seized up. I feel his arm twitch with the thought of reaching for his gun and press the blades deeper.

'I'm going to back you into the room now, and then you're going to close the door. Nod so I know you're listening.'

He nods begrudgingly, and I step back until we're out of the doorway.

When he hesitates, I press the blade so firmly that a millimetre deeper and I'll pierce the skin. His pulse drums against the metal, travelling up to the handle in my grip.

'I said shut the fucking door.'

He slowly reaches out for the handle, and the door squeals on its hinges. By the time it clicks shut, I've got the gun free from his holster and raise it fast, then crack the handle on the back of his head. I watch as he slumps down, out like a light before he's even hit the floor.

I chuck the gun and scissors onto the bed and begin to undress him, wriggling out of the hospital gown before slipping it over his head. It takes all of my strength to lift him into the bed, bolts of pain rushing to my shoulder that make my eyes water. I turn him over onto his side with his back to the doorway and step out of the hospital room dressed in his police uniform.

The hallway is as bright as the room had been, blinding me as I pass the nurse's station with my head down. The nurse who had fitted the cannula in my hand is patting down her pockets, anxiously looking for the scissors she'd left behind. I see her look towards the room and head for the door; I walk quickly towards the elevator, and only when the doors close do I allow myself to release the breath I'd been holding.

I haven't got long to find Evelyn. She won't have stayed at home; it would be too much of a risk, in case I finally decided to confide in the police as my last resort; or maybe she knows I'm too weak and selfish to do that. No, she couldn't take that sort of risk, not after coming this far. She'll have taken Aaron somewhere. She won't make his death quick; she'll want to drag out, to make him feel the pain we've felt all these years. She'll want to be alone and undisturbed, meaning she'll likely wait for nightfall. My heart jumps a little with a bout of hope I daren't feel.

The elevator doors open on the ground floor, and I step out, briefly looking up to follow the signs to the exit. It smells of smoke down here. Along one of the corridors, I see people being wheeled in on gurneys, black with soot and with oxygen masks over their noses and mouths. The fires are getting closer, smoking us out.

Where would you go, Evelyn? You've got your way, and you'll want to do it perfectly. So where would you go?

I reach the doors to the drop-off bay for emergencies, passing the security guard at his station; he nods, believing me to be an officer, so I nod back, making sure I don't hold his gaze for long enough to be remembered.

I step outside, out of the air conditioning and into the heat, and look up at the furious sky: waves of hot smoke billowing in, the wildfires returning to where it all began.

The realization comes to me suddenly.

Where it all began.

Evelyn is going to take Aaron to where Joshua died.

A Mercedes pulls up in the bay, and a frantic mother jumps out of the car with a toddler in her arms. 'Which way for the ER?'

I glance down at the uniform. She thinks I'm a cop too.

'Through the doors, take a right.'

'I'll be right behind you,' an equally frantic man calls from behind the wheel.

I crouch down and look through the open window.

'Go in with them, I'll park up for you.'

'A-are you sure?'

'David, hurry up!' the woman shouts, heading towards the doors.

The man scurries out of the car, handing me the key with shaking fingers.

'Thank you so much, officer. Our son is asthmatic . . . and with this smoke . . .'

'I get it, sir. We do everything we can for those we love.'

He gives me a grateful nod before rushing in after them.

I walk round the car to the driver's side and get behind the wheel. The tyres scream as I slam my foot on the gas pedal and speed out of the bay.

It's time to go back to where this all began.

50

Aaron

I don't know where we're going, or how long it will take. I only know that the result of this journey, the final act waiting for us at the other end, is inevitable. Evelyn told me so, down in the dark basement, and worst of all, I accepted it. She shut off the lights and closed the door, and I sat there bound and gagged, and waited for death. When she appeared again at sundown, she untied me slowly and matter-of-factly. She didn't tease or taunt me; she didn't drag me or push me. She simply untied the restraints and guided me from the basement to the car. I didn't fight her, not even for a second.

She drives in tense silence, out of the city and into the desert. The buildings have been replaced by mountainous terrain; in a strange way it almost feels like coming home. Beside me, her breaths are fast and shallow, no doubt from the adrenaline coursing through her veins. Her breath smells; like rot or infection. I wonder if that's the cause of the swelling to her face.

She's sadder than I thought she'd be. I'd been expecting a woman hardened by her hate and anger, but as we drive along the desert highways, she keeps breaking into tears, as if she's been holding them in all this time and it's all finally coming out. I should hate her, shouldn't I? This is the woman who took my brother from me after I'd finally got him back; the woman who hurt Kyle, the only man I've ever felt safe with and come close to loving. I should loathe every movement she makes, every sound. But the only emotions I can muster are fear and pity. I don't say a word, too scared to provoke the anger I know is in her. I sit with my eyes on the road and pray for a merciful death when it comes.

My mom used to say that she was tired all her life, and death would be like the long sleep she'd been chasing after. She told me never to miss her, because she'd be happy finally being at rest. As my death comes knocking, I try to think of it like that. It makes sense to me, now more than ever; I've never been so tired.

Wherever we're going, it's close to the wildfires. When we began driving, I could still see the clouds in the sky, with glimpses of blue beyond the setting sun. Now everything is smothered by smoke, illuminated yellow by the approaching flames, getting hotter and thicker with each mile we drive. It isn't long before I spot burning embers and ash falling like snow. We pass several cars heading in the opposite direction, but no one is driving towards the flames like we are. We follow a bend in the highway and slow at the sight of a cordon. All traffic is having to turn around and head back the way it came.

The sign reads 'Evacuation Zone'.

Evelyn pulls to a stop, a hundred feet or so from the barrier, until the cars that had been turning around are gone, and it's just us and the troopers guarding the cordon. One of them begins the trek towards the car, no doubt to tell us to return the way we came. Evelyn sits behind the wheel, grinding her teeth quietly in her mouth. Just as the trooper approaches the driver's side, she slams her foot on the gas pedal, thrusting us both back in our seats, squealing tyres smoking against the road. The car speeds towards the barrier. The second trooper has to jump clear of our path, landing on the hard ground just as we break through and speed off down the highway.

*

A rumble of thunder groans from overhead. It's tough to tell what's smoke and what's cloud up there; the sky is a hot, bright yellow from the heat of the flames, smudged over with black smoke creeping on the breeze. But that was definitely thunder. A fork of lightning cracks through the haze.

'Do you recognize where we are yet?' Evelyn asks, after almost thirty minutes of silence.

I look out at the endless desert, but I can barely see anything through the smoke. Burning embers float within it for miles around, flickering like fireflies.

Then we reach a bend, and a flash of a memory sparks in my mind.

It's 2013, and I'm driving Billy's car. He's sitting beside me, shouting so loudly that his spittle sprays against my face.

You're so stupid. You're so fucking stupid.

I tell him I'm sorry through my tears, repeating myself until the words clog into one unintelligible jumble and I'm hyperventilating behind the wheel.

'You look like you do,' Evelyn says, her voice breaking through my thoughts.

I stare out at the road, shaking violently in my seat. I'm sweating and yet I feel cold. My knees are knocking together, similar to the sound Billy's knuckles made against my head.

She's taking me back to the scene of the accident.

'No,' I say. 'No, please—'

She puts her foot down on the pedal.

'*Please*—'

'Imagine how scared he would have been out here,' she says. 'Were you driving at this speed, Aaron? Or were you driving faster?'

The car speeds up. Faster and faster until the pedal must be flat against the floor.

'Imagine how he would have felt, knowing you'd left him here to die. Alone in the dark. What do you think he would have been thinking? Do you think he called out for me?'

'Please . . . stop . . .'

I can't catch my breath. My throat has seized shut and air is trapped inside my lungs, swelling and swelling until I'm sure they'll burst. Tears fill my eyes until all I can see are the shimmering embers on the other side of the glass.

'I wake up in the night sometimes and hear him calling out for me. Crying for me, wondering why I haven't come to save him. Do you think that's what his last thought was as he lay dying? That his mother wasn't there to save him? Or could he only think of the pain?'

'I'm sorry. I'm so sorry.' My heart is racing so fast that I'm sure I'll vomit. I can barely hear my own thoughts over the drum of my pulse, the chattering of my teeth and the knocking of my knees. Bone against bone against bone against bone. 'Please, take me back. We can still turn back.'

'There's no way back, Aaron. Not for you, not for me. Not for Joshua. Not for any of us.'

I can't see the road through my tears. I sit in silence trying to breathe, as smoke starts creeping through the vents on the dash. Above, there's a second boom of thunder.

Another memory flashes, dragging me back.

I'm behind the wheel. We take the next bend in the highway. I can barely see through my tears and Billy's blows, my eyes rattling in their sockets. I feel the steering wheel moving with my grip as I'm knocked, the car swerving with each hit. He calls me an idiot. I keep telling him I'm sorry. He pauses mid-punch, curses loudly with shock.

I blink away the tears just in time to see the boy standing in the road.

In Evelyn's car, I vomit into the footwell. I blink and blink, but I can't shift the sight of him: his wide, terrified eyes looking at me beyond the blinding headlights. The gape of his mouth as he took his last free breath. I vomit again. Another fork of lightning splits the sky.

The car screeches to a stop.

'Get out,' she spits.

I hear her car door slam shut.

I rub my eyes and look through the windscreen. The smoke is thick and moving fast with the breeze. I sit in the car staring out in horror, just as I'd sat after hitting Joshua.

Drive, Billy had yelled. *Drive the fucking car!*

I'd looked back in the rear-view. At the small body lying on the ground.

His next punch came so hard and so fast, knocking my head into the window beside me.

I said drive!

I'd slammed my foot on the gas pedal and driven away as fast as I could, until I couldn't see the boy behind us anymore, until Billy finally stopped hitting me.

I snap back to the present as the door beside me opens: Evelyn stands on the other side, her gun pointed directly at my head.

'Get out of the car.'

I try to move, but my limbs feel useless; my hands shake as I search for something to hold on to. My legs threaten to fold beneath me as I stumble out, coughing in the smoke. I can breathe out, but I can't breathe in; I'm choking. She orders me to walk, and I take a few steps before falling straight onto the road.

'I'm sorry,' I sob. 'I'm so sorry!'

My chest rises and falls with each cry, just as Joshua's must have done as he lay dying, staring up through his tears at the stars in the sky. But all I can see is smoke. Evelyn appears above me. A boom of thunder crashes so loudly overhead that I feel the thrum of it against my back.

'This is how he felt,' she says; she's sobbing too. 'Lying here, knowing he was going to die. Do you understand now? *Do you?*'

She kicks me in the ribs. I scrunch up into a ball, but I don't make a sound; the kick knocked the wind out of me. 'Get up.'

I lie on the road without the strength to move. I wish she'd get it over with and kill me here. End it now, once and for all.

'*Get! Up!*'

The next kick is strong enough to knock stars into my eyes. She kicks me again. And again. I see flashes of the night I killed Joshua, feeling Billy's blows, then hers, then his, back and forth while all I can do is grit my teeth and cry, silently begging for the bullet.

She finally stops kicking and drags me up by the scruff of my neck.

'Walk. You owe it to me to walk.'

I stumble blindly through the smoke, across the highway towards the desert. We pass rocks and dips. Burning ash falls silently around us, flitting violently whenever the wind blows. The fire is so close I can see the flames on the mountains, creeping over the peaks, set to burn down the other side. With the thunder, the lightning, the flames and the gun, it feels like the whole world is caving inwards. The entire time, I can hear her behind me, breathing excitedly, the rotten smell of her breath creeping over my shoulders.

We walk for what feels like miles, until the car on the road vanishes into the smoke. She orders me to stop.

'Turn around.'

I do as I'm told, trembling and sobbing quietly. Death is imminent now. I can feel it in the smoke scratching at my lungs. Taste it in the air, acrid and burnt from the fire and destruction. The adrenaline in my body feels like poison, making my heart lurch. I'm both terrified of the bullet in her gun and begging for it, longing for this misery to finally end.

'I'm ... so ... sorry ...'

I'm weeping like a child. I feel the saliva strung between my lips and teeth, the rivers of tears and snot snaking down my face.

'Shut up.'

'Please forgive me. Please—I'm-so-sorry . . . You'll never know how sorry I am.'

'*I said shut up!*'

She lowers the gun and pulls the trigger. The bullet rips through my thigh and I scream. I collapse to my knees, looking up at her through the smoke, at the burning embers floating around her, the glow of the approaching flames glinting in her eyes.

Hot blood streams down my thigh and pools where my knee meets the dirt. I flinch as the scorching barrel of the gun is pressed against my forehead.

'You don't get to be sorry,' she says. Thick tears glisten on her cheeks, glowing like fire from the embers in the air and the flames in the distance. 'You don't get redemption. *You killed my child!*'

I close my eyes and cry, waiting for the end, jolting when a thunderclap cracks above us, so loud that I'd thought it was a bullet from the gun. But as the thunder eases and the lightning prepares to strike again, I hear a loud bellowing sound in the distance.

The gun leaves my head. I open my eyes. Evelyn isn't looking at me anymore, but back towards the road.

The sound keeps on blaring.

It's a car horn calling through the smoke from the highway.

51

Evelyn

I turn towards the sound of the horn and spot two headlights piercing the smoke. The sound dies, but the headlights remain. Aaron is kneeling in a pool of blood on the ground. I place the gun between his eyes again. He shuts them with a whimper, as if he's accepting his fate. But just as I'm about to fire, I hear a shout.

There's a dark silhouette running through the smoke.

Lightning flashes and lights up the ground. Thunder crashes in the clouds above. Aaron looks up at the sky, screwing his eyes up as the first drop of rain patters against his face.

I turn back to the running man. He's close enough for me to hear him panting for breath, and I recognize the police uniform as the figure slowly comes into view. Tobias must have told them about my plans. The final twist of the knife in his act of betrayal, the one thing I never thought he'd be man enough to do.

I lunge towards Aaron, snatching him up from behind with an arm across his throat and his back to my chest, feeling the racing of his heart. I hold the gun to his head as the man approaches.

That's when I recognize him beneath the uniform.

It's Tobias.

He looks awful. He is deathly pale and his face looks older, so much older; fear and stress ageing him over a matter of days rather than years. Long ago, I would have felt endeared to him. I would have wanted to protect him from the pain he's carrying. But now all I feel when I look at him is rage.

'Why won't you stop?' I hear myself shout. 'Why won't you just *fucking stop!*'

He comes to a halt twenty feet away, fighting the urge to double over to catch his breath. He coughs and spits on the ground.

Rain patters quietly around us; a drop here, a drop there. I'm sure I can feel it running down my face, until I realize the trails of water I feel are tears.

'Because I can't afford to lose you,' he replies through his panting. 'And if you kill that boy, there's no going back.'

'There's no going back, whether he dies or not.'

'But you'll still be *you*,' he says. 'If you kill Aaron, you're killing yourself. And you're killing me.'

'Is that what it'll take to make you stop? Killing you?'

I move the gun from Aaron's head, pointing it at Tobias with an outstretched arm. It wavers in my grip, speckled with fine drops of rain. I can feel the tears running down my face and beg for them to stop. But the emotions I've held back just keep coming and coming.

'This has gone on long enough. You've broken laws, stolen cars, you've *killed* people. Did you hear that, Evelyn? You've *ended people's lives.* Their families will be feeling the same way you feel right now. You've done so many awful things, and I've let you, because I was too scared to lose you. Even now, I can't bear the thought of losing you. But this ends now. Let him go.'

I will myself to pull the trigger, fire a bullet into his neck to stop his chatter.

'Do you think Joshua would want you to do this? Do you think he'd want you destroying your life and mine?'

'*It's what's right!*'

'You know that's not true. You know he would never want this.'

'You don't get to speak for him!'

'And you do?' Tobias takes a step forward. 'Have you really looked at the man you're set on killing? Or do you see only what you want to see?'

I feel Aaron shaking against me, his heart hammering through his back and into my chest. His flesh warming mine.

'He's sorry, Evelyn. He's more sorry than anyone I've ever known. He was young, he was reckless, and he made a mistake. A terrible, terrible mistake. But he doesn't deserve to die.'

'Stop!' I'm weeping now, sounds crawling out of me that a dying animal might make as Aaron continues to shiver against me. 'How can you be such a coward? He killed our child. He destroyed everything, took everything that we had. How can you look him in the eye? How can you be so weak as to forgive him?'

'I'm not the weak one, Evelyn. It's you. It's always been you.'

The tears keep coming. I gasp for air, but my lungs fill with smoke.

'Please, just leave me alone.'

'You know I can't. This isn't you, Evie, it never was. Where did my wife go? Bring her back to me. The woman who loved people, cared for everyone she met. The woman who was strong, and loving, and forgiving. Where is she?'

'*She's gone,*' I bellow.

We stand at odds, smoke and embers drifting around us, the rain growing heavier. I feel my hair sagging with it, see more and more drops collecting on the gun like dew.

'Do you think Joshua would want you to be doing what you're doing right now? Do you think he could love you like this?'

To my horror, his words cut into me, stabbing at my heart.

I'm shaking violently. Aaron could break out of my hold if he wanted to; I can barely keep a hold of myself. But still, he stays.

'Look at you. Look at who you've become. You would *terrify* him, Evelyn.'

'Enough!'

I fire a shot, the bullet exploding into the dirt. The sound cracks like thunder and echoes across the plains. Still, Tobias steps closer.

'But despite everything you've done,' he says. 'Despite all the lives you've destroyed, I still love you.'

'*Enough!*'

Real thunder booms overhead; Aaron jerks in my grip, and the rain really begins to fall. I can feel it plastering down my hair until it's flat to my head, pattering on my shoulders until the fabric of my shirt sticks to my skin and I'm dripping all over.

'I love you, Evie. Even though you've caused far more pain and destruction than Aaron ever has. What he did was an accident. What you've done was entirely by choice.'

'How can you say that?' I stammer, shouting through the rain. 'He murdered our *son*.'

'It was an *accident*, Evelyn. One he would take back if he could.'

'How can you speak for him? How can you excuse what he did?'

'I've forgiven him, Evie. And you should too.'

'I'll *never* forgive him for what he's done.'

'I'm not talking about Aaron,' Tobias says softly. 'I'm talking about Joshua.'

Thunder booms above our heads. I stare at him along the length of the gun; he's soaked through from the rain, his hair matted to his head and droplets hanging from his nose, his eyelashes. He steps even closer.

'It's time you forgave Joshua for dying.'

I stumble. A strange sound escapes my mouth. I can feel myself unravelling. My strength and anger unspooling at my feet. I can't see through the tears anymore.

'Forgive him, Evelyn. Forgive Joshua for leaving us. Forgive him for running into that road.'

'*Tobias, that's enough!*'

'Forgive our son for hurting you like this.'

'*No!*'

'Forgive him for not living for as long as he should have. Forgive him for making us love him only to leave us behind. Forgive him for tearing our world apart. Forgive him, Evelyn. *Forgive him.*'

The sobs grow, until I'm not holding on to Aaron anymore; he's holding on to me. I'm wailing and I can't stop. I slump down, bending at the knees until I'm on the wet ground and crumpled in his arms, the embers around us extinguished by the rain. I've dropped my gun, and I'm clutching my son's killer as if he's the last thing I have to keep me from splitting completely in two. I watch the rainwater washing his blood away, dragging it down into the cracks in the earth.

'And it's time you forgave yourself,' Tobias says, crouching down. I stare up at his rain-speckled face and wonder how we became so far removed from one another. The man I adored. 'Forgive, Evie. Forgive Joshua. Forgive Aaron. Forgive me. But most of all, forgive yourself.'

I howl into the desert, choking on the rain. Aaron is holding me tight, sobbing with me. I'm locked into the embrace of the man I've sworn to hate with every fibre of my being, holding on to his wet clothes in a death grip.

I can't open my eyes; I can't bear to see anymore, feel anymore. I sense Tobias's wet arms slipping under my knees, my back, the warmth of his breath on my neck as he picks me up with a pained groan.

'I forgive you, my darling,' he whispers in my ear. His wet lips press against my temple. 'I forgive you.'

He carries me across the broken landscape without another word, letting me unfurl in his arms, the rage I carried for so long shattering into pieces. So many pieces that I'll never be able to build it back together.

52

Tobias

We drive towards Sharp Memorial Hospital in silence, listening to the windscreen wipers drag across the glass, shivering in our wet clothes. The air smells metallic. Aaron's blood stains my hands from when I fastened my belt into a tourniquet and fixed it above the gunshot wound to stop the bleeding; I knelt beside him to do it, and the blood soaked into my trousers, cooling against my skin. He's sitting in the back of the car, suffering in silence and white as a sheet, droplets of rain still snaking down his face from his sodden hair.

Evelyn is in the passenger seat beside me, shivering violently. She hasn't stopped crying. Tears slip silently down her cheeks as she stares out through the windscreen, completely dissociated. I wonder what she's seeing: memories of the distant past, or of the more recent things she has done. Maybe she's finally thinking of the future. I'm not brave enough to do that; now the chase is over, there seem to be only two choices: face what we have done, or run.

When we began this journey, I never pictured the three of us like this; sitting in the same car, breathing the same air, forgiving each other without words for everything we've done. I wonder how we all became this broken; how we didn't see the signs before it was too late and we collided into each other's lives.

I drive towards the hospital, which shines like a beacon through the rain, desperately trying to plan what we do next. Evelyn and I could drive across the border and try to salvage what little freedom we have left. We could keep running, but together this time. The thought of having lost her for so many years and finally getting her back, only to lose her again, is unfathomable. No one can help her heal like I can. I'll keep her safe.

I pull up across the street from the emergency bay and turn off the engine. Aaron goes for the door handle without a word.

'Aaron,' Evelyn says, surprising us both.

I watch him in the rear-view mirror, his eyes wide. Evelyn's are still fixed ahead of her, as though she still can't bring herself to look at him.

'When you leave this car . . . I want you to have a good life. I want you to have the life that my son never could. Be happy not just for yourself, but for him, and for us.' She closes her eyes, bracing herself as she thinks of our son and the sadness envelops her. 'I want you to remember that I said that.'

'Yes, ma'am,' he croaks. He looks to me in the rear-view, asking for permission to leave. I nod silently and watch him get out of the car. I wish I could say more to him, after the time we spent together. But I let the moment pass and watch as he limps towards the emergency room, leaving a faint trail of blood behind him on the wet ground. I don't take my eyes off him until I see two nurses rush to his aid in the foyer. There are cops inside too.

'I've been thinking about what we could do next,' I say, my voice filling the void. 'The Mexico border is only seventeen miles from here. If we can just get across, then we can—'

She turns to me then, and for the first time in years she smiles at me. The smallest, saddest smile I have ever seen. She cups my face with her shaking hand.

'No more running,' she whispers, her tears flowing as if they'll never stop. 'It's time to face what we've done.'

She lowers her hand and takes mine, holding it tight. We listen to the rain hammering on the roof of the car. I can feel what's coming next, and tears scratch at my eyes. I have to stop myself from begging her not to say the words that are about to leave her lips.

'I can't grieve our son alongside you, Tobias. I need to do it alone. And you may not realize it yet, but so do you.'

My heart sinks, and she squeezes my hand tighter. I'm shocked, and yet deep down, I knew. I've known it all along. I knew it before we set off at the beginning of this terrifying journey, when it felt more like an ending in so many ways. And it makes sense that it's happening here. Where so much ended for us, and where all of this pain began. Sharp Memorial Hospital was where Joshua was taken after he was found.

'I love you,' she says. 'I have loved you for almost thirty years. But this love is destroying us.'

'You don't know what you're saying.' I can't stop myself from stammering. 'We just need to take a breath, that's all. To get away from here, and think about this clearly—'

'I am, Tobias. I'm finally thinking clearly. And this is the decision I've come to. Deep down, you know it's the right thing to do, too. You can't look after yourself when your sole focus is fixing me, and I can't heal if you're trying to do it for me.'

We sit in silence for a while, her thumb stroking the back of my hand.

'Our love used to bring out the best in us,' she says. 'But now it enables the worst. I'm so tired of fighting the need to fall apart, but I can't do it when you're waiting to catch me and put me back together. I need to do this alone, and you need to let me.'

A sob lurches up my throat. I had her back, I *finally* had her back, and yet I can feel her slipping away from me all over again.

'But . . . I don't know who I am without you.'

I'm crying now. Warm, heavy tears seem to fall endlessly

down my cheeks. I close my eyes, as if I'll be safe from the pain in the dark.

'Look at me,' she says. 'You'll be a much happier man without me than you have been for the last eleven years. We can never go back to how it was. How could we, without Joshua?'

I sniff back the tears, but they keep on coming. She's right, of course she is. It was foolish of me to hold on so tightly to the past, to the lives we lived before our trauma, before the birth and the death of our son.

'And you'll be a happier woman?' I ask.

She swallows hard, trying to keep the tears at bay.

'I'm really going to try.' She strokes my face and I close my eyes, resting in the warmth of her palm, wondering how I'll live without ever feeling her touch again. 'We need to let go of the past. But we can't do that without letting go of each other, can we?'

She reaches for me, and I for her. We hold on to each other as if our lives depend on it. We smell of smoke and sweat and rain; the sharp tang of infection creeps from her mouth with each breath, but I don't care. I want to hold her like this forever, feeling her heart beating against mine, her warmth and the wet bristle of her hair on my face. But I also know she's right. I know we have to stop hiding from the truth, the inevitable. I have to let her go.

She pulls away first, and we kiss briefly and tenderly, our teeth chattering and our lips wet.

'I'm sorry for everything I've put you through,' she whispers, stroking a hand through my hair. 'I want you to be happy, like Aaron. I want you to find yourself and to live the life you deserve to live. I want you to meet a woman who can give herself to you fully, in the ways that I no longer can. I want you to find peace.'

'You're my best friend,' I whisper.

'And you're mine. But sometimes the best thing you can do for someone you love is to let them go.'

She's right. I've leant on her for so long that I've forgotten how it feels to stand on my own two feet. But if this journey we've been on has taught me one thing, it's that both of us can do anything we put our minds to. If Evelyn can try to move on and heal, then I can try to go it alone.

We kiss once more and then she reaches for the door.

She gets out first. I follow, shaking with each step, and walk round the car to meet her. I take her hand and she squeezes it.

'Everything is going to be okay,' she whispers.

Then we walk together towards the hospital, squinting to see through the rain, towards the foyer and the police officers within. I take a deep breath, and despite the fear, and the pain, and the exhaustion, I can feel freedom slowly seeping in, the weight of all of our crimes and all of our secrets slowly lifting from our shoulders.

We look at each other one last time.

Then the sliding doors open, and we step inside.

53

Aaron

I come round from the anaesthesia slowly, blinking lazily. My throat feels rough and dry where the tube was during the surgery. I'm not sure how long I've been in the hospital, or how long the operation took. After I limped inside, I was whisked off pretty quickly. Judging by the pain in my thigh, they've done what they needed to do. The scans showed the bullet was still inside me and they needed to cut it out. I wonder if I'll get to keep it.

There's a soft knock at the door and I languidly turn my head.

My mom is stood in the doorway, holding a cup of coffee.

I wonder if I'm dead; that's my first thought. Maybe I died on the operating table, and all of this is the afterlife I wasn't sure existed. She sure as hell wouldn't be here for real. Maybe the drugs are making me see the things I want to see.

'Hey,' she says.

It's only then that I know I'm not dreaming.

There's a chair by the bed, and she sits in it. I wonder if she was sitting there before I woke up, before she went to get coffee. I can smell it in the cup, the bitter scent turning my stomach. Her eyes are red and puffy from crying.

'I'm still your next of kin,' she says.

'Sorry,' I croak. 'I didn't know who to change it to.'

'That's not what I meant. I'm glad that I am.'

She looks so much older now than when I last saw her. After she kicked me out at sixteen, the only other time I laid eyes on her was at the sentencing hearing before I went down. I was sure I glimpsed her at the back of the room, watching. Or maybe I saw what I needed to see in that moment; needing to believe that I had someone there to support me to make me feel less alone.

Now her face is wrinkled, her eyes hooded and her mouth downturned; there's a droop to her neck that wasn't there before.

'I have so much I need to say,' she says, her eyes looking anywhere but at me. 'But I don't know where to start.'

She puts the coffee on the side, the Styrofoam cup shaking in her grip, and pauses for a moment, as if unsure what to do with her hands. Then she reaches for me. I look down at her fingers over mine, feel the warmth of her palm.

'I am so sorry, baby.'

She looks up at the ceiling to keep her tears from falling, blinking furiously before looking back to me.

'I was a bad mother to you. I had so many chances to make it right, I know I did ... I could have stopped taking the pills. I could have left Tony. I could have moved you out of that town so you could've had a better start in life some place where people wouldn't have been so cruel to you. I could have accepted you when you came to me and told me the truth, rather than pushing you away. I could have visited you in prison, or sent you a letter, or come to you when you got out. I could have made it up to you so many times, but I failed you at every turn.'

She looks away again, her throat constricting, but the tears eventually fall. She huffs out a sigh and composes herself.

'I did come to see you when you got out. I heard you lived above the deli and I was going to see if you'd want to talk to me. I saw you walking home on the other side of the street, but ... I didn't have the guts to call out, or ring your buzzer after you'd gone inside. I was a coward, like I have been all these years. And when I almost lost you to that woman, like I've lost your brother ... I realized how many chances I'd had and thrown away. I don't want to do that anymore.'

She leans forward, holding my hand tighter.

'If you want me to go and never come back, I'll go. I'll understand if that's what you want. But if you'll have me, I promise to try and make it up to you. I'll never see Tony again, and I'll kick the pills. I'll do better by you in every way I can. You're a grown man now, you might not need your mom anymore. But if you want me around, I'll be here. I can't promise I'll be the perfect mom, but I promise you I'll try.'

I've watched her this whole time, listening to the words that I've dreamed of hearing since I was sixteen. I part my lips to speak; a sound escapes with my held-back tears.

'I've ... I've always needed my mom.'

And then I cry; I cry like I've never cried before. I feel her lowering the rail of the bed, and I move with the weight of her as she sits on the mattress and pulls me into her arms. I breathe her in, the only scent that reminds me of home, cigarette smoke and the same Avon perfume she always wore. For the first time in a long while, I finally feel safe. I let her rock me as I cry, feeling my tears and snot wetting her blouse and holding on to her for dear life. It reminds me of everything I've lost over the years, of all the time that has gone by and all of the pain I've carried. But it also reminds me of everything I can hope to gain from this point on; that beyond my chequered past lies an untouched future that's mine to claim.

'I'm here, baby,' Mom whispers, kissing me above the ear as she rocks me. 'I'm here.'

V

ACCEPTANCE

San Diego, autumn 2013

Evelyn has been awake all night, tossing and turning.

I'll drift off, be asleep for ten minutes, maybe a little more, and then wake to her turning over, the mattress moving beneath us. I'll hear her sigh heavily, or get up to use the bathroom, or hear the clock leave the bedside table as she picks it up to check the time before placing it back on the side. The whole time, the rabbit we bought scurries around in the hutch outside, the backdrop to her sleeplessness.

'He's going to be fine,' I tell her for the tenth time. 'He's going to be making friends. He needs this.'

I hear a sharp intake of breath and realize she's crying.

'What's the matter?'

She's lying on her back, looking up at the ceiling with tears slipping down her face.

'I don't know. I just . . . I feel like something's wrong.'

'You're just anxious, and that's okay. This is all pretty new, for all of us.'

'It doesn't feel like it's that . . .'

'Then what is it?'

'That's just it, I don't know.'

'Try and sleep,' I say, wiping away a tear. I kiss her forehead. 'You'll feel better if you get some shut-eye.'

I pull her into an embrace and breathe in the scent of her, enjoying the warmth of her against me.

I don't remember falling asleep. All I know is that I wake to a scream. A scream so loud, so piercing, that I bolt upright in bed.

Evelyn is pacing the room with the phone to her ear.

'We'll be there. Is he okay? Please tell me he's okay.'

My heart lurches. She'd said she thought something was wrong. I can't think of what might have happened, I'm too dazed by sleep and disorientated from the scream; all I can do is say his name over and over in my head.

Joshua Joshua Joshua Joshua Joshua.

She hangs up the phone and looks at me.

'What happened?'

'They won't say, but he's hurt. He's really hurt, Tobe. We need to go to Sharp Memorial Hospital right now. That's where they're taking him.'

She pulls open the wardrobe and snatches the first blouse she finds from a hanger, so forcefully that I hear it crack. She's shaking all over.

I get out of bed and go to her, cupping her face as it appears through the neck of the blouse. She jerks her head roughly out of my hands.

'I told you something was wrong, but you wouldn't listen.'

She's snatched up a pair of jeans and is headed out the door before I can respond, and I stand in the dark room in nothing but my underwear, feeling an aching sense of dread creep in. A sense of something to come, a sense of loss for the life we had before we dared to go to sleep.

54

Tobias

Central California Women's Facility, summer 2028

I've been out of Chino for six months, where I was remanded after all the felonies I committed chasing my wife through the desert, but stepping behind prison walls again brings the memories rushing back. Whether it's a men's or a women's prison, they all feel the same. Hard grey walls. Ice-cold air that prickles the skin and dries the throat, the overcrowding making it feel like there's never enough of it to go around.

I'm led to the visitor's room, a tight space with no natural light and a row of chairs facing windows of glass, through which you can see where the inmates will sit on the other side. I know how it feels to sit on both sides of these windows. On the convict's side, it's like watching a TV channel you're not allowed to change over: you can see freedom right there in front of you, taunting you from behind the glass, before you're ripped away and sent back to your cell. On the visitor's side, I already can't wait to get out, back to the sun and the fresh air. It's an experience that makes you never want to do wrong again.

I'm instructed to take a seat, and eye all of the scratches in the pane, the fingerprints smudged on the phone set into the wall.

My heart races with excitement, the kind of palpitations you get when you arrive on a date and sit waiting for them to walk towards the table.

This is the first time I'll have seen Evelyn since the night at the hospital. As soon as we were arrested, she was sent one way, and I another. We were driven in separate cop cars and convicted in different hearings. We've written each other letters, sent from prison to prison, the tone of each note loving yet distant. In her last letter, received the week I was set to be released, she instructed me to wait six months before visiting, to go out into the world and become my own person. Then she asked me to begin divorce proceedings. But despite knowing that we're better off apart, and that we'll never see each other again except through a pane of glass, I don't think I'll ever escape that fizzy, excited feeling in my gut when I'm near her.

A buzzing sound cuts through the room, and the door leading into the cell block opens. The inmates step through one by one in their bright, garish jumpsuits and take their seats. Evelyn steps through last, and our eyes meet.

The last time I saw her she was nothing but skin and bone, and her face was swollen beyond recognition. She'd lost that glint in her eye, that spark she always had. But as she sits down and picks up the phone, I see it flickering quietly again.

I pick up the phone on my side and stare at her, taking in her healthy complexion and the delicate smile pulling at the corners of her lips. She's gained weight, padding the gaunt cheeks that grief gave her and filling her jumpsuit in all the right ways.

'Hi,' she says.

'Hi.'

We stare at each other, taking in all the little things: remembering the old parts and drinking in the new. My heart aches, longing to embrace her.

I adore this woman.

'How are you?' she asks.

'I'm good. It's strange to be out.'

'Where are you staying?'

'Just a studio apartment in Little Italy, for now. Not much bigger than my old cell, but big enough for me.'

We'd had to sell the house in the end. The last time either of us saw it was the beginning of the end of our time together. I'd left our home in cuffs and never went back. But maybe it's good to keep it all in the past. To leave prison and start anew. That's something Evelyn will never get to do herself, serving consecutive life sentences for murdering Kyle Atkins and Chris Alexander.

'How are you doing?' I ask. 'You look . . . good.'

She laughs quietly. 'Was the pause necessary?'

I find myself laughing too. 'I wasn't expecting it, that's all.'

'I'm doing good. Really good. There's a psychotherapist that visits every week for group therapy for a bunch of us. I didn't think it would help, but it has. I think she plans to take me under her wing, let me be an assistant of sorts, so I can be working again. Helping others.' She plays with the phone cord, wrapping it around her finger. 'I feel safe in here.'

I wonder how prison makes her feel safe; I certainly didn't when I was inside. But slowly it dawns on me: she means she feels safe from herself, from everything she is capable of and everything she has done.

'Are the other inmates good to you?'

'There are a few bad apples, but they don't bother me. They've heard the stories.' She huffs a laugh. 'Most of the inmates are good people, and I've got some friends. I didn't realize how lonely I was, not having friends all these years.'

I swallow hard. It seems she's done better inside than I have on the outside. I've kept myself to myself mostly, not quite ready to let people in, to drop my anchor in a town I'm set to leave.

'I got the papers through last week,' I say. 'We're officially divorced.'

'The end of an era,' she says, with a smile.

'Yeah.'

We fall quiet, the mutter of others in the visiting room filling the gap.

'What do you reckon you'll do with yourself now that you're free?' she asks.

'That's kind of why I'm here.' I watch her take me in, trying to read my face. 'I've got the opportunity to go home.'

Her eyes widen a little.

'I've been offered a job with my old company. They heard I was out and got in touch. It's not the level I was at, but it's a start. A way to build myself back up again. And I'll be closer to Mum. She sounds so much older on the phone these days. It will be good to be with her while I still can.'

Her face is straight while I talk, though she gnaws anxiously on her bottom lip, but when I take a deep breath and ask her what she thinks, a smile creeps across her face.

'Good,' she says. 'That's good.'

'Is it?' I inspect her expression for every possible sign of a lie. 'Because if you want me to stay, I'll stay. You know I will.'

'I know. And that's exactly why you need to go.'

'I never thought I'd leave. But it never felt like home without Joshua with us, and now you're in here . . . it just doesn't feel like home anymore.'

'It never did, did it?'

I shake my head. 'No, it never did.'

We sit in silence for a while, staring at each other through the glass, trying to memorize every inch of each other's faces as though we may never see one another again.

'This really is the end of an era,' she says, choking up a little.

'I'll come back to see you. To see Joshua.'

I say his name and, for the first time in years, she smiles at the thought of him. She doesn't shut down; she isn't engulfed by the rage that ripped through our lives and put this pane of glass between us. Tears wet her eyes.

'I think you ...' She stops herself, gnaws on her lip for a moment more, collecting herself. 'I think you should take him home. He deserves to be with family and be looked after, to have loved ones bringing him fresh flowers every week, to be kept safe. He deserves to go home too.'

Her hand is shaking on the desk. I wish I could reach out and take it, squeeze it tightly in mine.

'Think about it,' I say. 'Don't make the decision right now. I won't go for another month or two. You can write to me and—'

'There's nothing more to think about. He deserves to go home. He's waited long enough.'

'Okay.'

The guard announces we have five more minutes before the visiting session ends. I want to demand an hour; a day. I've not seen my wife in all these years and—

I correct myself silently.

Ex-wife.

'Have you heard from Aaron?' she asks.

I didn't expect her to mention him during our visit. However far she has come, I didn't think she could bring herself to speak of him. But she looks at me through the glass with patient eyes, genuinely wanting the answer.

'He wrote to me a while ago. He's living on the East Coast now.'

She nods. 'That's good.'

I remember what she said to him the last time she saw him.

I want you to have a good life. I want you to have the life that my son never could. Be happy not just for yourself, but for him, and for us.

'Have you?' I ask. 'Heard from him?'

'I'm not quite there yet. Maybe one day.'

'Yeah. One day.'

The guard calls time, and the buzzer sounds as it had when the inmates entered. My heart lurches, and I feel my hand reach up for the glass. She places hers on the other side, just for a moment, before standing from her seat.

'I love you.' I say it into the receiver, but the phone lines have been cut off. But she is looking at me through the glass with a knowing look. I read her lips.

I love you too.

I watch as she is led back out the way she came in, lingering long after she has gone, until the officer taps me on the shoulder and guides me back towards the door.

*

I get back into my car in the parking lot and sit awhile, processing everything we said to one another. It will take a lot longer for me to digest how much better she seems within herself. I'm happy to see her better, but I can't shake the veil of shame I'd felt when I realized how I'd been part of what had been holding her back. I may have helped save her in the end, but I'd also driven her there, my grief manifesting itself in the need to keep her beside me, safe and contained, until she finally broke free.

I sit and think of home life back in London. Of having Joshua there, of being with my family and finally piecing myself back together after so many years in this agonizing purgatory. It's hard to picture what life will be like without Evelyn, as it has always been a struggle to exist without Joshua. But if I've learnt anything over the years, it's that it isn't about what lies ahead, but about mastering the art of putting one foot in front of the other. Then one day, I'll look up and see how far I've come, and somehow everything will be okay.

I reach into my backpack on the seat beside me and pull out the letter from Aaron. I carry it with me everywhere I go, and have read it so many times that the ink has smudged under my grip and the paper has wrinkled, each corner dog-eared from being repeatedly taken in and out of my bag. I take a deep breath and begin to read. I breeze over the pleasantries to the heart of it.

> I wanted to thank you. My mom came to the hospital after we got there and took me home. She told me that you were the reason for her seeing sense, and that you gave her a second chance she didn't know she deserved. I don't know what you said to her, but I wanted to thank you for bringing us back together. I don't think either of us would have had the courage to reach out if you hadn't helped. She isn't perfect - hell, who is? - but she's enough. Mom came to visit me at Christmas with Nikki and the kids, and I felt like I had a family for the first time in my life.
>
> I also wanted you to know that I'm doing what Evelyn told me to do. I'm living life for all of us. I'm in night school, working on my high school diploma after screwing it up the first time around, and hopefully one day I'll go to college. I think I want to be a writer. I'm not so good yet, but I want to learn, and I want to say everything that's been stuck inside my head all these years. Maybe I can help bring people together, the way you did Mom and me. I don't know what the future holds, but for the first time in my life I feel hope. I pray you get that too, wherever you end up.
>
> Aaron (and Lexy)

I fold up the letter, blinking the tears from my eyes.

Hope. I can't remember the last time I had that. When Joshua died, the prospect of hope died with him. There was nothing to hope for that could ease the pain of losing him. There was no hope for a future without him, because a future without him wasn't worth anything at all. But after seeing how Evelyn is healing, and knowing Aaron is on the right path, it makes me feel, for the first time, that I might be headed somewhere too. I feel home calling to me, and warmth being breathed back into my chest. I don't know what I'm supposed to do with my new lease of life just yet, but home is a great place to start.

I look at the photo of Joshua on the dash, holding his favourite plush rabbit in a tight embrace, his gap-toothed smile beaming for the camera. A single tear slips down my cheek. I take the photo and kiss it, before reattaching it to the dash.

'Come on buddy. Let's get you home.'

Thank you to everyone listed here, who helped to publish *Redemption*:

At Madeleine Milburn Agency:

Agency and Rights
Madeleine Milburn
Valentina Paulmichl
Georgina Simmonds
Rachel Yeoh
Olivia Maidment
Saskia Arthur

TV and Film
Hannah Ladds
Casey Dexter
Nicole Weinroth (WME)
Hilary Zaitz Michael (WME)

At Simon & Schuster UK:

Editorial
Katherine Armstrong
Georgina Leighton
Gail Hallett

Copyeditor
Cari Rosen

Proofreader
Gillian Hamnett

Marketing and Publicity
Harriett Collins
Sarah Jeffcoate
Richard Vlietstra

Sales
Heather Hogan
Madeline Allan
Jonny Kennedy
Rich Hawton

Art
Craig Fraser

Production and Operations
Karin Seifried
Mike Messam

Audio
Dominic Brendon

Rights
Amy Fletcher
Ben Phillips
Namrata Mistry

Finance and Contracts
Keely Day
Meshach Yeboah
Isabel Ireland
Maria Mamouna